# THE PAIN OF PLEASURE

"Did I hurt you very much, my darling?" Angus asked, as they lay quiet finally side by side.

"No," said Amalia.

"What is it? What are you feeling?"

Amalia did not answer. Now that her treacherous body had taken its pleasure, she was left with the realization of what she had done. She had betrayed the fine man who had married her. Betrayed him with his own best friend.

Then he kissed her lips. One hand stroked down her body and then upward to her breasts, finding her nipples already rigid. She began to feel again that inward melting, that growing urgency. And she knew she could not stop what was happening . . . did not want to . . . prayed it would go on and on and never end . . . even as she knew with agony it would. . . .

***WILD WINDS OF LOVE***

# VERONICA JASON

A SIGNET BOOK
NEW AMERICAN LIBRARY
TIMES MIRROR

## Publisher's Note

This novel is a work of fiction. Names, characters, places, and incidents are either the product of the author's imagination or are used fictitiously, and any resemblance to actual persons, living or dead, events, or locales is entirely coincidental.

NAL BOOKS ARE AVAILABLE AT QUANTITY DISCOUNTS WHEN USED TO PROMOTE PRODUCTS OR SERVICES. FOR INFORMATION PLEASE WRITE TO PREMIUM MARKETING DIVISION, THE NEW AMERICAN LIBRARY, INC., 1633 BROADWAY, NEW YORK, NEW YORK 10019.

SIGNET TRADEMARK REG. U.S. PAT. OFF. AND FOREIGN COUNTRIES
REGISTERED TRADEMARK—MARCA REGISTRADA
HECHO EN CHICAGO, U.S.A.

SIGNET, SIGNET CLASSICS, MENTOR, PLUME, MERIDIAN AND NAL BOOKS are published by The New American Library, Inc., 1633 Broadway, New York, New York 10019

First Printing, December, 1982

1 2 3 4 5 6 7 8 9

PRINTED IN THE UNITED STATES OF AMERICA

# 1

## South Atlantic Ocean, 1823

Only the endless swells moved the longboat, rocking it gently, monotonously. As it had most of the time for days now, the boat's tattered sail hung limp. In every direction the ocean stretched emptily to the horizon. There were no whitecaps on this day of flat calm, only those restless swells which gave back winking reflections of the brassy sun like the facets of some enormous gem.

Seated on a thwart in the sail's scant shade, Amalia looked across the curled bodies of the four semiconscious men in the bottom of the boat to where Angus MacFarlane sat on the midship thwart, red-gold hair and beard bright in the relentless sunlight. His big hands rested on the partially shipped oars, even though, to protect what strength he had left, he would not start rowing again until late afternoon brought some measure of coolness.

Most of the time these past few days, Amalia had felt a blessed apathy. But now, as she looked at those hands with the red-gold hair curling along their backs, a memory broke into her consciousness. That storm-lashed Long Island house thousands of miles to the north. Herself lying in his arms, brought by the caresses of those big hands to such a state of desire that she forgot, for a time, all the pain and bitterness he had caused her in the past. She had even forgotten that she was another man's wife.

Well, little chance of that ever happening again. Soon both she and Angus would lapse into torpor, like those motionless figures in the bottom of the boat. Soon after that they would die, as the ship's carpenter and so many others in this longboat already had died. One after another, their bodies had been lowered over the side.

Strange that the carpenter, a six-foot-four giant of a man, half Sagaponack Indian and half Fiji Islander, had been the first to die. Perhaps his very size had been the reason. His share of the ever-dwindling supply of hardtack and jerked beef had not been enough to sustain him. But Angus MacFarlane was almost as large. And yet there he sat, not only alive but also ready to resume rowing when the sun had declined.

He had been sitting with head bowed, eyes fixed on the inch or so of salt water sloshing gently in the bottom of the boat, but now he raised his gaze to Amalia. Where it was unprotected by his many weeks' growth of beard, his face was red and blistered. In that sunburned face his eyes looked all the bluer. A strange expression came into them—sad and wry and yet touched with mockery. She felt that he somehow had sensed her thoughts of a moment before. Somehow he knew that she had been thinking of that stormy night when he had managed to reduce her to a mindless creature moaning for the release his body could bring her.

Stonily she stared back at him. Never again, she thought. No, not even if a ship appeared on the horizon at this moment and eventually took them back to that Long Island village.

Because this time he had done the truly unspeakable and unforgivable. This time he had separated her from her child. Pain twisted inside her as she thought of Michael in that other crowded longboat, his one-and-a-half-year-old face contorted with weeping, arms raised beseechingly as she looked down at him from the deck of the burning ship. "Michael!" she had screamed, and struggled frantically in Angus' grasp. Then she realized that he was holding her away from him and aiming his big fist at her chin.

When she came to she was in this longboat—a crowded one then—and the boat that held her small son was a black shape many yards away over the sunset-streaked water. The swift tropic night had descended. Hours later two squalls had struck, brief but fierce, with lashing rain and the crackle of lightning. And when dawn came there was no sign of the other longboat.

Pray God some ship had found it. But even if it was still out there somewhere on the endless blue ocean, surely there was a chance that Michael had survived. He had been in the care of Lena—brown-skinned Lena with the razor-disfigured face—who had served both Amalia and her mother before her. What was more, the men in that boat, rough sailors though they were, surely would see to it that the little boy had enough food and water to stay alive.

But what if none of them were alive? What if their boat had overturned in one of those squalls? Or what if it still drifted, but with no one aboard it alive?

The thought that Amalia found least bearable was that of Michael suffering. Better that he had died. Better that many days ago gentle hands had lowered his small body over the gunwale and let it drift down through ever-darkening water to the black ocean floor.

Angus MacFarlane was still looking at her. She wanted to cry out, as she had yesterday—or was it the day before, or the day before that?—"Where is my son? Why did you separate me from my little boy?" But if she said that, he would make the same reply as before: "I did what I had to do. And anyway, he is my son too."

She wrenched her mind away from Michael, forced it to turn to other memories. Eyes closed now, she thought of that tiny Mississippi River town where she had spent her growing-up years. The seething sound made by the giant paddle wheels of passing steamers. The lumber mill beyond the end of the wide main street. The cool, dim chapel, redolent of beeswax polish and of burning candles, at the convent school she had attended.

And then, unbidden, came those few fragmentary memories of that place in New Orleans where, until shortly before her third birthday, she had lived with her mother and Lena. Because her mother had lied to her, she had not known for many years what sort of place that was. And yet even before she had learned the appalling truth, those bits and pieces of very early memory had held the power to make her uneasy.

Again she turned her thoughts aside. It always hurt her to think of the mother she had so dearly loved as a liar or anything else shameful. Better to think of the stories her mother had told in her gentle voice, stories of her own girlhood back in Spain. Those accounts were so vivid that Amalia had felt she could almost see the Cádiz streets and hear the sidewalk vendors' cries and the bells worn by the heavily burdened donkeys as they toiled upward over the cobblestones. Sometimes she almost felt that it was she rather than her mother, Juana Ramirez, who at the age of fifteen had left her impoverished home to work in the frowning castle across the valley from Cádiz. . . .

Her thoughts of her young mother in that harsh but romantic Spain she herself had never seen began to blur. As sometimes mercifully happened, she slid into brief slumber while still sitting upright.

# 2

## Cádiz, June 1799

Juana knew that in the city of Cádiz, only a mile away across the valley, the sun shone with almost tropic intensity on steep narrow streets, on palm-bordered squares, on private courtyards fragrant with orange blossoms. But the sun did not penetrate to this stone-floored corridor of Castle Villega. Since two centuries before Columbus sailed, Castle Villega had been standing here on its rocky promontory. In some places its walls were twelve feet thick. And even in summer those parts of it not warmed by hearth fires or by sunlight streaming through leaded windows were cold, like the heavy coldness that had settled around Juana's heart.

As she moved along the corridor in her peasant blouse and skirt, feet bare on the straw matting, thick dark braids dangling over her shoulders, she saw two porters emerge from young Don Enrique's room and walk toward her, each carrying one end of a trunk. It was, she knew, one of the trunks that would accompany him to Madrid, where, in a little more than a fortnight, he would be married. His future wife was a great lady indeed, nothing less than the ward of Don Enrique's distant cousin His Majesty Carlos the Fourth. Even though she already had known that he was leaving that afternoon and that she was unlikely ever to see him again after today, the sight of that trunk sent a fresh pang through her heart.

It never occurred to her, though, to protest his leaving in any way. This exalted marriage, arranged by Enrique's parents, the Duke and Duchess of Villega y Ortiz, was only right and natural for him. She would never dream of trying to interfere, even to the extent of telling him that she carried his child.

She walked into the lofty bedchamber. Back turned, Enrique Villega stood at a window—Pablo Enrique Francisco Villega y Ortiz, to give him his full name. She started across the room toward the bed which, as yet unmade, gave her a reason for being there.

He turned toward her, a slender youth of twenty with light brown hair, gray eyes, and a complexion much lighter than her own Spanish Gypsy coloring. Oh, how she prayed that her child would look like him rather than herself.

He said, his face lighting up, "Juana! I hoped I would see you before I left. No, don't bother with the bed. I want to talk to you."

Hands holding both of hers, he said, "I shall miss you, Juana."

She knew that he would not—not really—but she was grateful to him for saying it. But then, he had been gentle and kind to her from the first. She had been working at the castle for almost two years—from her fifteenth birthday to a few weeks short of her seventeenth—when Enrique returned from the University of Paris to his ancestral home. The first morning she had walked into his bedchamber, carrying his breakfast tray, she had realized that he found her attractive. But he had not made an immediate amorous advance, as most young men of his class would have.

No, she had nothing to reproach him with. At any time she could have asked old Pedro, who served Enrique's parents as steward, to assign another maid to the young don's room. Instead, more deeply in love each day with his young handsomeness and his gentle manners, she had gone on serving him his breakfast coffee and rolls. Then one morning, still half-asleep, he had reached up and caught her hand as she started to turn away from the big canopied bed.

Smiling, and with some sort of pleasant dream still lingering in his gray eyes, he had said, "Juana?"

He did not draw her onto the bed. It was of her own free will that she sank down beside him.

All the past winter, with the massive door locked against intruders and with morning light, gray or sunny, streaming through the tiny-paned windows, they had made love in the big bed with its dark blue velvet canopy and curtains. Even if she had chosen to, she could not have pleaded ignorance as an excuse for her behavior. Raised in three small rooms with her parents and five younger brothers and sisters, Juana even as a young child had acquired knowledge of sexual activity and its consequences. Furthermore, she'd had sufficient religious education to know that fornication was a mortal sin.

But she was deeply in love. What was more, she knew that young girls in the poor neighborhoods of Cádiz, even when they remained chaste, received no great reward for guarding their virginity. They were apt to find themselves married to men three times their age—either that or to young men who, after their first passion for their wives wore off, were inclined to take drunken pleasure in beating them. In all probability she would never again have the chance to lie in the arms of a man she loved, a young man smooth of skin and pleasant of voice who, when his desire was spent, still held her and stroked her hair rather than turning away from her as indifferently as if they had both been rutting animals.

Now Enrique said, "I have something for you."

He turned to a mahogany desk whose graceful lines marked it as French rather than Spanish, opened its drawer, and took out a small black velvet pouch.

"No!" Juana cried. She had an instinctive delicacy that made her shrink from the thought of taking money from him.

He pressed the pouch into her hand. "Please, Juana! If you choose to, buy with it something you would really like, something to remember me by."

As he spoke, he was looking down into her face in its frame of dark braids. It was not a beautiful face, except for the great dark eyes, but it held an appealing gentleness. Would life, he found himself wondering, be gentle with Juana? He had a sudden disturbing feeling that quite the opposite would be the case.

Reluctantly she dropped the pouch into her skirt's deep pocket. "I need nothing to keep me reminded of you." Then she added, "Besides, there will be the child."

She had not meant to tell him. The words had just slipped out.

Dismay leaped into his gray eyes. "Juana! You are sure?"

She nodded.

"But what will you do? Is there some man who will marry you?"

"Yes."

"A kind man?"

"Yes."

At least Manuel Moreno, a widowed shoemaker, did not seem unkind. Just old—in his late forties—and always smelling of shoe leather, and often dull, what with his long fulminations against the present Spanish government. Even though learning that she was with child by another man would be a bitter blow to him, she did not doubt that he would marry her. Manuel was thoroughly smitten. For a year now, whenever she went home for the day off allowed to her once every two weeks, she had known she would find him there, looking at her with the humid-eyed devotion of an aging hound.

"All the same," Enrique said, "I think I should give you more money, just in case you may need it."

This time as he turned to the desk she did not protest. After all, she might find herself in want. When he learned the truth, Manuel might not want to marry her. In that case she would need this money, money that Enrique would never miss, but which might mean the difference between life and death to herself and her child.

He had begun to place gold pieces on the desk's surface. Her gaze strayed to a display of miniatures on a nearby table. A miniature of Carlos the Third, able and enlightened father of the present incompetent king. Miniatures of the Duke and Duchess of Villega, and of numerous family connections. And a miniature of Enrique painted only a few months ago. In her almost two years at the castle she had never stolen anything. But now her hand reached out, closed around the miniature, and dropped it into the left-hand pocket of her skirt.

There was little likelihood that it would be missed. The artist had made two copies of the miniature for the duke and duchess. And she was sure that Enrique did not intend to take the original with him. In fact, he had told Juana that he considered having his miniature painted "a lot of nonsense."

Enrique's gold pieces would, if necessary, nourish her body and the body of her child. The miniature would nourish her heart for as long as she lived.

He had turned around now, a still-larger pouch in his hand. "This will make a hundred gold escudos, all told."

She placed the money in the pocket that held the other pouch. "My thanks to you, Don Enrique." In bed these past months she had called him "Enrique," and "dearest one," and sometimes "soul of my heart." But it seemed to her fitting that now, at this moment of farewell, she could acknowledge the vast gulf between them by using his title.

"Good-bye, Juana. Go with God." He tilted her chin and kissed her.

Out in the corridor, with the feel of his final kiss still warm on her lips, she hesitated for a moment, and then walked toward a branching corridor that led to the steward's office. Her day off was not until the following Thursday. But, unwilling to suffer the pain of watching Enrique's actual departure, she would ask the steward to allow her to go home at once.

Two hours later she climbed a street so narrow that even now, in early afternoon, the ancient buildings on its left-hand side shadowed it completely. She stopped before a structure of peeling brown plaster which housed, among others, the Ramirez family. On the sidewalk out front, little more than a narrow stone rim, her youngest siblings, three-year-old twin girls, squabbled over a wooden doll their father had carved. Juana went inside and climbed three flights of rickety stairs through sounds of people quarreling, crying, singing, through smells of wine and food and mice and mildewed wood. She pushed open a door. Beyond it was the small room, strewn with maize-husk pallets, where her three young brothers slept. The next room held her parents' bed with its heavily carved oak headboard, a much-prized object which had been almost the only legacy of three generations of Miguel Ramirez's family. The room also held a pallet for the twins and another one which, until she went to work at Castle Villega almost two years before, Juana had shared with the eldest of her sisters, Maria.

The last of the three rooms served the family as kitchen, dining room, and living room. When Juana entered it, her fourteen-year-old sister Maria was wielding a broom in one corner. Her mother, Constancia, was bent over the fireplace coals stirring a kettle of what Juana identified, from the smell, as rice and beans. She straightened up and turned around.

When Miguel Ramirez, that humble, pious man, had fallen in love with her, Constancia had been one of a band of Gypsies who slept in their gaudy caravans in the valley and by day climbed up to Cádiz to tell fortunes in the street and mend pots and pans and pilfer as many objects as they safely could. She had been slender, flashing-eyed, and scornful. Her figure had thickened, but her black eyes were still haughty.

She said, "This is not Thursday! What are you doing here?"

"I was not feeling well, so I asked if I could take today off instead."

Constancia turned to the younger girl. "Maria, leave us. And don't listen at the door. Go downstairs."

Unwilling to miss whatever her mother planned to say, Maria stood there sullenly for a moment. Then she propped the broom in the corner and went out, closing the door behind her.

Constancia did not waste time asking in just what way her daughter did not feel well. Perhaps it was because she knew that Juana was almost never sick. Or perhaps it was because she, who had grown up among master charlatans, could recognize a lie the moment she heard it.

She said, "I was talking to Granny Blanco yesterday." Granny Blanco was a neighbor who had two grandsons working as potboys at the castle. "She said she'd heard that you had not gone to mass with the other servants for many months now."

People who knew Constancia might have thought it strange that she should be interested in such a matter. She was not only irreligious. She was antireligious, with a fund of ribald stories about priests and a ready scorn for neighbors who from their meager resources bought candles to burn at the church's gold-encrusted altars.

Perhaps regret over having married such a woman increased Miguel's natural piety. Whatever the reason, he himself attended mass every morning. What was more, he had managed to send his eldest daughter during her seventh and eighth years to the school maintained by the Blessed Sisters of the Poor. As his family increased, he could no longer afford the school. But at least Juana was one Ramirez—the only one—who could read and write.

"Well?" Constancia said. "Is it true you've stayed away from mass?"

Juana remained silent. She had not gone to mass because she could not take communion. She could not take communion because for many months she had not gone to confession. And she had not gone to confession because she could not tell the priest she was truly contrite for her sin and would not repeat it. No, she could not tell the priest that, not as long as her last thought at night in the cell-like room she shared with another maidservant was always of the morning hours, when in Enrique's bed she would again experience a bodily ecstasy which, she somehow sensed, would have to last her for a lifetime.

Constancia asked, "Who is the man?"

Struck dumb, Juana stared at her mother. Could that irreligious woman have guessed the scruples that had kept Juana out of the castle's chapel? Evidently. But perhaps she would have known anyway. Perhaps the Romanies' claim of second sight, by means of which they gulled the "gentiles," or non-Gypsies, was in Constancia's case not just a claim.

No point in lying. Not now, when it was all over. "He is Don Enrique. Today he is . . ." Her throat closed with pain.

"I know. He is going to Madrid to be married. And you have his child in your belly. That's true, isn't it?"

Numbly the girl nodded.

"Juana, you imbecile. If you were so riggish that you had to bed down with some man, why couldn't he have been someone who might marry you?"

Stung, Juana cried, "I did not want just . . . just a man. I loved him. I'll love him until I die!" Tears burst from her. She raised her hands to cover her face.

Constancia did not touch her. But when Juana's sobs had quieted, she said, "Ah, yes. Love. I know, daughter. I was in love once."

Juana took down her hands and stared at her mother. Who was the man whose memory had brought that almost soft look to Constancia's haughty face? Surely not her plodding husband. Some young Romany? Some wellborn "gentile"?

The ironic light had come back into Constancia's eyes. "Well, matters could be worse. At least you will have a husband. Manuel Moreno will marry you. He won't like what has happened, but he will still marry you." She turned back to the fireplace. "Now, sit down. Your father will be here soon."

Miguel Ramirez came in a few minutes later, bent under the weight of the half-dozen brooms, bound together, which he carried on his back. During the brief winters he peddled charcoal from house to house during the day, and at night in this kitchen made the brooms which, throughout the long summer, he sold in the streets. He was a small man with a seamed gentle face that appeared older than his forty-three years. He looked anxiously at his favorite child, seated on a stool beside the fireplace. "Hello, daughter. Maria told me you were here." He slipped off his load by its leather carrying straps and leaned it against the wall of peeling plaster. "She said you weren't feeling well."

It was Constancia who answered. Leaving the big wooden spoon in the pot, she turned to her husband, hands on her hips. "That's right, husband. And you won't feel well either, once you know the reason."

She told him the reason.

Miguel looked with shock and sorrow at his daughter's bowed head with its glossy dark braids. Somehow he could not summon up the paternal wrath with which most men met occasions like this. Mostly it was because he felt the fault to be his rather than Juana's. He had chosen as the mother of his children a woman who scoffed at religion. It was a fit judgment upon him that his favorite among those children should have gone astray.

And yet even now he could not honestly regret his choice of a wife. Constancia still fascinated him, still brought to his life an excitement which had vanished years and years ago from the marriages of men he sometimes talked to over a glass in a nearby wine shop.

Constancia said lightly, with one of those swift changes of manner that were part of her appeal for him, "Don't look so downcast, husband. There is still Manuel Moreno, remember."

Miguel looked at Juana's bowed head for a long moment. Then he asked, "Daughter?"

She raised her gaze to his face and nodded. As she had toiled up the road that led from the valley to the city on its rocky promontory, she had kept telling herself that if Manuel would still have her, she would marry him, and gladly.

Her father still stood there looking at his best-beloved child. He had hoped for a different sort of husband for her than a shoemaker several years older than himself. He had wanted her to have a young man, perhaps even an educated man, an apothecary, say, or a schoolteacher.

Constancia said, "Well, are you going to Manuel's shop? Or do you want your dinner first?"

"I want no dinner," he said heavily. "I'll go to see Manuel."

"Good. If he will not marry her, it is best we know right away, so that we can decide what else to do. And when you go downstairs, give Maria three pesetas and send her to the market. We are almost out of rice."

He nodded, picked up his load of brooms, and left.

An hour passed, during which Maria returned with the rice, only to be ordered by Constancia to take the family laundry to a square a quarter of a mile away, where, with water from the public fountain, women washed clothes in wooden tubs. Another half-hour passed, during which Constancia, baking flat round loaves of bread on an iron griddle which rested on the coals, did not even attempt to converse with the girl who sat silently on the fireside stool.

Footsteps sounded in the outer rooms. Constancia straightened and turned. Manuel Moreno came in, a rather stoop-shouldered man of medium height with light brown, almost sandy hair which hinted that he was a descendant of one of those Germanic tribesmen who centuries ago had invaded the Spanish peninsula. His face, slightly pockmarked, was amiable enough except when he spoke on his favorite topic, the fecklessness and corruption of His Majesty's government. Then his face would darken with rage.

Today his face was neither amiable nor angry, but stricken.

"Hello, Manuel," Constancia said. Then: "Well? Did my husband tell you the news about our Juana?"

For the second time since he had come in, he threw a brief look at the girl who sat with gaze lowered to her clasped hands. "Yes, he told me."

The news had been a terrible blow, so much so that after Miguel Ramirez had left he had barred the door of his shop and just sat there in the leather-smelling dimness, an awl in his hand. For more than a year he had loved Juana almost to the point of adoration. In fact, except for his parents, now many years dead, she was the only person he had ever loved. Certainly he had not loved the woman he had married through an arrangement between his family and hers, a woman who had turned out to be both cold and shrewish. He had found himself unable to love their only offspring, a son who had been loutish as a boy and even more so as an adult, a son who sneered at his father's political convictions and who seemed content to pass his life as a private in the king's army.

True, Manuel had been able to love something inanimate—the fifty acres of land he once had bought in the hope of escaping a trade he had never enjoyed. But foolish King Carlos, egged on by his wife and his wife's lover, had decided to rearm, in the delusion that thus he would be able to face France's Napoleon as an equal. A big army meant big taxes upon the peasantry. Unable to pay, Manuel lost his acres before he had been able to turn them into a farm.

"Well?" Constancia said again. "Are you willing to help us? Although I suppose there is no need to ask. If you were not willing, you would not have come here."

She was right about that. It was agony to think of his Juana in that young aristocrat's bed. But on the other hand, if she had remained virgin, perhaps he would never have summoned up the courage to try to claim her. He might have just gone on visiting the Ramirez family on Juana's day off but never mentioning marriage to the girl or her parents, lest he be refused. And eventually he would have gone off to Louisiana alone.

He nodded to Constancia. Then he said, "Juana."

The girl looked up at him. "Yes, Señor Moreno?" Several times he had asked her to call him Manuel, but she kept forgetting.

"Manuel," he said. "You must call me Manuel."

He went on, "Juana, will you marry me? Before you answer," he added quickly, "perhaps I had best tell you that I intend to go to Louisiana."

Startled out of her unhappiness, she exclaimed, "Louisiana! In America?"

"Yes. It is Spanish territory now, you know."

It was. The French had ceded that far away territory in return for Spanish acquiescence in some of Napoleon's schemes. Juana had a vague idea, though, from something Enrique Villega had once said, that the French-speaking inhabitants of Louisiana still followed their former laws and customs, all but ignoring their Spanish governor.

"But why, Señor . . . But why, Manuel?"

"Because I think I may find myself in prison if I stay here. Already I have been warned not to speak against the king. And often in the wine shop I go to there has been a man sitting at the table next to the one I always share with my friends. He might as well wear a sign saying 'police agent.' And so I think I had best leave. A cobbler can make a living anywhere. And I can not stand the things that are happening to Spain."

Bored as Juana had been in the past with Manuel's political diatribes, she knew that he was right about the king. Enrique, although the king's distant cousin, had much the same opinions about him. She knew that Enrique was glad that he did not share in the tainted blood which had entered the Bourbon line through marriages in recent generations, blood that had produced not only weaklings like the current monarch but also outright imbeciles like his older brother. Instead, the ancestor that Enrique and King Carlos had in common was King Ferdinand. A daughter of that able and intelligent ruler had been Enrique's grandmother.

Juana caught her breath. There was something she had not realized until now. The child she carried would not be just her descendant, and the descendant of Miguel Ramirez, broom seller, and his Gypsy wife. It would be the great-great-grandchild of a king.

Manuel said, "Will you marry me, Juana, and go with me to New Orleans?"

"Yes, Manuel. I will marry you."

They exchanged smiles, but made no move to touch each other, partly because they were both shy and partly because they were aware of Constancia's sardonic gaze.

Suddenly Juana remembered those two velvet pouches. She took them from her skirt pocket and placed them on the table. "I have some money, one hundred escudos." No need to say from whom the money had come. That was obvious. "It could help us in America." She turned to her mother. "Unless you and Papa—"

"Keep it," Constancia said, with a shrug. "Let that be your dowry. Lord knows your father and I would never be able to give you one."

A dowry. Yes, Juana thought, whenever Enrique had time to remember her during the busy days ahead of him, surely he would hope that those coins had helped establish her in respectable wifehood.

Manuel was staring at the small black velvet bags. He hated the thought of touching money furnished by Don Enrique. On the other hand, he would need money—perhaps more than he had been able to scrape together—if he wanted to open a shop at a favorable location in that city five thousand miles away. And it would require a prosperous business to support not only himself but also Juana and the child, that child he would try to love just as much as he would love the future ones of his own begetting.

"The money will be useful," he said.

Juana smiled at him. "I am glad." She added silently: And I will make it up to you. I will be as good a wife to you as I possibly can.

# 3

The 120-foot Spanish merchantman *Esperanza,* with its flat stern and skyward-pointing bowsprit, had little of the grace of the clipper ships, those greyhounds of the sea which in only a few decades would speed between the ports of Europe, America, and the Orient. But when the *Esperanza* was under way, her square-rigged sails swelling in the wind, she had a certain awkward stateliness. One of her two holds carried cargo, mostly olive oil and Spanish wines. The other, with a bulkhead partitioning it into one large cabin for men and another for women and children, carried more than thirty passengers. In addition, the afterdeckhouse held not only the officers' sleeping quarters but also two cabins for passengers willing and able to pay a stiff sum for privacy, comparative comfort, and the privilege of sharing meals with the captain and mates.

Manuel Moreno and his young bride occupied one of the two private cabins.

He had known that booking the cabin was the wildest sort of extravagance. He also had anticipated that the ship's officers would look askance at the cobbler sharing their table, although as it turned out their displeasure was considerably lessened by the presence of the cobbler's gently charming young wife. But Manuel had shrunk at the thought of Juana, already two and a half months pregnant, shut up in that crowded hold for weeks and weeks. Even though it might mean that they would have to settle for cheaper living quarters in New Orleans, better to spend the money now for her comfort.

He had a more selfish reason, too. Now that she was his, he could not bear to be separated from her.

Often at night in their cabin's double bunk Juana found herself wishing—guiltily, and yet unable to suppress the wish—that she was one of the women passengers down in the hold. It was not that Manuel was in any way selfish or rough. But he was an awkward lover. Frequently he was impotent. And when he did manage to penetrate her, he usually reached his climax in two or three minutes. Once, hoping to please him, she tried to feign some of the passion she had felt in Enrique's bed. Instantly Manuel became motionless. Opening her eyes, she saw by the moonlight streaming through the porthole that his face looked profoundly shocked. Plainly he believed that virtuous women never enjoyed the carnal aspect of marriage. From then on, whenever he took her in his arms, she just lay passive, trying not to remember a castle bedchamber filled with morning light, nor the soaring delight to which Enrique's thrusting young body had carried her.

The days, though monotonous, usually were pleasant enough. As private-cabin passengers, she and Manuel were allowed to walk the deck at any time, not just for the two midafternoon hours allowed the passengers in the hold. During the daylight hours she spent in her cabin, Juana knitted garments and a small blanket for her child, or read laboriously from a copy of *Don Quixote* which someone, probably a former passenger, had left on the shelf above the washstand.

Mealtimes were somewhat uncomfortable. True, the gray-haired captain and his much younger mates were courteous to her, even gallant. Manuel, though, they all but ignored. Juana could understand why her fellow Spaniards, with their rigid sense of class, should behave in that fashion. But she was surprised and puzzled that a certain Samuel Higgins, who with his wife occupied the other private passenger cabin, should look down his thin nose at her shoemaker husband. Samuel Higgins, after all, was a citizen of the newly formed United States of America, that country where, Juana had heard, everyone was deemed to have been created equal. In fact, the United States had sent him on some sort of diplomatic mission to the Spanish court. Now he and his wife were returning to their own capital of Philadelphia, although, as Mrs. Higgins told Juana, they would not be there long. Soon the city of Washington would be the new nation's seat of government.

Charlotte Higgins seemed quite oblivious of social distinctions. A plump, dark-haired matron of forty-odd, she defied her husband's obvious disapproval by walking with Juana about the deck and advising her, in the fairly fluent Spanish she had acquired during a year in Madrid, about childbirth and child rearing, and home remedies for everything from colds to acute indigestion. She also gave Juana lessons in English. The ability to speak English was almost a necessity in Louisiana, Charlotte said, because of the many Americans who had flocked there to buy land or to engage in business.

Weeks passed. The *Esperanza,* long out of sight of land, moved slowly but steadily across a summer-tranquil blue ocean. Lulled by the not unpleasant monotony of the voyage, Juana began to feel a sense of timelessness, as if forever she would be moving across an empty blue ocean beneath a blue bowl of sky.

Then one morning she awoke feeling too feverish and leaden-limbed to leave the bunk bed. After refusing the breakfast that an anxious-faced Manuel brought to her, she fell into heavy sleep.

She awoke to see late-afternoon sunlight streaming through the porthole. Manuel sat beside her, fear deep in his eyes. She asked, "What is wrong with me?" and found that it hurt her swollen throat to speak even those few words.

He gave her a forced-looking smile. "It is a kind of pestilential fever, the captain says. Two crew members have it, and several of the passengers in the hold."

He got up, crossed to the washstand, and picked up from the shelf above it a glass half-filled with brown liquid. Returning to the bed, he said, "Drink this."

She asked painfully, "What is it?"

"A medicinal draft. The captain said it will help you." But she could tell from the near-panic in his aging face that he had little faith in the captain's healing skills.

The medicine did not help. In fact, that was her last lucid interval for many days. Burning with fever, she tossed in the bunk. Much of the time she was aware of being in the ship's cabin, with a distraught-looking Manuel seated beside her or forcing cool liquid or warm gruel down her swollen throat. But often it seemed to her that she was also somewhere else—moving about the crowded kitchen of the Ramirez family or dusting heavy ebony furniture in one of the castle's lofty-ceilinged rooms. Once she seemed to be back in Enrique's bed, feeling his lips on her lips and his hands caressing her body. She babbled his name and broken love words, and then became dimly aware of Manuel's pain-filled eyes looking down at her.

She had no idea whether it was days or only hours after that when everything changed. The bunk no longer rocked with an almost imperceptible motion, but pitched wildly, so that if someone—Manuel?—had not fastened a restraining band around her, she would have been hurled to the floor. There was a howling sound which she finally identified as wind. The porthole across the cabin no longer remained more or less on the same level as her face, but sometimes soared higher, showing dark gray sky through its glass, and sometimes plunged low through seething gray-green water.

She had another semilucid interval. Not only her husband but also the captain was in the wildly pitching cabin. Yelling to make himself heard through the tumult, Manuel was saying something about an apothecary.

"You can't go down there!" To Juana, the captain's voice seemed to fade in and out. "The hatches will remain closed until we get through this storm, if we ever do. And you're to stay in this cabin."

Manuel cried, "But he could help her! She's dying! I won't let her die."

The captain's voice was harsh. "If you or anyone opens that hatch, the ship may founder. And if you try to go out on deck, I'll put you in irons for the rest of the voyage."

Through the uproar of screaming wind and groaning ship's timbers, Juana did not hear the captain slam the door. She only knew, from the swiftness with which it closed behind him, the he must have slammed it.

She slipped back into semiconsciousness, into a world where cobblestoned Cádiz streets and the castle courtyard and this wildly rocking room seemed to merge and then disentangle and then merge again. After an unmeasured interval, though, she had a feeling that things had changed. Something dreadful had happened. That must be why it was not Manuel, but one of the mates, a plump, thirtyish man with a cast in his right eye, who forced liquid down her resisting throat. Where was Manuel? What was it the captain had threatened? To put him in irons? She tried to ask the mate if that was what had happened, but her clumsy tongue and lips could not form the words.

She did not know how many days passed before the morning she awoke to a universe that no longer shrieked and careened wildly. In the aftermath of the storm the ship still rolled, but far more gently. Through the porthole she saw blue sky, then sky plus an arc of darker blue ocean, then only sky again. Mrs. Higgins sat beside the bunk.

Juana said, "Manuel. Where is—?"

"Sh-h-h!" Leaning forward, Mrs. Higgins laid her palm on the girl's forehead. She smiled. "No fever. You are going to be all right, my child. But you must rest. I will be back in a moment."

She returned holding a tiny glass filled with dark liquid. "Take this."

"What—?"

"It is laudanum. It will put you back to sleep. When you wake up, we will talk."

Juana slid into dreamless sleep. When she awoke, afternoon light had filled the cabin. Again Mrs. Higgins sat beside the bunk.

"Please tell me," Juana said. "Where is my . . . ?"

"You must be brave, dear girl." Mrs. Higgins took Juana's hand, almost as thin as a bird's claw, in her own. "And you must be thankful that you did not lose your child."

The child! Juana's other hand flew to her stomach. Yes, the child was still there, swelling her thin body. Now it seemed to her that in her delirium she'd had a sense of the child, already born, here in the cabin with her. A boy? A girl? She did not know. Now she could recall only that she'd had a sense of someone very much apart from herself, someone more proud and spirited than she could ever be.

Her thoughts swung back to her husband. "Tell me where Manuel . . ."

"Juana, you must be brave," Mrs. Higgins said again. "You see, your husband overheard two of the officers talking about a passenger down in the hold, an apothecary who was rumored to have brought some of his medicines with him. This was during one of the worst days of the storm. The hatches had been battened down for almost a week, except for brief periods during lulls in the bad weather, when the crew opened the covers. Even though the captain ordered your husband to stay off the deck, he went out there, presumably with the idea of opening the hatch himself. A wave swept him overboard. There was no chance of saving him."

Arms flung across her eyes, Juana wept. She realized now that in a way she had come to love him, that amorously awkward man who in the end had been willing to risk—and lose—his life to try to ensure her own.

The woman allowed her to weep for several minutes. Then she touched Juana's shoulder. "My dear, you must stop. You cannot afford any further drain on your strength."

After a moment Juana lay quiet. She asked in a dull voice, "What about the other sick ones? Did some of them—?"

"Only two died, both of them crew members. Many down in the hold were sick. It must have been terrible down there with the hatch cover closed and people raving with fever. But by some miracle—or perhaps the apothecary's medicine!—they have all survived.

"And now, my dear," she went on, "do you feel strong enough to consider your future? Or would you rather we talked later?"

"No, now." For her child's sake as well as her own, she had to think of what lay ahead.

"Good. Now, forgive me for asking, but how much money do you have?"

"I don't know," she said drearily. "Manuel kept it in the portmanteau under the bunk."

Grunting slightly, Charlotte Higgins leaned over, opened the built-in cabinet under the bunk, and took out the leather portmanteau. She crossed to the table affixed to the bulkhead under the porthole, placed the portmanteau upon it, and took from the little trunk a leather bag.

Moments later she said, "You have fifty-two gold escudos, which equals about three hundred and fifty American dollars or—let's see—about thirteen hundred French francs. It's a respectable sum, Juana. It should keep you in comfort until well after your child is born, and for perhaps half a year afterward, if you are frugal. And I have thought of a way you can be frugal. But wait a moment, until I put the portmanteau away."

When the hand trunk was back in its place, Charlotte again sat down beside the bunk. "I have a distant cousin who lives a few miles outside of New Orleans. She is about twelve years older than I am. I haven't seen her for a long time.

Why, it must be almost twenty years since she and her husband—her first husband, I mean—visited us in Philadelphia. But we do correspond at Christmastime. That is how I know she was widowed about six years ago and remarried a year later. Her name is Mountjoy now, Dorothy Mountjoy.

"I'm sure that if I write you a letter to take to her," Charlotte Higgins went on, "she will be glad to give you room and board for a very nominal sum. After all, hers is a large house, and only she and her husband live there. Oh, there are the slaves, of course, but they have their own quarters. Living there, you could save nearly all of your money, so that after the child is born you could book passage, if you choose to, on a ship back to Spain.

"I'll leave you now, and see about your supper. Think over my idea, and decide if it is a good one."

Juana had decided even before the door closed behind her friend. Of course she would go to this Mrs. Mountjoy, and feel grateful for the opportunity.

And after the baby was born? Well, if she had to, she would go back to Cádiz, back to those overcrowded three rooms. Her mother would care for the child while she herself looked for work—any sort of work except that of a servant in Castle Villega.

But she found she did not want to go back. An adventurous streak she had not known she possessed made her think she might want to stay in the New World if she possibly could. Underneath her grief and anxiety, a hope stirred. She knew that she would be alone, and, except for that money, quite helpless against whatever disasters might come her way. And yet she felt that even for a seventeen-year-old widow with a child, that semitropical city at the mouth of a mighty river might hold something rich and strange.

# 4

Although the month was September, the New Orleans sun beat down on the wharf almost as intensely as it had in July. Mrs. Sara Davidson, however, seemed unaffected by the heat. She sat erect in her graceful landau carriage, eyes fixed on the Spanish merchantman which had just tied up at the wharf. She was waiting for some promising young woman who might or might not come down the gangplank, waiting in the same way that a cat crouches beside a field-mice run.

Dark-haired, and with a plump but well-proportioned figure clad in tasteful brown bombazine, Sara was a handsome woman, until you looked into her eyes. Black and lustrous, they appeared devoid of expression, as if curtains just behind their surface hid everything she thought or felt. Few people meeting her mistook her for that legendary creature, the bawd with a heart of gold.

There seemed to have been no reason, except sheer perversity, why she should have become any sort of bawd. One might almost think that sometimes a person, from earliest years, has been claimed by the devil for his own.

She had been born in Norfolk, Virginia, the third child and only daughter of a well-connected doctor and his wife. They were excellent parents, loving but not foolishly so, firm but not rigid. Outwardly she conformed well enough that they thought of her as a model child. True, there were rumors at the school she attended that she had stolen a bracelet from one girl and a sterling-silver bookmark from another. There was also a rumor that when the school's music master had threatened to report to her parents her failure to practice, she had made a false but highly effective counter-threat to tell that he had put his hand up her dress. But none of these rumors had reached her parents' ears.

She grew up into a gracefully mannered and very good-looking young woman. For some reason—perhaps those opaque eyes of hers—her suitors were not numerous. Still, she received a few proposals, notably one from a young man her parents favored, a young architect who had been a classmate of one of her brothers at Yale.

To her parents' incredulous consternation, Sara at the age of twenty announced her unshakable decision to marry Ephraim Davidson, a rich widower who owned Norfolk's largest retail store and who was more than three times her age.

They had been married less than six months when Ephraim died, helped out of this world by his bride. Not that there was anything for anyone to prove, or even suspect. When Ephraim, clutching his chest, went into his final attack, the butler and a housemaid as well as Sara were in the room with him. They saw her slip from his waistcoat pocket the box of pills prescribed by her own father. They saw her place the pill in his mouth and lift a glass of water to his pain-contorted lips, saw him swallow. The servants as well as his wife saw him die.

What no one but Sara ever knew was that days earlier she had removed from the box several of the pills, made of powdered foxglove, and put sugar pills of her own concoction in their place.

Weeks later, Sara discovered to her rage and disgust that her rich husband had not been rich at all. Two years before his marriage to her, the old fool, as his widow always referred to him in her thoughts, had mortgaged his store and even his fine mansion in Norfolk's best residential district. With the aid of his lawyer, a man of about forty, she salvaged what little she could from the forced sale of the store and the house, and then went home to live with her parents.

Two months later the collapse of a local bank took the few dollars she had. Three weeks after that she wrote a letter to her parents, a letter so cold and biting, so filled with details of exactly what she intended to do, that she felt sure it would keep them from ever trying to find her. She slipped the letter under their bedroom door early one morning. Then through the first gray light she walked down to the waterfront, where a south-bound merchant ship was getting ready to sail with the tide. Ephraim's lawyer, portmanteau in hand, waited for her on the dock. Infatuated with her even before her old husband's death, he gradually had come to feel that compared to Sara neither his wife nor his three young children held any importance for him.

The ship stopped overnight in Charleston, South Carolina, to discharge Long Island hides and take aboard furniture and fine china destined for New Orleans. Sara suggested that she and the lawyer spend the night ashore, and that lovesick individual of course agreed. That night at the inn she laced his supper wine with laudanum. When the ship sailed at dawn, Sara was aboard it, with the lawyer's fund of ten-dollar gold pieces tucked away in her smart little hand trunk with its cover of brown cut velvet. The lawyer himself was still snoring in his room at the inn.

Knowing him, she had been sure he would not track her down, and he did not. From that morning on she used to amuse herself occasionally by thinking of how he must have, sooner or later, crept back to his wife and children, with God only knew what story to explain his absence and the loss of his money.

In New Orleans she went to an establishment about ten minutes' walk from the waterfront.

During their brief marriage her old husband—perhaps in an effort to compensate for present shortcomings—had often boasted of his youthful exploits in the brothels of New Orleans, including one run by a Mrs. Prewitt. Some years ago, he told Sara, he had learned that the establishment had been inherited by Mrs. Prewitt's niece, a Mrs. Bolton. Before he had finished the first of his stories, Sara began to listen attentively. It appeared to her that prostitution was a field of endeavor in which a woman like herself, a woman both cold and highly intelligent, could achieve wealth and power almost effortlessly.

Hence her appearance, one autumn afternoon in 1780, on Mrs. Bolton's doorstep, where she asked the quadroon maid for admission.

Mrs. Bolton was an easygoing, rather stupid woman under whose proprietorship the brothel had slipped from the standards set in her aunt's day. She was both disconcerted and embarrassed by this obviously well-bred young woman who, seated in the garish parlor, calmly suggested that Mrs. Bolton hire her.

But the young woman was better-looking by far than any

of Mrs. Bolton's present girls. What was more, someone was needed to replace a girl who, only the week before, had run away with one of the American bargemen who guided their rafts up and down the Mississippi. Hesitantly Mrs. Bolton agreed to hire the young woman with the cultivated voice and strange, cold eyes.

Before long, Mrs. Bolton had reason to congratulate herself upon that decision. Sara was the perfect harlot. She never touched alcohol. She never got into hair-pulling spats with the other girls. She never tried to refuse a customer on the grounds that he was too drunk or otherwise too repulsive. And indeed, Sara had no impulse to do so. With no sexual feeling whatsoever, she did not care whether the customer who occupied her bed for a strictly allotted number of minutes was a young Apollo or a senile fumbler. The important thing was that each customer added to her carefully hoarded and swiftly growing fund of money.

Mrs. Bolton continued to congratulate herself—until the day when Sara announced calmly that she had rented a house in the next block, had recruited several girls, one of them a favorite of Mrs. Bolton's customers, and was about to open her own establishment.

It was a success from the very first. At Mrs. Bolton's Sara had learned a lot about what *not* to do. At Mrs. Bolton's the woodwork had been dingy and the chandeliers dull with dust. Sara's place sparkled with cleanliness. Mrs. Bolton's parlor was cluttered with elaborate furniture, heavy draperies, and amateurish paintings of simpering nudes. Sara's parlor was furnished in the serene style of the early 1700's, with an Aubusson carpet, graceful sofas, and slender-legged chairs and tables. In that well-bred setting the expertly painted and highly erotic nudes, commissioned by her from a local artist, were all the more stimulating.

But the chief difference was that Mrs. Bolton had refused certain customers. With a prudery that seemed to Sara laughable in a brothel keeper, the woman had refused to accommodate men of unorthodox sexual desire. As she often remarked, hers was not one of those "Frenchified houses."

Sara's establishment, on the other hand, drew the line only at sadists. And she made even that prohibition, not out of moral scruples, but out of unwillingness to risk injury to her stock-in-trade, her girls. Otherwise there were no prohibitions.

No matter how bizarre a man's sexual taste, he would be accommodated at Sara Davidson's.

On that September afternoon when she waited on the New Orleans dock, Sara had just turned forty. She was rich. She was powerful. She knew judges, top-ranking military officers, highly successful business and professional men. What was more, she knew things about them that no one else knew, not their wives, nor their doctors, nor their clergymen. So far she had never threatened to use any of that knowledge to bend these influential men to her will. She had not needed to. Just the awareness that she had certain facts in her possession made them want to stay in her good graces.

The only trouble with her business was the girls themselves. Things happened to her girls. They aged, and they took to drink or opium, and—in surprising numbers—they got married. One way or another, she had to keep finding replacements. It was in the hope of spotting a likely girl that she had driven down to meet an incoming Spanish ship, the *Esperanza*. European ships, their holds crowded with near-penniless immigrants, had yielded her more than one recruit.

The passengers were coming down the gangplank now. Suddenly she stiffened. There, except for one thing, was a girl who looked to be exactly the sort Sara sought. She was young, eighteen at most. She had a soft prettiness. She was poor, at least if one could judge by her clothing, a black poplin dress so ill-fitting that almost certainly it had been made for someone else. And apparently she had traveled alone, because it was not a husband or father or brother who, hand on her elbow, guided her down the gangplank, but a gray-haired man in the uniform of a ship's captain.

There was only one thing wrong with her. She was well-advanced in pregnancy. The birth of her child could not possibly be more than three months away, and probably less than that.

Well, even so, once she had the child . . .

Sara kept her gaze fixed on the gray-haired man and the girl.

Juana felt gratitude to the captain for more than his guiding hand on her elbow. Ever since Manuel's death, and even more so since Charlotte Higgins and her husband had left the ship in Philadelphia, he had been solicitous of her. He had seen to it that she had nourishing food with which to hasten her recovery. Whenever his duties permitted him to do so, he had chatted with her on deck, pointing out an occasional lighthouse as the ship moved slowly south along the North American mainland. Several times, holding the Spanish-English grammar Mrs. Higgins had given her, he helped her to practice her English.

Now, as they descended the gangplank, he asked, "You are sure you have the address of Mrs. Higgins' cousin?"

"I have it." Not trusting the precious slip of paper even to the pormanteau she carried, she had pinned it inside the pocket of her full-skirted dress. Until weeks ago, it had been Charlotte Higgins' dress. Because Juana had been upset over her lack of a proper garment in which to mourn her husband, Charlotte had altered her own black poplin for her young friend. Although the remodeled garment did not fit through the shoulders or anywhere else—Charlotte was not an expert seamstress—it did conform to Juana's idea of what was proper.

The captain said, "Then all you need is someone to take you where you're going. I'll put you in a hired carriage. As for the trunk, I'll have it carried to the warehouse over there." He meant the trunk which had carried all the rest of her possessions and her husband's too. "You can come to get it whenever you choose."

"Thank you."

They had reached the wharf and taken a step toward the line of carriages for hire when a voice called from the *Esperanza*'s deck, "Señor Capitán!"

He halted and looked up to where the first mate stood on the *Esperanza*'s deck. "Something must have gone wrong. I'm afraid I cannot see you into your carriage. But the driver of the one at the end of the line is reliable and speaks Spanish."

"Thank you," she said fervently. "Thank you for everything you've done for me."

He touched her cheek with a crooked forefinger. It was the first caress of any sort he had given her. "Go with God, little one."

"Go with God."

She looked after him for a moment as he hurried up the gangplank. Because he was to retire from the sea at the end of his return voyage to Spain, she knew that in all probability she would never see him again. She turned and began to walk along the wharf.

As soon as the captain had turned back toward the gangplank, Sara Davidson descended from her carriage, not waiting for assistance from her mulatto coachman. Threading her way through the crowd of dockworkers, ship's passengers, and sightseers, she hurried after the girl.

After twenty years in this polyglot city with its largely French populace, Spanish officialdom, and American businessmen and river-barge crewmen, Sara was almost as fluent in French and Spanish as she was in English. Now she called out, *"Hola! Señorita Ricardo! A donde vas?"*

Hearing a voice call out in Spanish, Juana turned around and waited for the woman in brown bombazine to approach.

A moment later Sara Davidson said, still in Spanish, "Oh, forgive me! I thought you were someone else." Then, with a smile: "But since I have stopped you, may I be of assistance to you? You are newly arrived here, aren't you?"

"Yes, señora."

"I cannot help noticing that you are expecting. Do you have a place to stay, and friends to look out for you?"

Raised in one of the poorest sections of Cádiz, and listening from the age of fifteen on to the rough talk of her fellow servants at the castle, Juana of course knew of the existence of prostitutes, and of the men and women who lived off their earnings. But there was nothing in Sara Davidson's appearance or manner to indicate that she was anything but what she seemed, a respectable matron taking a motherly interest in a young stranger.

Something, though—perhaps an instinct, perhaps that flat look in Sara's dark eyes—told Juana that she was faced with a creature of prey. She said, "Yes, I have a place to stay." Even though the woman obviously waited for her to continue, Juana did not elaborate.

"Well, I am well-known and well-connected in this city. If in the future you find yourself in need of someone, please look me up. My name is Sara Davidson and I live at 17 Rue de Chene."

Juana felt a flare of indignation that this woman should think that in the future she might become foolish enough, or corrupt enough, to turn to someone like her. But she felt too young and awkward, too intimidated by this strange place, to dare to express what she thought. "Thank you," she said. "Good-bye." She turned away.

The driver of the coach at the end of the line scrambled down as soon she stopped beside his vehicle.

"Could you take me to the house of a Mr. and Mrs. Mountjoy? The name of the house is Twin Pines, and it is several—"

"I know exactly where it is," the driver said. He was a small, swarthy man who appeared to have a tincture of African blood. "I used to take visitors to Twin Pines when Mrs. Mountjoy's first husband, Dr. Elton, was alive."

Not looking around to see if the woman in brown bombazine still watched her, Juana got into the coach.

# 5

While the carriage still moved through New Orleans, Juana had sat bolt upright, head swiveling from left to right as she tried to see what was happening on both sides of the street. After her many weeks on the water, where she had seen the same faces day after day, she felt overwhelmed by the sounds and sights swarming in on her. Carriages and carts and barrel-laden wagons rumbling over cobblestones. A seller of mussels and meat pies crying his wares in a strange tongue which, her driver told her, was a kind of French dialect called Cajun. A group of well-dressed men, some in knee breeches, some in the increasingly popular long trousers, talking in front of an impressive stone building which the driver said was the stock exchange. Graceful black women carrying bundles on their heads. Fine ladies in gauzy dresses and enormous hats laden with artificial flowers and fruits. Workmen in calf-length pantaloons and leather aprons.

But now that the carriage was out on a country road, she relaxed somewhat, leaning back against the cushions, which smelled of stale tobacco. The odor only slightly lessened her enjoyment of the other smells coming through the open carriage windows, smells of dark, rich earth and the green things growing from it. Once through a break in the trees she saw a great white bird swoop down to settle on a tussock in a swamp. To her, raised in arid Spain, the sheer fecundity of this half-drowned land was a delight.

"Here's the Mountjoy drive," the coachman said, and turned his vehicle onto a narrower road that ran between rows of giant oaks dripping with moss. It was Spanish moss, the driver told her, although why it should be called Spanish, he could not say.

The vehicle emerged into a wide clearing. In awed silence Juana looked at the sweep of velvety lawn, at the three-story house of rosy brick with its white shutters and pillared white porch. On each side of the wide steps leading to the porch stood a towering pine. It must be those two trees, she realized, which gave the house its name.

The carriage moved along a circular drive to the foot of the steps. The driver opened the carriage door, helped her to descend. From her reticule she took out an American half-dollar. So that she would have some less-valuable coins for purposes such as this, the *Esperanza*'s captain had changed a few of her Spanish gold pieces into American silver.

Evidently the driver had felt touched by the pregnant young girl in her ill-fitting mourning dress. After a hesitant moment he said, "You gave me too much," and handed back a small silver coin. She said good-bye to him and then mounted the broad steps. Behind her she heard the carriage moving away.

She let the brass knocker fall twice against the paneled door and then waited. No response. She knocked again.

The door opened. The grizzled old black man who stood there wore a butler's livery, but he had none of the hauteur of the upper servants at Castle Villega. In fact, he looked almost ill-at-ease.

Juana said, "I have a letter for Mrs. Mountjoy."

After a moment he opened the door wider. "Come in, ma'am."

She stepped past him into a wide, cool hallway paneled in what she later learned was rosewood. "I takes the letter," the butler said.

His accent made his words unintelligible to her, but she did understand the meaning of his outstretched hand. From her reticule she took the precious letter and laid it on his yellow palm.

"Just rest yourself," he said, and gestured toward a high-backed straight chair standing against the far wall. Then he turned, opened a door in the opposite wall, and closed it behind him. Seated in the chair, Juana looked at the gleaming floor, at a broad staircase sweeping upward, and at the portraits of a man and woman who wore the same sort of neck ruffs she had seen in two-hundred-year-old portraits at Castle Villega.

The door opened. "Mrs. Mountjoy sees you soon," he said.

He walked past the foot of the stairs toward the rear of the house.

Again his words had been unintelligible, but Juana gathered that she was to wait. Minutes passed. She felt a growing unease. The letter, which she had read many times, was only a few sentences long, informing "Dearest Cousin Dorothy" that the bearer was Juana Moreno, a young widow in need of a place to live until after her child was born. Why should Mrs. Mountjoy be taking so long to read it?

The door across the hall opened. In the fairly dim light Juana could make out only that the woman who stood there was small and thin and had either gray or gray-blond hair. She said in a bright, brittle voice, "Come in, please, Mrs. Moreno."

Juana stepped into a large room where late-afternoon sunlight lay on furniture covered in chintz, and on bowls and vases filled with dahlias and late-blooming yellow roses, and on a vast oriental rug of muted pastels. "Please sit there, my dear," Mrs. Mountjoy said, and indicated a chair. She herself sank onto one corner of a sofa. Beside her was a small table which held Charlotte Higgins' letter and its envelope.

Juana saw now that Mrs. Mountjoy must be in her middle fifties. Blue-eyed, and with pale skin like a finely wrinkled French kid glove, she had retained a certain prettiness. But her hands, clenched in her lap, looked almost ugly in their white-knuckled tension.

She said, "My dear, I am afraid I have sad news for you. It is not that I would not do anything in the world for a friend of Charlotte's. Why, Charlotte has always been my dearest—"

"Please!" Although unable to follow the swift flow of words, Juana had sensed that they boded ill for her. "If you please, señora, speak more slowly. My English, it is not good."

"What I was saying," Mrs. Mountjoy answered, spacing her words, "is that I am very sorry, but I will not be able to have you here. You see, my dear, I am not well, not well at all."

Then, as Juana gazed at her in consternation, the woman cried, "Surely you must have someone else here in New Orleans!"

"Señora, how could I? I have been here only three hours! Please, señora, I have money. I can pay you—"

"Oh, my dear! I don't want money. But since you have it, you can go to a boardinghouse. Yes! That is it! There are a number of comfortable establishments of that sort in the city. My coachman will drive you—"

"Señora!" In her desperation, Juana began to plead. "Look at me, señora. Anyone can see that I will have a child in a few weeks. An innkeeper might not want me in his place. He might fear he could not get rid of me before—"

"I tell you I can't have you here!" She began to fumble with the fastening of a ruby brooch pinned to the bosom of her dress. "Unfortunately I have only a little money in the house at the moment. But this pin is valuable. If you will allow my coachman to drive you into the city, you can sell the pin for enough to hire a suite of rooms and a servant until after your lying-in . . ."

She broke off, head cocked to one side. Those tense, thin hands fell to her lap. Juana heard it too, then, the sound of footsteps in the hall.

A man of about thirty-five, tall and handsome in fawn-colored coat and breeches and resplendent black riding boots, came into the room. He halted, smiling at sight of Juana. "Well! Who is it we have here?"

Mrs. Mountjoy said, in that bright, brittle voice, "Why, hello, Lawrence. This . . . this is Mrs. Moreno. She is a friend of my cousin Charlotte, and she just dropped by to . . . to give me a message from Charlotte. Mrs. Moreno, this is my husband, Lawrence Mountjoy."

Hoping her surprise did not show, Juana inclined her head. A few days before she left the ship in Philadelphia, Charlotte Higgins had mentioned that her cousin Dorothy's second husband was "a younger man." She had not said how much younger. Perhaps she hadn't known. After all, for many years she had been in touch with her cousin only by letter.

Lawrence Mountjoy bowed an acknowledgment. Then his smiling, quizzical gaze traveled from Juana to his wife, back to Juana, and then to his wife again. He said in a gentle tone, "Now, Dorothy. Something is wrong, isn't it? Hadn't you better tell me?"

The little woman looked up at her husband, lips compressed. Sensing a possible ally in this youngish, handsome man, Juana wanted to cry out, "I counted on staying here until my baby was born! For a long time I've counted on it. Please, please persuade her to let me!" But both pride and timidity kept her silent.

Lawrence Mountjoy said, "What is this?" and picked up Charlotte Higgins' letter. "May I read it?"

His wife had raised a hand as if to restrain him, but now it fell back into her lap. His eyes, of the same shade of light brown as his straight, smooth hair, moved rapidly down the page.

He replaced the letter on the table and then said, "You of course told her we'd be happy to have her stay with us, didn't you, dear?"

"No! Lawrence, I'm not well! You know I'm not—"

"Now, Dorothy! Of course you are sometimes ill. Just the same, how could Mrs. Moreno be a burden to you in this big house, with enough servants to care for a half-dozen visitors, let alone one young woman? And I'm sure Mrs. Moreno would never intrude upon you unless you sent for her." He turned to Juana. "That's true, isn't it?"

Caught between embarrassment and sudden hope, Juana could only nod.

"Please, Lawrence, please! She has enough money to stay at an inn. Please tell her she must—"

"Dorothy!" Near-exasperation came into his voice. "Just look at her! Forgive me, Mrs. Moreno, but I must say this." He turned back to his wife. "Obviously this young woman's confinement is not far off. Aside from anything else, do you want people to hear that you turned away a young woman in her condition to try to find some sort of public accommodation? It would be bad enough if she were just anyone. But she is a friend of that cousin you've always said you were so fond of . . ."

His voice trailed off. Then he said quietly, "It will be all right, Dorothy. Truly it will. Now, tell Mrs. Moreno you will be glad to have her here."

For a long moment the woman stared at him silently. Then her face seemed to sag, as if even her muscles had collapsed. Her blue, slightly faded eyes turned to Juana. "My husband is right, my dear. I am a foolish, worrisome woman. It is just that my nerves are so . . . so very bad. But of course you may stay here, just as long as you need to or want to."

Humiliation still mingling with her vast relief, Juana put her hands on the arms of her chair and pushed herself to her feet. As gracefully as she could manage, she curtsied. "*Gracias, mil gracias, señora.*"

Lawrence Mountjoy asked, "Where are your belongings?"

"I left my portmanteau in the hall. Our . . . my big trunk is down in a warehouse where the boat docked."

"We'll have it brought here tomorrow. Right now I'll show you to your room."

He turned to his wife, lifted her thin hand, and kissed it. "Now, just rest, dear. That's right. Lean back and close your eyes. I will be down in a few minutes."

Out in the hall he picked up Juana's portmanteau and then led her up that gracefully curving staircase. The upstairs hall, although narrower, was better lighted because of the tall window at its end. A few feet short of that window he opened a door and then stood aside for her to enter. She walked past him and then halted, awed and delighted.

All three rooms of the Ramirez family back in Cádiz could have fitted into this one bedchamber. True, Castle Villega had contained even larger and much loftier rooms, but none which had seemed to her as attractive as this one, with its highly polished floor spread with small scatter rugs, its graceful mahogany furniture, and its four-poster bed hung with floral-patterned curtains that matched the window draperies.

He set down her portmanteau and then crossed the room and opened another door. "A dressing room." He added matter-of-factly, "Perhaps you will choose to have the child sleep there later on." He moved across the bedroom to a window. "There's a garden below."

She went over to stand beside him. Still with that half-incredulous delight, she looked down at a hedge-enclosed garden where gravel paths meandered past benches and past flowerbeds set with pedestal-mounted reflecting balls. Along one path a peacock moved slowly, pecking at gravel. Even though his tail was not spread, Juana thought him as magnificent as any which had graced the gardens of Castle Villega.

Beyond the rear hedge was a tall stand of trees, and from somewhere beyond the trees smoke spiraled upward through the fading afternoon light. "They are making supper back there in the slave quarters," he said, and then added, "I mean the quarters of the house slaves. The field hands, of course, are housed near the plantation, five miles from here."

"Plantation?" She did not know the word.

"Fields, very extensive fields, where we grow cotton. Well, do you like your room?"

"So much," she said fervently. "I am so happy, and so . . . so relieved." With an inward shudder she thought of the bewildered panic she had felt only minutes ago down in that drawing room. "How is the way I can ever say thank you?"

"Why, in the way you have just said it." He smiled at her. "Now, I realize you must need to rest. But perhaps first we should sit down so that I can explain something to you."

They sat down in armchairs that flanked the small fireplace with its white marble mantel and its large white paper fan masking the empty grate. "My wife really does suffer from nerves," he said. "Like most neurasthenic people, she is subject to wide fluctuations in both physical and emotional health. Today happened to be one of her bad days. Tomorrow you may find her quite a different woman."

Juana nodded. By listening intently she had caught the gist of what he said, even though she did not know the exact meaning of every word.

"You must not think of her as one of these women who imagine their ailments. When I married her five years ago, she enjoyed excellent health. Then, when we had been married less than six months, she went out for a carriage ride one day. The horses bolted, tipping the carriage so that both my wife and the driver fell out and slid down an embankment. He struck his head against a rock and was killed. My wife was so badly injured that for a long time she was in too much pain to even try to walk. Eventually she recovered the use of her limbs. But ever since the accident she has been subject to these . . . these fits of nervous frenzy. While they last, she feels unable to cope with the slightest domestic difficulty, let alone an unexpected visitor."

Juana looked at him with sympathy-filled eyes. *"Que doloroso!"*

"That means 'how sad,' doesn't it? Yes, it was sad not only for her, but for me as well. Because, you see, I really love my wife.

"Forgive me for introducing such a personal note before we are really acquainted," he said. "But I saw the look on your face when Dorothy introduced me as her husband. Since you will be here for at least a number of weeks, I would like to explain to you how our marriage came about."

He paused for a moment and then went on. "My mother was a distant relation of Dorothy's first husband, Charles Elton. By the time I was sixteen, both my parents had died. I came here to live as Cousin Charles's ward. By the time I was eighteen I knew I was in love with his wife, even though she was twenty years older than I. Yes, I know that must strike you as strange. But it sometimes happens. For instance, have you ever heard of Ninon de Lenclos?"

"Ninon . . . ?" Juana shook her head.

"She was a Frenchwoman who lived in the seventeenth century. For about forty years she was sought after by some of the most influential men of her time. Toward the end of her life a young man, a son of her illegitimate daughter, fell in love with Ninon, not knowing she was his grandmother. When he learned the truth, he killed himself."

Again he paused, and then went on. "Anyway, I fell in love with Dorothy and stayed in love, resisting all of her and her husband's efforts to marry me off to one young lady or another. Then Cousin Charles died. It took me months to persuade her to marry me. Oh, it wasn't that she didn't love me. She confessed that all along she had been aware of what I felt. I hear that a woman is almost always aware when a man loves her. What was more, she had felt drawn to me for years. What worried her was what people would say. I finally persuaded her that the only two people whose opinion counted were ourselves."

Not knowing what to say, Juana said nothing.

"Well, there it is. Now, since you must be tired, and since Dorothy must still be in an agitated state, I think it might be better if you had your supper up here tonight, don't you?"

"Yes, much better."

"I'll send Mitty up with your supper. In fact, she can take care of you while you're here. She was once owned by a couple from Madrid, and so she speaks some Spanish."

With Juana following him, he crossed the room. In the doorway he turned and said, "Well, good-bye for now."

"Good-bye. And *gracias,*" Juana said earnestly. "*Mil gracias.*"

"What is the Spanish phrase for 'you are welcome'? *Por nada?*"

She nodded.

"Very well. *Por nada.*" He gave her another smile and then moved toward the head of the stairs. Heart swelling with gratitude, she looked after his tall, well-tailored figure for a moment before closing her door.

When the slave woman brought her a tall can of water, and then, minutes later, her supper, Juana felt brief disappointment. She had hoped for someone near her own age, someone she could chatter with in her native tongue. But Mitty was old, with a grayish cast to her black skin and a sullen look in her eye. She was somewhat deaf, or at least pretended to be. Juana realized that conversation between them probably would remain at a minimum.

But her supper, which she ate seated at the pretty little mahogany desk in one corner of her room, was excellent, a mixture of chicken, rice, tomatoes, and okra which reminded her of a dish Constancia used to make on feast days. Soon after Mitty had returned to remove the tray, Juana went into the dressing room and poured water from the tall metal pitcher into a big china basin. She undressed, bathed her swollen body in the cool water, and put on her nightshift. She returned through flickering candlelight to the four-poster bed, extinguished the candles in the three-branched candelabrum on the bedside stand, and stretched out. Almost immediately she began to drift off to sleep.

She had no idea of what time it was when she awoke, feeling frightened and confused. What had happened to the ship? Had it run aground? It must have, because the rocking motion to which she had been accustomed for many weeks now had ceased. Her hand groped for the bunk rail. Where was it? And how could the bunk have become so much wider?

And there was another change, a far more frightening one. She had a sense that from somewhere in the darkness beyond the cabin door an evil approached. It was as if some monster had managed to crawl from the black water onto the ship's deck . . .

Then she realized where she was—not in a cramped ship's cabin, but in the spacious bedroom of a beautiful house near a city she had never seen until today. For a few moments she went slack with relief.

But only for a few moments, because now it was happening again. Just as in her half-sleeping state, she had a sense of approaching evil. It rose now, not from the sea, but from the lower floor of this darkened house. Motionless and sweating, she sensed it slithering up those graceful stairs. Now it pressed against her door. So strong was the impression that she expected to hear the paneled wood creak. She heard nothing, though, except the pound of her own heart.

Gradually that sense of evil withdrew, faded away entirely. Lying there in the luxurious bed, and once more aware of the scent of night-blooming jasmine from the garden below, she scolded herself for being so silly as to let a grotesque impression from her half-dreaming state persist after she awakened. Furthermore, she could recall now the incident that must have given rise to that impression.

One day about three weeks before the *Esperanza* reached New Orleans, the captain had pointed out to Juana a creature swimming alongside the ship, just below the surface. To the horrified girl it had looked like a writhing bundle of long, thick snakes. It was a species of free-swimming octopus called argonauta, the captain told her. She had wondered if such a loathsome creature might, in the dark of night, reach one of those thick arms over a ship's gunwale and then haul itself aboard. That fleeting notion had lain buried in her mind these past weeks, only to emerge during her sleep so strongly that it had persisted even after she woke up.

Again her exhausted mind and body slid toward unconsciousness.

This time it was a prolonged, high-pitched scream that brought her awake.

She lay there, again aware of sweat on her forehead and her upper lip, waiting for the sound to repeat itself. It did not. Nevertheless, she was still sure that the sound had come from somewhere beyond her open window—the garden, or the trees beyond it, or the slave quarters beyond the trees.

Then, remembering that peacock, she smiled with relief. The peacocks at Castle Villega used to give that same scream, a cry that sounded like that of a human in the grip of rage or pain.

She again fell asleep, and this time she knew nothing more

until sunlight, streaming through the window, awoke her to a sense of well-being, even lightheartedness, which she had not known since the morning when Charlotte Higgins had told her of Manuel's death.

# 6

Almost immediately Mitty arrived with Juana's breakfast. She place a tray holding sweet rolls and a pot of hot chocolate on the bedside table, and then said, in Spanish thick with an accent Juana knew must be African, that Mrs. Mountjoy would like to see her on the garden terrace in about an hour.

"Thank you," Juana said. "Lovely morning, isn't it?"

The black woman stared at her with real or feigned incomprehension. "What?"

Juana raised her voice. "I said thank you."

Not answering, Mitty turned and shuffled from the room.

An hour later by the gilt clock on the fireplace mantel, Juana went downstairs and turned back along the wide ground-floor hall. Passing a partly open door, she looked inside and saw a slave woman almost as old as Mitty making a bed, a narrow one with a dark mahogany headboard but neither canopy nor posts. Near the bed the open doors of a wardrobe revealed coats and breeches hanging in neat rows. Mr. Mountjoy's room? Undoubtedly. So he did not even share a bedroom with his beloved wife. She thought: How sad!

Through a pair of open doors at the hall's end she could see a sun-flooded terrace. Nerves tightening with the memory of Mrs. Mountjoy's behavior the afternoon before, Juana moved out into the sunlight.

One look told her that Mrs. Mountjoy, seated in one of a pair of white wicker chairs, was indeed a different woman today. Her blue eyes were calm. Her face looked years younger, as if serenity had smoothed out some of its lines. Only her hands, busy with knitting needles, retained that ugly look of tension.

"Good morning, Juana. You don't mind if I call you Juana, do you? Sit here by me." Then, when the girl had sunk with awkward care into the other chair: "First of all, my dear, I must apologize for my behavior yesterday. There are times when my nerves are very bad."

"I know. And I am very sorry."

"My husband told you?"

"Yes. He told me about the carriage accident. I am so very sorry."

Mrs. Mountjoy's head, more gray than blond in the sunlight, nodded an acknowledgment. For several moments she knitted in silence. Juana's gaze moved to the garden, where the peacock, his magnificent tail spread today, strutted down a path.

"When do you expect your baby, my dear?"

Juana turned back to the older woman. "I think it will be about six weeks."

Dismay, quickly veiled, came into the blue eyes. With returning anxiety Juana realized that the woman must have hoped the birth would be sooner than that. Why was Mrs. Mountjoy, at least seemingly a gentlewoman, so unwilling to give another woman desperately needed shelter?

Could it possibly be that Mrs. Mountjoy feared that her husband might become susceptible to a young girl? It was a measure of Juana's diffidence that the idea had not even occurred to her until then. And as soon as it did, she dismissed it. How could Mrs. Mountjoy doubt her husband's long and well-proved devotion?

"And after the baby's birth? What plans do you have for the two of you?"

"Perhaps I shall go back to Spain. I have enough money for passage. Or perhaps I can work as a maid. There must be families in New Orleans who would hire me, even if I do have a child."

"Oh, my dear! I think it would be much better if you returned to your own country. You are so young to be making your way alone. And surely at least one of your parents is alive back in Spain."

Juana felt a small flare of stubbornness. What she did after she left this woman's house was her own business. But all she said was, "Yes, both of my parents are alive. Perhaps I will go back."

She would write to them very soon, she resolved, telling of her safe arrival in America and saying that she would write again when she had a permanent address. Her parents would give her letter to the parish priest, Father Ernesto, and he would read it to them. She would write also to her friend Charlotte Higgins in Philadelphia.

"Señora, if I write two letters today, will I be able to post them?"

"Of course. Give them to me and I will see to it."

For a while neither woman spoke. Then Juana said, "Yesterday your husband said something about having my trunk brought from the dock."

"Yes. Before he left for the fields this morning, I heard him tell the butler to send someone down to the docks with a wagon. I am sure your trunk will be here before the day is out."

Thinking of the docks reminded Juana of the woman in brown bombazine who had accosted her the day before. She said, "Do you know a woman named Sara Davidson?"

Mrs. Mountjoy's head jerked up. "Sara Davidson! I know *of* her. Everybody in and around New Orleans does. But how is it you have heard of her?"

Juana told her of the incident on the wharf the day before.

"Oh, my dear!" Mrs. Mountjoy said. "It is good that you turned away from her." She lowered her voice. "The woman runs a bad house, the most expensive one in the city. And people say that she is powerful, more powerful than the police and than most men in the government, because one way or another she can get them to do whatever she wants."

Juana said, feeling rather pleased with herself, "I knew she was bad. I could tell."

Again there was silence, except for the click of knitting needles. Looking at a far corner of the garden, Juana saw that the peacock seemed to be admiring his image in one of the reflecting balls.

She said, "Did you hear the *pavo real* . . ." She broke off, nodding in the direction of the resplendent fowl. "I do not know how to say it in English."

Mrs. Mountjoy followed the direction of Juana's gaze. "Oh! The peacock."

"Did you hear the peacock scream last night?"

Mrs. Mountjoy had dropped a stitch. She recovered it and then said, "He screamed? Oh, yes. Now that you mention it, I think I did hear him. But then, I'm used to it. He does that whenever a weasel or cat or something of the sort comes near that orange tree at night, the one over there in the opposite corner of the garden. That is where he roosts."

She began to roll up her knitting. "Lawrence will want to look over the household accounts when he comes back in the early afternoon."

"Does he go to the fields every morning?"

"Yes. He does not believe in leaving things entirely to an overseer."

"And is it a large . . . ? What is it called? Oh, yes . . . a large plantation?"

"The largest in the territory. By his wonderful management, Lawrence has doubled its size since it was left to me by my first husband."

"Mr. Mountjoy must be very smart."

"Oh, yes. He is very, very smart." She stood up. "Oh, no, my dear, don't you get up. Why not stay out here? The fresh air will be good for you."

Early that afternoon Juana's trunk arrived. She did not know about it at the time. Accompanied by the strutting peacock, she was making a delighted and detailed inspection of the garden, from the plots of stately rosebushes to an herb bed where fat bees hovered above sage and rosemary and thyme. But when she climbed the stairs to her rooms, she saw the open trunk, gutted of its contents. Mitty was hanging garments in the tall mahogany wardrobe with its elaborately carved doors. On the bed was a tangle of garments—poor Manuel's two extra homespun shirts and one pair of underdrawers, Juana's two extra shifts and two pairs of drawers, and the blue muslin dress that had been part of her meager trousseau. Without a word, Mitty scooped those garments up in her arms and headed toward the door.

Juana said, "Where are you going with those?"

Not pausing, Mitty answered, "Washerwoman," and left the room. Moments later, watching from the window, Juana saw the black woman unlatch the gate in the tall hedge at the garden's foot. Evidently beyond it was a path leading to the slave quarters.

By late afternoon Mitty had returned the garments, smelling of sun and fresh air and a hot iron. Juana wore the blue muslin down to supper that night.

Because of her native shyness, and because she feared that

Mrs. Mountjoy's mood might have undergone another change, Juana had felt apprehensive when she heard the supper gong, a sound Mitty had told her to expect. But when she entered the candlelit dining room next to the drawing room, she saw that Mrs. Mountjoy, if anything, looked even more relaxed than she had that morning.

Lawrence Mountjoy said, "My dear Mrs. Moreno, you look charming."

Juana threw a somewhat apprehensive glance at her hostess. But there was no flicker of resentment in Mrs. Mountjoy's blue eyes. Plainly, whatever the reason for the woman's strenuous objection to Juana's presence the day before, that reason had not been jealousy. And even if Lawrence Mountjoy had found her attractive, Juana realized suddenly, still his wife would have no real reason for jealousy, because Juana felt no pull of attraction to him. True, he was a good-looking man, and pleasant-mannered. Furthermore, Juana, like any normal woman, felt a certain amount of sexual awareness in the presence of most men. But in Lawrence Mountjoy's presence she felt only a blankness where that awareness should have been.

During most of the meal of baked fish and steamed okra he chatted easily about the continued hot weather, and the need for rain, and about the progress of the cotton harvest. Grateful that he did not seem to expect her to talk, Juana contented herself with smiling and nodding. Mrs. Mountjoy spoke a sentence or two now and then, but most of the time just looked dreamily at the candle flames.

Near the end of the meal he said, "I hope you won't find me objectionable, Mrs. Moreno, if I say that my wife has told me that you expect your child in about six weeks."

Because he had spoken slowly, Juana had grasped the gist of his sentence. She nodded. "That is so."

Lawrence Mountjoy turned to his wife. "My dear, don't you think that we should ask Dr. Hiram to have a look at her?"

"What? Oh, yes. Dr. Hiram. By all means."

He turned back to Juana. "And I think that as the time draws close, you had best have Mitty sleep in your dressing room. That way she can have someone fetch Dr. Hiram at any time of the day or night. He lives not much more than a mile from here."

The days that followed were on the whole pleasant for Juana, even though, like any woman in the last weeks of pregnancy, she felt a vast weariness of her clumsy girth and of the long, long waiting. Dr. Hiram, a short, fussy little man who wore spectacles attached to a black velvet ribbon, called on her twice, each time confirming her estimate of the approximate date when she could expect her child's birth.

Every day she studied her English, sometimes alone, sometimes with Mrs. Mountjoy helping her. Mrs. Mountjoy, too, taught her to crochet. With both of them crocheting squares that Mrs. Mountjoy later joined together, they completed a coverlet for the baby's crib in less than a week. Sometimes they worked in companionable silence. Other times Mrs. Mountjoy, in a soft, relaxed voice, asked questions about Juana's growing-up years in Cádiz, or reminisced about her own childhood in Virginia. Often Juana found it hard to believe that this was the same woman who had tried so hard to turn her away the day of her arrival.

Most evenings, only the Mountjoys and Juana were at the candlelit supper table. Several times, though, there were guests. Once it was a New Orleans judge, once the city's leading banker, once a United States senator and his wife. From the deference with which these distinguished people treated their host, she gathered that Lawrence Mountjoy must be a very rich and important man indeed.

She also learned from the table talk that Louisiana was no longer a Spanish possession. By some arrangement whose details she could not follow, the territory had reverted to the French.

Only twice during those weeks did Dorothy Mountjoy experience a spell of "bad nerves." One afternoon Juana was passing Mrs. Mountjoy's bedroom, near the opposite end of the second-floor hall from her own room, when the door opened and Mrs. Mountjoy's personal maid, Flossie, came out. Before the maid closed the door Juana caught a glimpse of Mrs. Mountjoy walking the floor with tears streaming down her face.

The second incident came almost two weeks later. Juana came in through the front door that afternoon after having taken the daily walk—twice around the circular front driveway—which Dr. Hiram had recommended. As she stepped into the lower hall, she heard a shriek from beyond the partially opened door of the drawing room, followed by a rhythmic pounding. Alarmed, she hurried forward, and halted in the doorway. Ignoring the maid, who with hands on her mistress's shoulders was trying to restrain her, Dorothy Mountjoy stood close to the wall, pounding her fists against it. "Where is he?" she screamed. "It's past four. Where is he?"

Juana must have made some sound, because Dorothy Mountjoy turned her head. Her face was that of a madwoman, eyes distended, lips drawn back in what seemed half-snarl, half-grin. Tears rained down her cheeks.

She cried, "You little fool, you! Why don't you go? Have your baby anyplace, have it in a ditch! Just go!"

As if the woman's words had held some strange sort of power, Juana felt pain grip her body. She turned and, hand on the railing, pulled herself up the stairs. Mitty, who for more than a week now had slept in the dressing room, was wielding a feather duster over the ornately carved wardrobe doors. Juana grasped one of the bedposts. "Mitty! Have them send someone for Dr. Hiram."

The old woman shook her head.

"But, Mitty! The baby—"

"No. It is not time," Mitty said in her strangely accented Spanish. She pointed to the bed. "Lie down."

Helplessly Juana obeyed. A few minutes later another spasm gripped her, a much weaker one. After that, nothing. How the old slave woman recognized that Juana's was false labor, the girl never knew.

After a while she became aware that there was no sound from below. Perhaps Lawrence Mountjoy had returned and managed to quiet his wife. Still later, the supper gong sounded through the silent house. When she went downstairs, Juana again was not surprised to learn from Mr. Mountjoy that his wife felt too ill to be present.

Four days later, the day after her own eighteenth birthday, her child was born shortly before noon. Her labor, which was difficult, had lasted sixteen hours. Afterward that sixteen-hour ordeal seemed to Juana a prolonged dream in which faces floated, looking down at her through changing light—lamplight, and then lamplight mingled with dawn grayness, and then full sunlight. She could remember Mitty's face, and Dr. Hiram's, and that of a woman she did not recognize. It was only later that she learned that the woman was a local midwife who sometimes assisted Dr. Hiram.

Finally she saw Dr. Hiram holding a small red shape by its ankles. She heard a cry. Then almost immediately she slid into exhausted sleep.

She came awake to find midafternoon sunlight filling the room. Mitty sat beside her bed. Why, Juana thought, something has happened to her face. After a moment she realized what it was. Mitty, who always wore a look of dour stupidity, was *smiling*. The black woman got up, went into the dressing room, and came back with the blanket-wrapped newborn in her arms. She laid the infant beside Juana. "You had a little girl."

As she looked down into the small, squirming face, Juana felt a pang of disappointment. Oh, not because of her child's sex. It was because the wispy hair on the round little head was dark. The closed eyes, Juana felt sure, also were dark. And she had so hoped that her child would have Enrique's light brown hair, fair skin, and gray eyes.

Then every other thought was overwhelmed by a wave of love, of almost fierce tenderness. You have only me, she thought, and yet you are going to have a good life, the very best of life. I, Juana Elena Ramirez Moreno, promise you that.

Mitty asked, "What will you name her?"

"Amalia."

She had decided that months ago. If a girl, her child would be called Amalia. If a boy, he would not be Enrique, much as she would long to name him that. Instead he would be called Manuel, after that man who had not only given her and her unborn child the respectability of marriage but also lost his life because her life had been in danger.

She asked, "Mitty, did you ever have children?"

The black woman's smile vanished. Some memory brought the old dourness, intensified now, back into her face, deepening its lines. "I had three. I don't know where any of them are."

"Oh, Mitty! I'm so sorry."

Mitty shrugged. "It is no use to talk about it." She fell silent, while Juana realized that there had been another change in the black woman. The deafness which had made conversation with her so difficult apparently had vanished.

Mitty's smile came back. "Amalia. That is a pretty name."

For nearly three weeks the slave woman continued to sleep in the dressing room on a cot beside Amalia's cradle. Then one afternoon she came to Juana, her face again set in those dour lines. "The mistress says I must start sleeping back in the cabin. Three girls back there are going to have babies, and the mistress says I must be ready to help."

Juana felt surprise. Mrs. Mountjoy seemed far too detached a person to concern herself with pregnant slave girls. Then Juana decided that it must have been Mr. Mountjoy who had realized that Mitty would be needed back in the cabins. He merely had felt it would be more fitting if the order came from his wife.

"I'm sorry, Mitty," Juana said. But secretly she was glad. The black woman had become far too possessive of Amalia. She had sulked these past few days whenever Juana, long since fully recovered, wanted to change or bathe the baby. Now she would have her child all to herself.

# 7

Afterward, looking back, Juana realized with wonder that those weeks when she and Amalia were alone together in those two rooms of the Mountjoy house were the happiest days of her life. Yes, even happier than the times when, awakening in her servant's cubicle at Castle Villega, she had known that in about an hour she would be lying in Enrique's arms. Her healthy daughter seemed to grow more beautiful every day. And despite Amalia's brunette coloring, Juana could see an emerging resemblance to Enrique in the well-marked brows and the wide spacing of the eyes. Juana began to feel a growing optimism, a sense that Amalia was a kind of talisman, ensuring that nothing could go too wrong for either of them.

She had only one cause for sadness during those weeks. Samuel Higgins, replying to Juana's letter to his wife, reported that Charlotte had died in a fall in their Philadelphia home. Juana felt sorrow not only for Charlotte but also for herself. She had liked to think that on this vast continent there was at least one woman whose friendship she could trust. She was so happy with her little daughter, though, and so comfortable beneath the Mountjoy roof, that she could not harbor sadness for long.

True, she was aware that soon she must leave this fine house. Mrs. Mountjoy seemed friendly enough in her often abstracted fashion, and even fond of the baby. She had taken Amalia in her arms a few times, holding her in the gingerly manner of a woman unused to infants. But Juana knew that any day now Dorothy Mountjoy might turn upon her, that mad look in her eyes, and rail at her for being here. No, she must not stay here much longer. Surely, though, some New Orleans family would want to hire her, despite her baby daughter. She even began to hope for marriage to some good man.

And if by any chance things did not promise to turn out well for her in Louisiana? Then she would return to Spain. She had the passage money. But if possible she wanted to remain in this opportunity-rich country rather than return to that poor street in Cádiz and to an Old World class system that would doom Amalia, no matter how beautiful and spirited she might become, to the hard, narrow existence of a poor man's wife.

One night at supper she said, "Now that I am strong again, I think I should go to New Orleans as soon as possible and find work there." As she spoke, she felt proud of herself. Only a few weeks ago she would not have been able to frame an English sentence that long. She added, "But first I will need one more kindness from you. We will need someone to take us there."

An odd silence. Eyes regarding her through the candlelight. Lawrence Mountjoy's light brown eyes. Dorothy Mountjoy's blue ones, only a moment ago dreamy in the candlelight, but now wide with tension, as if some anxiety had broken through her abstraction.

Mr. Mountjoy said, "Of course our coachman will take you and the baby into the city. But hadn't you best wait a few days, so that I can obtain a position for you before you leave here? I know all of the finest families in New Orleans. I am sure that any one of several of them will be glad to hire you."

"No, Lawrence!" Mrs. Mountjoy cried. "No, no!"

Juana felt chill bewilderment. Was her presence that great an affliction to Mrs. Mountjoy, so great that she could not bear the thought of Juana staying here even an additional few days?

Lawrence Mountjoy stood up, his chair scraping backward over the floor. "Now, Dorothy! Now, my dearest!" He moved to where she sat and, with hands on her upper arms, raised her to her feet. "You had best go to your room."

She was weeping now. "Please, Lawrence. Please!"

"Come, now, dearest." Arm around her, he led her from the room.

Juana sat in worried silence until his return. When he had resumed his place at the table, she said, "Mrs. Mountjoy doesn't want me to stay here for even a few more days, does she?"

He sighed. "Frankly, I'm seldom sure just what it is that my wife wants."

"I had best leave in the morning. I can hire a room for Amalia and myself until I find work. I have money, you know, more than three hundred dollars."

"Nonsense! Accommodations in New Orleans are expensive. You will find that three hundred dollars is no great sum. It might take you many days, and a good part of your money, to find a suitable position."

Juana kept a dismayed silence. Guarding that money was a life-and-death matter to her and Amalia. Without it she would have no way of retreating, if need be, to those three crowded rooms in Cádiz.

"Best to let me drive into New Orleans tomorrow and call upon a number of my friends. Perhaps before the day is out I will have arranged for some family to hire you. Certainly I should be able to arrange it before the week is over."

"But Mrs. Mountjoy wants me to leave right away. I can tell!"

"Now, Juana. You know her well enough to realize that by tomorrow her mood may have changed entirely. If it has not . . . well, in that case perhaps it would be best if I drove you to someplace like the New Orleans Inn. But let us wait and see, shall we?"

In the morning she found that he had been right about his wife's mood. At seven-thirty, as usual, Mitty brought Juana's breakfast, and then moved quickly into the dressing room to hang adoringly over Amalia's crib while Juana drank chocolate and ate sweet rolls. Soon after Mitty removed the tray, Juana carried her blanket-wrapped daughter down to the garden terrace. Even though it was now December, warm sunlight still fell on the mellow bricks.

Dorothy Mountjoy was there, her knitting in her lap, her gaze fixed on the garden, where a recent frost had killed all but the most hardy of the annuals. As Juana stepped onto the terrace, the woman turned her head. For a moment something stirred in the blue eyes. Then they became even more dreamily remote than usual. She said, "Good morning," smiled, and again looked out over the garden.

Juana sat down in a chair a few feet from Mrs. Mountjoy.

Cradling the baby in her lap, she made a few awkward attempts at conversation, and received brief, abstracted replies. Convinced that Mrs. Mountjoy did not expect her to talk, Juana sat in silence, enjoying the sun's warmth and the sight of her daughter's seraphic although toothless smile. Finally, after a murmured farewell to Mrs. Mountjoy, she went into the house.

She spent most of the rest of the day studying her English so that she could communicate as well as possible with her employers in the highly likely event that they, as friends of Mr. Mountjoy, would be English-speaking. Surely he would offer her services to French-speaking people only if he could not place her with an American or Spanish family. Around four she heard the clop of hooves and the rattle of coach wheels going past the house toward the stables beyond the hedge at the far end of the garden. Her heartbeats quickened. Lawrence Mountjoy must have returned from New Orleans.

Minutes later he knocked on her door. When she opened it, he said, smiling, "I have good news for you. An American couple named Baker will be glad to hire you. They will pay you six dollars a month, plus room and board, of course."

Six dollars! She would have been content with half that. In her excitement she forgot her English. "Oh, señor!" She opened the door wide. *"Favor de—"*

"No, I won't come in. I have some business matters to attend to down in my office. At supper I will tell you all about the Bakers. In the meantime, perhaps you had best get your things together so that you can leave in the morning."

When he had gone, she opened the old trunk standing against one wall and began to fill it with clothing from the wardrobe and the chest of drawers. There was more room in it now than there had been when she came here. She had given Manuel's garments, including the brown broadcloth coat and breeches he had worn at his wedding, to Mitty to distribute among the slaves. She was sure that Manuel would have preferred to have his clothing used rather than left lying in a trunk.

When the trunk was packed, she placed her portmanteau on the bed, intending to put into it the few articles strewn across the top of her dressing table—a comb, hairpins, and a little case for needles and thread. She opened the portmanteau, reached down to its little tray to lift it out, and then paused, hand in midair.

The tray no longer held the leather bag containing her money.

Stomach contracting into a sick knot, she lifted the tray out, upturned the little hand trunk onto the bed, and pawed throught the spilled contents. No leather bag.

She searched the trunk next, thinking it barely possible that she had placed the money there and then forgotten about it. After that she searched the floor of the wardrobe, and through the pockets of all her clothing, and then—careful even in her panic not to disturb her napping daughter—she searched through the small chest of drawers in the dressing room.

At last she returned to the bedroom and sank trembling onto the bed. Someone had stolen her money, the precious money that was to be her shield against whatever might threaten her and her baby.

She forced herself to try to think clearly. The first thing to do, she realized, was to tell Lawrence Mountjoy. If anyone could recover her money, he could.

She descended the stairs, stopped in the open doorway of Lawrence Mountjoy's office, a small room next to the dining room. He sat at his desk with a stocky red-haired man standing beside him. Since she had seen him in the house on a few earlier occasions, Juana recognized him as the plantation's overseer.

Mountjoy turned his head, took one look at Juana's stricken face, and said, "That will be all, Mullins."

As the overseer moved toward the front door, Mountjoy got to his feet and said, "Come in." He closed the door behind her. "Better sit down, Juana." He sat down beside the desk. "Now, what is it?"

"My money! My more than three hundred dollars! It is gone!"

"You are sure?"

She nodded. "I looked everywhere."

After a moment he said, "It must have been one of the slaves. Mitty would have had the best opportunity."

Juana cried, "Oh, no! Mitty would not have done that."

"Perhaps you are right. There are seventeen servants quartered out back, if you count the coachman and stableboys and gardeners, and any of them could have slipped upstairs to your room."

She tried to remember if the butler or one of the downstairs maids had been in the dining room when she mentioned her money the night before. She could not remember. And anyway, she suddenly realized, it did not matter. She'd had no reason to open her portmanteau for weeks and weeks. The money could have been stolen at any time during that period.

"Now, Juana. Don't look like that. I will get your money for you."

Hopeful but dubious, she asked, "How?"

"The slaves themselves will recover it for you. I shall tell them that unless they produce the thief and the money, they will all be punished."

That seemed unfair. But she was too distraught to worry a great deal about such fine points. "Oh, I hope you can get it back! I . . . I would be afraid to take that fine position you found for me if I had to go there penniless. What if your friends dismiss me? What would Amalia and I—"

"Juana, you will not have to leave here until your money is restored to you. I promise you. Now, will you please excuse me? I have some papers to look over before suppertime."

Dorothy Mountjoy did not appear for the evening meal. Throughout it Juana stayed mostly silent, trying to listen as he talked of her future employers, the Bakers, trying not to worry about that vanished leather bag. When supper was over, she returned to her room and restored the wildly strewn contents of her trunk and portmanteau and the wardrobe to their proper places. For a while after that, still fighting her anxiety, she sat beside the cradle where Amalia lay on her stomach, one dimpled hand curled near her face. Then Juana went into the bedroom and undressed. She had expected to lie awake for a long time, but apparently shock and worry had exhausted her. She slid almost immediately into sleep.

She never knew at just what hour her waking nightmare began. She knew only that she came abruptly out of sleep to see a figure standing beside her bed, a deeper dark against the darkness. A scream rising within her, she sat bolt upright.

The scream never reached her lips. A hand struck the side of her face a sharp blow, rocking her head to one side, making points of light swim before her eyes through the darkness.

Then the hand covered her lips, forcing her head down onto the pillow.

"When I take my hand from your mouth, don't make a sound. Your baby is only a few feet away. And babies are very, very fragile."

Through her shock and pain and fear, an even more paralyzing terror rose. She lay motionless, heart hammering in her breast.

She heard the scratch of a flint against the flint box. Candlelight struck upward into Lawrence Mountjoy's faintly smiling face. For a moment he stood there, not touching her. Then he bent. His hand, catching the neck of her nightshift, ripped the garment down to its hem. He gave another tug, tearing the swath of homespun completely free. Then he stood up and let the length of material fall to the floor.

Rigid, terrified eyes never leaving his face, she lay there while his gaze roamed down her naked body. Then, quite calmly, he sat down beside her on the edge of the bed.

"I intended to wait several more nights, but I find I cannot."

Her shocked mind began to work. Several nights. Then he had not intended for her to leave here to go to work for the Bakers. Perhaps there were no people named Baker.

She whispered, before she knew she was going to, "You are the one who took . . . ?"

"Your money? Yes, four or five days ago, when I sensed you'd begun to think of leaving for New Orleans."

He still smiled. His eyes had a peculiar shine, which she knew was not due to the candlelight. With a kind of weird detachment she reflected that now she knew why she had never thought him attractive, this handsome, well-dressed, youngish man. The reason was that until tonight she had never even met him. Until tonight what he really was had been hidden by the facade of a highly successful planter and long-suffering husband, devoted to a neurasthenic wife much older than himself.

He said, "Now, I want you to understand the situation from the first, Juana. You will stay here just as long as I want you to, because I hold all the cards. I have everything—money, long-established reputation, influential friends. You have nothing—no money, no friends, only a child who makes you all the more helpless." He paused as if to let his words sink in. Then he went on. "If you succeed in leaving here, I will charge you with theft and have you hunted down and arrested. You will deny it, of course, but who will the authorities believe, their friend Lawrence Mountjoy or an obviously lower-class immigrant who landed here only last September? And after you are in prison, what becomes of your child?"

He paused again, and then asked, "Now, are you going to be quiet, or must I gag you?"

She lay there, dark eyes enormous in her white face. She thought of Amalia, "fragile" Amalia. Just one blow of the sort she had suffered a few minutes ago would kill her little girl. She whispered, "I'll be quiet."

Those strangely shining brown eyes considered her. "Perhaps. But I don't think I will run the risk." He took a white handkerchief from his coat pocket. "Open your mouth."

Half-paralyzed with fear, she was slow to obey. He drew back his hand. "Open it!" She parted her lips and teeth. He slipped the gag into place, told her to raise her head, and then knotted the handkerchief at the back of her neck.

Lying rigid, she watched him undress. With that same weird detachment she noted that his body was much thicker than it appeared when he was clothed. Even though his erection showed how aroused he was, he took time to fold his coat, shirt, breeches, and underbreeches neatly over a chair back. Then he launched himself upon her, thrusting her legs apart with his legs, grinding himself into her. To her body, dry with shock and revulsion and terror, each stroke was painful. The ordeal seemed to go on for a long time, even though she knew it could not have been more than a few minutes. In fact, when he finally collapsed upon her, a disgruntled sound he made in her ear indicated that he had hoped to last longer.

He rolled off her inert body and stared up at the ceiling through the candlelight, as if debating whether or not to stay in her bed longer. Then he got up and quickly dressed.

Not smiling now, but still with that peculiar shine in his eyes, he looked down at her and said, "I will be back tomorrow night, and as often after that as I choose to." He looked toward the open door of the dressing room and then down at her again. "And remember to be very, very careful."

He leaned over her, unknotted the gag, and stuffed the

handkerchief in his coat pocket. He went out, closing the door quietly.

She lay still for a moment more. Then, on legs that felt scarcely strong enough to support her, she stood up, lifted the candelabrum from the bedside stand, and hurried into the dressing room. As if she feared that after all he had somehow managed to harm her child, she held the candelabrum above the cradle. Amalia still lay on her stomach, small body scarcely stirred by her breathing.

Juana returned to the bedroom and sank down on the bed. She felt an almost irresistible urge to gather up her baby, creep down the stairs, and run from this house as far and as fast as she could. But he would be expecting her to do that. He must be waiting right now, on the lower floor or perhaps outside the house, to intercept her.

And besides, where could she go, an immigrant without money or friends or even a firm grasp of the English language? And when the police hunted her down and arrested her, how could she defend herself? Even though she had only the vaguest notion of what a courtroom looked like, she imagined him in one, standing to address a judge he might well have entertained at Twin Pines. "Where this young woman hid the money she stole from me, I have no idea. But two of my slaves saw her take it from the safe in my office."

Mrs. Mountjoy, Juana thought. Go to her right now. She had seemed friendly enough except when her nervous fits were upon her. And she had shown actual tenderness toward Amalia. Surely she would help now, surely she would.

But for Juana to go to Dorothy Mountjoy's room would mean leaving Amalia alone, unguarded. That madman might come in . . . On the other hand, if she gathered up the baby and started to carry her down the hall, Amalia might wake up and cry. She could imagine that shiny-eyed man, sitting down there on the lower floor in his office or on the edge of his bed, waiting for just such a sound.

She made her choice, praying that it was the right one. She shed the ruined nightshift, leaving it in a heap on the floor, and dressed in her most serviceable clothing, a dark blue blouse and full skirt she had worn when she worked at the Castle Villega. Then she soundlessly opened her door, closed it behind her, and moved down the dark hall. A three-quarters moon, shining through a window at the hall's end, gleamed on the paneled door of Mrs. Mountjoy's room.

The doorknob turned under Juana's hand. She eased herself into the room, closed the door behind her with an almost inaudible click. The room was not completely dark. On a stand beside the bed a candle flickered inside a hurricane lamp of dark blue glass. The bluish light wavered over Dorothy Mountjoy, lying in the bed on her back. Her harsh breathing was loud in the room.

Heart pounding, Juana crossed the room, bent over, placed her hand on the woman's lips. Her rasping breath caught. Her eyes flew open.

"Please! Please!" Juana whispered. "Don't make noise. You must help me. You won't make noise, will you?"

The gray-blond head moved from side to side. Juana removed her hand. Instantly the woman said in a fierce whisper, "Go away!"

"No!" Juana whispered back. She sat down on the edge of the bed. "You must help me. Your husband came to my room tonight . . ."

Even in that dim light Juana could see the despairing pity that leaped into the woman's face. It told Juana that there was no need to recount the rest. Dorothy Mountjoy said, "I knew it last night at supper. When you said you were ready to leave, I knew he would not wait much longer."

"You've got to help me get away from here!"

Mrs. Mountjoy whispered harshly, "I can't."

"You can! You must know some family near here that would protect my baby and me."

"Even if I did, I would not tell you. Juana, Juana! I am more helpless than any of the slaves back there in the quarters."

"How can you be? You are rich! Your first husband left you this house and the largest plantation in—"

"It is not mine." Bitterness in the whispered voice now. "I signed it over to Lawrence soon after we were married, when I was still too infatuated to let myself see what he was."

Her dry, tense hands grasped Juana's. "Let me tell you about Lawrence. Then perhaps you will see that . . ." She broke off, and then went on. "The accident which left me crippled for so long. It was not an accident. Lawrence told me so after he knew that I could no longer do anything about it."

He had treated the coach horses' harness, she went on to say, with a chemical that remained inert for about fifteen minutes after the harness was in place. Then it began to burn the horses so painfully that the crazed animals bolted.

"He must have hoped that I would be killed, just as the coachman was. But all along, too, he must have known what he would try to do if it turned out that I was only injured, which of course is what happened. He began to give me pills for the pain. By the time I realized that they were opium pills, it was too late. I *had* to have them."

She released Juana's hands and lay back, eyes staring at the ceiling through the bluish glow. "Sometimes, just to teach me how helpless I am, he will delay coming home from the plantation. I won't be able to get the pills because he keeps them locked in the safe. By the time he gets here I have become . . . something scarcely human."

Her gaze moved to Juana's face. "Don't you understand? He can make me do anything, just by withholding my pills. To get them, I would betray you even if you were my own daughter. And so even if I did know someplace safe for you to go, it would do you no good. A few hours from now, by keeping those pills from me, he could have me babbling everything. He would follow you, and tell whatever clever story he has made up to destroy you in other people's eyes. The slaves would know they had better back any story he chooses to tell. And I . . . Oh, God, Juana, I would confirm his story too!"

Her whispered voice was feverish now. "So get back to your room before he suspects that you have come here. Do as he says! Do *anything* he says. Remember, Juana. He's a madman."

Juana sat rigid for a moment. Then she sprang to her feet. With a terrifying picture in her mind she sped across the room and opened its door, almost too agitated to remember to close it quietly. She hurried down the hall. Perhaps even now he was bending over that cradle . . .

She entered her room, forced herself to close the door silently. Stomach a sick knot, she hurried through the candlelight into the dressing room. Enough light came through the doorway to show her that Amalia still slept peacefully.

Shaking all over, she went back into the bedroom. She undressed, took her other nightshift from the chest of drawers, and put it on. The ruined shift she rolled up and placed in one corner of the wardrobe's floor.

She looked at the bedroom door. No latch, and a keyhole but no key. There would have been no point in locking the door anyway. He would be able to get in sooner or later. She lay down and stared unseeingly at the opposite wall.

Then, beneath her leaden despair, a hope stirred. Mitty! Mitty liked her, and adored Amalia. Mitty would help them, no matter what the consequences. And never mind that she was only a slave, and a decrepit one at that. She would know of someone, black or white, who would be willing to shelter Juana and her baby.

She lay there staring at the wall until the candle guttered out. She still had not slept when dawn grayed the room or when, well after sunrise, she heard Mitty turn the doorknob.

Juana sat up in bed. As the door opened, she cried softly, "Mitty! Oh, Mitty!"

But it was not Mitty who carried the breakfast tray. It was a fat girl of fourteen or fifteen, her yellowish complexion marked with brown patches. Juana had glimpsed her once or twice before and had gained a vague impression that she was one of the kitchen maids.

Juana watched numbly as the girl placed the tray on the bedside table. Then she asked, "Where is Mitty?"

The girl looked down at her with a stupid expression like the one Mitty used to wear. But Juana was sure that in the girl's case the stupidity was real.

"Mitty? Mitty left near evening yesterday." She spoke in a dialect that made the words sound like, "lef' neah evenin' yistiday."

It took Juana a moment to realize the girl's meaning. Then she asked, "How can it be that she left?" It seemed unbelievable that a slave so aged would have run away. Nor was it likely, for the same reason, that her owner had found a buyer for her.

"Massa sent her away in a wagon."

"Sent her where?"

"Other plantation Massa's got."

"*Where?*"

The fat girl shrugged. "Someplace upriver." She turned and went out.

Juana lay back. From a map which the *Esperanza*'s captain had showed her she knew that the Mississippi was many hundreds of miles long. An "upriver" plantation could be near any one of the numerous settlements strewn along its banks.

For a long while she lay there in wooden despair. What could she do except stay in this house, hoping that sooner or later Lawrence Mountjoy would begin to suffer pangs of conscience or grow tired of her?

But she knew that madmen do not suffer pangs of conscience. And if he grew tired of her, he would not let her go, lest she find people to believe her story. He would get rid of her, and of Amalia too.

So there it was. Dorothy Mountjoy would not help her. Mitty could not. But staying here would mean not only degradation. Ultimately it might mean death for herself and her little girl. Therefore she must try to escape him as soon as possible, no matter what the consequences if he caught her.

But even if she managed to reach New Orleans safely, what then? He could still track her down, have her jailed, have Amalia taken from her. Unless . . .

Unless she could find someone able and willing to protect her.

And there was someone powerful enough, someone who might still be willing . . .

Grimly she stared at a patch of morning sunlight on the wall. It was a terrible way out of her dilemna. But she would take it if she had to.

Because she knew she was going to need her strength, she drank the chocolate and ate two sweet rolls, even though she had no appetite. Then she dressed, went into the next room, and lifted Amalia from her cradle.

She spent most of the day seated beside the bedroom window. Holding the baby in her arms, she stared down into the garden and made her plans. As the day waned, she began to wrestle with the question of whether or not she should go down to supper. She feared that Mountjoy, looking at her across the candlelit table, would read her intentions in her face. Or if his wife was at the table, some look passing between Juana and the older woman might arouse his suspicion.

On the other hand, she might provoke his anger by staying away. If so, there was no way of knowing what form his punishment of her might take.

The question was solved when, after sunset, the yellow-skinned girl knocked and then came into the room. "Massa says, you wants your supper up here?"

"Yes, please."

When he came into her candlelit room—shortly after nine, by the clock on the fireplace mantel—she was in bed, face expressionless, thick dark braids lying on her shoulders. He looked at her with approval. He undressed, again folding his clothes neatly over a chair back, and then sat naked on the bed's edge.

Whether to excite himself, or to intimidate her even further, or merely for the pleasure of boasting, he began to talk. He told her what she already knew—that Dorothy Mountjoy's accident had not been that at all. He talked of his occasional visits to various women in the slave quarters.

A smile on his lips, he had been looking at the candelabrum. Now, brown eyes holding that peculiar shine, he turned to her. "The first night you were here I became so excited, thinking of my plans for you, that I went back to the quarters around ten o'clock and visited Hully." Juana knew that Hully, a very black girl of thirteen or fourteen, was the butler's granddaughter. "It was her first time, and she put up quite a fight. I had to almost break her arm before she would lie quiet."

So it had not been the peacock screaming that night.

He said, "Take off your shift."

She hesitated only a moment before stripping the garment off over her head and dropping it on the counterpane. Instantly he fell upon her, driving hard into her unresisting body. Again the onslaught was brief. He looked down at her, and she could see angry disappointment with his performance in his face.

She held her breath. Would he take his anger out on her? Slap her as he had the night before? Sink his teeth into her neck or breast?

After a moment the threatening look faded from his eyes. He shrugged. Then he got up, dressed, and without looking at her again, left the room.

She blew out the candles and then just lay there, struggling with an impulse that almost overwhelmed her, an impulse to dress immediately, snatch up her child, and leave this house. But she must wait. All day she had kept warning herself that she must wait until there was little chance that anyone, black or white, in the Mountjoy house and its slave cabins was still awake.

She heard the tall clock in the downstairs hall strike eleven, midnight, twelve-thirty. Now! With shaking fingers she lighted one candle and then dressed in her dark full skirt and blouse. Then she hesitated. She dared not burden herself with the portmanteau or even a bundle of extra clothing. She would need both her arms and hands to carry Amalia and, as they moved along a woodland path, to protect the little face and body from whipping branches. But there was one article in the portmanteau which she could not bear to abandon.

She placed the little hand trunk on the bed, lifted out its tray, and burrowed with her fingers through layers of under-clothing and heavy knitted stockings to an object in one corner. She brought it out. Holding it on one palm, she quickly freed it from the frayed length of dark red ribbon in which it was wrapped. For a second or two, holding the miniature close to the candlelight, she looked down at Enrique's beloved young face with its wide-set gray eyes and engaging smile. She rewrapped the miniature, dropped it into the pocket of her skirt, took down her brown knitted shawl from the wardrobe.

In the almost completely dark dressing room she lifted the baby's soft, warm body into her arms. Amalia gave a whimper. Juana's heart leaped into her throat. The baby must not cry, she simply must not, until they were well clear of this house.

"Sh-h-h, my darling. Sh-h-h, my heart."

Amalia sighed and went back to sleep, head pillowed on her mother's breast.

In the bedroom Juana blew out the candle, opened the door softly, stepped out into the hall. Moonlight flooding through the window at its western end showed her the head of the stairs. Aware of the pulse hammering in the hollow of her throat, she hurried forward, footsteps noiseless over the thick carpeting. When she reached the stairs she checked her pace and descended cautiously, keeping close to the banister to avoid the center portions of the steps, which sometimes creaked. The moonlight in the ground-floor hall was dimmer, but still bright enough for her to see, with a surge of relief, that the door to Lawrence Mountjoy's room was closed. Even so, as she neared it her heart pounded with the fear that it would open and his tall figure would step out to block her way.

His door remained closed. She hurried down the hall. The door leading onto the terrace was locked and barred, as she had known it would be. Left arm cradling Amalia, she turned the key in the lock, cautiously drew the bolt. The grate of metal against metal seemed loud in the utter stillness, but that couldn't be helped. She stepped out into cool air and into the bright—far too bright—radiance of an almost full moon. To get out of this flooding moonlight as quickly as possible was the important thing now, even though her running footsteps over the flagstoned terrace and gravel path would make more noise than slower ones. At the foot of the garden she reached out to push open the white wooden gate in the tall yew hedge.

From her left came a high-pitched scream.

For a moment she stood frozen. Then she realized that the cry, with its metallic sound almost like that of a brass trumpet, could not have issued from a human throat. The peacock. Her intrusion into the garden at this after-midnight hour had disturbed his slumbers there in the dwarf orange tree in an angle of the hedge. As she pushed the gate open, she wondered fleetingly how she had ever been able to convince herself that the scream her first night here had come, not from the slave quarters, but from the resplendent fowl that by day strutted up and down these garden paths.

She moved through the gate, turned left, hurried along the shadowed strip between the tall hedge and the grove of trees that hid the slave cabins. Ahead was the carriage house and stables. As she passed the structure, one of the horses, apparently catching the human scent, gave a whinny. Thank God, she thought, that Mountjoy, busy making money out of the plantation his once-infatuated wife had given him, kept no pack of hunting dogs.

She turned the corner of the hedge, keeping close to its shadow. When the hedge gave way to the house's northern wall, she decided to make a dash through the moonlight to the trees on the other side of the drive, rather than to risk creeping past Lawrence Mountjoy's window.

The drive swerved to join the circular one that swept around the wide front lawn. She did not follow it but kept close to the shadow of the wood that formed the lawn's northern boundary. A few yards ahead, a path angled away through the trees toward the public road. She had discovered the path on one of the walks which, obeying Dr. Hiram's orders, she had taken while she awaited her daughter's birth.

For an anxious moment she thought she had missed the small opening and would have to retrace her steps. But no, here it was. Right hand shielding Amalia's small head and face, she plunged into the deeper darkness beneath the overarching branches of pine and broadleaf trees. At first she moved cautiously lest some root or fallen branch trip her up, but as her eyes grew more accustomed to the dim light filtering down through the trees, she quickened her pace.

Perhaps fifteen minutes later she emerged from the path into the shallow ditch that bordered the public road. New Orleans, she knew, lay about eight miles to her right. How long would it take her to walk eight miles with the baby in her arms? Would Lawrence Mountjoy, an early riser, discover her absence before she reached the city? Perhaps he had discovered it already. Perhaps the peacock's scream or the horse's whinny had sent him upstairs to look in her room. Perhaps even now, astride a galloping horse, he was turning from the long Twin Pines drive onto the public road . . .

But she would not let herself think about that. She would just keep to the ditch, so that at the first sound of hoofbeats she could scramble back into the shelter of the trees.

The ditch, though, offered rough going. Low bushes growing in it grabbed at her skirts. She kept stubbing her toes against what felt like rocks or chunks of wood. Then something, probably a tree root, almost sent her sprawling. She saved herself and the baby only by freeing her right hand in time to catch a tree's dangling branchlet. After that she knew she must keep to the road, despite the flood of blue-white moonlight. She climbed to the road and started walking as rapidly as she could. A minute or two later she knew that she must be passing a swamp, because from beyond the road's opposite side came the deep roar she had come to recognize as that of a bull alligator. Soon after that a ghostly egret, long legs dangling, snowy plumage dyed bluish by moonlight, flew across the road at treetop level. She heard the faint sound of his beating wings. Otherwise, except for her muffled footsteps, there was silence.

Then, from somewhere behind her, she heard the creak of wheels. She plunged down into the ditch, crouched. Now the thud of hooves mingled with creaking sounds. Amalia, jostled by Juana's swift descent into the ditch, woke up and began to wail.

"Sh-h-h!" Juana whispered frantically, rocking and patting the small form. Amalia wailed all the louder. "Sh-h-h," Juana said again, still crouched, but with eyes fixed on the bend in the road.

A wagon came into view, drawn by a white or gray horse which, even from fifty yards away through that uncertain light, appeared old and spavined. On the driver's seat sat a man with a black face and white kinky hair. Beside him was the thin figure of a woman, her face shadowed by the brim of her hat.

Stay hidden, lest they, in hope of a reward or for some other reason, hurry back to Twin Pines to betray her? Or appeal to them, in the hope that they would take her safely to New Orleans before Mountjoy discovered she was missing?

It took her only seconds to make up her mind. With her left arm cradling Amalia, whose wails had ceased as abruptly as they had begun, she used her right hand to help herself scramble up onto the road.

The old horse, startled by the sudden appearance of a shawled figure in its path, reared in the traces, whinnying. The driver said soothingly, "Sam, you old fool, nothing to be scared of, just a gal." Like nearly all the blacks Juana had encountered, he pronounced "scared" as "skeerd" and "just" as "jes'."

The horse quieted. As Juana moved closer, the driver said testily, "Gal, ain't you got no sense, popping up out of a ditch like that? I got half a mind to . . ."

Apparently she had come close enough that he could see beneath the shadow of her shawl to her face, because he said in a bewildered voice, "Why, it's a white lady." He turned to the thin black woman beside him. "Dicey, this here's a white lady."

Juana said, "Please! I must get to New Orleans. Will you take me there?"

After a moment the driver said, "Ma'am, it ain't fitting you ride with us."

"Please! I have run away from Twin Pines. Do you know Twin Pines? There is a man there, Lawrence Mountjoy. He . . . Oh, please! Help me!"

She broke off, wretchedly aware of the resistance, the fear, in the black face beneath the white woolly hair.

The woman beside him spoke for the first time. "We knows him, ma'am. White folks don't really know him, but black folks does." Her voice thickened. "He's not a man, he's a *devil.*" She turned to the driver. "Zach, you get down, help the lady up here."

"Dicey, if Massa Mountjoy finds out what we done—"

"Just shut your mouth, just shut your ugly mouth and get down off this here wagon. Best she and the little one hides under the seat. Nobody sees her there."

The man climbed down. So did the woman. Juana had become aware now that the rear of the wagon was piled high with those large tubers Louisiana people called yams. The black woman, a wispy little thing not even as tall as Juana, said, "You climb up, now, and hide under the seat. I spreads my skirt, nobody see you. Here, give me that baby."

Transferred to strange arms, Amalia again wailed. Juana climbed into the wagon and lay, knees drawn up, under the seat. The feisty little black woman held the baby up to Juana's reaching hands. Seconds later, after Dicey sat down on the seat and spread her skirts, after Zach urged the old horse back into its plodding walk, Amalia fell asleep, seemingly as content as if the swaying wagon were a cradle.

For perhaps a minute there was no sound but that of plodding hooves and creaking wheels. Then the woman up on the wooden seat asked, "Ma'am?"

"Yes?"

"Where you going in New Orleans? Someplace special?"

After a moment Juana said, "Yes. But just leave me anywhere inside the city. I'll find my way from there."

"We be there before daylight. Can't just leave you and the baby alone in the dark streets."

Juana remained silent. She shrank from telling anyone, even these black country folks, where she intended to go.

And yet, the thought of wandering through strange dark streets until daylight . . .

The little woman said, "Looky here. Suppose we leaves you at my sister's. They live next to her man's blacksmith shop. You stays there till morning, then goes where you wants to."

"Thank you," Juana said fervently.

The wagon rattled on. Then, through the squeaking of the wheels, she heard another sound, one that made her heart leap with terror. Hoofbeats, pounding hollowly on the dirt road. Almost as clearly as if she had been able to look back, she saw him in her mind's eye astride a galloping horse, eyes in his rage-pale face still holding that peculiar shine.

She heard the two up on the seat conferring softly. Then the woman said in a low voice, "It's him, all right. But you just keeps still."

Juana became aware that the sound of her surging blood was almost as loud in her ears as those pursuing hoofbeats. She heard him shout something, heard the black driver say, "Whoa!"

The wagon came to a halt. Juana heard Lawrence Mountjoy ask, "Have either of you seen a white woman with a baby?"

"White lady with a baby? No, massa, no."

"Don't lie to me! You see this pistol? You lie to me and I'll use it. Whose niggers are you, anyway?"

"We's free niggers." There was fear in the man's voice, but a certain dignity, too. "I'se Zach Green, and this here's my woman, Dicey. We sharecrops for Massa Biglow."

There was a creak of leather, as if Mountjoy had leaned forward in the saddle. "Yes, I think I've seen you at the Biglow plantation. Where are you going now?"

"We takes these here yams to market."

Juana heard horse and rider move to the rear of the wagon. There was the sound of several objects thudding onto the road. With helpless fear she realized that he was not taking the black couple's word. He had dislodged several yams, thinking that she and the baby might somehow be concealed back there. And now he would order her rescuers to get down. He would look under the seat . . .

But he did not. Instead she heard him say, more to himself than to the black couple, "Sly bitch must have gone in the other direction." Then, more loudly: "Do you know who I am and where I live?"

"Oh, yes, massa, we knows."

"If you see her, offer her a ride and bring her back to Twin Pines. You ought to be able to manage that between the two of you. Bring her to me, and I'll give you fifty dollars."

For a moment Juana's heart seemed to stop beating. Fifty dollars! It was a huge sum, probably more money than those two had ever possessed at one time in their whole lives. Surely they could not resist it. Surely now they would get down from the wagon and . . .

"Massa, we sees her, we sure brings her back to you. For fifty dollars, we does almost anything. But we ain't seen her yet."

For a moment Juana went limp with relief. Then Amalia sighed, squirmed in her mother's arms, let out the faintest whimper . . .

Juana's whole body turned cold. If the baby cried now, those two brave people up there on the plank seat would die. In his fury, that madman might kill her and Amalia right on the spot too. And perhaps that might be preferable to being taken back to Twin Pines.

She thought of covering the tiny mouth with her hand. But unless she pressed hard, hard enough to perhaps injure the little face, she might provoke Amalia to even louder sounds.

"Blessed Virgin," Juana prayed silently, "don't let her cry, don't let her cry."

Perhaps the Virgin heard her prayer. Or perhaps Amalia, lying warm in her mother's arms, decided that those voices were not annoying enough for her to wake up entirely and make a vigorous complaint. Whatever the reason, Juana became aware after a moment that the baby had slid back into sleep.

"Remember, I'll pay you fifty dollars."

Juana heard his mount's bridle jingle as he wheeled around. Then the sound of galloping hooves was dwindling away in the distance.

After a while the black woman said, "You all right, ma'am?"

Juana managed to say, "Yes, I'm all right."

"Zach, you get down, see about them yams." A few moments later she asked, "He break any?"

"A couple busted, that's all."

"That ain't bad. Put the others he throwed out back in the wagon, and then we goes. Ma'am?"

"Yes?"

"You and the young'un best stay there. Somebody sees you up on the seat, word might get back to that devil."

Worn out, Juana actually slept for a while after that, despite the jolting, creaking ride over the dirt road. She did not come fully awake even when she realized that the vehicle moved over city cobblestones. It was only when the wagon stopped, and she heard her rescuers descending to the ground, that she became fully conscious.

Dicey said, "Hand the baby down, ma'am. Then you gets down."

Feeling cramped and chilled, Juana descended to the ground. They were in the fenced yard, she saw, of a one-story house. From the fence opposite the door a roof projected, forming a shed. Even though the moon was down now, she could make out, inside the shed, the dark shape of a blacksmith's forge.

"You wait here, ma'am. I tells the whole thing to my sister."

Juana stood there with the still-slumbering Amalia in her arms while the couple moved to the door of the house. Zach knocked. After a few moments lamplight bloomed beyond a window. The door opened and the couple went inside. Perhaps three minutes later the door opened. "Ma'am?"

Juana carried the baby over the threshold of a lamplit kitchen. In the fireplace banked coals gave off a pleasant warmth. "This here's my sister," Dicey said. "Her man's asleep." She nodded toward the closed door of an inner room.

Numb with exhaustion, Juana mumbled an acknowledgment.

The sister, a brown-skinned woman no taller than Dicey, but much plumper, smiled and said, "I puts a mattress right by the fire, ma'am, and I spreads a nice clean sheet, washed this morning. You sleeps long as you can, and then goes where you wants to go."

Dicey and Zach bade Juana good-bye then, saying that

they hoped to deliver their yams to market and then reach home not too long after sunup. Juana realized that her thanks were woefully inadequate. Despite her bone-weariness and her dread of what lay only a few hours in the future, she was able to think: Maybe someday I'll have enough money that I can give them fifty dollars.

# 8

At a little past eleven that morning Sara Davidson sat at the desk in her office, account book spread out before her. Unlike the rest of her house, her office had a Spartan plainness. No pictures on the walls, no vases of flowers, no ornaments of any kind. Just the big oak desk with its many cubbyholes, and two straight chairs.

There was a knock at the door. "Come in," Sara said.

The door opened and someone stepped into the room. Only then did Sara look up from the rows of neat figures. "Close the door behind you, Solange."

A mulatto freedwoman from Martinique, Solange Thierry was good-looking enough to have been the star attraction of some less expensive brothel. Instead she chose to wear a maid's uniform and open the front door of number 17 Rue de Chene.

But her job was more important than it appeared to be. Where the domestic staff was concerned, Solange served as Sara's eyes and ears, reporting to her employer if she suspected the cook of padding the butcher bills, or if she saw the cook's assistant, a Dutch seaman who had jumped ship in New Orleans, stealing the brandy reserved for Sara's most distinguished and generous customers. But it was at the front door that Solange was most valuable. She had developed a sixth sense about clients. She could judge within seconds whether or not a man would behave himself in an acceptable manner. If she decided he would not, it was her task to persuade him, ever so tactfully, that he should go to one of the establishments down the street. On the rare occasion when she was confronted by some drunken or overly insistent caller, she had to make up her mind swiftly whether she could handle the situation or would have to summon Jack Creelson, a huge ex-dockworker who stayed discreetly in the background except for those times when it became necessary to employ force.

Right now there was an odd expression on Solange's light brown face. Sara said impatiently, "What is it?"

"There is someone on the front steps."

"Tell him to go away."

It was a house rule that any client who stayed overnight was to have finished his excellent complimentary breakfast and left the premises by eleven o'clock. Nor were other clients admitted until four in the afternoon. During those five hours the elegant salon was aired to rid it of alcohol and tobacco fumes, and floors were swept and polished. During those hours, too, Sara devoted herself to account books and business correspondence.

"It isn't a man, Mrs. Davidson. It is a woman, a white woman, asking for you. When I asked her name, she said that you would not know it, but just the same you had asked her almost four months ago to come to see you."

"What does she look like?"

"Dark, pretty, very young. Could be as young as seventeen. But the strangest part of it is that she has a baby in her arms."

Sara said after a moment, "Tell her to come in."

Seconds later, after Solange ushered the caller into the office and then left, Sara Davidson thought: Yes, the same girl. She looked different, though, and it was not just because her body was no longer swollen, or because she carried an infant in her arms, or because she wore a homespun blouse and skirt instead of that ill-fitting black garment. Her face now had a rigid look, as if she were willing herself to become some substance less sensitive than flesh and blood. Wood, perhaps.

"Sit down, my dear."

Juana sat in the straight chair three or four feet from the desk. Amalia looked up at her mother with placid dark eyes.

Sara Davidson said, "So you remembered my address."

"Yes." Juana did not feel it necessary to add that she had remembered the house number, seventeen, because she herself had been born on the seventeenth day of the month. "You told me to come to you if I needed help."

"Yes, I did." Something in the girl's manner made Sara certain that she knew what sort of place this was. Perhaps she had guessed that day on the dock. Perhaps someone had enlightened her since then. Anyway, she knew.

Sara waited for the girl to describe whatever straits had decided her to come here. Instead Juana said, "I have heard that you have much power, more than rich men and judges and such."

Although her face did not betray it, Sara was startled. She said calmly, "That is true."

"Have you more power than Lawrence Mountjoy?"

"Mountjoy! Now, why on earth should you ask that?"

"Do you know who he is?"

"Of course. Everyone knows. He has the biggest plantation within fifty miles. But why should you want to know if I have more—"

"Please, lady! Please tell me. Because if you don't, there is no reason why I should stay here . . ."

Her voice trailed off. Sara said, "All right, I will tell you. Mountjoy came to my place just once, several years ago. He hurt one of my girls, and I had him thrown out. He was furious, of course. He tried to have my place closed on the trumped-up charge that I had kidnapped a girl. He couldn't persuade any of the highly placed people he knows to help him in the scheme. I'm sure some of them were afraid of him, but they were even more afraid of me. Finally he dropped the whole idea.

"There. Does that answer your question?"

"Yes."

"Why did you ask it?"

"Because my baby and I need protection against Lawrence Mountjoy. And only someone more powerful than he is can give us that."

"Isn't it time you told me how it is you know him, and what happened between you?"

Juana told her.

Sara listened without surprise. For years now she had known what sort of man Mountjoy was, not only from her personal experience with him but also from stories about his forays in the slave quarters at Twin Pines.

"If I had money," Juana said, "Amalia and I would go back to Spain right away. But I have no money, and no friends." Her voice speeded up. "And he told me that if I ran away, he would find me and tell the police I had stolen from him, and have me put in jail. And then my little daughter . . ."

She broke off and then asked, "Will you lend me money to take us to Spain? I will repay you as soon as I can."

"No." Sara's voice was calm. "I am a businesswoman. I don't make unsecured loans."

Well, Juana had never had any real hope that this woman would lend her money.

The girl was silent for several seconds. Again Sara had the feeling that she was trying to will her young flesh into becoming something hard, insensate.

"Then can I work for you here?"

"I think that can be arranged."

The girl was not beautiful, but Sara had a premonition that many of her clients would find her more appealing than they found Anna-Maria, a stunning beautiful strumpet who, five years ago at the age of sixteen, had somehow managed to make her way from a Neopolitan slum to New Orleans.

No, this girl was not a beautiful strumpet. In fact, Sara was sure that a harlot was about the last thing this girl had been cut out to be. Unless she turned to drink or fancy clothes, she would save as much as she could of whatever she earned here. As soon as she had accumulated enough money and had become convinced that Mountjoy had forgotten her, she would leave. Even so, Sara might hope to employ her for four or five years.

Juana said, "But I must keep my little girl with me."

For once, Sara was openly surprised. "Keep her *here?* Why, for a dollar or so a week some woman would be glad to care for her in her own home. And I would be willing to lend you the first week's—"

"No! If that dreadful . . . if he should find out where . . . No! She must stay with me."

At last Sara said, "There's a separate attic apartment. It was here when I bought this house. I had it fixed up a few years ago because I thought it might help me keep the housekeeper I had then, the best one I ever employed. She quit, though, and the ones I've had since haven't wanted to climb all those stairs. So you can have it.

"Of course," she went on, "with you getting all that space, I'll have to take more for board and room out of your earnings. If I charged you the same as I do the other girls, there would be jealousy. And another thing. You'll need someone to look after the baby when you're not in your apartment. You can have Lena."

Lena was a twenty-four-year-old from Trinidad. Like the rest of Sara's black servants, she was not a slave. Slaves might be all right for a plantation, Sara felt, but their sometimes sullen behavior would cast a pall over an establishment like hers.

For much the same reason, she had assigned Lena to kitchen duties. Lean was capable enough to have performed domestic tasks anywhere in the house. Unfortunately, at some time in the past, and under circumstances which she never divulged, she had acquired a hideous knife scar along one cheek, running from her temple to her chin. Therefore Sara kept her out of sight of the clientele.

"You'll have to pay part of Lena's wages, of course, since you will be keeping her from her other duties."

What with those extra expenses, Sara reflected, the Spanish girl would have trouble accumulating money. The establishment could count on her services for a good long time. No malice accompanied Sara's thought, just the satisfaction of a merchant concluding what promised to be a profitable business agreement.

"Do you know," Sara Davidson said, "that you haven't even told me your name?"

For a moment Juana remained silent. Perhaps she should not use her name any longer, that name her parents had told to the priest, so that, as he sprinkled water on her infant self, he could say, "In the name of the Father, and the Son, and the Holy Ghost, I baptize thee——" But ever since she had decided that perhaps she had no recourse except to come to this place, she had felt too distraught, too frightened, to decide whether or not to use a new name.

Then, through her misery, she felt a surge of rebellious pride. She would not let the world strip her of even her name. She said clearly, "I am Juana Ramirez Moreno, and this is my daughter, Amalia."

# 9

The human mind seems to possess an innate self-protectiveness. It is said that a soldier, after a few battles, can perform without emotion deeds that once would have driven him mad with self-loathing. It is as if the mind, splitting away from the body, can view the body's acts with almost complete detachment.

Quite early in her almost three years at Sara Davidson's, Juana achieved that detached state.

Sara helped her to achieve it, not out of any sense of compassion, but only out of concern to protect a valuable asset. She realized that a girl as sensitive as Juana, if subjected to too many severe shocks too soon, might turn to drink, or run away despite her fears of Mountjoy, or even leave her infant daughter in the courtyard of some monastery and then take her own life.

And so from the first she saw to it that Juana was not subjected to the establishment's least pleasant customers—the very ugly ones, or the semi-senile, or the overdemanding. Oddly enough, Sara's seeming favoritism did not arouse resentment in the other girls. Perhaps it was because they knew that Juana, charged for her third-floor living quarters and for the services of Lena, kept only a small part of her earnings. Perhaps it was because, harlots though they were, they were still women, and so were touched by the thought of the little girl up there in those attic rooms—rooms off limits, by Sara's order, to everyone except Juana herself and Lena. After all, several of the girls at Sara's had children, but in each case the girl was fortunate enough to have a relative or friend willing to care for the child.

Or perhaps it was Juana herself who kept the others from resenting her. Anyone looking into that small face, with its big, tragic dark eyes, would have found it hard to envy her.

True, she learned to smile, just as the other girls did, whenever Solange ushered clients into the elegant salon. But it was not a smile which ever touched her eyes.

There were times, though, when she was almost happy. In those two rooms under the eaves—a bedroom, and another room with a plain oak table and straight chairs and a brazier for cooking—Juana would sit in her bedroom rocker with Amalia in her arms, and sing her a Spanish lullaby, and dream of the day when her daughter would be a happy and beautiful young lady. Because she never doubted that Amalia, unlike herself, would be beautiful. She had regretted that her child did not have Enrique's fair coloring. But by the time Amalia was a year old it became apparent that she was indeed her father's daughter. Already Juana could see Enrique in the classically cut features and the poise of the head. What was more, Juana felt that the little girl, ranging gleefully if somewhat unsteadily over the two rooms, showed the blithe self-confidence of her young father. Or perhaps her spirited ways also were an inheritance from her grandmother Constancia. Certainly noblemen in their castles and Gypsies in their caravans were alike in one respect. Neither of them felt obliged to conform to the ways of ordinary people.

Lena, too, helped make Juana's life bearable. The brown-skinned woman with the puckered scar along one cheek from the very first seemed enchanted with Amalia, and Amalia with her. Juana liked her too, this young woman only six years older than herself. Often in the mornings, when it was time for Lena to report for a few hours' duty in the basement kitchen, she and Juana nevertheless would steal fifteen minutes or so to chat with each other. They talked of Amalia. They talked of Juana's childhood in Cádiz and Lena's on her lush tropical island. They talked of the flower garden visible from the tiny balcony outside the kitchen window where, with one or the other of them holding Amalia, they often sat. They talked, too, of Lena's difficulties with the temperamental cook down in her basement realm.

What they did not discuss was Juana's harlotry. It was as if for them the house consisted of only this attic aerie and the basement. The rooms on the two floors between, including the one where, for varying lengths of time and varying amounts of money, Juana shared a bed with a succession of men, simply did not exist. And so, because of her daughter, and her chats with Lena, and that strange, numb detachment she had achieved after only a few days in this house, she was able to endure her life.

One other consideration helped her to endure it. When she had been there about a year and a half, she learned through Anna-Maria, the beautiful Neapolitan, that Lawrence Mountjoy was still keeping an eye out for her. In a New Orleans gambling house Mountjoy had talked to one of Anna-Maria's frequent customers about a "Spanish slut named Juana Moreno" who had robbed him, and of how he was sure he would run across her someday. Anna-Maria's client had repeated the conversation to her.

"Don't worry," he had added, "I didn't tell Mountjoy there was a Spanish girl named Juana at Sara Davidson's. In the first place, I don't think she ever robbed anyone. And even if she had, I wouldn't help the likes of Mountjoy to track her down."

Well, Juana reflected, when Anna-Maria told her of the incident, even if Mountjoy did learn where she was, he could not harm her, not as long as she was under Sara Davidson's protection. And as soon as she had enough money, she would board the first Spain-bound ship.

But her savings, which Lena took to the bank for her each week, grew so slowly. Unlike the other girls, she spent no money on drink or jewelry or expensive scent. True, she'd had to repay the money Sara Davidson had lent her to buy a crib and mattress and bedclothes for Amalia. Also she'd had to pay for the evening dresses which Sara ordered for her—surprisingly demure ones in her case, in contrast to the provocative ones worn by the other girls. But she bought no dresses on her own initiative. Nevertheless, the sums Lena took to the bank each week remained discouragingly small. Perhaps some of her customers, guessing that it was some form of grim necessity that held her to this place, might have given her extra money. But Sara Davidson had declared that surreptitious giving was against the rules. A donor of such presents might find himself barred forever from Sara Davidson's exclusive portal.

Nevertheless, by the time she had been there two years, Juana had saved almost two-thirds of the amount needed to take her and Amalia to Spain. Then one morning when Lena unlocked the attic apartment door in answer to Juana's knock, the black woman said, "Oh, Miss Juana! I'm afraid she's caught cold."

Seconds later, looking down into the flushed face of the child lying in her crib, Juana knew with chill certainty that it was more than a cold which ailed her little daughter.

The doctor who treated Sara Davidson's girls was summoned. Since it had been years since he'd had experience with childhood ailments, he sent for a colleague, a pious Huguenot who had never thought to enter such premises for any reason whatsoever. He pronounced Amalia's ailment to be "lung fever," and then, addressing Juana as if from a great height, ordered a croup kettle, medicine to pour into the boiling water, and a sheet to spread over the top and sides of the crib to confine the steam.

For more than two weeks Juana did not leave her attic rooms. She seldom even moved from Amalia's side except when Lena's presence allowed her to get a few hours' sleep.

On an evening about ten days after the Huguenot doctor's first visit, an evening when Juana felt frozen by the terror that each rasping breath of her child would be the last, Sara Davidson climbed the steep stairs to the attic door and knocked. Hair disordered, and with the circles under her eyes appearing almost black in her white face, Juana opened the door.

Sara said, "Lena will be up here in a few minutes. There's no need for both of you to attend the child. And your gentlemen friends have been asking for you. Now, tidy your appearance, Juana, and come down to the salon."

"Go away," Juana said quietly. "If you try to force me away from my baby, I'll kill you."

Sara turned and went down the stairs. Knowing power as she did, she knew that no amount of power would prevail against the fierceness she'd read in that until now gentle face.

Four nights later Amalia's fever broke and she appeared to lapse into normal sleep. The doctor, summoned by Lena, pronounced the child out of danger. For three more days Juana stayed in her attic rooms. Then she returned to the ornate salon, and to the almost as ornate bedroom where, for a fee, men made use of her body.

Amalia had been saved. Therefore she must not mourn over the deep inroads into her bank account. Because she had earned no money during her child's illness, the weekly charge for her attic rooms and for Lena's services had come out of her savings. Medicine had been expensive. And the doctor, on the theory that the wages of sin should be as punishing as possible, had tripled his usual fee. There was no help for it, she told herself grimly. She would just have to go on, praying that nothing else would interfere with her slow accumulation of money.

Amalia was two years and eight months old when something happened that made Juana realize that her child could not stay here much longer. One way or another, she had to find a means of freeing them both.

That evening, in her second-floor room, Juana had just said good-bye to a client, a rather shy widower, the owner of a small plantation, who always asked for Juana on his infrequent visits to Sara Davidson's. After his departure, Juana dressed, stepped out into the hall, and then stood motionless with shock.

A few feet to her right, on the opposite side of the hall, the door to Carrie's room stood open. A blond, thirtyish American who sometimes said she was from Boston, other times from Trenton, Carrie three months later was to be dismissed by Sara for excessing drinking. That night, though, Juana had seen her about half an hour earlier down in the salon, matching glass for glass with a bibulous French cloth merchant. Now, apparently, they were in Carrie's room, too drunk to realize that they had broken one of Sara's most inflexible rules: while entertaining a client, a girl must keep the door of her room closed.

In front of the open door, staring in, stood Amalia.

With a strangled cry, Juana darted forward and scooped her child up in her arms. Startled, Amalia let out an indignant wail. "It is all right," Juana soothed as she carried her child toward the attic stairs. "Mama's not angry."

At the top of the stairs she opened the unlocked door to the attic apartment. Lena sat there in the lingering summer twilight, head sunk on the arms she had crossed on the kitchen table.

"Lena!" Then, when the brown-skinned woman woke up and straightened, face still bleary with sleep: "You forgot to lock this door after me! You know this door is never to be left unlocked. Do you know where I found Amalia? In the second-floor hall!"

Appalled, Lena stared at the still-indignant child in Juana's arms. "Oh, I'm so sorry! But it was so hot in the kitchen today, Miss Juana, and I worked so hard. I guess that's why I forgot. Anyway, I was going to undress Amalia and put her to bed, but I thought that first I'd rest just a second . . ."

"It's all right. I know how tired you must be."

Juana carried Amalia into the other room and put her to bed. For half an hour she sat beside the crib singing a Spanish lullaby about bluebirds, even though she knew that by now Sara Davidson would have missed her. She did not return to the salon until after Amalia's long lashes had swept down to lie like dark fans on her cheeks.

# 10

At eleven-thirty the next morning Juana went to her employer's ground-floor office. Although she had been able to retire to her attic room not long after midnight, Juana had slept little. Instead she had stared upward through the darkness, thinking about what she must say in the morning to Sara Davidson. Now, as Juana sat there in the austerely plain office flooded with morning sunlight, there were dark circles under her eyes.

She said, "Mrs. Davidson, I must make more money."

Before answering, Sara studied the girl for a moment. Despite the dark circles, Juana looked well. She had gained back the pounds she had lost during her child's illness. In fact, except for the weight of experience in the big dark eyes, she looked scarcely older than when she had first come here, a frightened girl just turned eighteen.

Sara asked, "Why do you want more money?" although of course she knew why. Juana still wanted to get away from this place as soon as possible.

"It is my little girl. She is getting to an age where . . . where she must not stay in a place like this."

Sara thought: Then board her out someplace. There wouldn't be much chance of Mountjoy finding the child. As nearly as Sara could judge from information furnished her by various sources in recent weeks, Mountjoy was no longer hell-bent on punishing "that little Spanish bitch." Apparently even an obsessed man could not keep his rage at white-hot heat forever.

But she did not suggest boarding the child out. Ever since that day when Juana, with that fierce light in her eyes, had ordered Sara away from the attic door, the woman had known it was useless to argue with the girl where her child was concerned.

And so she said, "Just how do you propose to make this additional money?"

Juana drew a deep breath. Then she said, with a rush, "I want you to let me entertain the special clients."

Hiding her surprise, Sara let her cool gaze rest on Juana's face. It was true that the girls who entertained special clients earned more, much more, because such men were resigned to paying considerable sums for the satisfaction of their needs.

Even though she barred sadists from her premises, Sara welcomed men of a diametrically opposed temperament, men who needed to suffer punishment of some sort—humiliation, or at least the threat of pain—before they could find sexual release.

Sara long had been aware that such men were often community leaders, intelligent, hardworking, and scrupulously honest. Over the years she had formed theories as to why these men could obtain full sexual satisfaction only when a woman treated them contemptuously or even brutally.

Sara still studied the face of the girl seated a few feet away from her. Juana did not look in the least like the sort Sara usually would choose for her special clients. Such girls were taller than average, with faces that could easily assume a cold, demanding look. And certainly it was impossible to imagine Juana wielding a whip across the back of some man prone on the floor. But not all of such clients needed the release of physical pain. For instance, there was the prominent surgeon who visited Sara's every ten days or so. In the room of one or another of the three girls who entertained the "specials," he would change into the housemaid's uniform which the establishment kept for him. He would brew tea on a spirit lamp, also kept for him by the house, and serve it to the girl as she sat at a table covered with impeccable white linen. Then he would change back into his masculine garments, pay the bored or idly amused girl her considerable fee, and leave the house.

Often Sara had noticed a patient sadness in the eyes of such men as they walked out of her establishment. It had occurred to her that she might be able to charge even stiffer fees if the girls could keep them from feeling sad and ashamed afterward. But that was asking too much of any strumpet she had ever met.

Except perhaps for Juana.

Sara said, "All right. You'll earn a minimum of triple your usual fee." True, the girl might accumulate money at an alarming rate. But if she proved as valuable as the woman suspected she might, Sara would devise some other means of holding on to her.

After a moment she went on. "Now, I'm sure the other girls have told you how ridiculously some of these men behave."

Juana hesitated, then nodded.

"But I'm also quite sure that they did not venture any guesses as to why such men behave that way. I doubt if it would ever occur to those featherbrains to wonder."

Juana said nothing.

"But I've thought about it. I have an idea that when they were very little boys they were more than ordinarily attached to their mothers, or perhaps to a nursemaid. I think that this person, whoever she was, treated them harshly. Somehow they grew up wanting that sort of treatment from women. You could never expect respectable wives to understand such needs, let alone fulfill them, and so they come to places like mine."

And lucky for me that they do, she added mentally. Far more so than any of her other customers, these men had placed themselves in her power. If she ever chose to talk of the French general who during his prolonged visits meticulously polished the shoes of about half the girls in the place, or the lawyer whose wish was to be ordered to sit on a high stool with a dunce cap on his head. . . .

She went on, "Yvonne once told me that a customer, just before he left, suddenly blurted out that when he was a little boy his mother would not speak to him for days at a time. And do you know what Yvonne said?"

Juana shook her head.

"Yvonne laughed at him and then said, 'And you're still thinking about it fifty years later, you silly old fool.' "

Juana made no comment, but the look that came into her eyes, a look of mingled indignation and sympathy, caused Sara to think that the girl might indeed work out well with the "specials."

Sara was right about that.

True, Juana found them strange, these men who for some reason had been impelled down such bizarre erotic byways.

But she never found them laughable. Perhaps it was because she could tell how ashamed they felt, and how much they envied Sara's other customers, no matter how crass or stupid, who needed only to bed down with a woman for a few minutes.

Not much time passed before the "specials" began to realize that Juana did not despise them. Instead of departing as soon as they had completed whatever ritual they found necessary to bring them sexual release, they began to linger to talk to Juana. They seldom talked of anything personal or crucially important. Instead they would talk of some happening in the news—a fire on the city docks, say—or of some not-too-intimate family matter, such as a son's departure for college in the eastern United States or in Europe. Juana sensed that it really didn't matter to them what the talk was about. What mattered was that here was a woman who knew the terrible truth about them, and yet neither laughed at them nor despised them.

Aware that these clients lingered, Sara told each of them that the fee had increased. Without argument, they paid.

One of Juana's clients was Howard Whitelaw, an American jurist who recently had arrived in New Orleans to aid in the transition of the territory from French to American rule. In fact, it was not until Whitelaw told her about it that she knew that Louisiana—once French, then Spanish, then French again—had been bought by the United States. He was a big man with a gently dignified face and a bald head fringed with gray hair. During his visits to Juana he required only two things of her. First, she was to wear clothing that he'd had made for her, a dark dress and white frilled cap of the sort that might have been worn forty-odd years earlier by a housekeeper or other upper servant. Second, she was to lock him inside the closet in her room, releasing him only when he called to her to unlock the door.

She soon realized that in Howard Whitelaw she had something she had not had since Charlotte Higgins left the *Esperanza* in Philadelphia. She had a friend. Often after she unlocked the closet door he would linger for almost an hour. He would talk of the function of the new, American-style legislature. He would talk of his son at Harvard and his two daughters still at home. And he would talk of his wife, whom he loved very much, and who would leave him instantly if she learned of the compulsion that over the years had brought him to various establishments like Sara Davidson's.

On his fourth visit he began to talk of his early childhood. His mother, he said, had died before he was a year old.

"Then who raised you?"

"Until I was five, a housekeeper took care of me. I remember being so fond of her that I followed her about all day, even though she often scolded me and even slapped me for being in the way. She left us soon after my fifth birthday. My father told me that I woke up screaming every night for more than a week, and ate almost nothing. I don't remember that. To me it seems that one day she was there, and the next day gone."

Juana did not ask whether or not the much-loved, much-feared housekeeper had locked him in closets. Perhaps he did not remember whether she had or not. But Juana was sure that the woman had.

Just as Whitelaw confided in her, Juana began to tell him things which she had told no one else. Ever since she came to this luxurious house, men had asked her about herself. They had wanted to know where she was born, and why she had come to America, and how it was that she had become one of Sara Davidson's girls. Always she had answered as briefly as possible. She had left Cádiz, she told them, because her family was poor, and she had wanted "to better" herself. And she had entered Sara Davidson's employ because what little money she had ran out, and she could find no work. She never told any of them of her marriage and widowhood. And of course she never told them about the little girl behind the locked door at the head of the attic stairs.

But she told Howard Whitelaw all of it. Her love for Enrique, a love that was rapturous even though she knew from the start that it was doomed. The death of poor Manuel. Her weeks at Twin Pines, that beautiful house that had turned out to be a nightmarish prison. And finally her decision to flee to Sara Davidson, in the hope that at least she and her child would be protected.

"You say his name is Mountjoy?" Whitelaw said the first time Juana confided in him. "He must be staying close to his plantation. I haven't run across anyone of that name."

Juana found the news hopeful. Howard Whitelaw had been here long enough to have met every person of prominence in

New Orleans. If he had not encountered Mountjoy, it must mean that the handsome, well-spoken plantation owner whose eyes could take on that strange shine had given up looking for her. Perhaps he had sold his property and taken his drug-addicted wife to some other part of the country. Perhaps—although Juana felt this was too much to hope for—he had died. But she knew that for Amalia's sake and her own she must not assume the danger was over. She must not make that assumption until she and her little girl were well away from New Orleans.

But she was still far from her financial goal. And Amalia was almost three now, an age when she would begin to ask questions and retain memories. . . .

Sometimes Juana felt an almost irresistible impulse to tell Lena to draw her savings out of the bank. Then she would take Amalia upriver as far as their money would carry them and come ashore in one of the small settlements that dotted the banks of the Mississippi. But once there, what could she do, a penniless, friendless young woman with a small child? Perhaps she would be lucky enough to find immediately some family who would employ her as a domestic. If she had been alone, she would have taken that chance long ago. But because she had that small hostage to fortune up in the attic, she dared not risk it.

No, the safest course was to stay in this place until she had accumulated enough for their passage to Spain. Increasingly, though, she dreaded the thought of returning to those crowded three rooms in that steep Cádiz street. In letters to her family she had written of her job as a "housemaid" to a rich American lady named Mrs. Davidson. But Juana felt that Constancia—shrewd, cynical Constancia—would need to take only one look at her daughter in order to guess the truth. And what of Juana's father, that gentle, pious man who loved his eldest daughter best of all his children? Juana knew that her father would rather think of her as dead than as a harlot.

And yet for Amalia's sake she must return to Spain as soon as possible. There, surrounded by people of her own blood, her daughter would grow up safely and perhaps even happily.

It was Howard Whitelaw who showed her there might be still another way out for her.

On an October evening he said, "Juana, ever since I last saw you, I've been thinking of your problem. I may have a solution." He paused. "You know about Napoleon, don't you?"

Bewildered by the seeming change of subject, Juana said, "Of course." Even shut away in Sara Davidson's she had heard of how the great French general had swept through Europe like a devastating whirlwind.

"Then as you probably know, France is at war with England. English men-of-war have blockaded the Continent so successfully that only a few American ships have been able to deliver their cargoes of cotton from New Orleans and the Atlantic-coast states to European ports. And that is where you come in. Juana, how much money do you have?"

She said, still bewildered, "Two hundred and eleven dollars."

"How would you like to turn that into two thousand or more?"

She stared at him. Two thousand dollars was an unimaginably vast sum.

"Let me explain, Juana. There is a large shipment of cotton sailing from New Orleans to France about ten days from now. What makes this ship different from those that have been turned back by the blockaders is that Washington is furnishing it with both cannon and the gunners to fire them. So equipped, the ship is almost sure to get through with its cargo. The English would not want to risk renewed war with the United States, not when their armies are so hard-pressed on the Continent.

"So far, very few men know that this merchant ship is to be armed. Therefore you can buy shares in the venture at the very low prices which have prevailed ever since the blockade became effective. But once the news is out, the price of shares will shoot sky-high."

Juana said, past the hopefully quickened pulse in the hollow of her throat, "But suppose it doesn't work out that way? Suppose the government changes its mind, and I can't sell my shares, and the ship sails unarmed, and is turned back. . . ."

"Then you will lose your money. But there is small chance of that happening. Oh, Juana!" He leaned forward and clasped her hands in his. "If I were a well-to-do man, I would put up the money for you. But I am not. Few people know it, but I am deeply in debt. Ten years ago a good friend—at least I thought he was a friend—asked me to cosign a note for a large sum of money. He never paid it back. In fact, he disappeared, although I heard that he has been seen in Brussels.

"Ever since, I've been paying off that loan. Because of my bad judgment, I've had to deny my wife and children things they needed. And so I feel I have no right to advance you money for this venture. As it is, I feel guilty enough. . . ."

He broke off, but she knew what he meant. He felt guilty enough over the money he spent here at Sara Davidson's.

"Think about it, Juana. But don't think too long. Once word is out that the ship is to sail armed, you'll have lost your chance to buy shares cheaply."

He went on. "Now, I have offices at 230 Bourbon Street. Can you remember that number?"

Juana nodded.

"If you decide to buy in, get the money to my office as soon as possible."

After twelve almost sleepless hours, Juana came to her decision. In the hope of being able to take her daughter away from this place before she was even a month older, she would risk everything she had. She sent Lena out with instructions to present to the bank a draft for the entire amount of her savings. After that, Lena was to take the cash to Howard Whitelaw's office. Around ten-thirty Lena returned and climbed through the quiet house to the attic rooms.

"Mr. Whitelaw says for you to come to his office next Thursday morning. If you can't, he'll come here Friday night."

Thursday, a whole week away. How could she get through that week, not knowing whether or not she had condemned herself and Amalia to two or three more years in this place?

Somehow she did get through it, although afterward in her memories of that week she seemed surrounded everywhere—in the salon, in her attic refuge, in that second-floor room where she lay with men whose names she didn't know—by that cold, ominous light that fills bad dreams.

Thursday morning at eight she left the house, walked a few hundred feet, and hailed a carriage-for-hire. As long as they behaved themselves, Sara Davidson did not object to her girls going out for airings or for shopping. Juana seldom had availed herself of the privilege. For one thing, she had feared that she would see—looking at her from a passing carriage or coming toward her along a street—the handsome owner of Twin Pines. For another, it seemed to her—although she was wrong on that point—that what she had become was written on her face, so that women she passed would feel an impulse to draw their skirts away from her, even if they did not actually do so. But today in her sick fear over her two hundred and eleven dollars she gave no thought to the chance of meeting Mountjoy, let alone to what strange women might read in her face. Unseeingly she looked at the sidewalk crowds moving along past the stately houses with their wrought-iron balconies. Even at this early hour the street vendors were out crying their shrimp and meat pies and bananas, mingling with businessmen and workmen and laundresses, black women who with the grace of caryatids balanced bundles of laundry on their heads.

The carriage let her out at 230 Bourbon Street. Heart pounding, she entered a narrow staircase beside a clockmaker's shop and climbed steep, narrow stairs, to a door which bore Howard Whitelaw's name. She was sure he would be there. He had told her he never reached his office later than eight. She knocked.

A split second after he opened the door, she knew that her money was safe. He would not smile at her like that if it were not.

"Come in, Juana, come in! The news is good."

His office was bathed in bright October sunlight. When they had both sat down in straight chairs near his tall desk, he said, "You have a little more than eleven thousand, three hundred dollars."

She stared at him incredulously. No one had that much money. Oh, the King of England, perhaps. But no one else.

"Child, child! It is not the vast fortune you obviously think it is. But if you handle it wisely, it will keep you in modest comfort for a long, long time, perhaps for the rest of your life."

She said, half-convinced now, "How is it . . . how on earth did you. . . ?"

"I pyramided it. New Orleans is a city of gamblers, remember. After news of the armed merchantman spread, shares changed hands so fast, doubling in value each time, that within two days I was able to sell your shares for two thousand.

"I suppose," he went on, "that the really prudent thing to have done would have been to turn that sum over to you. But by that time I'd heard rumors of still a second merchant ship to be fitted out with cannon. I verified the rumors and then . . . well, I guess I've caught the New Orleans gambling fever myself, because I invested all your profits and my own also in shares of the second cargo of cotton. Those shares shot up in value even faster than the first lot. The result is as I told you."

As she sat there, dazed, he added, "Do you realize what this means? It means you won't have to go back to Spain unless you want to, and I don't think you do."

Astonishment opened her mouth. "How did you know. . . ?"

"Oh, Juana, Juana! Don't you know that your face shows everything you feel? When you talked of your parents, I could tell you feared what they might guess about you, or what you might feel compelled to tell them.

"But you needn't go home," he went on. "Sixty miles up the Mississippi there is a pleasant little sawmill settlement named Belleville. It's really more than a settlement. Besides the sawmill, it has a bank, and a comfortable inn, and a Catholic church, and a convent school attached to a nunnery.

"Sixty miles is a good distance from New Orleans," he went on. "It takes almost a week to tow a barge that far against the current and past the sandbars. And swamps and thick forests make those sixty miles slow going too for travelers on horseback. There is almost no chance that Mountjoy would find you there, even if he is still interested in looking for you. And there is also little chance that you would be recognized there by some visitor from New Orleans. And even if you are, you can just keep saying that it must be a mistake, that you never heard of anyone named Sara Davidson.

"You could stay at the inn until you find a permanent place to live. A pleasant little house there shouldn't cost you more than six hundred dollars. You can turn the rest of your money over to the banker in Belleville—he's a friend of mine—to invest for you. It should bring you about five hundred a year, certainly enough to keep you and your little girl, and even that Lena you keep talking about, if she wants to go with you. And when your daughter is old enough, she can enroll in the convent school."

Juana sat speechless, so happy that she longed to put her head down on his desk and weep. She could see it all. The quiet river town. The little house where she and Lena would raise vegetables and flowers in the backyard. And the convent school where Amalia would grow into a beautiful and happy young lady.

She hoped that the nuns at the school would not mind that she herself did not attend the Belleville church. It was not the thought of her past sins which would keep her away. From early childhood she had been taught that God could and would forgive sins, even though they were "as scarlet." But somewhere along the line—perhaps when Lawrence Mountjoy stared down at her shiny-eyed through the candlelight, perhaps as she clutched her child in terror beneath the seat of that farm wagon, perhaps as she submitted to still another client in Sara Davidson's opulent brothel—somewhere along the way, she had lost her faith. How could she go into God's house when she no longer believed in him, when instead she had become convinced that all she could count on was the kindness of a few rare people like Howard Whitelaw and Zach and Dicey Green?

The Greens. Before she left New Orleans she would go to that blacksmith's cottage and leave fifty dollars with Dicey's sister.

Howard Whitelaw was speaking. "And you could marry again, Juana. You would be far from the first . . . well, woman of pleasure who has done so. You are still very young, and you are pleasing to the eye. And you're a *good* person, Juana. There is no reason why you shouldn't remarry."

Juana found her voice then. "No, I want nothing more to do with men, not in that way. That part of my life is over. From now on I want nothing but peace and safety for myself, and a happy life for my daughter."

# 11

Juana's final interview with her employer took place three mornings later in Sara Davidson's office. In a dark green cloak and bonnet, and with a newly purchased portmanteau on the floor beside her, Juana sat in one of the two straight chairs.

"Mrs. Davidson, I came to tell you that I am leaving."

Sara was aware of that. For three hours she had known that Lena and the child had left the house at dawn and now awaited Juana aboard a craft tied up at the New Orleans dock.

"Then you have your passage money to Spain?"

"Yes." If Sara Davidson chose to think that she was returning to Cádiz, all the better.

Sara, of course, thought nothing of the sort. She knew that the child and Lena were aboard, not an oceangoing ship, but a flat-bottomed barge which would travel laboriously up the Mississippi, sometimes propelled by men wielding poles, sometimes pulled by mules slogging along a towpath. Since little of importance went on in New Orleans without her knowing about it, she was also aware of Howard Whitelaw's successful gamble with Juana's money as well as his own.

Sara, of course, was highly displeased that she was to lose a valuable asset. As she looked at the small face framed by the green bonnet—a face trying very hard to appear composed despite the mingled trepidation and joyous hope in the dark eyes—Sara thought of the several ways in which she might keep the girl here. She might threaten, for instance, to get word to Lawrence Mountjoy that Juana was going upriver, and that he might learn her destination by following along on horseback as the barge moved slowly north. But to do that would mean coming into direct conflict with Howard Whitelaw. And it would be stupid to alienate such a man, just for the sake of a strumpet. Whitelaw, although a relatively poor man, was well-liked and able. He might even become governor of Louisiana Territory someday. Best not to provoke the antagonism of such a man unless she had to.

She said, just to see what the girl would answer, "You've told Lena you are leaving?"

Juana said, after a moment, "Lena is going with me."

Even though Sara already knew that, the idea brought her anger, or at least the nearest thing to anger that she ever permitted herself. She was losing not only a successful harlot but also a capable servant.

Sara asked, "Do you have anything else to tell me?"

"Nothing else." Juana got to her feet. "Good-bye, Mrs. Davidson."

Sara remained seated. "Good-bye."

For a moment Juana stood motionless. She had spent almost three years in this house. Here she had changed from a terrified young girl to a self-controlled creature able to withdraw, mentally and emotionally, from what happened to her body. And here, finally, she had become a woman of property, with the means as well as the will to live the rest of her life as a celibate.

And yet at the end of those years, all that she and Sara Davidson had to say to each other was good-bye. She turned and went out.

For perhaps a minute Sara Davidson looked at the closed door. For now, she would waste no more thought on Juana Moreno. But if she ever had an opportunity to even the score with the little Spanish slut without too much cost to herself, she would seize it.

She turned back to her desk and opened her account book.

# 12

## Belleville, Louisiana Territory, 1808

Outside a window of the convent dormitory, a mockingbird saluted the new day. In the torrent of sound pouring from his throat, thrushlike trills and goldfinch warbles alternated with the jeering calls of blue jays and the plaintive cries of catbirds. Amalia's eyes with their long silky lashes flew open. Lying there in her narrow bed, she listened with delight. She knew how the mockingbird felt. For three days rain had poured down. But now the sun was out. She could see reddish sunrise light on the dormitory's opposite wall.

For a few moments she resisted temptation. Then the mockingbird's song, and the thought of all that sunrise glory outside, became too much for her. Very quietly, so as not to awaken the girls in the beds on either side of her, she swung her feet to the floor. She took down her underclothing from one of the hooks at the head of her bed and then dressed as she had been taught by the nuns, pulling on her drawers and her petticoat under her nightgown so that no one, not even herself, could glimpse her unclothed body.

"Amalia!" It was a shocked whisper. "What are you *doing?*"

Amalia looked across the dormitory to where her best friend, Esther MacFarlane, had sat up in bed, gray eyes wide, light brown curls showing beneath the edges of her nightcap. Like Amalia, Esther was eight years old. Also like Amalia, she was pretty. There the resemblance ended. Esther, the daughter of a prominent New Orleans family, did her lessons slowly and with painstaking care. Amalia, knowing that she could do hers swiftly and easily, often postponed them to the last minute, with the result that sometimes they did not get done at all. Esther never broke any rules. Amalia often found herself unable to resist breaking them. And yet Esther worshiped the ground that Amalia's wayward feet walked on, or, more accurately, danced over.

"I'm going down the drainpipe," Amalia whispered back. She pulled off her nightgown, hung it up, drew her dark blue woolen uniform over her head.

"You'll get in trouble!"

Fingers busy with buttons, Amalia whispered, "No, I won't. Sister Elizabeth probably won't come in to wake us for at least half an hour. And I'll climb back up in five minutes."

She tiptoed to an open window. Leaning out, she grasped the drainpipe with one hand, then put her right leg over the sill and rested her foot on one of the drainpipe's metal supports. She drew herself the rest of the way out of the window and then through the ruddy sunrise light, descended the ivy-covered convent wall to the ground.

She truly had meant just to stand in the kitchen garden below the dormitory windows for a minute or so, listening to the noisy bird, inhaling the scent of dew-wet grass and vegetables and herbs, and feeling the sun on her face. She had intended after that to climb the pipe, strip off her dress, put on her nightgown, take off her underclothing beneath it, and be lying in bed when Sister Elizabeth came in to awaken them to another day of studies, prayer, and plain, nourishing meals.

But the gate in the garden wall was open, and beyond was the woodland, and somehow Amalia was soon moving down the path between the tall trees. The reddish light slanting through the tree trunks made her think of light from rose windows falling on cathedral pillars. She had never seen a cathedral, just the Belleville church, but in the mother superior's office there was a framed watercolor of the nave of Notre Dame.

Along the path, ferns still held drops of dew, shining like rubies when they caught the sunrise light. The air smelled of those ferns, and last year's fallen oak leaves underfoot, and of aromatic pines. Here in the woodland also birds were awake, some of them just barely so. She came to an alder branch where a towee sat, feathers fluffed, eyes still too fogged with sleep to be alarmed by the sight of her. He gave her a drowsily friendly chirp as she passed. When she had walked a few more yards, a blue jay arrowed across the path.

Evidently he had been up to no good—nest-raiding, perhaps—because behind him in hot pursuit flew a male cardinal, his body an even fierier red in the warm light.

Amalia laughed. Then suddenly she halted and looked up through the trees to where a small rosy cloud floated in the deepening blue of the sky. She experienced then one of those moments of self-awareness which can come even to quite young children.

She thought: I am Amalia Moreno. I am eight years, five months, and—let's see—eleven days old. I am happy. And all my life I am going to remember standing here and thinking this.

If anyone had asked her why she was happy, she would have answered, puzzled, "But how could I help but be?" She had Mama, soft, pretty, gentle Mama, there in their snug white clapboard house. She had Lena, who in Belleville's only carriage-for-hire fetched her from the convent for her one day at home each week and then brought her back. And she had the school.

At first, of course, she had hated it, or rather, hated not being still at home. Like almost every new girl, she had cried herself to sleep for two nights. Then her interest had been caught by her new surroundings. The cool chapel with its flickering altar lights. The wide corridors with their lustrous floors smelling of beeswax. The flower and vegetable gardens, so much larger than those Mama and Lena kept at home. The pleasure of mingling her voice with those of the sisters and the other girls at evensong.

She had been here nearly two years now, and she enjoyed almost everything about the school. Oh, a few of the girls were horrid. And there was Sister Mary Joseph's ruler. Sister Mary Joseph taught Amalia's favorite subject, literature, and Amalia admired her greatly. But the good sister was dismayingly quick to wield her ruler across the palms of the inattentive, the pert, or the merely stupid. Almost every day someone in her class heard the command, "Hold out your hands!" followed by a sharp *thwack* which made every girl in the room wince in sympathy. But aside from that ruler, and those few horrid girls, the school was a wonderful place.

The mother superior sometimes said, "Amalia Moreno thinks life is a banquet." She meant the words to sound censorious, but somehow they did not. Perhaps it was because she found herself unable to disapprove sufficiently of Amalia's blithe spirit. Oh, the reverend mother knew that the world was a vale of tears, and that existence here should be regarded as a time to prepare for the perfect life beyond. But sometimes she wondered why that God, if he had not wanted any of his children to delight in the world, had created people like Amalia, whose senses reveled in almost everything she saw, heard, smelled, tasted, or touched. The mother superior never communicated such thoughts to the sisters in her charge, of course. Not for anything would she voice thoughts that might disturb their strong and simple faith. It was only with Father Jean-Claude Dupres, who came regularly to the convent to hear confessions, that she discussed such troubling ideas.

There on the woodland path, Amalia suddenly realized that she had left the dormitory far longer than five minutes ago. Already the light had lost its rosy sunrise cast. She turned and hurried back along the path, through the garden gate, and up a graveled walk toward the convent wall and its drainpipe.

"Amalia!"

She halted. Sister Elizabeth looked down at her from a dormitory window, her young face distressed in the frame of her white wimple. "Go around to the front door!"

Amalia obeyed. She waited by the dormitory door until Sister Elizabeth unlocked it and told her to come inside.

"My child, my child! You know it is wrong to break the rules. When are you ever going to stop doing it?"

Made suddenly wretched by the distress in Sister Elizabeth's face, Amalia said, "I don't know, sister. There just seemed to be no good reason *not* to climb down. And I intended to get back before you'd had a chance to find out that I'd gone."

"You'd still have broken the rules, whether I knew about it or not. And it's not your place to question whether there's a good reason for your not climbing down the drainpipe. The rules are there to be obeyed, not questioned."

She paused and then added, "If the reverend mother didn't have so much else to cope with, I would report you to her. Well, since you are already dressed, you might as well go to breakfast."

"Thank you, sister. And I will try not to break rules. I will really and truly try."

For several months Amalia managed to curb her wayward impulses. Then, shortly after her ninth birthday, came the Episode of Hannah Moffat's Drawers.

The first part of the episode was in no way Amalia's fault. Hannah Moffat, daughter of one of the several American families who had settled in Belleville since Louisiana had become part of the United States, was a pale, overly plump girl. All sorts of foods, from shrimp to bananas to strawberries, made her break out in spots. What was more, she repeatedly suffered misfortunes not of her own making. Amalia thought that in heaven there must be angels especially assigned to making people like Hannah happy, so that they would be compensated for their earthly miseries.

On a late-November morning Hannah Moffat stood near Sister Mary Joseph's desk, reading aloud to the class in a dull monotone from *Lives of the Saints.* Suddenly the edge of something white appeared below the hem of her uniform. Then her cotton drawers slithered the rest of the way down her plump body to lie in folds around her high-topped shoes. The class tittered, then broke into laughter.

Sister Mary Joseph thwacked the desk several times with her ruler. "Class! Stop that!" Then, to the scarlet-faced Hannah: "Pick up you. . .ah. . .garment. Go up to the dormitory, take out your sewing kit, and do what is necessary."

When the door had closed behind Hannah, she said to the now silently apprehensive class, "By next Friday each of you will write a poem about a saint. It need not be long, but it must rhyme. Is that clear?"

Unlike many of her classmates, who looked stunned and outraged, Amalia was excited by the novelty of the assignment. Nearly everyone else, she felt sure, would choose either St. Theresa of the Little Flower, or St. Francis of the Birds, whose statue stood in the little glass-roofed courtyard outside the mother superior's office. It would be more fun, Amalia decided, to take some less-well-known saint, like Ursula, the patron saint of young girls. Amalia was fascinated by the legend of Ursula, a British Christian princess of a thousand years ago who, to escape her betrothal to a pagan king, gathered a thousand young maids together and set sail with them for Europe. (Reading that, Amalia had reflected that parents in those days were certainly lenient. You'd never catch any of the parents *she* knew letting their daughters run around like that.) They had marched to Rome, where the pope blessed them, and then turned toward home. They never got there, because an army of pagan Huns killed the lot of them. Even though she knew that they could not have received their martyrs' crowns otherwise, Amalia felt sad over their deaths. Still, they must have had a good time up until then, with Ursula leading them through strange towns and over mountains and across rivers. She would write her poem the next day, Thursday, which was her day home with Mama and Lena.

This time her day at home was even more enjoyable than usual. Mama and Lena had begun to make Christmas mincemeat, and all morning Amalia worked beside them in the kitchen. In the afternoon, because the day had turned chill, Amalia was allowed to kindle a fire in the parlor hearth. She and Mama sat beside it, Mama with a red shawl she was knitting. For a while Amalia, who was not good at any sort of "Fancy work," dutifully tatted a few more inches of the pink lace she had been working on each Thursday for several months. Then, caught up in the story her mother was telling about her childhood in Cádiz, Amalia laid her shuttle aside.

Juana often talked about Cádiz, and about that long sea voyage, during the course of which Amalia's poor papa had died in a violent storm. By contrast, the first years following Mama's arrival in New Orleans had been very quiet, apparently. After Amalia's birth, Mama said, Lena had come to live with them in rooms on the top floor of an inn. Amalia had a few fragmentary memories of those rooms. A balcony where she and Mama or Lena sometimes sat and looked down at a garden below. A door, with a knob which Amalia sometimes reached up to touch, but which would not turn. Not long ago she had asked Mama about that door, and Mama had said, "We kept that door locked because the attic stairs were very steep. We were afraid you would fall."

Just before Amalia turned three, they had traveled on a river barge up to Belleville. Amalia had one exciting and quite detailed memory of that journey. The barge had stuck on a mud flat, and it had taken the mules on the towpath, plus the bargemen, plus all the male passengers, to get it afloat once more.

What with the dancing fire in the hearth, and Mama's stories, and home food which was always such a joy after the convent's nutritious but dull fare, the hours flew by. Suddenly it was time to travel with Lena through the early dark back to the convent.

It was not until she entered Sister Mary Joseph's classroom the next morning that she remembered she had not made up her poem about St. Ursula.

There might still be time, she told herself frantically, for her to make up a poem. If only she weren't called upon too soon. . .

"Amalia, we will start with you."

With a sense of doom, Amalia got to her feet and walked up to stand beside the big desk.

"About which saint is your poem?"

Amalia managed to say, "Saint . . . Saint Ursula, the patron saint of young girls."

Sister Mary Joseph looked surprised. Evidently she too had anticipated that the entire class would pay tribute to either St. Francis or St. Theresa. "Very well. Proceed."

In desperate search of inspiration, Amalia let her gaze roam over the class, coming to rest upon Hannah Moffat's plump face.

Words formed in Amalia's frantic mind, popped out of her mouth: "St. Ursula, St. Ursula, the young girls' friend,/Why did you let Hannah's drawers descend?"

A moment of silence. Then the class exploded.

"Stop that!" Sister Mary Joseph shouted. "Stop immediately!"

The laugher ceased except for one final titter.

"Amalia, come here. Hold out your hands." *Thwack.* "And you'll have only bread and water for supper tonight."

The ruler caused her pain, and so did the prospect of hunger. But what caused her even greater and far more prolonged distress was the memory of poor Hannah, sitting there with a face like a scarlet moon, while for the second time the class rocked with laughter at her expense. At the first opportunity Amalia pleaded for the other girl's forgiveness, and Hannah, a surprisingly amiable creature despite her chronic bad luck, granted it. Nevertheless, Amalia still sought to make it up to Hannah. For the rest of the term she gave Hannah the answers to difficult arithmetic problems. That, of course, was a grave violation of the rules, and would have landed her in considerable hot water if she had been apprehended. Being good, Amalia decided, was an immensely complicated business. Trying to atone for hurting Hannah, she had involved herself in more wrongdoing. How was it that the saints managed to be good all the time?

The sisters did not learn about the arithmetic problems. And the next year Hannah and her parents went back to South Carolina. It was not until she was several weeks past her twelfth birthday that the Episode of the Miraculous Birds landed Amalia in trouble again.

It was the reverend mother's custom to interview each student in her office at least once every two weeks, extending praise where it was due, admonitions when necessary, and in general exhorting each girl to greater piety and studiousness. This gray morning it was Amalia's turn. The mother superior had begun to speak approvingly of Amalia's French compositions when someone knocked. Bidden to come in, a freckle-faced young novice opened the door and said, "Oh, Reverend Mother! Sister Gertrude and Sister Agnes are in the henhouse with Jobie." Jobie was the convent's ancient fox terrier. "He has cornered a weasel, but he seems afraid to really attack, and the sisters wonder what to—"

"I'll go there." Then, to Amalia: "Wait here for me."

Left alone, Amalia moved over to the cage that housed Dicky, the reverend mother's canary. After she had coaxed him into song, her attention strayed to the window. Just beyond it, in the little glass-roofed courtyard, a statue of St. Francis stood, with little stone birds perched on the fingers of his outstretched hands.

Amalia looked back at Dicky. The paper on the bottom of his cage was dotted with dried droppings.

An idea came to her. She could no more resist it than she had been able to resist climbing down that drainpipe through the sunrise light. Swiftly she raised the window sash. She opened Dicky's cage. She slipped out the cage's paper lining, leaned over the windowsill, and shook the paper until many of the dried droppings had fallen onto the flagstones beneath the saint's outstretched hands.

She restored the paper, fastened the cage door. She could hear the reverend mother's measured footsteps now. Swiftly and quietly she closed the window.

It was not until the next morning that one of the novices discovered the strange phenomenon in the courtyard. Soon there was a little knot of nuns and novices gathered a respectful few feet from the saint. With nervous awe their eyes traveled from the droppings beneath the stone tails of the saint's little friends up to the glass roof, through which no mortal bird could have entered the courtyard.

Composing a letter to the bishop, the mother superior was at first unaware of the little group outside her window. When she did notice them, she raised the sash and said, "Sister Margaret! Sister Barbara! What is all this?"

Sister Barbara, the convent's youngest nun, said in a shaken voice, "Oh, Reverend Mother! We think there has been a miracle." She pointed to the flagstones beneath the stone birds perched on the saint's outstretched fingers. "Look!"

The mother superior looked. "Miracle, my foot!" she snorted. "Send Amalia Moreno to me at once."

This prank, all the nuns felt, deserved a stiffer penalty than her earlier ones. Amalia was denied the next two of her visits home, which for her was severe punishment indeed. But the furor caused by the St. Francis episode did not last long, because soon there was so much else to talk about. The young United States, infuriated by Britain's continued blockades and by her kidnapping of American seamen, had declared war on the Mother Country.

As far as one theater of the war was concerned, the sleepy little town of Belleville had a front-row seat. Craft bearing arms and soldiers, destined to help American ships run the blockade, kept moving down to New Orleans. What was more, empty craft kept moving past on their way upriver, not slowly and laboriously, like the barge that had brought Amalia and her to Belleville, but swiftly and easily. Less than a decade after Robert Fulton's first steamboat had chugged along the Erie Canal, steam had come to the Mississippi. Towns along its banks already were used to the seething sound of paddle wheels and the tooting of boat whistles.

Because New Orleans streets now were thronged with soldiers and with crewmen of both frigates and merchant ships, the parents of Amalia's best friend, Esther MacFarlane, had decided that the city was no place for an attractive young girl. Consequently Esther spent the three summers of the war at the convent, seeing her parents only when they came upriver on the steamer. Amalia was sorry for her friend's sake, but glad for her own. Esther's exile from the elegant MacFarlane house in New Orleans meant that she spent days at a stretch each summer in the modest clapboard cottage Amalia shared with her mother and Lena. Amalia could tell that Mama was pleased and proud that she had such a friend, a pretty, gentle-mannered girl from one of New Orleans' most respected families.

The peace treaty between the two warring powers was signed in Holland on Christmas Eve 1815. But before the news could make its slow way to New Orleans, General Andy Jackson and his men had soundly thrashed an invading British army in a battle three miles from the city. New Orleans and all of Louisiana went wild. Even if they had been aware that the war was over before the battle began, they would still have celebrated the Battle of New Orleans as a great victory. That night in settlements up and down the river, fireworks spangled the darkness.

On a Thursday three weeks later Amalia came home from the convent for her weekly visit. To her puzzled dismay, she read anxiety in her mother's face. "Mama, what is it?"

Juana looked at her daughter. On her next birthday Amalia would be sixteen, the same age as the century. She was tall for her age, and beautiful for any age. As Juana had anticipated, the once round baby face had been transformed. Like Enrique's, her cheekbones were high and her jawline was clean. Her manner was Enrique's manner, high-spirited and friendly, with just a touch now and then, in her rare angry moments, of Constancia's fiery hauteur.

"Nothing is wrong, darling. Nothing at all."

"Oh, Mama! Don't pretend. You're no good at pretending."

Juana said reluctantly, "A letter from Mrs. MacFarlane came today."

"Esther's mother? What did she say?"

Juana went to the desk in one corner of the small parlor and took out a folded sheet of heavy white paper. Amalia took it, unfolded it, and read:

My dear Mrs. Moreno,

My husband and I have been so grateful for your

many kindnesses to Esther over the past summer. Will you let us repay you, next summer, by having your daughter as our houseguest during the month of July?

Surely by that time our city will have regained all its peacetime tranquillity and charm. I am sure your Amalia would enjoy it. There is so much here in the summer for young people—band concerts and parties and picnics at nearby Lake Pontchartrain.

I know you will want to think about this, and so I won't press you for an immediate answer. But do please write to me when you have made your decision.

Your. obed. s'v't,
Caroline MacFarlane

Pulse racing, Amalia looked up from the page. "Oh, Mama! How wonderful." Then her voice went flat. "But you don't want me to go, do you?"

"Dear, it is just that our summers together mean so much to me."

"I know." And she did. Juana never complained of the dullness of her life or made self-pitying references to her widowhood. And yet these past few years Amalia had become aware that she was her mother's whole existence.

But, oh, how she wanted to make that visit! To take the steamboat downriver. To see smart city people moving down crowded avenues, instead of neighbors she had known for as long as she could remember, gathered in gossipy little knots on the wide, dusty street that led up to the sawmill on the hill.

"All right, Mama. I won't go."

"Now, Amalia. I did not say that I feel you shouldn't go. I just want to consider it for a day or two."

That night, a few hours after Amalia had returned to the convent, Juana lay awake, staring into the dark. It would be absurd not to let the girl go. After all, weren't the MacFarlanes offering what she herself had wanted for Amalia, a chance to mingle with fine people and to become acquainted with young men worthy of her, rather than just the few sons of farmers and tradesmen, not one of them with much to recommend him, in this little town. Belleville had offered her own battered spirit a refuge. It had proved to be a safe place in which her daughter could reach near-womanhood. But she had long since realized that it would be a terrible waste for a young woman of the sort Amalia was becoming to spend her life in this little town.

And surely there was no valid reason for the fear Mrs. MacFarlane's letter had reawakened. In all these years, she'd had only one bit of news about Lawrence Mountjoy. In 1805 a weekly newspaper, brought by a visitor who had ridden up from New Orleans on horseback, had circulated through the village. In it Juana had read that Mrs. Lawrence Mountjoy, née Dorothy Haines, had died of a heart attack at her husband's plantation a few miles outside the city. Since then she had had no word of Mountjoy, even though in recent years she had read all the New Orleans papers, which now arrived regularly by steamer. Perhaps after his wife's death he had sold the plantation and left Louisiana. Perhaps, as Juana grimly hoped, he was dead.

But suppose he were alive, and had remained in the New Orleans area. It still would seem unlikely that even an obsessed man like himself would have carried a grudge all these years. And even if by some wild coincidence he actually met Amalia, would he be likely to connect her with the infant born in his house all those years ago? Probably he had forgotten, if he had ever known, that Juana had named the child Amalia. And the Spanish surname Moreno was common indeed, even more so than its English equivalent, Brown.

For the same reasons, it was almost unbelievable that Sara Davidson, if her path by some even wilder coincidence crossed Amalia's, would realize who the girl was. And it could well be that Sara Davidson had retired, that she no longer sat, emotionless except for her greed, in that plain office in that otherwise luxurious house. More than likely, after several profitable decades, she had gone to some Eastern or even European city to live out her life as a rich and respectable woman.

Yes, it was absurd, this fear that in New Orleans this child she loved more than her own life would sooner or later meet disaster.

Tomorrow she would go to the convent and tell her darling that of course she could have that month in New Orleans.

# 13

## New Orleans, April 1818

In her big, airy bedroom on the second floor of the MacFarlane house, Amalia looked wonderingly at her image in a mahogany-framed pier-glass mirror. So that is what it does to you, she thought. That is how loving a man makes you look.

Surely her dark eyes had never been that brilliant before. Surely her face, usually the shade of magnolia petals, had never before been touched with rose on the cheekbones. Even her throat and shoulders and the beginning swell of her breasts, revealed by the décolletage of her white dress, had an unfamiliar sheen, a pearly look. And all because in a few minutes she would see Angus MacFarlane, dance with him, feel the warmth of his big hand not only through the back of her thin silk dress and her camisole but even through her stays.

The windows of her room were wide open. Even though it was still spring in most of the northern hemisphere, almost summertime warmth had descended upon New Orleans. The night breeze, ballooning the white lace curtains inward, was laden with the scent of jasmine and orange blossoms. Underneath was another smell, that of rich subtropic earth and of the swamps not far outside the city. That blended smell was something she had become used to during the past three summers.

She had loved her month-long New Orleans visits each of those summers. She had loved the afternoons which she and the feminine members of the household—Esther, and Mrs. MacFarlane, and two aunts of Esther's—had spent languidly in the downstairs sitting room, sipping cold tea, chatting, and stirring the air with palm-leaf fans. Light filtering through the jalousies had a dim, aqueous look, as if the room were underwater.

She had loved the evenings, when boys of her age and a little older had flocked to the MacFarlane house, drawn by Esther's prettiness and the exciting beauty of her friend from upriver. There on the semidark veranda, illuminated only by lamplight from the drawing-room windows, the young people would sing to the accompaniment of banjos which two or three of the boys always brought. They would sing "Yankee Doodle" and "Camptown Races" and "Drink to Me Only with Thine Eyes." Amalia would laugh, and flirt, and tease and be teased. And all the time she would have a dim sense of herself ripening toward some dark and wonderful excitement, something to which these nice but callow boys were only a prelude.

These past two summers after she had come home from the MacFarlanes', Juana had questioned her closely. Which of the boys had she liked especially? John Wentworth? Oh, yes, the boy whose family owned most of the shares in a Brazilian diamond mine. Did Amalia think that someday she and John might . . . ?

At this point Amalia would be apt to laugh and say something like, "Oh, Mama! Are you so afraid you'll be stuck with me?"

Juana, who often took her daughter's teasing seriously, would say, "Oh, my darling. I can't imagine anything I would like more than to keep you here forever. But that wouldn't be fair to you, spending your life with Lena and me."

"Mama, there is no need to worry, really there isn't. I'll find someone I'll want to marry. And who knows? He might even be willing to marry me!"

But she hadn't met anyone like that on her summer visits, not even her last one, when she and Esther, both nearing their eighteenth birthday, found themselves sought after by older admirers. Some were just out of college, some already launched in business or professional careers. They brought expensive bouquets and candies. Several of them had the purposeful gleam of the wife-hunter in their eyes. Unable to compete, the young boys faded one by one, disgruntled, into the summer darkness. Much as she enjoyed the attentions of these older and more sophisticated young men, Amalia did not feel strongly attracted to any of them, and so, while she flirted with all of them, she was careful not to encourage any of these almost nightly callers to the point of a proposal.

But a week ago she had met him, that man whom she had sensed, as she sat in the veranda's warm darkness those summer nights of her growing up, was waiting for her in the future. His name was Angus MacFarlane, he was a distant cousin of Esther's father, and he had come to New Orleans both for business reasons and to attend Esther's coming-out party.

Esther's debut, which Amalia had traveled from Belleville to attend, was one of the few such balls to be held in April. Most New Orleans debutantes were presented during the Christmas season. But it was not until early March that Esther had reached eighteen, the age Mrs. MacFarlane felt a girl should achieve before her formal introduction to society. By then Lent had begun, and so the party had to be postponed until after Easter.

Arriving a week before the party, Amalia had found the house bustling with activity. Servants polished windows and floors and stair rails. Wine sellers and florists and caterers hurried in and out. Because the maids were busy, Esther helped Amalia unpack the small trunk she had brought, filled with clothes sufficient for a three-week stay.

Esther said, as she hung a yellow muslin dress in the wardrobe, "We've got some real Yankee houseguests. One is my cousin Angus from Sag Harbor, Long Island."

"Angus? I never heard you mention him."

"Probably because I'd never seen him until now. But he exists, all right. He's twenty-five, and he's been captain on various trading ships his fathers owns. I guess he's been all over the world, even Hong Kong. He has a friend with him, a shipbuilder, and he also brought his twelve-year-old sister, Ruth."

"You mean she's Angus' sister?" Esther nodded. "And she's twelve? It isn't usual for someone twenty-five to have a sister or brother so young."

"She's a half-sister. Her mother died last winter, just as Angus' mother did years ago. In fact, I think that is why he brought her along with him. To help her get over her grief for her mother, I mean."

"And the friend?"

"Tom Fulmer, the shipbuilder? Angus may order a ship

from a New Orleans shipyard while he's here, and he wants Mr. Fulmer to advise him. They are all out sightseeing now, but you'll meet them at dinner."

Esther had lifted a white dress from the trunk. "Oh, Amalia! How beautiful! Is that what you'll be wearing to the ball?"

"Yes." Her voice softened. "Mama and Lena made it for me." She had a vision of them, heads bent over the white silk day after day, fingers making tiny stitches as they constructed the tight bodice with its off-the-shoulder neckline, the wide skirt with its many flounces. Two women determined that their Amalia would not be put in the shade by any of those rich New Orleans girls.

She said, "Tell me, Esther, is Paul Darrel coming to the ball?"

Esther's fair skin flushed. "Yes. Mama and Papa didn't want to ask him, but I insisted."

Paul was one of the young boys who had gathered on the MacFarlane veranda on summer nights. Only twenty now, and years away from the medical degree he planned to acquire, he seemed to the elder MacFarlanes far too young and inconsequential to be considered as a son-in-law.

Amalia asked, "Then you still like him?"

"More than ever." Her round little chin firmed in a way that Amalia knew quite well. "And someday I'll marry him. You'll see."

A bit tired from her steamboat journey, Amalia took a nap that afternoon. Thus she did not meet the Long Islanders until she walked into the dining room that night. Because she had slept until only a few minutes before the gong sounded, she arrived at supper late and more than a little flustered. She had tried to dress her hair carefully—smooth on the top and sides, but falling in a cluster of curls at the nape of the neck—for her first meeting with her fellow houseguests. A tendril, though, had escaped to curl over her forehead.

"Oh, Mrs. MacFarlane, I'm so sorry I'm late." And then she broke off, forgetting her tardiness, her gaze fastened on the tall man who had risen from his seat at the table.

"Why, Amalia honey," Mrs. MacFarlane said. A plump little woman in her late forties, she had retained most of the airs as well as traces of the prettiness of the Southern belle she once had been. "You're not really late. We haven't started yet. Amalia, these are our kinfolk from up north. That's Angus MacFarlane, and that's his sister Ruth, sitting beside him. The gentleman here on my left is Cousin Angus' friend Mr. Tom Fulmer. This is Amalia Moreno, everybody."

Dimly, but only dimly, Amalia was aware of the pretty blond child and of the man who stood beside Mrs. MacFarlane's chair, a thin man, pleasant-faced and gray-eyed, of thirty-odd. The only person in the room she really saw was tall, smiling Angus MacFarlane, with the brilliant blue eyes and the red-gold hair. She was suddenly reminded of something she had read. Centuries ago the Vikings had raided Scotland again and again. Some had even settled there, intermarrying with the Celts, and leaving a physical heritage of height, blue eyes, and reddish-blond hair.

At the school in Belleville, when the other girls wondered aloud if they were destined to "fall in love at first sight," Amalia had sometimes said that she did not think that anyone did. Apparently she had been wrong about that. If this tingling awareness of a man, this heightened sense of your own aliveness, added up to love, then there could be love at first sight.

She murmured something and then took her place beside Esther's father, a jovial man with graying side whiskers and the alert gaze of a successful merchant. She ate mechanically, not really tasting her food. A few times her eyes encountered Angus' brilliant blue ones, and each time she felt an almost physical shock.

Since he was seated at the opposite end of the table, on Mrs. MacFarlane's right, he and Amalia said nothing directly to each other at supper, and exchanged only a few words afterward as they moved from the dining room to the drawing room. For perhaps twenty minutes Mrs. MacFarlane played the spinet for them. Then, seeing that the child Ruth appeared to be already half-asleep, she suggested that perhaps it would be best if they all retired for the night.

Upstairs, Esther accompanied Amalia into her room for a bedtime chat. As soon as she had closed the door, Amalia said, "Now, tell me all about him!"

Esther, who had seen the glances which passed between her friend and Angus MacFarlane at supper, did not need to ask who "him" was. Uneasily she observed the luminous look on Amalia's face. In the past, observing how Amalia's only response to various smitten young men had been a light flirtatiousness, Esther had feared her adored friend might turn out to be an old maid. Now she felt an opposite fear, a fear that Amalia, in her headlong way, might be falling in love too soon, or too deeply, or both.

"Well, that branch of the MacFarlanes are Presbyterians." Esther's family were Episcopalians. "His family was always very straightlaced and devout, apparently. His father is a deacon."

"Then how lucky I am that I have never even been baptized! I can be anything, even a Presbyterian."

She spoke lightly, and yet she was aware of that faint shadow which every now and again passed over her spirit. From her mother's stories about her Cádiz childhood, Amalia knew that Juana had been baptized and raised in the Catholic Church. Why had she not had her child baptized?

During her growing-up years, Amalia had asked her mother that question two or three times. On one such occasion, when Amalia had just turned thirteen, Juana had answered vaguely, "Everything was so confused right after you were born. As I've told you, I was staying with strangers, friends of that woman aboard ship who had been so kind to me after your father died. And later on, after Lena and I rented those attic rooms, I kept putting it off, and finally I decided to just leave matters that way. But, darling, you can be baptized now if you like, and confirmed too."

"No," Amalia had answered after a moment, "I don't think so. I believe in God, of course, and I like the sisters, and I'm happy at their school. But I think I will wait awhile before I decide what sort of church I would like to belong to, if any."

One day about two years later, when their talk again had turned to religion, Juana had said, "I don't go to church here because . . . well, I just lost my faith, that's all."

Something in her manner had kept Amalia from further questioning. But she had found it hard to accept what her mother had said. Juana did not seem the sort to worry over theological matters. In fact, if there was ever a woman one might think sure to cling to the simple faith of her childhood, that woman was Juana Moreno.

Now Esther said, "Amalia, please! I know almost nothing about my cousin. This is the first time I've ever seen him. For all I know, he's engaged to some girl back there on Long Island."

"He isn't," Amalia said. "Unless he was a complete scoundrel, an engaged man wouldn't look at a girl the way he looked at me tonight." Then, seeing the added anxiety her confident tone brought to her friend's face: "Oh, Esther! Don't worry about me!"

The MacFarlanes had organized a picnic party at Lake Pontchartrain for the next day. It turned out to be quite a large party. Mrs. MacFarlane had invited a number of young people, including, at her daughter's insistence, the too-young-to-be-eligible Paul Darrel. To keep Ruth MacFarlane company, she had also invited the neighbors' children, twelve-year-old twin girls and a boy of ten. After the picnic meal of cold fowl and cheese and fruit, Angus said to Amalia, "Would you like to walk for a few minutes?"

"Why, yes," Amalia said, and silently willed the others not to accompany them.

No one did. They moved along the shore of the vast lake, with the water, glass-smooth on this windless day, on their left, and on their right a subtropical tangle of live oaks, pines, and flowering vines. A great blue heron winged over the water, wild parrots flashed from tree to tree, and somewhere in the distance a bull alligator roared. He said, "It's certainly different from eastern Long Island."

"What is Long Island like?"

He spoke of sometimes long and severe winters that made the blossoming springs and lush summers and colorful autumns all the more pleasurable. He told her of villages already almost two hundred years old. "They are farming settlements, except for Sag Harbor. That is a port, and a busy one." He paused and then said, "See that rock up ahead? Would you like to sit up there for a while?" He added, smiling down at her, "We'll be in full sight of the others, so that no one can be scandalized, and yet far enough off that they can't hear what we say."

If they had continued on for a few more yards, a bend in the shoreline would have hidden them from the rest of the picnic party. How nice of him, she reflected, to be that mindful of her reputation. Then came the disturbing thought: but what if he'd had another reason? What if he actually did have a fiancée—some prim miss of whom his Presbyterian father approved—and feared word might get back to her that he'd been indiscreet with some minx in New Orleans?

Hands spanning her waist, he boosted her up to the rock's fairly flat top and then climbed up beside her. She said, "And you sail as captain on your father's ships?"

He nodded. "I've been on five voyages so far, three to the West Indies and two to the Orient."

"Somehow I hadn't thought of sea captains as young."

"In Sag Harbor they are. I'd say that four out of five of them are under thirty. Of course, most of those are whaling captains."

"How is it your family are not whalers?"

"We once were. In fact, my first voyage, when I was nineteen, was aboard a MacFarlane whaler. When I got home I persuaded my father to sell his whale ships and go into the West Indies and China trade."

"But why? I've heard that men make vast fortunes in whaling."

"Some do. But it's a hard and dangerous life, which is why so many men, although still alive, don't return from those three-year voyages. They prefer exile on some tropical island to spending more months aboard a whaler. As for the romance of whaling people talk about, it's actually a dirty and smelly business. When a whale ship is cooking blubber at sea, you can smell it from twenty miles away. And then, there are the whales themselves . . ."

"What about them?"

After a moment he said, "It seems to me that what happens to the whale is so wasteful. Here is this creature weighing hundreds of tons, the largest living thing on earth. You kill him, or possibly her. The first one killed on my whaling voyage was a mother with a calf. We left the calf swimming in circles after the kill. But anyway, you harpoon the whale and bring him alongside. From his body you take enough blubber to melt down into a number of barrels of oil and enough whalebone to provide stays for a number of ladies. You've used about twenty percent of his vast body. What's left, you just cut loose and let drift away. Now, that's not very economical, is it?"

He had spoken in a light, even jesting tone, and yet to Amalia his disgust was plain. Disgust with an activity which could transform one of nature's most awesome and yet most gentle creatures into a bloody carcass to be discarded as soon as possible.

Until now, she realized, it had been his physical attractiveness which made her skin tingle at his slightest touch. Now she was beginning to *like* him.

Ruth MacFarlane and the other children had wandered down the shore. Now they had removed shoes and stockings. The boys with rolled-up pantaloons, the girls lifting their long skirts to mid-calf, they waded in the shallows. Amalia watched them for a few seconds and then turned back to Angus. She said, "But if we don't use whale-oil lamps, how can we light our houses?"

"The way most people have for most of history. Using olive oil, or other vegetable oils, or fat from the animals we kill for our food." Then he smiled and said, "But that's enough about whales, perhaps too much. I want to know about you. Mrs. MacFarlane said that your mother was born in Spain."

"Yes." Better to make some things clear from the first. "She was born in Cádiz. Her father made and sold brooms, and her mother was a Gypsy."

"And your father?"

"He was a shoemaker. He died on the voyage to America, months before I was born."

He felt surprise. Strange that this classically lovely girl should be the daughter of a shoemaker and the granddaughter of a broom seller. "And you live in—what's the name of the town?—Belleview?"

"Belleville. My mother bought a house there when I was very small." She knew he must be wondering how a shoemaker's widow could afford to buy a house and to send her daughter to a school attended by well-off girls like Esther MacFarlane, and so she said, "A friend of my mother's advised her to invest what money she had in a cargo of cotton. She did, and he was able to sell the shares for many times what she paid."

Amalia might have added that she did not know the name of the friend who had given her mother such excellent advice. Amalia had been about eleven when Juana explained to her the source of their modest means. If Juana had mentioned the friend's name, Amalia did not remember it. She recalled only that her mother had said that he was a judge and that, according to a New Orleans newspaper which had reached Belleville, he recently had died.

"Angus . . ."

Amalia became aware that his young sister, again wearing shoes and stockings, her hat dangling down her back by its yellow ribbon ties, stood on the sand looking up at them. The sidelong glance her blue eyes gave Amalia said quite plainly that she was not happy over her brother's attentions to this lady he had met only the night before. "Angus, could I . . . ?"

"Of course, Muffin."

Reaching down, he grasped her hands and drew her up to sit between himself and Amalia. "You didn't get sunburned, did you?" He tilted her chin and looked down into the pretty little face in its frame of silky blond hair. "No, I guess not. But you should keep your hat on." He put the hat on her head and tied the ribbons under her chin. Amalia watched the two of them, aware of his competently paternal air and of the child's obvious pleasure in his concern.

She thought: Someday he will be that way with his own children. Then she felt a little frightened by the thought of how unhappy she would be if it turned out that some other woman already was destined to give him those children.

# 14

At the MacFarlane house, the family and guests served their own breakfasts from the buffet in the dining room. Sure that Angus must be an early riser, Amalia came downstairs at eight-thirty. Only Thomas Fulmer was in the dining room, helping himself to sausages.

"Good morning," Amalia said. "Are we the first?"

"No, Ruth was still here when I came down a few minutes ago. She's gone to visit the children next door. Angus has had breakfast too. He left to keep an appointment with some old friend of his father's."

"Oh."

Tom Fulmer said in a dry voice, "He'll be back. Not for lunch, I'm afraid. He and I are meeting at Drake's Coffee House at noon. But don't worry, he'll be back sometime today."

"Oh," she repeated, and felt hot color in her face.

He said with swift contrition, "I'm sorry for embarrassing you. I guess I'm just an envious old man. I'd like to think of some girl looking that disappointed because she didn't find me here."

"Old? How old are you?"

"Thirty-two."

"Why, that isn't old, not really old."

"Thank you." Again his tone was dry.

Aware that she had blundered, Amalia tried to set things aright. "I meant to say, it actually isn't old at all."

"Thank you," he repeated, this time with a smile on his thin face. He reached for one of the stacked plates. "Can I serve you some shirred eggs? Kippers? Sausages?"

"A little of each, please."

When they had carried their plates to the table and sat

down, Amalia said, "I suppose Mr. MacFarlane is much admired by the young ladies of Sag Harbor."

"You suppose correctly."

"And he? Is there any young lady he especially admires?"

He turned to her with a smile. It started in his gray eyes, she noticed, and then spread to his lips. "As far as I know, the field is all yours."

"Oh!'

"And even if it were crowded with entries, I would still bet on you."

Gratified but embarrassed, she changed the subject. "Do you like being a shipbuilder? Oh, I suppose that's a silly question. Why would you do it if you didn't like it?"

"It's not a silly question at all. When I was a boy I wanted to own and sail ships, not build them. In fact, by the time I was twenty-one I had gone to sea long enough to qualify for my master's license. But then my father put pressure on me to join the family shipbuilding firm.

"My father's dead now," he went on, "so I no longer feel obliged to devote full time to the firm, not when I've got capable associates. If the right chance comes, I may become a sea captain again after all."

Smiling, he looked at her near-empty plate. "I can see you are not one of those ethereal young ladies who disdain anything as gross as food. Shall I get you some more sausages?"

"No, thank you. This should last me until early afternoon."

He left soon after that. Amalia was still dawdling over a cup of hot chocolate when Esther came into the dining room. She said, ladling food onto her plate, "Mama has one of her headaches, so it's going to be very quiet and dull here today. Would you like to go shopping this afternoon?"

Amalia hesitated. Her mother had not been able to supply her with money for serious shopping. But she could buy a bottle of scent. "I'd like to, Esther."

From her very first visit, Amalia had loved New Orleans. The quiet residential streets with their wrought-iron gates opening onto flower-filled courtyards, and the smart shopping streets where highly polished carriages whirled over cobblestones, and people in the sort of finery seldom seen in Belleville—tall hats and full-skirted coats and tight breeches for the men, narrow dresses sashed high under the bosom for the women—strolled past the display windows.

Around three that afternoon Esther's search for a milliner whose address she had forgotten had led them down a side street. They had gone only a few yards when a low voice called to them, "Young ladies!"

Both girls halted. Just inside a doorway, at the foot of narrow stairs stretching upward into dimness, stood a woman of about twenty-eight. She wore a purple blouse and a skirt with layered ruffles of green and orange. A green scarf covered most of her dark hair. "Read your palms, young ladies?" Her voice was furtive. Obviously she knew of a recent city ordiance, aimed at Gypsies, which outlawed fortune-telling. "Only ten cents for each of you."

"Oh, let's!" Esther said.

Amalia started to object, then smiled and shrugged. Even she could afford to spend a dime on nonsense once in a while. The Gypsy woman said, "Just come in off the sidewalk, please."

The girls stood with the woman at the foot of the stairs. Esther was the first to hold out her palm. She seemed pleased by the Gypsy's prediction of marriage to a tall, dark man—brown-haired and five-feet-ten, Paul Darrel might possibly be considered tall and dark—and three children, and two long journeys.

From her reticule Esther took a dime and gave it to the Gypsy. "Now you, Amalia." Then, playfully, to the woman: "Do your best. Amalia can probably tell the difference between a true fortune and the other kind. Her grandmother was a Gypsy."

Already holding Amalia's outstretched hand, palm up, the woman raised suddenly alert dark eyes to the girl's face. "Is that true?"

"Yes." With an odd unease she remembered something Juana had once told her. Gypsies blithely tell a "gentile" anything they think he or she wants to hear. But that does not mean they have no belief in their own supernatural powers. They tell each other's fortunes—reading tarot cards, crystal balls, palms—with complete faith that what they predict will come true.

The woman stared at Amalia's palm and then said abruptly, "There is someone who wishes you evil."

A chill rippled down Amalia's spine. After a moment she

managed to laugh. "Who wishes me evil? Is it a man or a woman?"

"I cannot be sure. But the signs for evil and for danger are there in your palm. It will be with you like your own shadow for years. You must always be wary." She dropped Amalia's hand and turned toward the stairs.

It was Esther who protested. "Well! I don't call that much of a fortune. What about marriage? What sort of husband will she have?"

The woman turned back to them. "I don't want to talk about her marriage."

"Good!" Amalia said. She was annoyed now, and in spite of herself, a bit apprehensive. "I would just as soon not hear anything you might say about my marriage." She reached into her reticule and then held out a dime.

"I don't want your money, young lady. Just remember what I said, and be as careful as you can." She turned and climbed through the shadows toward the floor above.

As they moved away down the sidewalk, Amalia said, "Cheerful sort, wasn't she?"

Esther threw her friend's somewhat somber face a worried side glance. "Oh, Amalia. At school you were the one who always made jokes when the girls tried to read tea leaves and so forth. You said you thought that sort of thing was all nonsense."

"I still think so."

But she was unusually quiet for the rest of the shopping expedition. It was not until they turned in through the MacFarlanes' high wrought-iron gate, and saw Angus tossing a ball back and forth with his young sister, that the sense of oppression caused by the Gypsy woman's words slipped from her.

The enchanted days passed. Amalia awoke each morning to the glad knowledge that in a few hours—or, if she was lucky, only a few minutes—she would see Angus MacFarlane's brilliant blue eyes and reddish-blond hair, hear his full, ringing laugh. It was the laugh of a man whose confidence and whose zest for life matched her own.

There were long carriage drives over roads walled with almost jungle-thick grouth. Usually there was not just one carriage but three or four, holding a dozen or more young people and Mrs. MacFarlane and her sisters and whoever else was acting as chaperon. There were evenings when they gathered around the spinet and sang. Often Angus stood so close to her that his broadcloth sleeve brushed her bare arm, sending an odd thrill along her nerves. And there was a second picnic, during the course of which Angus managed to draw her behind a thick-trunked tree. His arms went around her and his warm, firm lips came down on hers in the kiss she had been longing for, aching for. Her arms tightened around his neck. Her hand, cupping the back of his head, pressed his mouth even closer to her own.

After a moment he lifted his head and held her a little away from him. In the near-sunset light his face looked startled and pleased, but just a shade disquieted. He said with an unsteady laugh, "I hope you don't go around kissing lots of young men like that."

"Oh, no!" It was a low, distressed cry.

"I know you don't. I just meant that you should remember men are not made of wood. At least I'm not. We had better join the others. They're putting the picnic hampers in the carriages."

On the way home through the spring twilight, Amalia worried. Had she been too bold? But when they all gathered around the spinet that evening, she somehow knew that Angus was remembering that kiss and wishing that right then and there he could take her in his arms again.

Now, less than twenty-four hours later, she was aware that the tension between them had reached the breaking point. Standing before the pier-glass mirror in the white silk gown Mama and Lena had made for her for Esther's debut, she felt confident that before the evening was over he would ask her to marry him. And when she went out onto the landing and saw Angus in the hall below, the look that leaped into his face at sight of her made her more sure of him than ever.

But when she reached the foot of the stairs, other young men gathered around her. Confident amusement in his face now, Angus stood aside while they secured her promise for the first polka or waltz or mazurka. Thus it wasn't until late in the evening that Angus said, as they waltzed over the crowded floor, "I must talk to you." He whirled her through the open French doors onto the flagstone terrace that ran along the rear of the house. "Let's walk."

For a few moments there was no sound except the music

from the ballroom and the crunch of their feet over the gravel path. Then he said, "If I have your permission, I want to go up to Belleville. I want to ask your mother for your hand in marriage."

She halted. "Oh, yes! Yes!"

He looked down at her for a moment and then drew her to him. Arms around his neck, lips stirring beneath his, she pressed her body close against him.

Lifting his head, he gave an unsteady laugh. "I did not plan to go to Belleville until the middle of the week, but now I think I'll take the early steamer tomorrow. The sooner you and I are married, the better."

Here a hundred feet from the house the light from the ballroom was dim but she was still able to make out his expression. He looked much as he had the first time they had kissed, pleased and aroused, and yet just a trifle disconcerted.

She said, "You mean, I was too . . . too . . . But, Angus! We're engaged."

He smiled. "Not yet. Not until I have your mother's permission to marry you."

"Oh, *Angus*."

"Amalia, perhaps I had best make one thing clear." He was no longer smiling. "I find you very desirable indeed. What is more, I've led anything but a chaste life. What sailor has? But in my eyes you are apart from all other women. We are to marry and spend the rest of our lives together. That is why I am being conventional. These conventions, these formalities, help form the foundation we'll need through all the years ahead of us. Do you understand?"

"Of course, Angus. And you needn't worry about what Mama will say. She'll be so happy. Oh, I wish I could go up to my room right now!"

"Why?"

"So that I could write a letter for you to take to her."

He smiled. "The ball will be over in another hour. Well, shall we go back in?"

# 15

Late-afternoon sunlight filled the parlor of the little house in Belleville, lying warm on the well-polished furniture and on the red-gold hair of Juana's visitor. She felt that in much the same way, happiness was flooding her heart.

He had told her about himself, answering each of her questions without hesitation. Very soon she realized that here was the sort of young man she had hoped and prayed might fall in love with her daughter. Apparently he came from a sound and fairly prosperous family. Despite his ready smile, he impressed her as a serious and responsible man. And he was handsome, perhaps as handsome, in an older, more rugged way, as the young Spanish aristocrat who, on one of those long-ago mornings, had become the progenitor of Juana's beautiful child.

She looked at Amalia's letter, lying on the small table beside her. Angus MacFarlane had handed it to her almost as soon as he had introduced himself. With a tender smile, she thought of phrases from that letter: ". . . so happy, Mama. . . . Please, please like him. But what am I saying? How could you help but like him?"

Juana said, "There is one thing I must tell you, Mr. MacFarlane. I will be unable to give Amalia a dowry."

"It does not matter, Mrs. Moreno. As I explained to you, I receive the captain's share of the proceeds from my voyages on my father's ships. Amalia and I will have more than enough income."

"Just the same, I would like to explain why there is no dowry. My income is small, and I would not have even that if it were not for a friend who years ago advised me about making an investment. His advice turned out to be very good indeed."

Angus wondered if the friend had been in love with her.

Quite probably. Not for the first time since the brown-skinned woman with the scarred face had ushered him into this modest but pleasant parlor, he had wondered why Mrs. Moreno had no husband. Even though there was gray in the thick dark braids wound around her small head, she obviously was still under forty. In fact, the gray only emphasized the freshness of her face with its dark eyes, as large, although not as wide-spaced, as Amalia's. Strange that she had chosen to live in this little town, most of the time with only that servant as a companion.

Juana went on, "Have you and Amalia discussed setting a date for your marriage?"

"No. If you and Amalia insist, I will sail for Long Island in ten days, as I planned to do, and then come back here at a later date for the wedding. But for my part, I would like to have it quite soon. I could extend my visit to Louisiana an additional week, say. If that would give you time to plan a small wedding, Amalia and I could leave for Long Island immediately afterward."

"I think that could be arranged." Certainly, she thought, remembering fervent phrases from that letter, Amalia would be pleased by an earlier date. The thought was accompanied by a familiar faint unease. She wished her child were not such an intense person. People who could feel so much joy were equally open to pain.

She went on, "Are you going back to New Orleans tomorrow?"

"Yes, on the morning steamer. I have already booked a room at the inn for tonight, and told them to call me at daylight."

"I think Lena should go to New Orleans on the same steamer. She has New Orleans relatives she can stay with. She and Amalia could spend a few days shopping for a small trousseau. I'll stay here to start preparations for the wedding." She hesitated. "If it is to be in only two weeks, there won't be time for members of your family to travel to Louisiana."

"My half-sister is already here. So is my best friend. Aside from my sister, I have no immediate family except my father. He had pneumonia last winter, so I doubt that he would want to travel here even if we postponed the ceremony until late in the summer."

Juana smiled. "Then it will be a small wedding, because Amalia has no one but me and Lena, plus her school friends, of course, including Esther."

No one else, she thought, on this side of the Atlantic. And through letters from Father Ernesto over the last few years, she knew that her family in Cádiz was reduced and scattered. Constancia had died suddenly of a heart attack. Juana found it almost impossible to think of her proud, spirited mother as dead. One of her brothers, who had become a stonemason, had died when a wall he was working on collapsed. And all her other brothers and sisters were now married and had started families of their own, even the twin girls she remembered as squabbling three-year-olds. Only her father still lived in those once crowded and noisy third-floor rooms.

Angus said, "You'll be lonely after I take your daughter to Long Island, won't you?"

All Juana could manage to say was, "Yes."

"Why don't you come to visit us as soon as you can. And perhaps after that you and your servant—what is her name? Lena?—would like to move back there permanently. We MacFarlanes know everyone in town. Before long you would have many friends. Do you think that you would like that?"

Juana's face lit up. He felt he could tell how she had looked when she was as young as or even younger than her daughter was now. "Oh, yes! I would like that so very much."

What a nice woman, he thought. What a very nice woman Juana Moreno was.

At about the same hour, Amalia sat on a stone bench in the rear garden of the MacFarlane house in New Orleans. On her lap was a copy of Richardson's *Pamela*, lent to her by Esther's mother. Every once in a while she would read a sentence or two, but she had spent most of the last half-hour staring dreamily into the distance and wondering what Angus and her mother were saying to each other.

Footsteps over the gravel. Amalia looked to her right and saw Ruth MacFarlane approaching. She stopped in front of Amalia and said, "Are you going to marry my brother?"

Amalia looked into the child's troubled face. "Yes, Ruth. Do you mind?"

"Yes!"

Even though she knew about children's jealousy—she herself, at Ruth's age, had secretly feared some man might come along and marry her mother—Amalia felt disturbed by Ruth's vehemence.

"Oh, Ruth! Why?"

"Because he won't love me anymore."

"But he will! He must have loved you from the day you were born. Marrying me won't change that."

"But he won't live with Papa and me any longer. He'll live in a different house, with you."

"Probably. But you can stay with us anytime you like."

Ruth seemed to think that over. Then she asked, "Are you going to go along on Angus' next voyage? Captains' wives do, you know."

Amalia hadn't known. But instantly she began to think of how wonderful it would be to take a voyage as Captain Angus MacFarlane's wife. She said, "If he wants to take me with him, I'll go."

"Will you promise to make him take me too?"

Amalia said, disconcerted, "Why, Ruth! I couldn't make him take you along. But I would certainly suggest it."

After a long moment Ruth said, "I'll bet you I never get to go." Then she burst out, "I don't see why he has to marry anybody. In a few years I'll be old enough to keep house for him."

Amused now, Amalia looked at the pretty, stubborn face. A few years from now, she thought, you'll have so many boys flocking around you that you will seldom give a thought to your brother.

Aloud she said, "Please don't feel bad." She hesitated, wondering whether to use Angus' nickname for her, Muffin, and then decided against it. "You and I are going to be good friends, Ruth. Just you wait and see."

For Amalia, awaiting her lover's return, the rest of that day and evening dragged by with agonizing slowness. When she went to bed, sleep eluded her. Finally, though, she slipped into unconsciousness, only to be awakened by a knock on her door. Her eyes flew open to see late-morning sunlight pouring into the room.

"Who is it?"

"Esther. Angus is back. He brought a letter from your mother. I'll slip it under the door."

# 16

The next three days passed in what Amalia considered a thoroughly satisfying bustle. With the help of Lena, who was spending her nights at the home of an aged aunt, Amalia shopped for hours at a time, trying to make the trousseau money her mother had sent go as far as possible. Sometimes Esther accompanied them. More often, caught up in parties now that she had made her bow to society, she did not.

A few times, fingering a length of silk or fine muslin which she could not afford, Amalia felt a certain wistfulness. But by the time she started back to the MacFarlane house, knowing that soon she would sit beside Angus at supper, not a trace of her discontent remained.

Only one really disturbing thing happened during those three days. In a glove shop one afternoon, the proprietor left Amalia and Lena standing at the counter while he went into the back room to see if he had elbow-length white kid gloves of the proper size. Amalia stood looking at the shelves of boxes along the wall, a dreamy smile on her lips.

"Child, what are you smiling about?"

"Oh, Lena!" Turning, she put her hand on the woman's arm. "I'm so happy! You could never know how happy I am."

After a moment Lena said in a dry, cool tone, "That's right, Miss Amalia, I could never know."

Amalia felt startled. Except when strangers were present, Lena never before had addressed her as "Miss Amalia." Instead she had called her "child," or "honey," or just "Amalia." She looked into the woman's face, feeling that she saw a certain aspect of her for the first time. Always to Amalia Lena had been just Lena, someone who had been part of her life as long as she could remember, someone she loved almost as much as she loved her mother. Only when others commented upon it had she become conscious of Lena's race, or the long scar down one cheek. But now Amalia was seeing her in a new light, a brown-skinned woman of forty-odd with a disfigured face and no real life of her own.

Lena went on, in that dry tone Amalia had never heard her use before, "My face is the wrong color for your kind of happiness, isn't it? And besides, there's the scar—"

"Oh, Lena, Lena! I didn't mean it that way. You must know I didn't.

After a moment the woman said, "I know you didn't, honey." That other Lena, cold and bitter, who for a moment had looked out of her eyes, was gone now, and in her place was the Lena Amalia had known all her life. "I guess it was being back here in New Orleans that made me feel mean and sad for a minute. For me this was a mean, sad town. But I feel fine now. You forgive me, honey?"

"Oh, Lena! Of course I do."

The proprietor came back just then with three boxes of gloves. By the time Amalia made her selection, she had forgotten that there had ever been a moment's unpleasantness between herself and Lena.

It was the next night that Amalia's whole world collapsed.

That afternoon, at the end of their final shopping expedition, Lena had taken their purchases with her to her aunt's house. The next day they would meet on the docks and take the steamer upriver to Belleville. Through the late-afternoon light, Amalia returned in a hired carriage to the MacFarlane house. It did not surprise her to learn that Angus was not there. He and Tom Fulmer several times had spent the entire day on the waterfront, visiting shipping offices, and chandler shops, and boatyards.

Around six, Tom Fulmer returned alone. No, he did not know where Angus was. Angus had left him around two that afternoon, saying only that he had "an appointment."

Angus was still absent at supper. Tom smiled at Amalia across the table. "Don't worry. I think his appointment may have been with an old business associate of his father's. In that case Angus might have felt obliged to take supper with him."

Despite Tom's words, anxiety still weighed on her. Even though they would of course see each other tomorrow, it seemed odd to her that he should stay away on this, her last evening in New Orleans. After supper, unwilling to burden the others with her unease, she went to her room. She was at the window looking down on a garden flooded with the light of a newly risen full moon when someone knocked. She crossed the room and opened the door.

Esther stood there, looking upset. "Angus is here. I mean, he was in the house a minute ago. He asked me to tell you that he is waiting for you outside the gate in a hired carriage."

After a bewildered moment Amalia said, "Thank you, Esther." She went to the wardrobe and took down a white shawl. Then she hurried past her friend, down the stairs, and out of the house. As she came through the wrought-iron gates, Angus got out of the carriage standing there and opened the door for her.

"Angus, what on earth—"

"Please, Amalia." His voice had a constricted sound. "Please just get in."

As the carriage moved away down the street, she cried, "What is it? Have you heard from Belleville? Is my mother—"

"I have not heard from Belleville. Your mother, as far as I know, is perfectly all right. Please, Amalia. I'll talk to you about this just as soon as I can."

After that, she sat silent in the corner of the seat. Even though the night was fairly warm, she felt so chilled that she wrapped the shawl tightly around her. Soon the horse's hooves sounded, not over cobblestones, but a dirt road walled by trees on both sides.

Angus reached up and knocked against the trapdoor. When the driver's bewhiskered face appeared in the opening, Angus said, "Stop here and then wait for us."

He helped Amalia to alight. Too bewildered and frightened even to speak, she walked beside him up the road for perhaps two hundred feet. Then he stopped and turned to her.

"I wanted to make sure that no one else could hear this." His voice still had that constricted sound, as if something had tightened around his throat. "Amalia, I can't marry you."

Enough moonlight filtered down through tree branches for her to see his rigid face. She stared up at him wordlessly.

"I . . . I've been deceiving you, Amalia. There is a girl back in Sag Harbor. We quarreled just before I left. I thought it was all over between us. But today I received a letter from her. She'd sent it by a ship that left Sag Harbor only two days after I did."

He drew a deep breath and then went on. "She still loves me, Amalia, and I find that I still love her. I'm going back home and marry her."

Falsity in his voice, falsity in every line of his face. Beneath her shocked bewilderment she felt a surge of relief. "Why are you lying to me? There's no other girl. You love me! I can *feel* it, Angus. Why are you trying to make me think you don't?"

His voice held a desperate note. "Amalia, believe me, please believe me. I know how terribly wrong I was not to at least tell you about her before—"

"Angus, stop it! Stop lying, and tell me what the trouble *really* is."

When he didn't answer, she went on more quietly, "Darling, do you think you can fob me off with a lie? Do you think I'll stand meekly by and let you ruin both our lives? I won't. If I have to, I'll follow you back to Sag Harbor. What will you do then, when you have to produce a girl who doesn't even exist?"

Again he didn't answer. She said, "I'll find out the truth, one way or another. And so you'd better tell it to me right now."

After a long moment he said, "I hoped you would believe me. Oh, God, how I hoped you would."

Defeat in his voice now. Defeat in his face, making it look slack, and years older. "Yes, I was lying. The letter I received wasn't from a girl in Sag Harbor. I don't know who sent it. It was anonymous."

He wasn't lying now. A nameless dread tightened her throat.

"The letter advised me to talk to a Mrs. Sara Davidson. Do you know who she is?"

She shook her head.

His voice was anguished. "No, I can see you don't. I'm going to have to tell you. Sara Davidson runs a brothel. Do you know what that is?"

She managed to nod.

"It is on Oak Street, although I hear that until a few years ago the street was known by its French name. Her establishment is supposed to be the finest in New Orleans," he said bitterly, "and I suppose it is. Crystal chandeliers and oil paintings all over the place, except in that office of hers." He paused, and then said abruptly, "For about three years, your mother was a prostitute in her employ."

After a while Amalia said in a whisper, "You must be insane."

He didn't answer, but just looked down at her with that agonized face. Even though the very sickness in the pit of her stomach told her that his words were true, she said, "Yes, insane. Why else should you tell me a filthy, filthy lie about my mother?"

"Oh, God! Don't you think I would give anything to make it be a lie? But it is not. You lived there, too, Amalia, in rooms in the attic. That woman Lena took care of you during the hours when your mother was . . . was with customers."

Memories moved through her tortured mind now, certain fragmentary memories which always had puzzled her. The sound of distant music and laughter drifting up through that door which was always locked. No, not always, because there was that other memory of going down steps, each of which seemed very high. She had stood in a hall staring through the open door of a room at . . . what? She could not remember. But she did remember her mother emerging from another room and then rushing at her, sweeping her up against the bosom of a fine, silky dress she had never seen before, and climbing the stairs with her.

Several times she had almost asked her mother about that particular memory. Each time something had made her check the impulse.

"And that man who advised your mother how to invest her money," Angus was saying. "He was a client of Sara Davidson's, but not a regular client. He was some fancy kind of pervert. Oh, God, Amalia! Do you think I would or even could make this up? It's true. The Davidson woman described your mother, described Lena. She showed me a sample of your mother's handwriting, some sort of receipt your mother had given her for a loan of three dollars. It looked to me like the handwriting on the envelope of your mother's letter, the one I brought to you when I came back from Belleville.

"Oh, Amalia! None of this is your fault. And yet because of it I cannot marry you. For generations ours has been an honorable family. I have to live up to that, Amalia. I cannot bring children, your children and mine, into the world, children with a grandmother who has been a harlot. If I were alone in the world, perhaps it would be different, although I am not sure. But there is my father. I love and honor him. How can I give him grandchildren who would also be your mother's grandchildren?"

Blind with pain, she raised both her fists. She took a step toward him and began a rhythmic pounding against his chest. "I hate you. Oh, God, how I hate you. I'd kill you if I could."

He made no move to defend himself or even to step back from those pounding fists. After a few seconds her arms fell to her sides and she stood with hanging head. Her breathing was harsh and ragged, almost like sobbing.

He said in a dull voice, "Of course you hate me. I'm sure you always will." He added, not touching her, "Let's go back now."

Side by side, but with at least two feet of space between them, they walked back to the carriage. He spoke to the driver, helped her inside, got in beside her. As the carriage turned, he said, "I'll go to an inn tonight. Tomorrow I'll get word to Tom. He can bring my trunk and portmanteau to me." He added after a moment, "There is a ship sailing for New England ports the day after tomorrow."

She said nothing.

"Rest assured that I will never tell Tom, or anyone, about what has happened between us. And I hope that for your sake you will tell no one. You can just say that we have broken our engagement because of a quarrel."

Still she said nothing.

"Amalia, I would give my right arm if this had not happened. I know people are always saying that. But I mean it. I would gladly go through the rest of my life with one arm if thereby I could wipe out what I've had to do to you tonight."

She heard the sincerity in his voice. But it did nothing to lessen her agony. She wanted to hurl more words at him. Just how many brothels all over the world, she wanted to ask, have you been in? And yet because my mother, who must have been hard-pressed indeed. . . .

But what was the use in saying it? The world, she knew, would feel that he had made the only sort of decision that a man of his sort of family could make.

They were in the city now. She looked out of the carriage window at moon-silvered cobblestones, moon-silvered housefronts studded with the orange-colored rectangles of lamplit windows. Everything looked to her somehow grotesque, like the landscape in an evil dream. For a moment she wondered if she were not actually in the grip of a nightmare. After all, only hours ago she had been so happy that she would not have traded places with anyone else alive. And now she was . . . what? A whore's daughter, and as such, rejected by the man she had loved. Yes, surely it was a bad dream.

The carriage turned into the MacFarlanes' street. She knew she must stop trying to pretend she was in the toils of a nightmare and start thinking about how she was going to get through the rest of her life.

The carriage stopped. Angus got out and helped her to the ground. They looked at each other through the bright moonlight but said nothing, not even good-bye. She turned and went through the gate. After a moment she heard the carriage start up.

Someone was standing on the moon-whitened courtyard path. She saw the glow of his pipe and knew who he was. Tom Fulmer, having a prebedtime smoke, and having it in the open air, out of respect for Mrs. MacFarlane's curtains. As she approached him, he took the pipe from his mouth and said, "Amalia?"

To her surprise, because she had not known it was going to happen, she gave a great, shuddering sob.

"Amalia!" He looked down into her pain-twisted face. "What is it?" Then, swiftly: "No, don't tell me here. Let's go around to the rear garden."

He knocked his pipe against the sole of one shoe until he had dislodged its embers. Then, after putting the pipe in his coat pocket, he took her arm and led her around the house and down a graveled path to the garden's end. They sat down on a circular wooden bench built around the trunk of a big oak. At least a hundred yards separated them from the MacFarlanes' windows.

"Now," he said.

Broken and confused, the story tumbled out of her. He did not interrupt, even to ask a question. Only his arm, now encircling her shoulders, conveyed to her his sympathy and his shock.

When she fell silent he asked, after perhaps half a minute, "What are you going to do?"

She said, her voice dull, "Go home. Lena and I were going to take tomorrow afternoon's steamer anyway, so we could help Mama with preparations for . . ." She broke off for several seconds and then went on, "We arranged to meet down at the wharf where the river steamers dock."

"Promise me one thing, Amalia. Do as Angus suggested about telling no one what has happened. Just say that you two had a disagreement, or however you want to phrase it, and that you don't wish to talk about it. And stick to that. Someday you will be glad you did. You have told me. Let the story stop right here. I'll tell no one. And if I know Angus, he won't either."

He fell silent. Then, as if unable to find anything, anything at all, to say to comfort her, he stood up. "Come." His voice was gentle. "Let's go into the house."

They parted at the foot of the stairs, he to go to a bedroom at the rear of the house, she to climb to the second floor. She had reached the door of her room and was starting to turn the knob when Esther stepped from her room out into the hall.

"Oh, there you . . . Amalia! What is it."

Amalia said in a thick voice, "Angus and I are not going to be married, after all."

"Amalia! How can that be? What on earth . . . ?"

"We had a terrible quarrel, that is all. It made us both realize that we don't belong together. Now, please, Esther. If you care about me, don't ask me to say anything else."

She went into her room and closed the door.

# 17

Around eleven the next morning Amalia walked hesitantly down Oak Street through misty sunlight. Even though her departure from New Orleans was only a few hours away, she carried none of her belongings except a reticule. Early that morning the MacFarlane coachman had taken her portmanteau as well as her trunk down to the wharf where the river steamers were berthed and where, at three o'clock, she would meet Lena.

Although she didn't know quite what she had expected, she was dully surprised that this street looked like any other middle-class New Orleans street. How would she know Sara Davidson's house? Even if the girls at the convent school had been right when they whispered about such establishments displaying a red light, the light would not be burning at this hour.

A small black boy was moving toward her. He pulled a small wagon that held two paper-wrapped bundles. Evidently he was a washerwoman's son, delivering laundry to her customers. "Just a moment, please," Amalia said. The boy halted. "Do you know where a Mrs. Sara Davidson lives?"

"Sure do." He couldn't have been more than ten, and yet a certain slyness in his voice told her that he not only knew where Sara Davidson lived. He knew what sort of woman she was. He turned and pointed at a house across the street and about fifteen yards away in the direction from which she had come. "That's where she lives."

"If I give you a five-cent piece, will you take a note to her house, and hand it in, and wait for a reply? I'll be waiting for you here, over by that tree."

"Sure will, ma'am. You watch my wagon?"

"Yes."

With eyes that burned slightly after a sleepless night, she

watched him hurry across the street, climb steps, stand on tiptoe to reach the knocker. A uniformed mulatto maid who looked handsome, at least from a distance, answered the door and took the note from the child's hand.

Amalia's heartbeats were heavy and uncertain, as if her emotional anguish had translated itself into a bodily illness. But she had felt she had to come here, had to get from that woman herself a confirmation of what Angus had told her. True, Lena might have been able to give it. But whether she would or not was another question. And so, wanting to have at least the grim comfort of absolute certainty, Amalia had sat in her room in the morning light and written a note, and then brought it here.

As always at this hour, Sara Davidson sat at her desk, ledgers spread out before her. Someone knocked, and Sara said, "Come in."

It was not until the door opened and then closed that Sara looked up and saw Solange standing there. Older and harder-faced now, and with hair dyed to an unnatural glossy black, Solange was nevertheless still good-looking.

"Well?"

"A little colored boy brought you a note. He says the lady who gave it to him asked him to wait for an answer."

Sara unfolded the note and read:

> Dear Mrs. Davidson,
>
> I need very much to talk to you. Will you meet me in the cemetery at one o'clock this afternoon? I will be on the bench nearest the main gate.
>
> Your obed. s'v't,
> Amalia Moreno

Well, Sara thought, the girl seemed to have a head on her. A cemetery was one of the few places where two women—even a brothel keeper and a convent-bred maiden—could meet seemingly by accident and fall into conversation, with no chance observer thinking it strange.

Despite Juana's naive hope, Sara Davidson had not forgotten the name of the child who for almost the entire first three years of her life had lived with her mother in that attic apartment. But then, Sara seldom forgot anything. She had been amused when, several years ago, she had begun to see on the newspaper's society page such items as, "Mr. and Mrs. James MacFarlane have as a houseguest Miss Amalia Moreno, a classmate of their daughter, Esther, at the convent school in Belleville." Sara knew that the girl had to be Juana Moreno's daughter. Within days after Juana's departure with the child and Lena White that morning years ago, Sara had made it her business to learn at what upriver town the steamer had deposited them.

She had been even more amused yesterday when Angus MacFarlane came to see her. Cold as her temperament was, she still could realize that he was an extraordinarily handsome man, and a lusty one. She also recognized in his speech and self-confident bearing the stamp of a Yankee aristocrat. How was it, she still wondered, that a man like that had fallen in love with a Spanish strumpet's offspring, even allowing for the fact that he had not known what her mother was?

She reread the brief note. There was no reason why she should not be away from the house for an hour this afternoon. She dipped her quill pen into the ink bottle and wrote at the bottom of the note, "Very well. At one o'clock."

She signed the note, refolded it, and handed it to Solange. "Give this back to the boy."

Amalia had taken care to reach the cemetery several minutes before one o'clock. She sat on a bench feeling exhausted but keyed up, her tired eyes staring unseeingly at someone's family tomb, one of those marble structures where the dead rested aboveground rather than in the boggy New Orleans earth.

The cathedral clock struck one. While the vibrant sound still lingered in the air, Amalia heard the crunch of footsteps approaching over the gravel path. She looked to her right and then sprang automatically to her feet. A stout middle-aged woman in a dark green dress and bonnet was moving toward her. Surely this could not be a brothel keeper. She looked like some respectable widow come to mourn her late husband. Then she halted beside Amalia, and the girl looked into those dark, strangely opaque eyes, and knew that this woman was capable of anything.

"You are Amalia Moreno?"

Speechless, the girl nodded.

"I'm Sara Davidson. Let us sit down. I hate standing."

They sat down on the bench. Sara turned and looked intently into the girl's face. She no longer wondered at a man like Angus MacFarlane falling in love with Juana Moreno's daughter. Juana had been pretty enough in a soft, rather childish fashion. But her daughter was beautiful, even with the marks of fatigue and strain in her face.

"You wanted to see me?" Sara asked.

"You must know why. Did my mother and I . . . did we really live in your . . . your . . . ?"

"If her name is Juana Moreno and yours is Amalia Moreno, you certainly did, along with that brownskin with the knife scar, Lena White."

For a long moment Amalia was silent. Then she said in a low voice, "What I wanted to ask you is, why."

"Why what?"

"Why did my mother come to your place?"

Sara remained silent, considering. If she chose to, she could tell the girl about Lawrence Mountjoy. But Mountjoy was still around. In his mid-fifties now, and far gone in dissipation, but around. And this girl had a desperate look about her. If she knew what Mountjoy had done to her mother, no telling what she might try to do to him. There was just a chance that, feeling that her life already was ruined, she might go with her story to one of the sensational weeklies which flourished in New Orleans. She might even go after him with a pistol. It was unlikely, but still possible. And if anything like that happened, Sara would find herself involved in the sort of public scandal she had always thought it wise to avoid.

Besides, why should she oblige Juana by justifying her behavior in her daughter's eyes? The day that Juana walked out on her, she had promised herself that if she ever had the chance to get even without going to too much trouble, she would take it. She had a hunch that Juana worshiped this beautiful daughter of hers. Probably nothing could make her suffer as much as knowing that because of her own past her child's life had been shattered.

She shrugged and said, "Do you think that I bother to remember the stories that harlots tell me about how they got into the business? In my experience there has been only one real reason, no matter what fancy excuses they gave. They preferred turning harlot to going to work."

Color flooded Amalia's face and then drained away, leaving her whiter than before. She managed to say in a fairly even voice, "Mr. MacFarlane mentioned receiving an anonymous letter suggesting that he see you."

Sara nodded. "He showed it to me. It was printed in block letters, and it said he would learn something of importance about Amalia Moreno if he came to see me."

"Who wrote it?"

"My dear girl, how should I know? There may be scores of people in New Orleans who know that your mother was once at Sara Davidson's. Oh, don't look so startled. I don't mean people like the MacFarlanes. I mean people of the servant class. Over the years I've dismissed cooks and housemaids and coachmen. A good many of them must have found employment in private houses, taking their Sara Davidson stories with them. They wouldn't tell such stories to their employers because they wouldn't want the master and mistress to know that they had worked for someone like me. But they must certainly have told them to their fellow servants."

Amalia said, "I believe you sent Angus MacFarlane that anonymous letter."

Sara said calmly, "I tell you I did not."

"I don't believe you."

The woman shrugged. "Believe what you like." She stood up. "I will say good-bye now. I have things to do."

Still seated on the bench, Amalia numbly watched as the woman went down the walk accompanied by her shadow, moving foreshortened and inky black beside her on the graveled walk.

# 18

Two hours later Amalia and Lena stood at the steamer's rail watching the dark green riverbank slide by. Lena said, "All right, child. As soon as I saw you there on the dock, I asked you what was wrong, and you almost bit my head off. But aren't you ready to tell me now?"

After several moments Amalia said, "I am not going to marry Angus MacFarlane."

Lena said matter-of-factly, "Well, I knew that you two must have had some sort of ruckus. But probably it can be fixed up."

"It can't be! How can you fix up something that happened eighteen years ago?" She swung around to face the brown-skinned woman. "Lena, where did I spend the first three years of my life?"

Lena's face seemed to freeze. She said nothing.

"In the attic of a house owned by a woman named Sara Davidson! That's where I lived as a baby, didn't I, didn't I?"

"Child, how on earth did you hear about—?"

"Angus told me! And Sara Davidson herself told him."

Lena said in a low, shaken voice, "Oh, honey, honey! After all these years, your mama and I had come to think . . . Oh, child! I know what you must feel."

"Do you? Do you know what it is like to love a man the way I loved Angus, and then have him throw you over because your mother was a harlot?"

"Sh-h-h!" Lena looked around, apparently to make sure there was no one else within earshot, and then said, "Amalia, you must not be hard on your mama. She was never a light woman. She did what she did because she felt she had to. Now, do you want me to tell you about it?"

"No! I want *her* to tell me about it!" After a moment she added, "But you can do one thing for me. When we get to

Belleville, please don't come to the house right away. I want to talk to her alone."

"All right, child." Her voice sounded heavy. "I'll stay on the dock for an hour, and then drive up with your trunk in the hackney. But, girl, girl! Don't be hard on your mama."

"Don't interfere! This is between her and me."

Amalia turned, walked a few feet, and opened the door of the long deckhouse cabin.

Darkness had long since fallen by the time the steamer tied up at the Belleville wharf. Amalia walked the length of the wharf and then up the wide, unpaved main street, past the bank and Courtney's General Store and the post office and the shoe shop. The business establishments were darkened for the night, but there were lighted windows above the general store, where the owners lived. Apparently some clerk was working late at the sawmill, because light shone from an upper window of the tall structure on its hill. Beyond the shoe shop she turned onto a side street lined with small houses, each spaced a comfortable distance from its neighbors. A dog barked at her, but otherwise the street seemed asleep, with no lights showing.

Except in the house where she had grown up. There light shone from the parlor windows and through the front door's fanlight. Her mother was waiting behind that door, ready to welcome her daughter, and to inspect the trousseau purchases made in New Orleans, and to talk of her own preparations for the wedding. With pain and bitterness like a brassy taste in her mouth, Amalia went up the walk.

Juana must have been listening for her steps, because she opened the door a second after Amalia reached the small porch. "Oh, darling, darling!" She threw her arms around the girl, aware as she did so of how lissome and tall her daughter was, at least four inches taller than herself. Then she said, stepping back, "But where is Lena? Where is your luggage? Didn't the hackney coach . . . ?"

"Lena's down at the wharf with the luggage. She'll be along later."

"But why . . . ? Oh, never mind. Tell me inside. I can't wait to look at you."

In the short entrance hallway Juana looked up into her daughter's face and then halted. "Oh, darling! Oh, my baby. What is it?"

Amalia said thickly, "Angus threw me over."

Juana's face went white. "Threw you . . . Oh, Amalia, he couldn't have. There must be . . . Come in here, darling. Tell me what the trouble is."

They went into the warmly lighted little parlor. "Sit here beside me on the sofa, Amalia. That's right. Now, tell me, darling. You two had a quarrel. Is that it? Well, it can be fixed. He loves you, Amalia. I know he does. And so just because you both lost your tempers over something—"

"Mother, tell me about Sara Davidson."

Silence. Detached in her young fury and pain, Amalia watched her mother seem to age ten years before her eyes. At last Juana said, "Oh, my God. Oh, my little girl. Who told you?"

"Angus. He got an anonymous letter, and he went to see Sara Davidson, and she told him everything. And then he said he couldn't marry me." In her agony she lashed out cruelly. "And I understand that. How many people could you expect to say that Angus MacFarlane should be expected to marry a harlot's daughter?"

Juana would have preferred to have a literal knife thrust into her heart. Here it was, the moment she had feared for many years. It was also the moment which, in her love, her hope, her blind optimism, she had persuaded herself would never come.

How could it be that she, who adored her child, had ruined that child's life? It was because of sin, of course. But which sins? The ones committed in that luxurious house on Oak Street? Surely not. She'd had no alternative, or at least thought she did not. Then it must be the sins of those long-ago mornings in young Enrique Villega's bed.

And yet even now, in all her suffering, she could not regret or truly repent those mornings, because they had brought her Amalia.

She managed to move her numb lips. "Amalia, when I went to Sara Davidson's I did not know what else to do. I was young, and ignorant, and without money. I was in a strange country, and alone except for you, a tiny baby—"

"Surely you could have done something else! You could have been somebody's housemaid. If nothing else, you could have gone to the workhouse."

Looking into that bitter, suffering young face, Juana saw

that she must speak in detail of events she had hoped to keep forever hidden from her daughter. "Listen to me, Amalia." Each word was an effort. "When I was several years younger than you are now, I went to work in a castle across the valley from Cádiz . . ."

She went on, telling of her long-ago love for Enrique, the only love she had ever had. She spoke of how, already pregnant, she had married Manuel Moreno. She told of his death at sea, and then of those weeks—pleasant at first, later nightmarish—under Lawrence Mountjoy's roof. Finally she told of her flight to Sara Davidson, the one person she had heard of who might be able to protect her against that clever and powerful madman.

"I might have been able to find some other solution—although even today I don't know what—if I'd been older, or less ignorant, or had even a little money. But I was so terrified, Amalia, more for what he might do to you than to me if he could get at us."

For a moment Amalia just sat there, her mouth trembling. Then she cried, "Oh, Mama, Mama!" and collapsed with her head in her mother's lap. How could she have said such vicious things to the gentle creature who was the source of her own life? "Forgive me, forgive me. I didn't know. . ."

"Of course not. How could you have known?" Juana stroked her daughter's hair. "And we need not talk of it any longer. Instead we must discuss what is to be done. Do you think that if you go back to New Orleans on the early steamer tomorrow you might catch him before he sets sail for . . . what is the name of that place, Sag Harbor? You could tell him what I have just told—"

"No, Mama." Amalia straightened up. "Even if I thought it would make him change his mind, and I don't think it would, I couldn't bring myself to run back to him and plead with him."

Juana's face twisted. "Then what are you going to do?"

"Do?" Amalia's voice was calm now. "Why, I shall go on living here with you and Lena."

Juana looked into her daughter's face. It was just as beautiful as it had been before she left for New Orleans. And yet it had changed. The blithe, high-spirited Amalia was forever gone. No, Juana thought, that wasn't exactly the case. Rather

Amalia's self-confidence had been hardened by pain into something steelier. Pride. Looking out at her from her daughter's eyes Juana saw the pride of Constancia and the pride of the Villegas.

# 19

During the next few days Juana and Amalia and Lena packed the items bought in New Orleans and sent them back to the shopkeepers, accompanied by letters requesting whatever payment the merchants thought was "fair." It was painful to Amalia to handle the ivory-colored silk intended for her wedding dress, and the alpaca which was to have been made into a warm dress for the Northeastern winters, and the sheer muslin which was to have become nightgowns. But Amalia and her mother could not afford the emotional luxury of packing the material away in a trunk, to lie there until it became yellowed. Over the next few weeks merchants sent them sums of money, most of them small, because a length of yard goods diminished sharply in value once it was scissored from the bolt. Still, salvaging a little money was better than losing it all.

Spring gave way to summer, the breathlessly hot summer of southern Louisiana, with a ghostly mist hovering above the black river after dark, and the woods loud with insect voices. Amalia received a letter from Esther MacFarlane, a plaintive letter that said in part, "I've been expecting to hear from you. I know you forbade me to ask you what happened between you and Angus, but, Amalia, we have been friends since we were six! If you will confide in me, there may be some way in which I can help."

Amalia waited ten days and then wrote a brief, cool letter saying that she still preferred not to discuss her broken engagement, and that there was no possible way in which Esther could help. She knew the letter would offend, and that she would not hear from Esther for a long time, if then. But perhaps that would be best. Surely if Esther ever learned where Amalia had spent the first three years of her life, she too would conclude, however painfully, that their association should end.

For a while Amalia had recurring dreams in which Angus came to her, smiling, and said that it had all been a mistake, that there was no such person as Sara Davidson. The joy with which she awoke from such dreams made her sudden awareness of reality all the more painful. Gradually, though, such dreams became less frequent.

For a while Amalia managed to keep busy helping her mother and Lena keep the house clean, and to preserve the produce of their little garden—beans and sweet peppers and okra. In September, though, the convent's mother superior sent her a message. Two novices had left the convent, and so now there were vacancies on the teaching staff. Would Amalia care to take charge of the youngest ones, the six-year-olds?

Amalia loved working with the children. Sometimes, as she led the little girls in reciting simple poems, or read aloud to them from *Children's Lives of the Saints*, she would realize that for a while she had forgotten herself and was almost happy.

It was Juana who seemed unable to recover from the blow she had received that night Amalia came back from New Orleans. As fall merged into the brief but chill Louisiana winter, Juana grew thinner and paler. She never spoke Angus' name, but it became obvious in other ways that his jilting of her daughter was seldom far from her mind. For instance, on Sunday afternoons, when the eligible young men of the village—all four of them—were more apt than not to call at the Moreno cottage, Juana was eagerly cordial to each of them, as if hoping they would overlook her daughter's polite but definitely cool manner.

One late Sunday afternoon in December, when the door had closed behind Jim Courtney, the son of the owners of the general store, Juana said diffidently, "Don't you think that Jim is rather nice?"

"Oh, yes. He talks through his nose, and he holds his fork handle in his fist, and it's hard for him to get across our parlor without stumbling over something, if only his own feet. But he's nice enough."

After several seconds Juana answered, "He's the best of the lot. And he'll have the general store someday."

"Mama, Mama! I can't understand you. How could you possibly suggest that I marry Jim Courtney?"

Juana said, with a fervor that Amalia did not understand until later, "It is just that I want to see you settled."

"Please, Mama! Where is the law that says a woman has to be married? I would much rather go on living here with you and Lena the rest of my life than marry any of the young men in this town."

Juana was silent for perhaps half a minute. Then she said, "I think I will go to my room now, instead of having supper. No, no! I am all right. I just feel a little tired, and not in the least hungry. But will you come to my room after supper? There is something I want to show you."

Two hours later Amalia came into Juana's lamplit room and sat down beside the bed. With a shock she suddenly realized that her pretty mama was no longer pretty. The thick braids lying on the pillow were far more gray than black. She was pale, and her round face had a pinched look, with lines bracketing her mouth that had not been there only months before.

She said, "Here is what I wanted to show you."

She opened the drawer of her bedside table, took an object out, and placed it in Amalia's hand. Amalia looked down at the gold-framed miniature of a very young man, gray-eyed and wearing a powdered wig. His face was not only handsome but also extraordinarily pleasant, self-assured without being haughty, and amiable without being weak.

"That is your father, Enrique Villega."

Amalia stared down at the miniature, trying to feel some connection between herself and this Spanish aristocrat whose name she had never even heard until that dreadful night the previous spring. After a moment she said, "So young! He looks like a mere boy."

"That is what he was, although neither of us thought of him as such. When that miniature was painted, he was about the age you are now. Would you like to keep it in your room?"

"Oh, no!" Amalia held it out. "You keep it."

"All right." Juana replaced the miniature, closed the

drawer of the bedside table. "I just wanted you to know where it was."

Three afternoons later Amalia came home to find Dr. Sean Miller, a physician with patients in Belleville and two towns farther upriver, talking to Lena in the little entrance hall. The look on their faces made Amalia's heart give a frightened leap. "What is it? Is my mother. . . ?"

Dr. Miller said, "Come into the parlor, so we can talk."

Lena turned and moved swiftly toward the kitchen. Amalia went into the parlor with the doctor. When they were seated, he on the sofa, she in an armchair facing him, he said, "My dear, I am sorry to tell you this, but your mother is gravely ill." He paused and then said, "I fear a malignancy."

Stunned, she looked into his face, a thin, fortyish face with tired gray eyes. After a moment she found she could move her lips. "What sort of malignancy?"

"Of the brain, I think. She has told me her symptoms. Dizziness, blurred vision, and several fainting spells, although none so prolonged as she had this afternoon. She had forbidden her maid to talk to anyone about it, lest you learn of it. But this afternoon her maid could not bring her back to consciousness, and so she fetched me."

"What . . . what is. . . ?"

"I cannot say what will happen. Perhaps my diagnosis is wrong. Let us hope so. A woman still young, a woman who has been healthy until now. . . ."

He broke off, and then said, "Tell me, has your mother received any kind of severe shock not too long ago, say, sometime within the past year?"

Unable to speak, Amalia nodded.

He did not ask what kind of shock. Instead he said, "I thought so. So often I have seen formerly healthy people who, a few months after some severe emotional blow, develop a tumor. My colleagues laugh at me, especially the older ones. How could a person's emotions affect his body like that? But I think that someday medicine will find that there can be some sort of connection."

Amalia sat motionless. If Angus had not rejected her, probably her mother would still be well.

That moonlit night on the road outside New Orleans, she had pounded her fists against Angus MacFarlane's chest and cried out that she hated him. But it was only now that she knew the true taste of hatred, an actual bitterness in the mouth.

She said, past the hard tightness in her throat, "Can I go to her now?"

"I gave her a sleeping potion. Best to wait until she wakes up and asks for you."

# 20

On a spring morning almost a year to the day after Amalia and Lena's return from New Orleans, they stood beside an open grave in the Belleville churchyard. A surprising number of others had gathered there, most of the adult villagers, and several nuns from the convent. Despite her quiet and withdrawn life, gentle Juana had somehow won the affection of her fellow townspeople.

At the end, Juana had turned back to the faith of her childhood. She had sent for the local priest, and he had heard her confession and given final absolution. He stood at one end of the grave now, reading the burial service. Even as she tried to draw comfort from the words that had solaced millions upon millions, Amalia was aware of the cruel beauty of the day. This morning the atmosphere lacked its usual humidity. The broad river beyond the foot of the village's sloping main street sparkled. Not just birdsong from the churchyard trees but the chime of a ship's bell, distinct on the clear air, mingled with the priest's words.

He gave the final blessing. Someone handed Amalia a small shovel. Feeling a grief and bitterness too deep for tears, she let a shovelful of earth fall on the casket. Then, with Lena, she walked the few hundred yards from the church to the little house where she had lived all but the first three years of her life.

She returned to her duties at the convent the next day. Now more than ever it seemed to her important that she fill up her life with work. Besides, the stipend she received from the convent, although small, was a welcome addition to the income she had inherited from her mother.

She tried hard to be as content as possible. After all, she told herself, she was far, far more fortunate than her mother had been. It was Lena who, only weeks after Juana's death, began to nag Amalia about the future.

One breathless August night as they sat in the parlor, hands busy with needles and darning eggs, mending baskets on the floor near their feet, Lena asked, "You going to keep turning up your nose at those boys?"

She meant Amalia's local admirers. One of the four, a clerk at the mill, had given up and married another Belleville maiden. The others still came calling now and then, although not so often as in the days when Juana's nervous friendliness tempered her daughter's aloof courtesy.

"Yes," Amalia said.

Lena was silent for a moment. Then she placed a darned stocking in the basket, straightened up, and said, "We could sell this house and go somewhere else to live."

Amalia noted the "we." Ever since her mother's death, Amalia had felt that Lena was trying to take Juana's place. Far from resenting that, Amalia felt comforted by the increased closeness between them.

She said, "Go where? Some town farther upriver? It would be much like this one. And I hope you are not suggesting that we go to New Orleans!"

"No, of course not. But we could go *some*place. Raleigh, say, or Charleston. I've heard tell those are real big places, big enough you might find men you wouldn't turn your nose up at."

"Lena, will you stop worrying about me? After all, you've managed to get along without men."

"Had to. Men don't like a gal with one whole side of her face puckered up. Leastways, not men I'd look at."

Not knowing what to say, Amalia remained silent. After a few moments Lena went on. "Those last weeks with your mama, when she and I were closer than ever before, I told her how I got this scar. I figure I might as well tell you."

"Oh, Lena. You don't have—"

"It's all right. For a long time I didn't want to talk about it, but now it don't seem to matter so much. Anyway, as you know, my mama and papa were free coloreds in Trinidad, and that made me free too. They both died when I was fourteen—some kind of fever that killed a lot of people that year—and I went to work in a white lady's kitchen. I slept in a shed out back. Well, when I'd been there almost a year, the lady's husband came fooling around. I figured there was nothing I could do about it. Everybody knows that's what happens to colored gals, and nobody thinks anything about it. 'Cept that lady. She sure did. She came to the shed one night when I was asleep and laid the whole side of my face open with her husband's razor. I can still hear myself screaming and her saying, through the screams, 'Now see if anyone's husband wants to go to bed with you.' "

"Oh, Lena!"

Lena shrugged. "There was nothing I could do about it. If I'd gone to the law, they'd have believed her, not me, specially since everybody knows it's the coloreds who use razors and knives, not white ladies. When it got daylight, I went to stay with some free coloreds who'd known my mama and papa. I didn't want to stay in Trinidad no more, so when my face was almost healed, they snuck me aboard a ship sailing for New Orleans. I was found when the ship was only a few hours out, and the captain was awfully mad, but finally he said he wouldn't ship me back to Trinidad if I'd work for a year for some kinfolk of his in New Orleans. Between then and the time I . . . I met your mama, I worked in a lot of New Orleans kitchens."

She paused and then added, "One thing that lady in Trinidad was sure right about. Since I was fifteen I ain't been troubled with men, black or white, hanging around bothering me."

After a while Amalia said, "Hasn't it made you feel . . . ? I mean, I should have thought you'd have felt hatred for white people, or at least for white women."

Lena bent over, picked up a woolen stocking from her basket, and drew it over the darning egg until the yellow wood was revealed by the ragged toe. "No use in hating," she said finally. "Hate don't put no food in your stomach. But to get back to you, child. I think we ought to leave this town."

"Perhaps. Someday."

Lena laid her mending in her lap. "If you keep waiting for someday," she said, "you'll wake up some morning and realize there ain't no use in going someplace else, because nearly all your somedays are behind you."

Summer heat turned to brief autumn, with cool, almost dry air, and then to the chill damp of early winter. Esther

MacFarlane wrote again—a short, stiff letter—and after an interval Amalia sent an even briefer reply. Her heart ached at the thought of the puzzled hurt her friend must be feeling. But better that than the resumption of an intimacy that might lead Amalia, at some weak moment in the future, to divulge the story Juana had tried so hard to conceal.

In late December the convent's reverend mother studied the stoic face of the once high-spirited girl who had created the Miracle of the Birds. Christmas in that too-quiet house would be an ordeal for both Amalia and that brown-skinned woman with the scarred face. Accordingly she asked Amalia into her office one afternoon. The reverend mother's former canary had long since expired, but Dicky the Second poured melody from his cage into the sunlit room.

"Amalia, would you and your serving woman . . . what is her name?"

"Lena White. But she has always been more of a friend than a servant."

"I see. Anyway, would you two care to spend Christmas Eve and Christmas Day at the convent?"

"Oh, thank you, Reverend Mother," Amalia said fervently. "Thank you."

That was the one break in Amalia's routine. With one day much like the one before it—six hours teaching at the convent, then home to a few household chores and to supper with Lena—she found that time slipped rapidly by. There was not even the novelty of a letter from Spain. She had written to her grandfather Miguel Ramirez, telling him of Juana's death. She had expected that, as when Juana was alive, he would take the letter to his priest, and ask that it be read to him, and that the priest would write a reply. But no reply came. Perhaps, she thought, her letter had gone astray.

One day she realized that it was April again, and that almost two years had passed since the moonlit night when Angus had told her he could not marry a whore's daughter.

It was on a Sunday morning in May that Howard Lipson arrived.

When the knocker sounded, it was Amalia who opened the front door. She found a plump, well-dressed, rather embarrassed-looking man in his late twenties standing on the front porch. "Miss Amalia Moreno?"

"Yes."

"My name is Howard Lipson. I am a friend of Mr. Thomas Fulmer. I also handle his legal affairs."

Tom Fulmer. A bench at the foot of that New Orleans garden that nightmarish evening. Tom's arm around her while she gasped out her agony and humiliation. His voice saying, "Promise me one thing, Amalia. Do as Angus suggested about telling no one what has happened."

She opened the door wide. "Please come in, Mr. Lipson."

"Thank you, but not just now. Tom asked me to give you this letter, and then leave you alone until you had had a chance to read it and think it over."

He reached inside his coat and brought out an envelope. Wondering, she took it. He said, "I'll spend an hour down by the riverfront and then come back here. If you still want more time to think—and you probably will—I will go to the local inn tonight and then come back tomorrow."

From his manner it was obvious that he knew what was in the letter. "I see," she answered, although of course she did not. "Thank you, Mr. Lipson."

He lifted his tall hat briefly from his head and then turned and went down the walk. Amalia closed the door. Poking her head out of the kitchen, Lena asked, "Who was that?"

"Someone with a letter from Tom Fulmer."

"That friend of . . ." She broke off. Angus' name was not mentioned in that house. "You mean that Yankee shipbuilder you told me about?" Amalia nodded. "Well, don't you want to see what he has to say?"

"Lena, if you don't mind. . . ."

"All right. Tell me about it when you're ready."

Amalia went into the parlor and sat down in a chair beside the unlighted fireplace. Heart beating fast, she opened the envelope. Tom had written:

Dear Amalia,

I hope you will forgive me if this letter sounds awkward and abrupt. I have so much to say that I don't know how to do it except to plunge straight in.

Angus MacFarlane is no longer in Sag Harbor. For months he has been in Boston, making brief trips as captain of ships in the Atlantic-coast trade. A recent letter of his tells me that he is engaged to the daughter of the shipping firm's president.

For a moment the neatly written lines seemed to blur. What was she like, this girl who would soon be sleeping in Angus' bed and bearing his children? She forced herself to go on reading.

You see, about eighteen months ago MacFarlane ships began to suffer bad luck. One foundered in a Caribbean storm. Another ran aground on a reef near Australia and had to jettison valuable cargo in order to float free. Finally the MacFarlanes decided to sell their remaining ships, the *Goodspeed* and the *White Falcon*. That was when Angus joined the Boston firm.

Matthew MacFarlane, Angus' father, is still here. So is Ruth MacFarlane, that little girl you will remember, although she is not so little now.

As for the MacFarlane ships, I bought them. Not, I might add, without opposition from my brother, Richard, who felt the money should be spent to expand the boatworks we jointly own. But as I think I once told you, I have always wanted to sail ships, not just build them. So now I am about to sail as the *Falcon*'s captain.

That brings me to the point of this letter. I know that the last thing you would want to do if Angus was still here would be to come to Sag Harbor. But he is two hundred miles away now, and about to marry another woman.

And so, Amalia, will you marry me, and come to live with me on Long Island?

Always I have been inept where women were concerned, and this time I have run true to form. As soon as Angus went to Boston, I should have asked you to marry me. But I thought he might come back here. I also feared that you might not want to marry me, or anyone, not as long as there was a chance you might have Angus, after all. But he is pledged to someone else now, and so I am writing to you.

The awkward part, the stupid part, is that I am sailing on the *Falcon* next week on a long voyage that will take me first to the Caribbean, then to Cape Horn, then to Australia, then back to Sag Harbor. I absolutely must sail, or find myself in breach of contract with a number of shippers. And of course there is no time for us to be married, either here in Sag Harbor or in Belleville, before I sail. I hope to be back in seven or eight months, but it may take as long as a year.

I don't want to wait a year before trying to bind you to me. Any day now you may marry someone else. In fact—tormenting thought!—perhaps you already have married. After all, it has been two years since we saw each other. For all I know, you will be reading this seated across the breakfast table from your husband.

But if you are still free, and willing to marry me, I want to marry you right now, not a year from now.

This brings me to Howard Lipson, the bearer of this letter. He is a lawyer. He tells me that proxy marriages are legal in Louisiana, and that of course the state of New York recognizes the laws of Louisiana. And so will you marry me by proxy, with Howard as my stand-in?

Then, at your leisure, you can come to Sag Harbor and wait for my return. I realize you probably will want to bring your mother with you, and perhaps that maid—I forget her name—who came down to New Orleans from Belleville two years ago. I don't know how to say this gracefully, but your mother should not be afraid to come here. I have told no one about the reason for the rift between you and Angus, and I am sure he has not either.

Heart twisting, Amalia looked up from the letter. How she wished she could go into her mother's room and say to her, "Mama, here's an offer from a nice man, a very nice man. I think that perhaps I should take it."

Her gaze went back to the page. The next paragraph read:

Whatever your decision, you or Howard can let me know by letter. As you may or may not be aware, Sag Harbor ships keep crossing and recrossing paths in all the oceans of the world. Letters from home are passed from one ship to another. At the very least, I would be sure to get letters addressed to me in Sydney, Australia, because several Sag Harbor ships will be sailing directly there within the next few weeks, and will arrive in Australia well before my indirect route brings me there.

If you accept this offer, Howard will explain to you what provisions I have made so that you, as my wife, will live comfortably in Sag Harbor until my return. He will also arrange for someone in Belleville to handle the sale of your mother's property there.

As I once said to you, I know I am no figure of romance. But if you will marry me, I will love you and cherish you my whole life long.

Yours devotedly,
Thomas Fulmer

The letter still in her hand, she looked around the little parlor, the too-neat, too-quiet parlor of two women who lived alone, and who might still be living alone here twenty years from now. She thought of Tom Fulmer's thin face and gray eyes and pleasant smile touched with wryness. She thought of the bitter night when she had felt that his arm, placed around her shoulders, was all that kept her from disintegrating into pieces.

She would not need until tomorrow morning to make her decision. When Howard Lipson returned in a few minutes, she would give him her answer, and it would be yes.

She got up and went toward the kitchen to tell Lena.

# 21

In her cabin aboard the *Silas Bascombe*, Amalia was cramming the last of her belongings into her portmanteau. Fear and self-scorn had tied her stomach into a knot. I've been a fool, she was thinking, an utter fool.

How could she have been stupid enough to come anywhere near Angus MacFarlane's town, the town where this ship would dock within a few minutes?

Quite suddenly she had become convinced that when she emerged onto the deck she would look down to the wharf and see Angus' upturned face. If she did, what would she feel? Bitterness, of course. But would she, even though she was Mrs. Thomas Fulmer now, feel that stirring of the blood, that sensual hunger, which still invaded her body whenever Angus appeared in her dreams?

She had managed to turn her waking thoughts away from him these past weeks. When she stood beside her bridegroom-by-proxy, Howard Lipson, in the office of a New Orleans justice of the peace, she had thought only of Tom—gentle, humorous Tom—and of what he probably would feel when he finally received her letter telling him that she had become his wife.

After that ceremony in New Orleans, Amalia and Howard and Lena, who had acted as a witness, returned to Belleville. Within a few days Howard had arranged to have the local bank handle the sale of the little clapboard house in which Amalia had lived since her third year. And less than a week after that he ushered Amalia and Lena aboard the *Silas Bascombe*, a sleek three-masted schooner bound for the Caribbean and Atlantic coastal ports.

All through the six-week voyage Amalia had managed to keep her waking mind busied with other matters than Angus MacFarlane. As the ship carried her closer to his native town, though, he appeared in her dreams frequently, more frequently than at any time since those first anguished weeks after he had jilted her. During the several nights when the schooner lay at anchor in Kingston, Jamaica, her dreams were especially vivid. A dream in which he seemed to be with her in her cabin, making love to her in the bunk that rocked gently in the tropical darkness, was so real that she awoke. For a long while she lay there, her body quivering inwardly with a mixture of humiliation and remembered pleasure.

But even the most vivid dreams can be blotted out by the waking mind. As the graceful ship sailed north, paralleling the summer-green Atlantic coast, Amalia filled her days by reading the books she had brought with her, and by hemming, not very expertly, the dish towels and sheets cut from the bolt of linen she and Lena had selected in New Orleans just before the schooner sailed. Sometimes she spent an hour or more hanging over the ship's rail, half-hypnotized by the seethe of foamy green water past the hull, while she planned her new life. She would be a good wife. She would hold in check that willfulness, that occasional flamboyance, which Juana often had attributed to "your Grandmother Constancia coming out in you." She would do everything to please her Yankee neighbors, no matter how pious and sober, and to make Tom proud of her. And in time, please God, she would come to love him as he deserved to be loved.

She maintained her calm hopefulness as the ship sailed along Long Island's Atlantic shore and past the Montauk Light and turned into Long Island Sound. But about an hour ago, as she stood with Lena and Howard at the rail, he had said, "See that small lighthouse up ahead? It's at the end of Cedar Point. Once we round the point, we'll be able to see Sag Harbor."

It was then that panic had overwhelmed her. Mumbling an excuse, she had gone to her cabin, closed the door, and sat down on the bunk, hands clenched in her lap. In a few minutes she would see Angus' town. She would be looking down on that dock he had told her about, Long Wharf, and then moving up the village's wide main street, past the house his father had built. And suddenly he seemed close, so close that she felt he must be, not in Boston, but standing right there on Long Wharf, along with others curious to see what cargo and passengers the newly arrived ship had brought. Or perhaps he already knew she was aboard. After all, Howard Lipson had written about the proxy marriage to Tom's older brother, Richard, and he must have spread the news widely.

And if Angus was there, what would become of all her resolutions about starting a fine new life?

She went on sitting there even after she heard footsteps running along the deck, and the first mate bawling orders, and felt the gentle impact of the ship's bumper-protected side swinging against the wharf. She got up then and began to stuff articles from the shelf above the washbasin into her portmanteau. She had just packed her brush and comb when Lena tapped on the door and called, "Child, you going to stay in there all day?"

She had to face up to it. Aware of her thudding heart, she picked up the portmanteau, accompanied Lena down the passageway, and then stood at the rail in the late-morning sunlight, flanked by the gaunt brown-skinned woman and plump Howard Lipson. A sea of faces down there. ("Whenever a ship is sighted rounding Cedar Point," Angus had told her, "half the town flocks down to Long Wharf.") But after a moment she realized, with an inward shudder of relief, that Angus was not among them. Of course he was not. Why had she felt that fear that he was in Sag Harbor instead of in Boston with that girl he was to marry—if, indeed, they were not already married?

But there was one face down there which, after a moment, she recognized. Ruth MacFarlane's, framed in a bright blue bonnet which matched her summer frock. The first thing Amalia noticed about her was that at fourteen she was even prettier than she had been at twelve. The second thing she noticed was Ruth's strange expression as her blue eyes met Amalia's dark ones. It was an odd blend of excitement, pleasure, and something else, something that Amalia could not identify, although it looked rather like anxiety. A tall man of about sixty, with graying muttonchop whiskers, stood beside the girl. Like Ruth's, his gaze was fixed on Amalia. Pulses quickening, she wondered if he was Ruth's father—and Angus'.

Then she became aware that a man with gray-flecked dark hair showing beneath his tall hat had stepped from the gangplank onto the deck and was walking toward her. He halted and said, "Hello, Howard." Then: "You must be my brother's wife."

"And you must be Richard."

He bore a certain resemblance to Tom, the same thinness, the same gray eyes. But he was older—about ten years older, Howard had said—and he had a look which Amalia immediately thought of as "more Yankee." Even when he smiled, as he was doing now, he had an aloof appearance.

In the letter which had contained his proposal of marriage, Tom had said that his brother had opposed his purchase of the two remaining MacFarlane ships. How was it, she wondered, that Tom, soft-spoken and humorous and a decade younger than his stern-faced brother, had managed to prevail?

She said, "And this is my companion, Lena White."

Perhaps if she had referred to Lena as her maid, Richard would have been less disconcerted, but as it was, he nodded briefly in response to Lena's dignified inclination of her head, and then looked away. Apparently he held it unsuitable for a white woman to have a brown-skinned companion, especially one with what was obviously a knife scar puckering one side of her face. Well, Amalia thought, she was willing to adjust to Sag Harbor in every other way. But as far as her relationship with Lena was concerned, Sag Harbor would have to do the adjusting.

Richard Fulmer asked, "Where will you stay until you are settled? Mrs. Arnshaw's boardinghouse?"

"I think so." She turned to Howard. "Isn't that the place where you live?"

Howard nodded. With the faintly old-maidish air Amalia had noticed in him frequently these past weeks, he added, "Mrs. Arnshaw offers the only public accommodations in Sag Harbor where you can be sure of meeting respectable people."

Richard shrugged. "What can you expect? This is a seaport. Nearly all of us respectable people make money out of shipping or shipbuilding. We have to put up with the sort of waterfront life every seaport offers."

He turned back to Amalia. "Since you are my sister-in-law, I do wish I could offer you the hospitality of my house on Union Street. But that would not do. Except for a serving couple who come in by the day, I live alone, now that my brother has decided he must sail the seven seas."

His sardonic tone made Amalia wonder just how strenuously the brothers had argued over Tom's acquisition of the MacFarlane ships. "Please don't apologize. I'm sure I will be very comfortable at the boardinghouse. Besides, Mr. Lipson has promised me that as soon as possible we will look for a suitable house for me to buy."

"I'm sure you will be able to find something." He raised his hat. "Well, good-bye for the moment, Amalia."

He had hesitated before the last word, as if finding it uncomfortable to call a woman he had just met by her first name.

"Good-bye, Richard."

Tom's brother turned away. Howard Lipson said to Amalia, "If you'll excuse me, I'll make sure that our trunks will be delivered to the boardinghouse. Then we will go ashore."

Less than two minutes later Amalia and Lena and Howard moved down the steep gangplank. When she stepped onto the wharf, Amalia halted and said, "Ruth? It is you, isn't it?" How tall the girl had grown. Her face was almost on a level with Amalia's. "How nice of you to meet our ship."

"I've been waiting and waiting, thinking every morning that this was the day you'd get here."

Why, Amalia wondered, had Ruth awaited her arrival so impatiently? Certainly during those days in New Orleans Amalia had not been aware that Ruth was developing any fondness for her. But perhaps, in spite of her childish jealousy, she had.

Ruth rushed on, "Are you really married to Tom Fulmer? I mean, really married? After all, you were down in Louisiana, and he's off on the *Falcon* somewhere—"

"Ruth! I see that I must introduce myself, as well as apologize for my daughter's manners. I am Matthew MacFarlane, Ruth's father."

And Angus' father. That stern Presbyterian father who, his son had felt, must never be afflicted with grandchildren who were also Juana Moreno's grandchildren. She had thought of Richard as "Yankee-looking," but Matthew MacFarlane was even more so. In fact, the rough gray hair showing beneath his tall hat, the long seamed face, the hazel eyes set deep beneath heavy brows, made her think of one of the harsher-tongued Old Testament prophets. Jeremiah, perhaps.

He added, "Welcome to Sag Harbor, Mrs. Fulmer."

"Thank you, Mr. MacFarlane."

"Welcome home, Howard. What sort of voyage did you—?"

"Amalia!" Ruth's hand in its lacy blue mitten fastened on Amalia's arm. "You didn't answer me. *Are* you married to Tom Fulmer? Just as married as if you'd stood up with him in church?"

"I have a paper that says so."

"Ruth!" her father said. "Mrs. Fulmer, I hope you can forgive Ruth, and forgive me for having such an undisciplined daughter. A child of a man's later years is apt to be overindulged, especially if her mother is no longer . . ." He broke off, and then went on sternly, looking down at his daughter. "Of course Mr. and Mrs. Fulmer are married. I explained all that to you. A proxy marriage is just as legal as any other sort of marriage."

Apparently Ruth was at last convinced, because then tension left her pretty face. But why, Amalia wondered, had the child worried about the genuineness of a proxy marriage? Surely she could no longer fear that Amalia would marry her brother. He was in Boston now, engaged to another girl. . . .

Or was he?

Again that surge of panic, oddly mingled now with hope. Unable to endure it, Amalia said to Matthew MacFarlane, "I understand that your son is in Boston."

"Yes. Or rather, he is now captain of a coastal trader that sails out of that port. I suppose you also know that he is engaged to marry a Miss Barbara Weyant, his employer's daughter."

Embarrassment in his voice. Amalia could understand it. Almost certainly he knew that his son and Amalia had once planned to marry.

Amalia managed to keep her own voice quite steady. "Yes, of course I knew Angus was engaged." Then, belatedly: "Mr. MacFarlane, this is my companion, Miss Lena White."

More courteous than Richard Fulmer had been, Matthew MacFarlane tipped his hat. Then he said, "If you will excuse us now, we will say good-bye. But I would like to call on you very soon, Mrs. Fulmer. This evening, in fact, if you feel you will not be too tired from your journey."

Wondering why he should be in such haste to see her again, she said, "I won't be too tired. Will around eight be convenient?"

"Perfectly." He tipped his hat again, bade them good-bye, and walked away with his tall young daughter beside him.

Howard Lipson said worriedly, "I can't very well leave you two alone here." He raised his voice. "Boy! You with the red hair."

A barefoot urchin of about ten, fiery hair bright in the sunlight, ran toward them across the wooden planks. "Yes, sir, Mr. Lipson?"

"Go tell the livery stable I want my surrey brought here."

He flipped a coin through the air. The boy caught it. "Yes, *sir*!"

A few minutes later Howard handed Amalia into the front seat and Lena into the backseat of a four-wheeled vehicle drawn by a bay horse. Amalia soon realized why the dock was called Long Wharf. It was long indeed, its outer reaches lined on both sides by berthed ships—merchantmen and small fishing boats and broad-beamed vessels Howard identified as whalers. Farther along on the wharf they passed roofed sheds where blacksmiths and sailwrights plied their trades. Then the surrey's wheels rattled off the wharf and onto the hard-packed earth of Main Street.

With wonder Amalia looked at the sidewalk crowd moving past open-fronted grog shops, past stores displaying oilskins and duffel bags, and past a brick structure with a faded sign, "Harbor Hotel," on its veranda roof. Most of the pedestrians, Howard told her, were sailors off those merchantmen and whalers tied up at the wharf. Many of them were staggering drunk, but that was about all they had in common. They appeared to be of almost every nationality and race. There were tall, bronze-skinned men with braided hair. (Sagaponack Indians, Howard told her, and probably harpooners off the whaleships. For some unknown reason, Sagaponacks made good harpooners.) A very black Fiji Islander with a bone through his nose. Three blond men reeling along, arms about each other's shoulders as they bawled out a song in some Scandinavian tongue. In the street in front of the hotel, cheered on by spectators lining the veranda, two struggling men rolled in the dirt, screaming curses in a French patois that Howard identified as "Canuck, French-Canadian." Most of the men, though, appeared to be Americans. Amalia heard them calling to each other in Yankee accents, and a soft drawl that reminded her of Hannah Moffat, her plump and unlucky South Carolina classmate at the nuns' school. She even heard a voice that brought her an unexpected pang of homesickness for the swamps and bayous of Louisiana.

There were no women on the sidewalks, at least at the moment, but Amalia did see a hard-faced blond leaning out a second floor window of the hotel. And she caught a glimpse of another woman, face indistinct under a plumed hat, at a table just inside the doorway of a grog shop.

Howard said, "No respectable woman ever passes through this lower part of Main Street except on her way to or from a ship, and even then she has to be escorted. The rule for ladies is, never go north of Tinker's Alley alone."

Moments later he said, "This part of the business district is quite different, of course."

She could see that it was. A dry-goods store. An apothecary. A milliner. A general store. A window above a shoemaker's shop bearing the legend "Howard Lipson, Attorney-at-law." Here respectable-looking women as well as men moved in and out of the shops.

A few yards farther on the street divided, with the left-hand branch sloping upward past small houses toward a white church steeple. Howard took the right-hand branch. Even though he said that this was still Main Street, its character again had changed. Here there were only houses, many of them fine indeed. One of them, a tall gray clapboard with a white-pillared porch and white shutters, its spacious grounds guarded by a tall wrought-iron fence, was almost as handsome as any house she had seen in New Orleans.

"Captain Hannibal Allerdyce's house," Howard said. "He built it ten years ago, after he got rich off whaling. A lot of whaler and merchant-ship owners are planning to build houses along this stretch of Main Street. People are beginning to call it Captains' Row."

She shrank from asking the question. But sooner or later she would have to know, and so she said, "The MacFarlanes live on Main Street, don't they? Which house is theirs?"

"It's just up ahead." A moment later he pointed with his buggy whip. "There."

The house standing on the west side of Main Street was

neither new nor a mansion. But it looked gracious and solid with its brown clapboard facade and white trim, its one-story wings flanking the central portion. The paneled front door was wide, and topped by an exquisitely leaded fanlight. Later Amalia was to learn that Sag Harbor craftsmen prided themselves on making beautiful front doors, each with a fanlight different from any other in town.

So that was the house where she might have lived, as Angus' bride, until they built or bought a house of their own. To distract herself from the thought of being Angus' wife in that house—dining with him and his little sister and his stern-faced father, studying with him the plans of the house they would build, lying in his arms at night—she turned to Howard and said, "I understand that Richard Fulmer didn't want Tom to buy the MacFarlane ships."

"No. He wanted to expand the Fulmer Boatworks instead."

"I don't understand. Richard is the elder brother. How is it that Tom won out?"

Howard chuckled. "Because Tom was the one with the money. Three years ago a rich aunt of the Fulmer brothers died. She'd never cottoned to Richard, and so she left all her money to Tom. Richard has been pretty riled about it, I guess, even though he's no worse off than before. A little better off, in fact. He not only still has his share of the boatworks, he gets a percentage of the shipping profits by acting as business agent here while Tom is at sea.

"Poor Richard," he went on. "He must feel that life is always short-changing him, one way or another. When he was twenty-four the girl he was engaged to left him standing at the altar. I mean literally standing there. He was still waiting at the church when word came that she and a former suitor had taken the stagecoach to New York." The slightly malicious smile of the born gossip hovered around his lips. "I guess Richard never got over the humiliation. Anyway, he never married anyone else."

A moment later he said, "I'm taking you the long way around to the boardinghouse. I thought you might want to see Otter Pond. That's it, up ahead."

She looked to her left. About twenty mallards, the males resplendent in iridescent green and blue, floated on a lake bordered by weeping willows. Amalia reflected that only

Yankees, with their love of understatement, would call a body of water that size a pond.

At the far end of the pond he turned left onto a narrow road. On its right side stood a thick wood of oaks and maples, now clothed in the dark green of full summer. "Gypsies camp in there every year in early June. People are always getting up committees to try to get rid of them. But every year they are here again, the women going from door to door to tell fortunes, and the men trading horses with farmers between here and Bridgehampton."

A few hundred feet farther on he turned the surrey left again, back toward the center of town. They moved between rows of small but attractive frame houses, most of them with shutters at the windows, and many with prim gossip benches flanking the front door. These, Howard explained, were the homes of Sag Harbor craftsmen and of men who sailed as mates or boatswains on Sag Harbor ships. Finally he drew rein in front of a tall gray house on a street which sloped down toward the business district.

A brunette of about fifty-five, plump body encased in dark blue alpaca, opened the door. "Why, Mr. Lipson! Welcome home." As she looked from him to Amalia and then to Lena, a startled expression came into her eyes, but she recovered quickly. "Come in, please."

In the broad front hall she said, "I'm Mrs. Arnshaw. And you must be Mrs. Thomas Fulmer."

Amalia smiled and nodded. "And this is my companion, Miss Lena White."

Mrs. Arnshaw's brown eyes still looked disconcerted. Obviously Howard's letter to her had asked merely that she reserve rooms for Mrs. Fulmer and "companion," with no mention of the companion's race.

"How do you do," she said. "I suppose you ladies would like to go to your rooms immediately. They are on the second floor." As if to emphasize the respectability of her establishment, despite all those drinking, wenching, brawling men only a half-mile away, she said, "The entire second floor is occupied by single ladies only, or those unaccompanied by their husbands."

As they moved toward the foot of the stairs, she waved her hand to the left, where open sliding doors revealed one long white-clothed table and several smaller ones. "That is our dining room. And over here, opposite, are two parlors, where boarders are permitted to entertain guests of the opposite sex."

On the second floor she opened a door. Howard Lipson placed Amalia's and Lena's portmanteaus inside the room, bade the three women a polite farewell, and walked away. Stepping over the threshold, Amalia saw that the room assigned to her was an airy one with new-looking floral wallpaper, a large oval rag rug on the random-width pine floorboards, and a bed, chest of drawers, and dressing table of black walnut. An open doorway led to an adjoining room. Although it looked smaller, it also appeared to be freshly papered and comfortably furnished.

"The other room," the landlady said, "is of course for your . . . for Mrs.—"

"Miss," Lena said firmly. "Miss Lena White."

"Yes, of course. Now, when your trunks come from the ship, you can store them in the basement. Let's see, what else? Oh, yes. Dinner is at one and supper at six-thirty. Well, I guess that is all, except that I wanted to tell you that I think it is so romantic, Mrs. Fulmer, getting married by proxy like that."

"Yes," Amalia said, although in fact she could not see how one could consider it romantic to be married to a man one had never even kissed. Strange, yes, and a little frightening, but not romantic.

"We're losing our bachelors fast," Mrs. Arnshaw went on, "what with Tom Fulmer married, and Angus MacFarlane engaged to that Boston girl."

Something in the woman's eyes made Amalia sure that Mrs. Arnshaw knew that this was Angus' second engagement. Well, probably the whole town knew about that earlier broken one. That did not matter as long as they did not know why it had been broken.

"Well, I'll leave you now."

When the door had closed behind Mrs. Arnshaw, Amalia said, "Lena, I hope you don't mind."

"Mind?"

"The way some people up here seem to react to you."

For a moment that other Lena looked out of the brown-skinned woman's eyes, that embittered Lena who perhaps had kept a mental record of every injury, every injustice or slight, dealt to her by the white world. Then she smiled. "Honey, before I came here I told myself I wasn't going to mind. You see, us free coloreds have a saying. Down south white folks don't care how close you get as long as you don't get too high. Up north they don't care how high you get as long as you don't get too close."

She paused, and then added, "I hope there won't be any ruckus about where I eat my meals here. If we sit at that big table—"

"Why should we? I'll ask that we be placed alone at a small table. I would prefer that anyway." Until she felt on a firmer footing in this unfamiliar place, she wanted to avoid the questions of curious strangers as much as possible.

Shortly after eight that evening, Amalia sat with Matthew MacFarlane in one of the little parlors off the ground-floor hall. Facing each other, they sat in high-backed chairs which flanked a small fireplace. An oil lamp, its round pink globe ornamented by a large red rose, shed warm light on MacFarlane's face, softening a little its Old Testament sternness.

He said, "I know I should apologize for asking to see you so soon after the end of your long journey."

"No apology is necessary. But of course I did wonder . . ."

"Why I felt an urgent need to talk to you? It is because of my son. You see, Mrs. Fulmer, I know that you were once engaged to Angus. He wrote to me from New Orleans saying that he had fallen very much in love with a young woman named Amalia Moreno, and intended to marry her." Matthew MacFarlane paused. "I hope you will not mind if I comment that now that I have met you, I can well understand why any young man might fall in love with you."

"Thank you."

After a moment he went on. "But only days after that letter reached me, Angus and Ruth arrived home. Angus told me that you and he had decided you were not suited to each other. And that is all he would ever say, no matter how I pressed him for details."

He paused. But Amalia, clasped hands tightening in her lap, said nothing.

"*Was* it like that, Mrs. Fulmer? Or did he behave so . . . so outrageously in some way that you were forced to break with him?"

She was able to tell the lie in a matter-of-fact voice. "No. Just as your son told you, we decided we were not suited to each other."

Matthew MacFarlane did not appear quite satisfied with her answer. Nevertheless he said, "I am glad to have my mind set at rest on that score. I have worried about it. You see, Angus wrote to me at the time that you were only eighteen, and had gone to convent school from the age of six onward. And when I met you today, I felt even more distressed by the thought that he might have treated you . . . lightly.

"Although I hate to say it of my own son, Angus is a wild young man. Perhaps it is not entirely his fault. Women seem to find him attractive. And any man who goes to sea is assailed by temptations of the flesh in every port."

The hazel eyes beneath the jutting brows took on a brooding look. Amalia had the impression that he was remembering times in his own seagoing days when, on some tropical island or in some South American port, he himself had had to wrestle with the Devil. And sometimes, perhaps, the Devil had won.

"Angus and I have failed to get along over more than his attitude toward fleshly pleasures. There is that strange notion of his about whaling. Why shouldn't man hunt whales? The first book of the Bible tells us that God gave man dominion over the birds of the air and all the creatures of land and sea."

Amalia said nothing. No wonder that Matthew and Angus had "failed to get along." To Matthew it was a terrible sin for a man to commit fornication, even a lusty young man who, after several celibate months aboard ship, found himself surrounded by willing girls on some tropical island. But to slaughter the globe's largest living creature so as to obtain a few barrels of oil was in full accordance with God's law. Why had He put the oil in the whale if not for man's benefit?

"It was Angus who persuaded me to sell our whale ships and buy merchantmen, you know."

"Yes. He once mentioned that to me."

"I would never have let him have his way if I had been in my prime. But whaling is a young man's game, and I had realized by then that my own whaling days were over. And so I went along with his ideas. If we had stayed in whaling, we might have been rich enough to weather the loss of one ship and the jettisoning of another's cargo. But as it was, our only alternative to bankruptcy was to sell our two remaining merchantmen to Tom Fulmer."

"I'm sorry, Mr. MacFarlane." She was. In spite of everything, she could not help but admire and envy him for his inflexible code. Even as a child she herself had been afflicted by moral uncertainty, and had found it impossible to judge, for instance, whether doing poor Hannah's arithmetic problems for her was an act of wickedness or of Christian charity.

What was more, she liked him for having worried that Angus might have treated her "lightly."

"It is all right," he said. "Tom dealt generously with us. There is enough money that I can maintain my household and give Ruth a respectable dowry when some young man claims her a few years from now. And certainly there's no need to worry about Angus. He's an excellent captain, I'll say that for him, and besides, he is marrying a shipowner's daughter." He paused, and then added gloomily, "Unless the same thing happens again."

"A broken engagement, you mean? Oh, I very much doubt that." After all, she thought, with a bitter inward smile, no man was apt to discover that still a second fiancée had spent her earliest years in the brothel where her mother worked. No, Matthew had little reason to fear that the marriage would not take place. This time Angus must have been careful to make sure that his intended's early years held no ugly surprises. As for the girl herself—well, Amalia found it hard to imagine that any girl in love with Angus would break her engagement to him of her own accord.

"Well, Mrs. Fulmer, again I hate to say this, but I think you are going to be better off with Tom than you would have been with Angus. Tom is a fine young man. Everyone in town knows that."

"And I know it too, Mr. MacFarlane."

They said good night a few moments later, and Amalia climbed the stairs to her room. Lena, she realized, must be asleep, because the connecting door to her room was closed and no light shone beneath it. Amalia undressed, blew out the lamp. Then, wearing a robe over her nightdress, she went to a window, parted its heavy draperies, and looked down at a vegetable garden. A three-quarter moon was up, its light bright enough to show her tall rows of corn and part of a sprawling squash patch, evidence that the vegetables for future meals would be as fresh as the tomatoes and green peppers she had eaten at supper. Before she decided upon a house for Tom and herself, she would make sure that there was a sunny plot large enough for a vegetable garden.

Tom. What would it be like, his first evening back in Sag Harbor? What would it be like to take into her life, into her bed, a husband who had never even touched her, except for that brotherly arm he had placed around her shoulders that agonizing night Angus had jilted her?

Well, she would not worry about it. Tom was a mature man, and a gentle one. And she too, she hoped, had developed a certain amount of good sense and patience. Everything would work out, even the lovemaking part of it.

Her mind went over the day just past. Her witless panic as the ship neared Long Wharf. Her relief, touched with illogical disappointment, when she saw that Angus was not among the waiting crowd. Her meeting with Tom's disgruntled older brother, and with Matthew MacFarlane, and with Ruth, so puzzlingly eager to be assured that Amalia's marriage to Tom was a "real" one. And after that the drive through town, past the house where, if things had turned out differently, Angus might have brought her as his bride, past those woods south of Otter Pond where the Gypsies camped each early summer . . .

Gypsies. A young Gypsy woman in a shadowy New Orleans doorway, saying that she read the presence of a hovering evil in Amalia's palm. "It will be with you like your own shadow for years. You must always be wary."

Odd. The night Angus had dealt her that terrible blow, the thought of the Gypsy had occurred to her. And she could remember thinking of her the next day, as she sat on the cemetery bench with Sara Davidson, that woman with the opaque-looking eyes. But as nearly as she could recall, she had not thought of the Gypsy fortune-teller again until just now.

Sara Davidson. Amalia hated any recollection of that monstrous woman who, taking advantage of a young mother's helplessness, had kept her in virtual slavery. In fact, sometimes it hurt too much to think of the pain and fear her mother had suffered in her too-short life. Tonight was one of those times. She wrenched her thoughts away from Juana Ramirez Moreno to her own future in this small town, this strange town with its waterfront dives at one end of Main Street and, at the other, stately houses inhabited by pious Presbyterians. She would have a good life in this town, she and Tom and their children.

She turned and walked back to her bed.

# 22

Sleep eluded her for a time that night. Thus she did not wake up until someone tapped on her door. Thinking it must be Lena, she said, "Come in."

A smiling Mrs. Arnshaw stepped into the sunny room. "Five letters for you, Mrs. Fulmer. Mr. Lipson brought them from the post office." She laid the envelopes on the little stand beside the bed.

"Thank you."

Mrs. Arnshaw remained standing there, as if in hope that Amalia would open the letters immediately and perhaps share their contents. "I put them in order, the earliest letter on top. I imagine they are all from Mr. Fulmer."

Amalia knew they must be. She had recognized Tom's tall, firm handwriting. "Thank you," she repeated. "What time is it?"

"Almost nine."

"Then I suppose I have missed breakfast."

"Not at all. My guests serve themselves at breakfast, from the buffet in the dining room. The food will be there until ten."

With obvious reluctance she started toward the door and then turned back. "Oh, a couple of other things. Miss White said to tell you that she is going to look around the village this morning but will be back for one-o'clock dinner. And Mr. Lipson says he will take you house hunting at two-thirty, if that is all right with you."

Again Amalia thanked her. As soon as the door had closed behind the landlady, Amalia opened the topmost envelope. The letter's heading told her that it had been written in Sydney, Australia, about two months earlier. It read:

Dearest Wife,

It was not until two hours ago that I could be sure I had the right to call you that. When the *Falcon* docked here this morning the shipping agent handed me your letter and the one from Howard Lipson, mailed in New Orleans right after the proxy marriage ceremony.

I wish there was some word besides "happy" to express what I feel. After all, people say "happy to meet you" when introduced to a stranger, or that they are happy to see that the rain has stopped. What word is there to describe how I feel when I realize that you are going to be mine for the rest of my life?

Perhaps even now you are in Sag Harbor. Anyway, you will of course be there when you read this. As I think I explained to you in my letter of proposal, Howard Lipson will set up an account for you at the bank, and transfer money to it from my own account. And he will help you find a house for us. I don't care what house it is, my darling, as long as it pleases you.

I must attend to business now, my dearest. The sooner I can get the *Falcon* unloaded and reloaded, the sooner I will get back to you. But I will keep writing to you, sending letters from every port we touch, and whenever we encounter a Sag Harbor-bound ship at sea.

Your devoted husband,
Tom

Feeling an ache in her throat, she laid the first letter aside and opened the others, one after another. Apparently they all had been handed to passing ships, because each was headed "Aboard the *White Falcon*, at sea."

A paragraph from the second letter read:

I have just spent several idle minutes on deck looking at the stars. At this hour, and at this latitude and time of year, the Southern Cross blazes straight overhead. You have never seen it, have you, my darling? Well, some night not too long from now you will stand beside me on a ship's deck. I will have my arm around you, and I will point out not just the Southern Cross but those other stars with the beautiful names the old Arabs gave them—Achernar and

Al Na'ir and Al Suhail. That will be just one of the hundreds of things we will share, my dearest.

Midway of the last of the five letters he had written:

Do you know when I first fell in love with you? It was the night you walked into the dining room of Angus' cousins' house in New Orleans. I guess you hadn't had time to dress your hair as smoothly as you must have wanted to, because I recall a stray curl near one temple. I thought: I'll never again see anyone as lovely as her.

But it was plain from the first that you had eyes for no one but Angus. I kept saying to myself: Tom, you fool, what chance would you have even if Angus were not in the picture, a dull, thirty-two-year-old stick like yourself?

It is still hard for me to believe that you are mine. But since you are, I'm going to make you glad that you did not marry Angus. I'm going to make you happier than he ever could have.

Moments later, with tears stinging her eyes, she laid the letter aside. Tom was right. In time Angus would become just someone she thought of now and then. And in the meantime she would do her best to make him happy, this gentle, earnest man she'd had the good fortune to marry.

She placed the letter in the drawer of her bedside table and then got up and dressed.

That very first afternoon she found the house she wanted. Not that she decided right then to buy it. First, of course, she wished to look at other houses.

Over the next two weeks she and Howard Lipson, driving about in his surrey, looked at every house available, not only in Sag Harbor but across the cove on a point of land known as North Haven. Lena accompanied them on all those excursions, riding in the rear seat. It was true that Howard, with his almost epicene plumpness and old-maidish airs, could scarcely be considered a threat to a woman's virtue. Nevertheless, he did wear trousers. And as Tom Fulmer's wife, Amalia wanted to do nothing that could possibly make her an object of gossip. Hence Lena's conspicuous presence in the backseat.

As they looked at house after house, Amalia's thoughts kept returning to the first one they had inspected. It was on John Street, a narrow street which, as crooked as the cowpath it had been in pre-Revolutionary times, meandered westward from Main Street and then along the quiet waters of Upper Sag Harbor Cove. It was a narrow white clapboard house, perhaps a little too gaunt-looking from the outside, but flower-filled window boxes and green or blue shutters would remedy that. The lot was ample, more than an acre, and hedged in on three sides by boxwood. A stand of tall cedars at one corner of the house offered protection against the northwest winds which, Howard told her, howled across Long Island Sound to Sag Harbor during the winter months. From the northwest corner of the veranda a brick walk, wide enough to accommodate a wheelbarrow or even a pony cart, led back along the side of the house to the rear. A small ramshackle barn stood there, its walls bleached to satiny gray by decades of sun and salt air. There were a half-dozen apple trees, bushes of blackberries and gooseberries, and space for a large vegetable garden. Never mind, she thought, that the apple trees were gnarled and laced with honeysuckle vines, and that the garden space was covered with a tangle of knee-high grass, yarrow, and Queen Anne's lace. All that could be transformed. She pictured herself putting up vegetables and making jam, just as she and Juana and Lena had done in the little Belleville house.

But it was the interior of the house which really charmed her. The parlor and dining room were large, flooded with sunlight, and wainscoted in cherry wood up to a height of two feet. The kitchen fireplace, so wide it almost stretched across one end of the room, had ample hooks for kettles to dangle above the flames, and two iron-lined ovens set in its brick face. At one end of the fireplace a door led to a "hired girl's room." On the opposite side of the kitchen was a large pantry, with a door leading to a small outside shed. It was the sort of shed, Howard told her, in which Sag Harbor people placed ice chiseled from the cove each winter. Packed in straw, the ice usually lasted through August.

Upstairs there were six bedrooms, enough to accommodate a very large family indeed.

It was on a Saturday afternoon that she made up her mind to buy the John Street house. As she lay in bed that night, she suddenly wondered why she visualized Tom and herself as the parents of a large family. In the past she had never been conscious of a desire to have many children. Could it be that she feared that, married to Tom, she would have an empty space in her heart, a space that many children might possibly fill? She told herself sharply: No! It was just that Tom seemed the sort of man who could be an excellent father no matter how large his brood. But she would be happy with him whether they had six children, or one, or even none.

On Monday she would tell Richard that she wanted to buy the John Street house. It seemed only fitting that she consult him. After all, he was her brother-in-law. And he had been as cordial as she could expect a man of his temperament to be. He had called on her twice here at Mrs. Arnshaw's, and had offered to be helpful in any way he could.

As it turned out, she did not have to wait until Monday to see Richard Fulmer. She encountered him at a Sunday-afternoon reception given by Madison Street neighbors of his.

It was far from the first such party she had attended. Perhaps partly out of curiosity, but also out of their liking and respect for Tom Fulmer, Sag Harbor people had invited her to suppers, afternoon and evening receptions, and even a ball at the Allerdyce mansion. When the first few invitations had arrived only two days after she had taken up residence at the boardinghouse, she had been dismayed. Aside from the traveling costume she had bought for the journey from New Orleans, her wardrobe was the same as it had been during those two years spent alone with Lena in Belleville, years when her biggest social event had been Christmas dinner with the sisters at the nunnery.

When Amalia turned to her for advice, Lena said, "You buy yourself some nice clothes, honey. There's a second-story window on Main Street, above the cobbler's shop. It says 'The Misses Fanny and Bernice Weber, Modistes to the Bon Ton.' "

"They sound expensive."

"Child, you want to shame your husband before he even gets back here? That's what you'll do if you go to parties in the tacky things you got now."

Two hours later she stood in the Misses Weber's fitting room, having her measurements taken. Excited by gaining the patronage of Thomas Fulmer's beautiful proxy bride, they stopped work on clothing for other customers long enough to turn out three afternoon frocks and one ball gown for Amalia.

This Sunday afternoon, as she stood beside Richard Fulmer at the punch table provided by their Madison Street hosts, Amalia wore one of the afternoon frocks, a square-necked yellow silk with elbow-length sleeves. Richard said, with the air of a man fulfilling his social duty, "You look very nice, Amalia."

"Thank you." Something in his tone made her wonder if he thought she was being too extravagant with his brother's money. If so, he would not be at all pleased with her next words. "Richard, I have decided to buy a house on John Street."

"Must be the Farnsworth house. It's the only one for sale on John Street."

"That's the one. The Farnsworths left the deed with Howard, along with power of attorney to negotiate the sale."

"It's been on the market for three years. And no wonder! They are asking a fortune for it, a cool thousand dollars. Why, I know where you can buy a house and fifty acres of good farmland for that."

"I know the price is high. But Tom told me to choose what appealed to me. Besides, the house is partially furnished."

The Farnsworths, after occupying the house for forty years, had moved to Pennsylvania to live with one of their sons and his family. They must have taken most of their furniture with them, but they had left a few sofas and chairs and beds and bureaus. All the pieces had seen better days. But they would suffice for herself and Lena until they could furnish the house properly.

"Of course, if you think I'm being too extravagant . . ."

"You're not," he said grudgingly. "Times are good. If the orders coming in are an indication, Fulmer ships will have plenty of cargo. Much as I hate to admit it, perhaps Tom was right to buy those ships." He paused and then added, "Yes, I'm sure he would want you to have the Farnsworth house, even if the price is highway robbery."

Embolded, she said, "Do you think it would be all right if I bought a saddle horse too? Not a young, high-spirited one. I wouldn't be able to handle an animal like that. But I would like a gentle, older horse, one cheaply priced."

"Do you know how to ride?"

"After a fashion." Dressed in one of Esther MacFarlane's riding habits, she had ridden horseback with a group of New Orleans young people during those summers of her growing up. "I hate to be dependent on Howard to take me around. He has his law practice to attend to. I can keep a horse in the little barn behind the Farnsworth house. And I'll be able to ride it down to the business district whenever I don't feel like walking there."

The truth was that she wanted the horse mainly, not for shopping expeditions, but for solitary rides through the woods and across farmlands to the beaches. Ever since she had reached eastern Long Island, she had wanted to explore its countryside, unaccompanied by gossipy Howard or even Lena.

"I think there's still a six-year-old gray mare named Molly for sale at the livery stable. She might suit you. I'll see about it." For a moment as he looked down at her, envy of his brother was plain in his eyes. She found it easy to understand. Richard had been humiliated by a public jilting. His rich aunt's will had passed him over. No wonder he envied his brother, a man who was not only well-liked by everyone but also had been able to marry the woman he wanted.

He said, "I'm sure Tom won't mind your having bought the house, or the mare, or anything else you want." Then he abruptly added, "The Mapletons have just come in. I don't think you know them. I'll take you over and introduce you."

# 23

The next few weeks were the busiest of Amalia's life. Within hours after Howard, in exchange for her bank draft, had given her the deed to the house, she and Lena and a tall, silent woman from the Shinnecock village near Southampton were at work. They scrubbed floors, washed windows, polished the worn furniture, and wielded a carpet beater against some threadbare rugs Amalia had found in the attic.

The outdoor tasks were performed by a man of all work, Sam Thorpe, and his nephew Toby. Sam appeared to be of normal intelligence. But thirty-year-old Toby—more than six feet tall, almost two hundred pounds in weight, and looking much younger than his years—was definitely backward. Under his uncle's supervision, though, he was an excellent worker. Cheerful and almost tireless, he ripped honeysuckle vines loose from the gnarled apple trees. He mended holes in the roof of the small barn that was to shelter Molly, the mare she had bought, complete with sidesaddle, from the livery stable. And with a hand-driven plow he turned under matted grass and weeds, creating a thirty-by-sixty-foot plot of garden space. The summer was far too advanced for her to plant anything but peas and spinach for fall harvesting. Next year, though, she would plant everything from lettuce to corn to pumpkins.

One late afternoon, when the Indian woman had gone home for the day and Lena was hanging curtains in an upstairs bedroom, Ruth MacFarlane tapped at the back door. Amalia let her into the kitchen and offered her tea. "Or would you like me to show you through the house first?"

"Thank you, but I looked through the house three years ago, right after the Farnsworths moved out. I don't suppose you've changed it much yet."

"Not much. Oh, some of the furniture I ordered from New

York through Hobart's General Store has arrived. But chiefly all we've done so far is clean the place."

"I guess it would get dirty over three years, even shut up. It wasn't too bad when my friends and I went through it."

"Your friends?"

"Cora and Emma Watts and their little brother. We pried open a cellar window and went all through the place."

Looking at her visitor, tall and poised and appearing much older than fourteen, Amalia found it hard to realize that only three years ago Ruth had been young enough for such pranks as breaking into an empty house.

Teacups in hand, they sat at the kitchen table, its pine boards scrubbed so thoroughly by the strong-armed Shinnecock woman that they looked almost white. For a while Ruth chattered about a Sunday-school picnic she recently had attended. Then she said, "Amalia, would you mind if I asked you something?"

"Probably not. What is it?"

"Do you really love Tom Fulmer?"

Ruth *was* still a child, after all. Amalia could not imagine any of the adults she knew, except perhaps Lena, asking so personal a question.

For several moments she was silent. Only weeks ago a candid answer would have been, "I like and respect him and feel grateful to him, but I don't love him. At least not yet." Now, though, she realized that over the past weeks her emotion for him had deepened. His letters had continued to arrive, some with South American postmarks, but most handed to Sag Harbor-bound ships the *Falcon* had met at sea. His last few had mentioned receiving some of the letters she had dispatched by every ship that had a chance of encountering his.

His last letter, received only two days before, had said:

> The more I think of it, the gladder I am that you chose the Farnsworth house. Let's put in a grape arbor. And let's enlarge that barn into a carriage house, so that we can keep a surrey as well as a small gig for you to drive. I hope you don't know how to drive, because in that case I'll have the pleasure of teaching you.
>
> It looks now as if I should be home by Christmas, depending upon wind and weather and how long it takes me

to load and discharge cargo in the ports still on my schedule. We'll stand at an upstairs window of our house and look across the road and over that stretch of reeds to the cove. Probably the cove will be frozen over. My darling, have you ever seen moonlight reflected off a sheet of ice? I'm sure you haven't. You'll see that it has an unearthly beauty.

I wonder how long it will be before people start calling it the Fulmer house instead of the old Farnsworth house. Probably you and I will be grandparents by that time.

I must write up the log now, and then sleep. Good night, my dearest.

After reading that letter Amalia had sat with the pages still in her hand. Home by Christmas! She hoped that by then the house, fully furnished, would be beautiful. How wonderful it would be to see the look on his face when he first walked into the house that would be theirs for the rest of their lives.

She realized that just as the *Falcon* was bringing him closer and closer to her, each of his letters was drawing her emotionally closer to him. She thought: I won't have to learn to love him. I think it is happening already.

Now she said, "Yes, Ruth. I think I love Tom."

"I'm awfully glad." Apparently she meant it. Her pretty face seemed to hold nothing but pleasure at the thought of Amalia being married to a man she loved.

Ruth took a sip of tea and then asked, "Do you love him as much as you loved Angus?"

For a moment Amalia felt angry. Then she reminded herself that Ruth was only fourteen, too young to realize that such a question might be reopening an only partially healed wound.

"I love him just as much as I loved your brother, but in a different way." She hesitated for a moment and then asked, "How about your feelings, Ruth? I know you resented my engagement to Angus."

"Oh, yes. I was terribly jealous."

"Do you mind his engagement to Barbara Weyant?"

After a moment she smiled. "No, I don't mind."

"You see? Remember my telling you down in New Orleans that soon you'd be too taken up with your beaus to worry about your brother getting married?" She added teasingly, "How many beaus do you have?"

Ruth tossed her head. "I don't like any of them enough to call them beaus. But there are boys who seem to like me. At that Sunday-school picnic I was telling you about, each of the girls brought a box lunch and the boys bid on them. The money went to the church. If a boy's bid for a girl's lunch was the highest, he got to sit beside her while they ate it. Well, six boys bid for my lunch, and Danny Jameson—he was the boy who won—bid a whole dollar."

Amalia said, genuinely impressed, "Well, you may not like him enough to call him a beau, but it's obvious he likes you."

A few minutes later her visitor left. Amalia went back to two drunken Portuguese seamen to the lockup the other through Hobart's General Store.

Around ten the next morning she sat at a counter at Hobart's, looking through a catalog which held drawings of furniture offered by various New York cabinetmakers. Someone said, "Hello, Amalia."

With a start she looked up into Richard Fulmer's thin face. He said, "I've been thinking about you. In fact, I planned to visit you this afternoon."

"How nice. But did you have some particular reason?"

"Yes. I think you should have a pistol."

"A pistol! Why on earth should I . . . ?"

"Perhaps you haven't heard, but the constable had to take two drunken Portuguese seamen to the lockup the other night." The lockup, the nearest thing Sag Harbor had to a jail, was a shack with one barred window down near the waterfront. "They broke out, swam across the cove to North Haven, and for no reason at all set fire to a barn."

"Oh, dear. And I'd begun to think of this as such a peaceful village, in spite of the goings-on on lower Main Street."

"It is peaceful, mainly. A few drunken fights on the waterfront, but that's all. Sag Harbor's seagoing men know better than to invade other parts of town when they are drunk. But lately we've been getting a lot of foreign riffraff who don't obey the rules. And you and that colored woman are living alone, with no other house nearer than a couple of hundred yards. I think you need a pistol for protection."

"Oh, Richard! I'd be more afraid of a gun than of a drunken man. I've never in my life even held a pistol."

"There's nothing to be afraid of. I'll show you how to use it."

"But mightn't it go off?"

"Accidentally, you mean? No, you have to put a great deal of pressure on the trigger to make it fire. I want you to have a pistol for my sake as well as yours. I know that Tom, once he hears about the Portuguese and other such incidents, will feel that I should have provided you with some protection, and he'll be riled that I haven't."

She said reluctantly, "All right."

"Good." He raised his voice. "Mr. Hobart, Mrs. Fulmer would like to buy a pistol."

The storekeeper and Richard showed her how to ram the round shot in the pistol, fill the rest of the barrel with gunpowder from a small leather bag, and then tamp the gunpowder down with a ramrod. While the two men watched, she unloaded and reloaded the pistol.

"Now, leave it like that," Richard said.

"Loaded? But what if . . . ?"

"I told you. It won't go off unless you pull the trigger."

She looked at the gun with distaste. She would put it in a drawer of that newly bought desk in the parlor, she decided, and never touch it again.

Her brother-in-law left her a few minutes later. She turned back to the catalog and finished making out her order. When she finally rode home perched on Molly's broad back, the leather bag which dangled from her sidesaddle held the pistol, plus two pouches fo additional powder and shot. Despite Richard's assurances, she did not breathe quite freely until she had placed the pistol and the two pouches in the parlor desk and closed the drawer.

Much as she enjoyed furnishing the house, and going to parties, and sitting in the Fulmer pew at the Presbyterian church on Sundays, what gave her the most pleasure during those weeks of waiting for Tom were her solitary horseback rides. The gentle Molly carried her along Sag Harbor's narrow side streets, some of them as meandering as the footpaths they had once been. She rode through woods where, in natural clearings, orange butterfly bush and wild white daisies grew. Several times she rode through Bridgehampton, the little farming community four miles away, and then across open fields to Sagaponack, where the Atlantic's waves broke gently on a hidden sandbar and then rolled to shore. One late afternoon as she rode along between the water's edge and the dunes that lined the beach, she looked to her right and then caught her breath. Out there, near the horizon, was a line of large graceful shapes, black against blue sky and water. As if in a game of follow the leader, each of the creatures arched into the air, then disappeared beneath the water, then leaped again.

Quickly she slid to the beach, tethered Molly to the snaggled root of an upended tree stump that must have washed ashore years ago, and hurried to the tallest of the nearby dunes. Feet slipping in the sand, she climbed to the crest. From here she had a better view of those seagoing mammals out there which, apparently out of sheer joy of living, sported through water and sunny air. Thanks to conversations she had heard at Sag Harbor gatherings, she knew that they must be a species of whale, called blackfish, often glimpsed from Long Island beaches.

As she watched the huge playful creatures, she became more sharply aware of other delights. The salty breeze penetrating her riding habit of thin brown wool. A group of long-legged sandpipers skittering up the beach before an advancing wave. And the sun, turning the sea into a million-faceted gem, lying warm as a blessing on her face, and casting a reflection that ran like quicksilver along the curving blades of the dune grass at her feet. Suddenly she felt the sort of exhilaration that those soaring, diving creatures out there appeared to be feeling.

All this beauty around her. And that pleasantly situated old house, which her work was making lovelier and more comfortable by the day. And a husband, a fine, gentle man whose love she was sure now she could return.

She thought wonderingly: Why, I'm happy. For the first time since, on a moonlit road outside New Orleans, Angus MacFarlane had dealt her that paralyzing blow, she was happy.

The line of leaping, plunging whales had disappeared. Perhaps they had veered out to sea. Perhaps, having had their frolic, they now swam straight ahead, too low in the water to be visible from shore. Well, it was time she went home anyway. Already, near-sunset light was dyeing the beach and the white breasts of circling gulls. And she still had to go to the livery stable and arrange for a hired carriage to take her to and from the Allerdyces' party the next evening. She could scarcely walk the mile to their house in evening dress, let alone ride Molly there. Descending the dune, she untethered Molly and led her to a gray driftwood log, its satiny surface also turned pinkish by sunset, which would serve nicely as a mounting block.

A little more than twenty-four hours later her new confidence of enduring happiness was shattered to bits.

# 24

Because the Hannibal Allerdyces were the richest people in town, few ever declined their invitations. Amalia realized that it was a measure of the respect in which Tom was held that she, a stranger, had been accepted immediately by people like the Allerdyces. But grateful as she was, she could not help wondering if others secretly felt, as she did, that Allerdyce parties were almost stupefyingly dull. Most of the guests, like the Allerdyces themselves, were of advanced years and eminent respectability. In such company even the lively-minded confined themselves to generalities about the weather or the beauty and eloquence of last Sunday's sermon. After she had said for perhaps the tenth time that, yes, she was enjoying the fine weather, and, yes, she had thought last Sunday's sermon especially good, and, yes indeed, she was eager to see her husband, she felt that she had earned a respite. Raising her voice, she said to the Misses Lottie and Martha Stark, both quite deaf, "Could I bring you ladies some punch?"

"Oh, no, dear," Lottie said. "Punch does not agree with us."

"Well, if you'll excuse me, I'll have a cup."

She moved toward the table where a magnificent cut-glass bowl held nonalcoholic punch. Then, after making sure that the Stark sisters had turned their attention to another guest, she walked the rest of the way across the drawing room and entered a small side parlor.

The little room was deserted. Amalia walked over to the unlighted fireplace to look at the painting which hung above the black marble mantel. Its subject, a bewigged man in a tall military hat, blue coat, and buff breeches, apparently was an ancestor of Hannibal Allerdyce's, because an engraved plate on the lower edge of the frame said "Horace Allerdyce, Admiral of the Fleet During the Reign of Her Gracious Majesty Queen Anne."

She was still looking at the portrait when, although she had heard nothing, she became aware that she was not alone in the room. She whirled around.

Angus MacFarlane stood just inside the doorway. His face had turned pale beneath its sun-browned surface, giving him a muddy look. His pallor made his eyes appear even more intensely blue than she had remembered.

As she looked at him, numb with shock, her first thought was: I should have been prepared for this. It was inevitable that he visit Sag Harbor sooner or later. He had been born and raised in this village. His father and his young half-sister still lived here.

Perhaps it had been her fear of meeting him which had made her think he might not return to Sag Harbor for a long time, time enough that she would have become a settled matron. She had been right to fear such a meeting, because now, with him standing only a few feet away, she discovered that she was as vulnerable to him as ever. Vulnerable to her hatred of him, and vulnerable to her contradictory desire to have him gather her close and tell her that what had happened that night on the road outside New Orleans really had not happened at all.

She managed to move her numb lips. "Hello, Angus."

He took two steps into the room and then halted. "I didn't expect to find you here."

"In Sag Harbor? But surely you must have. Surely your father or Ruth must have mentioned in a letter . . ."

"I meant, I didn't expect to find you at the Allerdyces'."

Her voice shook. "You mean because they are so respectable? You feel they should have sensed that my background was—"

"No! I just meant that people like them are standoffish with anyone not raised here. But I suppose that because of Tom . . ."

His voice trailed off. She wondered what he had felt when he heard of that proxy marriage. Surprise, undoubtedly. But the shaken look on his face made her think that perhaps he had felt more than that. She thought: I hope he did. I hope he felt at least a tiny bit of the shock he once gave me.

When she spoke, her voice was cool and even. "Are your

fiancée and her parents with you? Or has the marriage already taken place?"

He looked at her, mouth compressed into a thin line. Finally he said, "There's to be no marriage."

Her heart lurched. Damn him, damn him. He had not only come back here. He had come back unencumbered. "So you jilted her too?"

"No. She broke the engagement."

She felt a surge of satisfaction. "Now, how can that be?" she asked mockingly. "How can that possibly be?" When he didn't answer, she went on, "Didn't the lady give you a reason?"

"Yes. But I'm not telling you or anybody else what it was."

She shrugged. "Very well." After a moment she asked, "When did you return to Sag Harbor?"

"I arrived yesterday morning."

And so yesterday afternoon as she stood on that sand dune, aware of her good fortune, aware of a new confidence that she and Tom could build a loving marriage, Angus was already here in Sag Harbor, ready to plunge her back into bitterness and pain and this shameful physical need of him.

A thickness in her voice now. "Do you plan to stay here?"

"For a while, at least. I won't be sailing on Weyant ships, of course, now that Barbara and I . . ." He broke off and then added, "But sooner or later I'll find a berth of some sort."

For several moments his blue eyes looked into her dark ones. Then he took a step toward her. He said, with what sounded like genuine pain in his voice, "Amalia . . ."

Her whole body stiffened. "No!"

He halted. She said, still in that thickened voice, "I hope you sign on a ship tomorrow. One which is bound on a three-year voyage. But as long as we are both in this town, I want to have as little as possible to do with you. Is that clear?"

After a while he said, "Entirely." Hardness in his voice now. "I'd thought that we might at least try to be friends. But if you—"

"Friends! After what you did to me?"

And to my mother, my gentle mother. But she would never be able to tell him about Juana's heartbreak and death.

"Very well." His tone was curt. "I'll do my best to stay out of your way. And you needn't curtail your social life, Mrs. Fulmer. I've never liked these upper Main Street parties. I came here tonight only to please my father."

Abruptly he turned and left the room.

Amalia faced the fireplace. Crossing her forearms on the cool marble, she rested her flushed cheek on them for several minutes. Then, realizing that she could not stay there all evening, she returned to the drawing room. There was no sign of Angus, although Matthew MacFarlane, his Old Testament face stern even on this social occasion, stood talking with several men in one corner. Amalia looked around for her hostess and finally saw her at the opposite end of the room, standing white-haired and buxom beside the spinet. Mr. Slight, the church organist, sat on the spinet's bench, which meant that soon Mrs. Allerdyce would launch into "Wind o' the Heather" or one of the other ballads in her repertoire.

Amalia moved to her side. "I'm sorry, Mrs. Allerdyce, but I fear I must leave. I have developed a headache."

"Oh, my dear, I am so sorry. You will miss the collation we are serving at ten o'clock."

"What distresses me more, I shall miss your singing." That was not as hypocritical as one might have thought. Despite their wealth, the Allerdyces served indifferent food, whereas Mrs. Allerdyce still had a quite pleasant contralto voice. "But I really must go."

She retrieved her wrap from the maid in the ladies' cloakroom, went out into the insect-humming August dark, and entered the hired carriage waiting at the curb.

# 25

The next morning, after an almost sleepless night, Amalia helped Lena transfer her belongings from one of the upstairs bedrooms to the "hired girl's room" off the kitchen. Days before, Lena had insisted upon the move. It would be "more proper," she said, especially after Amalia's husband came home, for her not to sleep upstairs. Besides, she would do most of the cooking, "just as I always have," and so the hired girl's room would be handier. "And it will cut down on my stair-climbing. I'm not as young as I used to be, you know."

Looking at the brown-skinned woman, Amalia saw that Lena indeed had aged. Her hair was now far more gray than black. The change made the old knife wound puckering her cheek look even more bizarre. "All right," Amalia had said, "if you think you'll be more comfortable in that room, take it."

Now, dusting the top of the chest of drawers which handyman Sam Thorpe and his "simple" nephew Toby had brought down from upstairs, Amalia became aware that Lena was watching her in the mirror. The scarred face had a narrow-eyed, speculative look.

Nerves raw, Amalia spun around. "Why are you looking at me like that?"

"Because I'm wondering what happened to you last night." When Amalia remained silent, Lena went on. "Something sure did. You've got shadows under your eyes, and you're nervous as a witch."

"All right! Angus MacFarlane turned up at the Allerdyces' party."

Lena's eyes became even narrower. "Is he married yet?"

"No, and he's not going to be."

"Why not?"

"He wouldn't say. Anyway, what does it matter?"

"Shouldn't matter a hill of beans to you, young lady. You've got a husband now."

"Don't you think I realize that?"

Not answering the question, Lena asked, "Is he going to stay here in Sag Harbor?"

"I suppose so, at least until he signs onto some ship."

Lena asked quietly, "You're not going to let him make a fool of you, are you?"

"What do you mean, make a fool of me? You think I am still . . . interested in him? Why, I hate him!"

"I don't like that kind of hating. It's too close to something else."

"Lena, mind your own business."

After a moment the woman said quietly, "I've known you all your life. Somehow I thought that did make you my business."

"Oh, Lena! Forgive me."

"It's all right, honey." In unconscious echo of Amalia's words to Angus, she added vehemently, "I hope that the next ship he signs onto is gone for years."

By means of staying away from the center of the village, Amalia avoided encountering Angus during the next two weeks. She stayed away from church on Sundays. She declined invitations, using as an excuse that Tom might return sooner than expected and that she wanted to have the house ready for him. Instead of visiting the Main Street shops herself, she dispatched Lena to buy whatever they needed. She continued to ride Molly almost every day, but never through the village.

On an afternoon a little more than two weeks after her encounter with Angus at the Allerdyces', Amalia was pruning the badly overgrown blackberry bushes beside the barn. She heard a voice say, "Hello," and turned to find Ruth standing there, looking especially pretty in pink muslin.

"Why, Ruth." Amalia laid her pruning shears on one seat of the grape arbor Sam and Toby Thorpe recently had built. "Let's sit down." When they were both seated, she said, "I haven't seen you in a long time."

"I know. But then, you haven't been seeing anyone, have you? At least I hear people saying they haven't seen you."

Looking into the bland face, Amalia wondered if the child

had any intuition of the reason for that. "I've been busy, Ruth."

After a moment Ruth asked, "Has my brother been here to your house?"

Amalia waited until she felt certain that her voice would sound matter-of-fact. "No. Why should he come here?"

"Well, he's not going to marry that Barbara Weyant now. And you and he used to be—"

"That was a long time ago. Besides, I'm married to Tom Fulmer." She hesitated, knowing it was wrong to try to extract information from one so young, and yet unable to resist asking the question. "Has your brother said why his engagement was broken?"

"No. He won't talk about it."

"Did you ever meet Barbara Weyant?"

"Oh, yes. Papa and I went up to Boston to see the Weyants as soon as Angus wrote that he was engaged. She was sort of pretty. She has brown hair and gray eyes and she's short, shorter than I am. She isn't beautiful like you, but she's all right. Anyway, I guess Angus thought so, until whatever happened did happen."

"I guess hearing that he wasn't going to get married after all came as a surprise to you."

Ruth shrugged. "You never know what grown-ups are going to do."

After a moment Amalia asked, "Has he signed onto a ship yet?"

"He hasn't been able to, so far." Ruth's voice quickened. "But the next time he signs on as captain for a long trip, he's going to take me with him."

Surely Angus wouldn't allow a girl like Ruth—unmarried and very pretty and very young—to take a long trip in a ship filled with men, especially since some of them were sure to be like those she had seen staggering in and out of lower Main Street grog shops. "Oh, Ruth! I thought you'd outgrown such ideas." Then, when the blue eyes shot her a resentful look: "Did Angus really promise to take you on a voyage?"

"Well, not exactly. But he'll take me. You'll see."

Disturbed by the intense look in the girl's eyes, Amalia tried to speak lightly. "But what about all those beaus of yours? What will they feel when you desert them for months or even years?"

The teasing seemed to have the desired effect. "They'll wait for me," Ruth said airily. Then: "Could I have a drink of water from the pump in your kitchen?"

"Why, of course. Let—"

"I can get it myself. And then I'll let myself out the front door. Good-bye," she added, and turned toward the rear of the house.

Ruth's visit, reminding Amalia even more poignantly of Angus' presence in the town, left her with a restlessness that lasted all evening and into the next day. In midafternoon she gave up trying to make a choice among the wallpaper samples Lena had brought her from Hobart's General Store. She dressed in her riding habit, placed the sidesaddle on Molly's broad back, and rode off down Sag Harbor Turnpike to Bridgehampton. From there she struck out across the narrow "potato roads," leading through the now-harvested fields, to the beach at Sagaponack.

Sometimes on that dune-sheltered stretch of sand she found children playing, or some Bridgehampton farmer casting a line into the water in hope of landing a striped bass. But children were back in school now, and farmers were too busy finishing up the harvest to fish. She had the beach all to herself. She dismounted, took a light blue blanket from the canvas saddlebag, and spread it on the sand.

She sat down. The sun was as warm, the sea as gloriously blue, as on that day when the sight of the whales had sent her spirits soaring. Would she ever feel like that again, so confident that she and Tom could be happy together? Perhaps, especially if Angus left Sag Harbor and stayed away a long, long time. But right now she felt numb to the beauty of the day, numb to everything except the warring emotions in her heart and a dull ache at the nape of her neck. After a moment she reached up, took the tortoiseshell pins from her hair, and let it fall like a thick dark curtain around her shoulders. There, that felt better. She lay back on the blanket, eyes closed against the bright sunlight.

She had been there perhaps fifteen minutes when she became aware of another sound besides the wash of surf. It was a crackling sound, as if someone moved through the tangle of beach-plum bushes, wild-rose vines, and eelgrass atop the dunes. The sound stopped. She sat up and twisted around on the blanket. Angus stood atop a dune, staring down at her.

Heartbeats fast, she sprang to her feet and stood facing him. "You! How did you get here?"

His gaze went to Molly, tethered to that half-buried tree root. "The same way you did, only I left my horse up on the road."

She knew he must mean the narrow road that ran through the potato fields to a gap in the line of dunes. "Why? Why did you come here? Have you been . . . ?"

"Following you? No, I had no idea you were here. I've been coming to Sagaponack since I was a child."

Feet sliding in the loose sand, he descended the dune. She waited for him, lips compressed. When he was a few feet away from her he halted and said in a harsh voice, "Put your hair up! With it hanging down like that you look . . ."

He hesitated. She said, heart pounding with rage, lips stretched in a smile that was not really a smile at all. "Like a whore? Or at least a whore's daughter? Is that what you mean?"

"No, goddammit! Of course I don't mean that. It's just that for a man, a woman with her hair hanging loose like that . . ." Again he broke off.

She said bitingly, "Why don't you leave here? Then you'd be spared the sight of me entirely." And I, she thought, would be spared the risk of encountering you.

"Don't you think I want to leave? But there are no berths available right now. I'd go to some other port, New York or Philadelphia, and see if they needed a man with a master's papers, if it weren't for . . ."

"If it weren't for what?"

"Haven't you heard about my father?"

"His fainting fit? Lena said the other day that she'd heard people in Hobart's talking about it."

"It wasn't just a fainting fit. Dr. Marsden says it was a stroke." Seth Marsden was one of Sag Harbor's two doctors. He was also Amalia's nearest neighbor, occupying an old house about two hundred yards from hers.

"My father doesn't want the whole town knowing it was a stroke. He also wants me to stay here as long as I can. Oh, he wouldn't stand in my way if I had a chance to captain a ship sailing out of Sag Harbor. After all, I have my living to earn. But until such a chance does come along, he wants me to stay here."

His father, she thought bitterly. Matthew MacFarlane, whose grandchildren must be of impeccable heritage on their mother's as well as their father's side.

And yet, despite the fact that she had every reason to hate Angus, she knew that if he reached out for her now and drew her close against him, knew that if that firm mouth with the full lower lip covered her mouth, she would find herself helpless in her need for him.

She said, "Well, if you won't leave town, you can at least get off the beach."

His blue eyes, anger kindling in them now, looked straight into hers for a moment. Then he said, "Put up your hair, Mrs. Fulmer, before someone else comes along and sees you like that."

He turned, climbed the dune, and disappeared over its crest.

With shaking hands she retrieved the tortoiseshell pins from the blanket and put up her hair. After that she waited until she was fairly sure he would be out of sight. Then, with the blanket restored to the saddlebag, she rode off the beach and across the potato fields. This time, though, she did not ride back along the turnpike. Seeking the distraction of a less familiar route, she took a series of narrow paths that led through woodland, past sunny clearings and small ponds where mallards and wild geese floated. She was nearing the northern edge of the woods when her eye was caught by something that lay among the scarlet Virginia creeper bordering the path, something that glittered. Glad to pay attention to something besides her inner turmoil, she reined in, unhooked her right knee from the saddle horn, and slipped her left foot from the stirrup. After sliding to the ground, she tethered Molly's reins to a branch of a small maple, walked back a few feet, and knelt. Yes, there it was.

She picked it up. A large brass earring, the sort she had seen Gypsies wear. And from where she knelt she could look through the trees at a kind of outdoor fireplace, a circle of fire-blackened stones set in a clearing. Yes, this must be the Gypsy campground Howard Lipson had told her about.

Gypsies. That Gypsy woman in that New Orleans doorway, telling her that there was an evil in her life, something that would follow her like a shadow for years to come.

On the busy New Orleans street that summer day, she had

not been frightened by the Gypsy's words, just disquieted. But now, here in these silent woods, she felt a kind of dread stealing over her, as if some kind of nameless, faceless menace was approaching through the leafy stillness. . . .

She dropped the cheap earring as if it had suddenly turned burning hot. She stood up. Not bothering to brush the damp earth from her skirt, she unhitched Molly, led her to a big oak stump, and used it as a mounting block.

# 26

Sara Davidson's establishment was wrapped in late-morning quiet. Emerging from her comfortable apartment at the rear of the second floor, Sara walked with rustling bombazine skirts along the corridor and descended the stairs.

Solange, her face older and harder but still handsome, stood in the lower hall. "I was just coming up to your rooms, Mrs. Davidson. There's a Mr. Mountjoy waiting for you in your office."

Sara frowned. "Mountjoy, Mountjoy . . . not Lawrence Mountjoy!"

"Yes, ma'am, that's the name he gave."

"Solange! You know you're not to admit anyone at this hour. And Lawrence Mountjoy is on the list of men never to be admitted."

"I know, ma'am. But he . . . he frightened me. It was something about the funny shine his eyes have, and the way he said, 'You'd better let me in, if you know what's good for you.' I had a feeling that he is sort of . . . crazy, and that if I didn't let him in he might watch the house until he saw me leave it alone . . . Anyway, I figured you would know how to handle him."

Sara said, meaning it, "You're going a little soft, Solange. Maybe you're not up to this job anymore." Sweeping past the suddenly worried-looking mulatto, she moved down the hall and into her office.

A man seated in the straight chair in once-expensive but now worn-looking brown broadcloth, a tall hat clutched in his hand, got to his feet. Closing the door, Sara said, "Hello, Mountjoy."

He bowed. "Mrs. Davidson!" His gaunt, lined face broke into a smile. "And just as handsome as ever."

"Don't talk nonsense. You and I are about the same age,

and time hasn't been any kinder than usual to either of us." She studied him for a moment, and then laughed. "Although I must say that your white hair makes a striking effect. You look like a devil who somehow has acquired a halo." She sank into the chair beside her desk. "All right. You can sit down again. Now, what are you doing back in New Orleans? Years ago, I heard you'd gone to Georgia."

"I did, soon after my wife died. You knew she'd died, didn't you?"

"Yes. Did you have anything to do with that?"

He didn't seem to resent the question. "No. Her heart just gave out. Why should I want to kill her?"

"No reason, come to think of it." One way or another, Sara knew about all there was to know about the Mountjoys. She knew that the poor ninny of a widow he had married had turned over to him everything she owned. What was more, the drugs he kept feeding her had kept her from ever trying to get anything back, so why should he kill her?

"I'd heard of this plantation in Georgia, bigger than the one I had here, and quite cheaply priced. At first the plantation prospered, but then I began to run into bad luck—ruined harvests, runaway slaves, and incompetent overseers. Finally I salvaged enough so that I can live modestly, and came back here. I had missed New Orleans from the very start, anyway."

Was that really why he left Georgia? Homesickness? Or had his proclivities so outraged his Georgia neighbors that ultimately he had found it wise to flee the state?

She said, "You still haven't told me the reason for this visit."

"I just happened to pass by here. Suddenly I was reminded of the girl who came to work for you . . . oh, twenty years ago or a little more. You probably don't even remember her."

Sara Davidson smiled. "I remember her. Her name was Juana Moreno. You raped her, and tried to hold her prisoner at your plantation, but she gave you the slip and spent the next three years working for me. So sometime during those years you heard she was one of my girls. I figured you would. But I also knew you wouldn't be able to do anything about it."

His lined face flushed, and that shiny look which had frightened Solange came into his eyes. But when he spoke, his voice was mild enough. "Nobody goes up against you, Mrs. Davidson, not with all those judges and legislators you've got under your thumb. But as I said, I wondered today what had become of that little Spanish slut."

Sara was enjoying herself now. "Oh, she married one of my clients, a Philadelphia millionaire. I hear President Monroe has been their houseguest."

Astonishment in the seamed face under the incongruously saintly white hair, and then rage. He swore at Juana, using language as foul as any Sara had heard in her long career.

She laughed. "I was just teasing. But she did do rather well. Through one of her clients, she made an excellent investment, and then took the proceeds up to Belleville, a small upriver town, and settled down as a respectable citizen."

"She still lives there?"

"No. Some months ago one of our clients, a riverboat captain, happened to mention Belleville as one of the towns he sometimes stopped at. I asked him if he'd ever heard of a Mrs. Moreno who lived there, and he said he had, and that she was dead."

She saw satisfaction in Mountjoy's face, followed immediately by disappointment. She thought: He wishes she were still alive, so he could get at her.

In a way, she could understand his persistent desire for vengeance against Juana, because she shared it, although not to the extent that she would ever put herself out for the sake of getting even. Getting even seldom made you richer. But she too hated the thought of being bested by Juana. A soft, ignorant little foreigner, Juana nevertheless had managed to outwit a sly madman like Mountjoy and a hardheaded businesswoman like herself.

He said, "There was a child, a little girl."

"Yes, Amalia Moreno. I know what happened to her. It was in the New Orleans *Tattler*."

The *Tattler* was one of several sensational weeklies that reported gossip about the bordellos and hig-priced saloons, along with any other event odd enough to interest its readers.

"The story had a headline, 'Beautiful Brunette Marries Sea Captain by Proxy,' and then it told how a Miss Amalia Moreno of Belleville had been married by Judge Watson to a proxy bridegroom. I forget the proxy's name—Logan or Lipton or something like that—but I remember the name of the real bridegroom. He was Thomas Fulmer, and he lives in Sag Harbor."

"Where's that?"

She smiled. "One can tell you were never a sailor. Sag Harbor is in New York State, near the eastern end of Long Island."

He sat very still for a while. "Well, I just wondered what had become of that little tart Juana." He got to his feet. "Thank you, Mrs. Davidson. I'll leave now."

She said, not rising, "Don't come back, Mountjoy. I'm sure there are plenty of people in this town who remember you. I don't want people thinking that Sara Davidson now accepts customers who beat up girls."

"Don't worry," he said, opening the office door. "I won't be back."

# 27

A few days after Amalia's clash with Angus on the beach at Sagaponack, Lena came home from grocery shopping to announce, with satisfaction, "Well, that MacFarlane fellow won't be around Sag Harbor much. He's signed on as captain of the *J. J. Paxton.*"

The *Paxton* carried passengers and cargo from Sag Harbor to New York and back twice a week, stopping at small Long Island Sound ports along the way. Quite a comedown, Amalia realized, for a man who had once been owner and captain of oceangoing ships. It was strange that she did not find the thought as pleasing as Lena obviously did.

But at least his job would make it much less likely that she would encounter him on the beach, or at a party, or anywhere else. Between trips, the *Paxton* laid over only forty-eight hours in Sag Harbor.

During the rest of that month she tried harder than ever to keep him out of her thoughts. She read and reread letters from Tom, which continued to arrive. She attended social functions on afternoons and evenings when she knew the *Paxton* was moving slowly along the sound. And she devoted many hours a day to such tasks as sewing draperies, revarnishing the stair rail, and arranging and rearranging the furniture she had ordered through Hobart's.

On the next-to-last day in September, Lena told her that Hobart's no longer ordered carpeting from the Connecticut Carpet Company. "I'll go over to New London tomorrow and bring back some carpet samples so you can choose."

"I don't think you should plan to go anywhere tomorrow. I think we're in for some bad weather."

"Rain? Everybody says rain is just what we need."

"I mean a hurricane."

"Hurricane! Child, you're not in Louisiana now. Why, I

never heard anybody even mention that they have hurricanes up north."

"Just the same," Amalia insisted, "I think there's a hurricane coming. Can't you feel the heaviness in the air? And it's so muggy and still, just the way it was in Belleville the day before that hurricane that flattened three houses. You remember. I was eight then."

"Yes, I remember. But I also remember that even down in Louisiana we had plenty of hot, muggy days in September, without no hurricane afterward. No, don't argue. I'm going over to that carpet factory. First thing you know, your husband will be home, and us with no carpets except those moth-chewed old things that half-wit Toby brought down from the attic."

Before eight the next morning Lena set out for Long Wharf, despite all of Amalia's efforts to dissuade her. Worried, Amalia sat in the kitchen sipping a second cup of coffee. Perhaps they *didn't* have hurricanes up north. But surely something was about to happen. The sky was completely clouded over. Beneath that gray dome the air seemed to press down, so hot and heavy that she could scarcely breathe.

Around two that afternoon, as she sat in the parlor hemming a tea towel, a light rain began to fall. Gradually it increased in intensity. Then the wind came, strengthening until the cove's usually placid waters became a miniature sea of tossing whitecaps. The day darkened, so much so that she lit the lamp on the mantelpiece. When gust-driven rain began to rattle like flung pebbles against the windowpanes, she laid her sewing aside. If this wasn't a hurricane's first stages, she thought grimly, it was an excellent imitation.

One thing to be thankful for. The ferry across the sound must have reached the Connecticut shore more than two hours ago. And it would not even attempt a return through this storm. Inconvenienced but safe, Lena would just have to find a place to spend the night over there.

Carrying the lamp, Amalia went back to the kitchen. In a wooden chest there, she and Lena kept a supply of old rags to be used for cleaning. Now she would stuff them under doors and around window frames to soak up as much water as possible if, as she was sure would happen, the wind started driving rain through even the tiniest cracks. Although still slamming against the house in gusts, the wind by now had set up another sound, a continuous high-pitched howl.

She bundled the cloths in a ragged brown window drapery the property's former owners had left behind. Better to start at the top of the house, she decided, and work down. Carrying the lamp and the bundle, she climbed through that unnaturally dim light up to the second floor. At the hall's end she set down the lamp, reached up, and grasped a dangling rope. Pulling on it, she lowered the steep, narrow stairs that gave access to the attic. She picked up the lamp, climbed through the opening to the attic, and placed the lamp on an old trunk. As she stuffed cloths around the frame of one of the two windows, she could see the tormented writhing of the giant juniper trees that stood beside the wide brick walk thirty feet below.

Five hours later, with oil lamps burning now in every room, she was still battling to save the newly papered walls, the new furniture. Carrying a wooden bucket in each hand, she moved from floor to floor, room to room, wringing out the soaked cloths and stuffing them back around window frames. When the buckets were filled, she carried them down to the kitchen and emptied them into the zinc-lined wooden sink, and then carried them from room to room until they were full again. The repetition of her motions, and the way lamp flames flickered in the wind which, along with the rain, penetrated every crack, gave her a dreamlike sense of unreality. Outside the walls of the house the wind sometimes rose to a high, rasping scream, like the tearing of some vast silken sheet. Other times the noise was not much louder than that of wind-driven surf pounding on a beach. But the sound never really stopped, not for a second.

It was during one of those comparative lulls in the storm that she became aware of someone pounding on the front door. Not quite able to believe her ears—who would be out in a storm like this?—she stood motionless for a moment in the upstairs bedroom. Then she set down the bucket she had been about to empty and descended the stairs. It was fortunate, she realized, that the front door was in the lee of the storm. Otherwise to open it would be to risk having the wind tear it from its hinges. Even so, when she drew the bolt and pulled the door back, the wind-driven rain blasting into the hall half-blinded her. It was not until the man on the doorstep had come into the house and slammed the door shut that she was sure of his identity.

Angus turned and looked down at her through the dim light coming through the parlor doorway. Rain had plastered his red-gold hair to his skull, and his white shirt and dark trousers to his body.

He said, speaking loudly enough to be heard through the uproar outside, "Are you all right?"

His nearness had set the pulse in the hollow of her throat to pounding. She said in a cold tone, "Of course I'm all right. This is not the first hurricane I have experienced. Now, I had better get back to work. You . . . you can wait down here until the storm is over."

He ignored her last sentence. "What work?"

When she had explained, he said, "I'll help you."

"No, thank you," she said, and turned to climb the stairs. A second later she realized with a kind of panic that he was following her.

On the landing she turned to face him. "I said, no, thank you. Now, please go downstairs."

He ignored that. "Where's Lena?"

"She went to Connecticut this morning."

"She sure picked a day for it. Now, where are the buckets? In here?" He strode into the bedroom she had just left.

She followed. "Put those buckets down! Didn't you hear me? This is my house, and I am asking you to—"

"Don't be a fool. You look exhausted. Now, sit down in that chair. Sit down!"

He moved toward her. Afraid that he would seize her shoulders and force her down into the chair, she sat. He left the room, a rain-filled bucket in each hand.

Because of the wind, she seldom heard the sound of his movements during the next half-hour or so. But she knew he was there, walking from room to room, sometimes passing the doorway of the bedroom in which she sat. The storm had already scraped her nerves raw. Now his presence here in this isolated, storm-racked house made her want to rush at him and scream, "Get out! Get out!"

At last he came back into the room. He pulled a sodden cloth blocking the tiny crack beneath a window frame, squeezed the cloth into a bucket.

Quite suddenly, as if somewhere in the universe a hand

had turned a giant valve, the storm abated. The wind died. The rain dwindled to a light patter, then ceased entirely. They looked at each other through the silence. "The eye of the hurricane," he said, and she realized that as a sailor he must have been through many of these cyclical storms in many parts of the world. He walked past her to the window. After a moment he said, "Come here."

She hesitated, then got up and stood beside him. A rent in the clouds was widening rapidly. Through it a first-quarter moon shone serenely on the still-agitated waters of the cove.

She said in a constrained voice, "Thank you for what you've done. But I can manage now."

"What do you mean? The storm's not over. After the eye has passed, the wind and rain will strike again from the opposite direction."

"I know. But usually the wind is weaker than before. So please go, while you have the chance."

"I'm staying. The wind will still be strong enough to drive water into the house. And with its roots weakened by rain, one of those junipers on the north side could come crashing down onto the roof."

Her nerves snapped. "When someone asks you to leave her house, don't you know you're supposed to go?" When he didn't answer, but just looked down at her, she said, "It's obvious why Barbara Weyant jilted you. I'll wager she couldn't stand your bad manners."

Anger was kindling in his own face. "That's a wager you'd lose. If you must know, she broke the engagement because she found and read a journal I was damn fool enough to keep."

"A journal?"

"Yes! One I started soon after I came back from New Orleans more than two years ago. I wrote in it because there was no one I could talk to, and I felt I'd go crazy, keeping it all bottled up. And so I wrote down how I was afraid I would never forget you, how I still loved you, wanted you."

She had begun to tremble. His eyes, somber now, were looking deep into hers. Frantically she searched her mind for something, anything, that would make him turn on his heel and leave this house. She said, "Am I supposed to regard that as a compliment? Am I supposed to fall into your arms, now that there is no danger you will have to marry me? Is that why you came here today?"

His face reddened, then went pale. After a moment he said in a controlled, deliberate tone, "Do you want to hear about my last half-dozen hours or so? I was still about two miles from Sag Harbor when the storm struck. I had to bring the *Paxton* through all that hell, and then get my passengers ashore, and then secure the ship so that she wouldn't pound herself to pieces against Long Wharf. After that I went to see if my father and sister were all right. And then I walked a mile through hurricane winds and falling branches to find out what was happened to you. And now you accuse me of coming here to try to seduce the wife of my best friend."

He paused. "It's not that you're a slut, Amalia. It's just that sometimes you think like one."

Slut. The word was like a lighted taper flung into a pile of tinder, igniting all her old torment and hate and humiliation. She swung her open hand at his cheek. He caught her wrist. Wildly she lashed out with her other hand, but he blocked that blow too, big fingers fastening around her left wrist. Silently she fought him, kicking at his legs and trying to free her imprisoned hands. Swiftly he released her wrists and encircled her with his arms, imprisoning her own arms at her sides, and holding the length of her body close against him.

For a few moments she still struggled, glaring up at him through the dim lamplight. Then she stood still, arrested by the change in his face. The angry look was giving way to something quite different, a kind of brooding.

He said, "Amalia . . ." and then, "Oh, God, maybe you were right. Maybe I did come here hoping . . ."

He broke off. After a moment he said, "You're pale and you look tired and your hair's coming down and there's a smudge of lampblack on your cheek. And you look so beautiful I can't bear it."

He kissed her then, his firm mouth with its full underlip warm and demanding on her mouth. She felt the shock of that kiss through her whole body. Aware that resistance was draining from her, she felt her lips softening and yielding to his.

He raised his head. "Amalia?"

She did not answer in words. She realized helplessly, though, that he must be reading assent in her eyes, eyes that felt strangely heavy-lidded.

He raised his hands, took the pins from her hair, and let

the dark, silky mass fall around her shoulders. He said in a thick voice, "I wanted to see your hair like this from almost the moment I met you. That's why, on the beach that day, I yelled at you to put up your hair. I was afraid I might . . . But you understood that, didn't you?"

She whispered, "Yes."

His big hands were fumbling with the buttons of her bodice. He undid them, pushed the upper part of her dress almost down to her waist, slipped the wide straps of her chemise from her shoulders. His warm hands cupped her breasts with their already erect nipples. It was spreading all through her now, a kind of near-fainting languor. She thought: I must stop him, stop myself—and then knew stopping was impossible.

She heard him make an inarticulate sound that was almost a groan. Then he was lifting her, carrying her, lowering her to the bed. He bent over her. Eyes closed now, she felt him stripping the rest of her garments from her, stripping them beneath her hips and down her slender legs. Eyes still closed, she heard the sounds of his own undressing. Then he was lying beside her, warm lips closed around one of those erect nipples, left hand caressing her other breast. That languor had changed now into an avid need deep inside her. Vaguely she realized that, without her volition, her hips had begun to stir.

Her heavy eyelids lifted. She looked into the brooding, almost somber face close above her own. "Please," she said, not knowing quite what she meant, "please."

He kept her waiting for a few moments more, hand stroking her flat belly and her silky inner thighs, lips and tongue teasing her nipples, bringing her a sense of inward melting. She heard a soft moan, and realized it had been her own voice. Then she felt the long weight of his naked body, felt his legs thrusting her legs farther apart.

He entered her. Briefly, but only briefly, she felt pain. Then his steady thrusting brought her only increasing pleasure, a pleasure so sharp that it was almost another sort of pain. She arched her body upward against him, because the ever-growing hunger deep inside her had become a torment now, and she knew instinctively that only his body, only the thrust of him against the swelling, hungry core of her, could bring her release.

He was carrying her higher and higher. She was aware of her head tossing and turning on the pillow. Then, just when she felt she could bear the sweet torment no longer, surcease came. Ripples of satisfied desire swept down her body. Through that ecstatic shuddering she felt the throb of his own release.

For a moment, body still weighting hers, he lay quiet. Then he kissed her mouth. She opened her eyes, and saw by the dim lamplight that he was still smiling and that his eyes had a tender look. Then he was lying beside her, hand clasping hers. "Did I hurt you very much, my darling?"

"No."

"What is it, Amalia? What are you feeling?"

She did not answer, but just lay there, hand cold and unresponsive in his. Now that her treacherous body had taken its pleasure, she was left with the realization of what she had done. She had betrayed the fine man who had married her. Betrayed him with his own best friend. Betrayed him with Angus MacFarlane, who had broken her heart, and her mother's, and—she was convinced—even brought about her mother's far too early death.

He said, his voice flat now, "You're thinking of Tom, aren't you?"

Tom, whom they had cuckolded in the house and in the bed his money had paid for. "Yes."

"Don't think I don't feel bad about that aspect of it. I do. But now we must think of what's to be done." He was silent for several seconds and then said, "You could get an annulment. It shouldn't be too hard in the case of a marriage by proxy, one that has never been consummated."

"And then?"

It took him a while to answer. "You and I could be married."

Her bitterness flared. "What an enthusiastic proposal! Would you really marry the daughter of a woman who had been one of Sara Davidson's girls?"

Again he was silent. Then he said, "Amalia, listen to me. I still hate that aspect of it, just as much as I did when I first learned of it. I wish your mother had been someone else, almost anyone else."

He paused. Should she tell him, she wondered, of what Juana's doctor had said about her malignancy? No, she decided. It was hard enough to acknowledge even to herself that only moments ago she had lain, senseless and moaning with desire, in the arms of a man she held at least partially responsible for her mother's death.

"But tonight has changed everything," he went on. "What's more, even though I felt I had to . . . to put you out of my life two years ago, I still love you, Amalia. Probably I always will."

When she didn't answer he said, "Well, haven't you anything to say?"

"Yes." Her tone was biting. "What about your father? Are you suddenly willing to saddle him with grandchildren who will also be a harlot's grandchildren?"

"No, not *willing*. As I told you, I still hate that part of the situation. But my father doesn't know and never will know about Juana Moreno. Besides, we could postpone our marriage until after his death, which I am afraid is fairly near now."

"Postpone it?" Her tone challenged him. "Why?"

"Because just the annulment of your marriage to Tom and your remarriage to me would cause at least a temporary scandal among the straitlaced people in this town. I'd like to spare the old man that if I could. We can wait until after his death and then marry."

"We could," she said crisply, "but we won't. I will never marry you at any time or for any reason."

At last he said, "You still feel that bitter toward me?"

"That bitter."

He said, his voice heavy, "The hell of it is that I can understand how you would be unable to forgive me." After a moment he went on, "What will you do about Tom?"

"I don't know yet. But anyway, it doesn't concern you."

He raised himself on one elbow and looked down at her. "All right, Amalia. As I said, I can understand how you would be unable to forgive me. But you love me too. If you didn't, you wouldn't be lying here with me now."

She said, trying to meet his gaze steadily and defiantly, "That was only . . . only . . ."

"A physical response? But, Amalia, you're not a light woman, ready to desire one man as readily as another. If you didn't love me, your body would not have responded to mine. Can you deny that?"

Looking up into the handsome face close above her own, she knew despairingly that she could not deny it, not and mean it. She continued to look at him. Vaguely she was aware that returning rain splattered against the windows and the first gusts of returning wind were striking the house.

His smile was touched with irony. "We might as well acknowledge that we love each other, in spite of your well-justified antagonism. And since this may be the last time I'll have a chance to make love to you . . ."

He kissed her lips. One hand swept down her body to its glossy dark triangle and then upward to caress her breast. She began to feel it again, that inward melting, that growing urgency.

While the storm roared with renewed fury, his thrusting body, answering her need, carried her to the heights and then the long, delicious descent.

# 28

For the next few weeks Amalia scarcely stirred out of the house on those days when she knew that the *Paxton* was tied up at Long Wharf. But avoiding the sight of Angus did not keep her from thinking of him. Over and over again she relived their parting moments. With the storm outside rapidly abating, they had descended the stairs, he fully dressed, she in a dark green flannel robe. In the lower hall he had looked down at her, his face somber in the light from the lamp still burning in the parlor. "We belong together," he said. "It's such a rotten waste that we can't be." He kissed her then, and although he didn't say so, she knew that he as well as she felt it would be their last kiss. They had clung together for a moment more. Then he had gone out into the diminishing wind, the slackening rain.

The first few early-October days following the hurricane were cool and clear, with bright sun beating down on debris-strewn front lawns and on giant uprooted elms bordering Main Street. Then there were nearly three weeks of Indian summer, with sunny days, serene skies, and trees which had survived the storm flaming with red and orange and yellow leaves, so that riding in the woods was rather like moving through the sort of light cast by stained-glass cathedral windows. Inevitably, though, November arrived, bringing gray days, frequent rain, and northwest winds that rapidly stripped the dying leaves from the trees.

It was around mid-November that a new worry began to weight her spirit. Before she had allowed him to quite literally sweep her off her feet, why hadn't she thought of the possibility that she might become pregnant? But she mustn't be, she mustn't be. She had known that it would be hard enough for her, no longer virgin, to face the man she had married. But if she was also carrying Angus' child . . .

Lena, who had not been able to get back to Long Island until a day and a half after the hurricane had passed, watched her with worried-looking eyes. Finally she asked, "Child, what's bothering you?"

"Nothing."

"Now, don't try to tell me that. You're worried about how you're going to feel when you finally face your husband. You're afraid you'll never be able to love him. But you will, honey, a fine man like that—"

"Lena! Will you please just stop talking? And stop looking at me like that. I'm fine. I'm not worried about anything."

Looking hurt now as well as concerned, Lena said, "All right, child. I won't ask you. But you can't fool me. I always know when you've got something on your mind."

Rainy November gave way to a December that was drier and even a little warmer. But the sun—each day traveling an arc a little farther south, each day setting a few minutes earlier—reminded her that Tom's ship must be coming closer and closer. Near the end of the first week in December she realized that no letters from him had arrived during the last ten days. That must mean he felt sure that he would reach her before his letters did. She continued to read his old letters over and over. And at night, in the bedroom she had prepared for Tom and herself—a room at the other end of the hall from where she had lain in Angus' arms—she knelt and prayed. She prayed for forgiveness, and wisdom, and strength to meet whatever the future held.

In mid-December Matthew MacFarlane died. Knowing that it would cause talk if she stayed away from the funeral of the man who had fathered her husband's best friend, Amalia was one of those who sat in the filled-to-capacity church that day. After the ceremony Angus and Ruth, her eyes swollen with weeping, stood at the church door shaking the hands of the congregation. When it was Amalia's turn she felt a kind of shock as her hand touched Angus'. For a second or two they stood looking into each other's eyes. Something that looked like alarm mingled with the controlled grief in his eyes. Afraid to risk more time in his presence, she did not attend the graveside rites in the Old Burying Ground, but went straight home.

That night a new moon hung in the western sky, shedding faint radiance on the winter-bare earth and the calm waters of the cove. Feeling tired and yet too keyed-up to go to bed, Amalia went out onto the porch. A warm shawl around her, she looked at Venus which, about to set now, cast almost as much light as the crescent moon.

Someone coming down the road, tall and wide-shouldered. He stopped at the gate, lifted the latch. Swiftly she descended the steps and went down the walk to meet him.

She said in a taut voice, "What are you doing here?"

"I had to come. That look on your face in church today. What is it? What's happened?"

She stood motionless. Tell him? She might as well. Very soon he and everyone else would know.

"Amalia, let's go in the house and talk. I have to know—"

"Not in the house. Lena is probably still awake, and might hear us. Let's walk."

They moved silently across the dead brown lawn toward the boxwood hedge on the property's northern border. They had almost reached it when he said, "Amalia, for God's sake . . ."

Best to say it swiftly. "I'm going to have a child."

She heard his sharp intake of breath. He stopped short and, hands on her shoulders, turned her to face him. "Are you sure?"

"Yes. These past few days I've become quite sure."

He said after a long moment, "That settles it. You'll have to get an annulment, or divorce, or whatever else is required. And then we'll get married."

Even now, in her anxiety and guilt, she was aware of her old and bitter grievance. "My child will be Juana Moreno's grandchild. Or doesn't that matter, now that your father . . ." She broke off, ashamed of herself.

"My father's death is not the reason," he said quietly. "And perhaps I'd better remind you that the night of the storm I suggested that we marry as soon as my father was no longer here to be upset. You rejected the idea, and I accepted your rejection. But everything has changed now. That is my child you are carrying."

She said after a moment, "I'm sorry for mentioning your father like that."

"It's all right. Under the circumstances, I can understand how you might say almost anything. But we must discuss the future now—"

"Angus, it's up to Tom to decide my future."

"Tom! What do you—?"

"I owe him that. We both do. Tom's the one to be considered first, because we're the sinners, and he's the one sinned against. If he wants to end our marriage—and I suppose he will—I'll make no protest. If by any chance he wants me to remain his wife, then I will do that."

After a moment he said, his voice harshly incredulous, "How can you say that? Are you forgetting the child? It's my child, not Tom Fulmer's!"

"Don't talk like a fool. How could I possibly forget my child, even for a moment?" She paused and then said more quietly, "If Tom wants me to stay with him, and wants to raise the child as his own, he will have that right." Again she paused. "I think you'd have to agree that Tom might possibly be a better father than you would."

After a moment he gave a laugh that held no mirth whatsoever. "I guess almost anyone would say you are right. But what if even Tom isn't generous enough to want to raise another man's child? What then?"

She looked up at him for a long, silent moment. At last she said, "I don't know. I only know I have to tell Tom before I decide anything. I'd better go in now. I'm cold."

They started back toward the house. After a while she said, "Until I have told Tom the truth, I don't think we should be alone together again."

"I suppose not. But you'll let me know as soon as you and Tom have come to a decision?"

"Yes."

They had reached the walk which led to the front porch. She halted and said, "Good night."

He did not answer immediately. For a frightened moment she thought he was going to reach out and draw her into his arms. But he did not. "Good night," he said finally, and turned and strode toward the gate.

# 29

Tom Fuller did not get home in time for Christmas after all. It was not until the afternoon of December 28, a cold, brilliantly sunny afternoon, that Amalia stood amid the crowd on Long Wharf and saw her husband smile down at her from the *White Falcon*'s quarterdeck. Heart bleak with the knowledge of what she must tell him, she stretched her lips in an answering smile. Vaguely she was aware of the bustle attendant upon any ship's arrival. On the main deck a uniformed first mate bawled orders. Seamen tossed hempen lines overboard, and dockworkers wound them around bollards on the wharf.

Stomach tightening into a knot, she watched Tom descend a ladder and then disappear inside the afterhouse. He emerged carrying a portmanteau and walked swiftly to the gangplank. Halfway down it he stopped short for a moment. His smile vanished. She knew then that already her expression had told him that something was very wrong.

But people on the wharf, friends he had known all his life, were calling out to him. With an effort that was perceptible to Amalia, he straightened his shoulders, smiled, and called out answers to their greetings.

When he reached the foot of the gangplank he stood face to face with Amalia for a silent second or two. She had forgotten just how pleasant his face was, the thin features clean-cut, the gray eyes clear and steady, the mouth sensitive. Finally she managed to say, "Welcome home, Tom." Then, swiftly: "There's a horse and gig waiting at the foot of Long Wharf."

"Fine." He took her arm, and they began to walk over the wooden planks. Plainly he too wanted to escape from all these friendly but curious faces. "Did you order the gig from the livery stable?" His tone was that of someone making polite conversation.

Her tone was equally stilted. "No. Howard Lipson did. He drove out to my—our—house in it and brought me here. He's sorry he couldn't be on hand to greet you. He had an appointment to draw up a will for someone in East Hampton."

"Then Howard has been helpful to you?"

"Oh, yes. So has your brother. I don't know why he didn't come to Long Wharf. Maybe he . . ." She broke off.

"Didn't want to intrude? Yes, I imagine that was it. Hello, Charles. Hello, Martha," he said to a stout, beaming couple who passed. Then: "Is this the gig?"

Once they were in the vehicle, with the reins in his hands, Tom's face lost that rigid smile. In silence they drove past the grog shops of lower Main Street and through the business district. Then, as they rode past the stately houses on upper Main Street, Tom said, "There's something dreadfully wrong, isn't there, my dearest?"

She thought: Oh, if only he wouldn't call me that! Aloud she said, "Yes. But please, Tom! Don't ask me to talk until we get to the house."

After a moment he asked, "Is Lena there?"

She nodded. "But you won't have to see her right away."

"You mean she'll keep out of sight? Why? Because she knows what you have to tell me?"

"Yes."

Three mornings before, Lena had cooked poached eggs for both herself and Amalia. Battling nausea, Amalia had sat at the kitchen table sipping coffee. At last Lena looked from the untouched plate to Amalia's face and said, "All right. Tell me the truth. You're in the family way, aren't you?"

Amalia did not answer. Lena persisted, "When did it happen? While I had to stay over in New London because of the hurricane? Yes, that's when it must have been."

Still Amalia was silent. Lena said, "And of course it was that MacFarlane devil."

"Don't call him that! It's not as if he forced me!"

"Then you just tell me how it was," Lena said levelly.

Amalia told her. "You see, it was my fault too," she finished dully. "I was stupid, stupid."

"I'll give you no argument about that! But the thing is,

what are you going to say to that good, good man who married you and had you brought away from that little town where you'd just have gotten older and lonelier every year? How are you going to tell him?"

"I don't know."

Now, three days later, she still did not know how she could bring herself to tell him.

When they reached the house on John Street, he did not drive back to the barn. "Might as well leave it out front," he said in that constrained voice. "I'll have to go back to the ship for a while this afternoon anyway." He got out, tethered the horse to the hitching post, and then, taking Amalia's ice-cold hand in his, helped her to alight.

As they went up the walk toward the porch, he said in that strained voice, "You've done wonders with the house. I like the shutters and the window boxes. This place looked pretty forlorn the last time I saw it."

She murmured an acknowledgment.

But when they went through the unlocked front door and into the parlor, he said nothing about the fine new turkey-red carpet, or the brown Empire sofa and matching Empire armchairs which flanked the fireplace. A newly laid fire flamed on the hearth. She realized that Lena must have lighted it when she saw the approaching gig, and then hurried back to her room off the kitchen.

He said, "I suppose we might as well sit down." His face was pale beneath its sun-bronzed surface. When they were seated facing each other beside the snapping fire, he said, "Now, tell me."

She realized that there was no way to tell it except straight out. "Tom, about six months from now I am going to have a child."

His face turned even whiter. But when he spoke, his voice was quite steady. "Is the child Angus MacFarlane's?"

"How did you—?"

"Letters I received from Richard and from Howard Lipson mentioned that he'd come back from Boston, jobless and with his engagement broken. When I learned that, I had a terrible premonition, but I tried to erase it from my mind." He paused. "Tell me all of it."

She told him. The hurricane. Angus' unexpected arrival.

The flare of hostility between them which had turned into a physical struggle, and then to something else.

At last she cried, "Oh, Tom! Don't look like that!"

He gave a smile that left his eyes as pain-filled as before. "How do you want me to look?"

"I'd rather you showed me you hated me, because of course you must."

"I suppose so, at least a little. And I suppose that at the moment I hate Angus enough to want to kill him. But you two aren't entirely to blame, especially you. You're still so young, Amalia. Fourteen years younger than I am. Even though I knew you didn't love me and that you might still be in love with Angus, I asked you to marry me and come here."

He added in a pain-filled voice, "But it might have worked. If my trip had not been such a long one, or if Angus had married that Boston girl . . ."

He had been looking at the fire. Now he looked at her. "What do you want? An annulment, so that you can marry Angus?"

She shook her head. "No. I've thought and I've thought, and the answer to that is still no. Oh, if it seems to me that that is the best thing to do for the child's sake, I'll marry him. But I don't want to."

Something like hope leaped into Tom's eyes. "Why not? Aren't you still in love with him?"

"Yes. But I've never forgiven him, Tom. I doubt that I ever could. And I would always be wary of him, afraid that he would hurt me again."

He leaned forward. "Then go on being my wife, Amalia! We can rest assured Angus will never tell what happened between you and him."

She said unevenly, "Then you still want me?"

"My dearest, don't you understand? I love you. This is far from the homecoming I expected, but that doesn't change my wanting you to remain my wife."

He paused for a moment and then went on. "What's more, I want the child, because it will be your child. We'll need to take no one into our confidence except our neighbor down the road, Doc Marsden. He's a cousin of mine, you know, or maybe you didn't know. Anyway, he'll have no hesitancy in saying the child is premature."

Tears spilled down her cheeks. "Tom, you're the most wonderful, the most generous . . ."

He laughed softly. "Generosity has nothing to do with it. I love you, and I want to hold on to you any way I can. Can't you get that through your beautiful head?"

He stood up, took her two hands in his, and drew her to her feet. His arms went around her, and he kissed her tear-wet cheeks and then her lips, warmly, tenderly. She thought: I have been married since last May, and this is the first time my husband has kissed me.

He said, "I must go back to the ship now, darling, and then talk to Richard. But I'll be home in plenty of time that we can look over the whole house before supper."

About seven hours later Tom lay beside her in the bedroom she had furnished for the two of them. Hands clasped beneath his head, he stared at the invisible ceiling and said, "I am sorry, my darling. I could tell that it was . . . not right for you."

Only minutes ago their bodies, linked together, had been as close as human bodies can become. He had been the most gentle and considerate of lovers. And yet she had felt no stir of response. She had lain there inert, wishing only that his lovemaking would soon be over.

She said, "Tom! Oh, Tom! It will be all right, in time. It is just that we scarcely know each other."

He said quickly, "I know it will be all right . . . in time. Once the baby is born, everything between you and me will be different."

"Yes, Tom. Of course it will."

He lay silent for perhaps two minutes. Then he said, "I'll be here ten more days, but perhaps from now on I'd better sleep in the bedroom across the hall."

"Oh, Tom! You don't have to . . ."

"I know I don't have to. You would accept my lovemaking every one of those ten nights. But the results might be that we would form a . . . a pattern in which I would be the one who desired, and you would be the dutiful wife. I don't want that, my dearest. And so I'm willing to wait."

"Wait?"

"Until after the baby is born. I'll be back here by then.

The *Falcon*'s next trip is a short one, just to England and back."

He took one hand from beneath his head and turned to face her. Enough light from a near-setting half-moon came through the window to show his smile and the faint shine of his gray eyes. Cupping her face with one hand, he leaned over her and kissed her. "Good night, my dearest."

He lay down down then and turned away from her.

# 30

To an outside observer it would have seemed that Tom's first week at home passed smoothly and pleasantly. He bought a gig to replace the rented one, and a bay horse named Buttons, younger and leaner than Molly, but almost as tractable. He taught both Amalia and Lena to drive. ("It won't be safe much longer for you to ride, Amalia, and so you'd better learn how to get around in the gig after I've gone back to sea.") Each day he spent several hours handling ship's business and conferring with his brother about their jointly owned boatyard.

Three times during that week he and Amalia had their evening meal out, once with a large party at the Hannibal Allerdyces', once with Richard in the tall, rather gloomy house in which he and Tom had grown up, and once with their neighbor, Tom's cousin Seth Marsden. A blond, stout widower, Dr. Marsden resembled Tom not at all. Although of course nothing was said about it at the supper table, Amalia sensed that Tom had told his cousin about the child, and that Dr. Marsden had agreed to pronounce the birth a premature one.

The remaining evenings they had supper at home, talking pleasantly, except for an occasional brief, awkward pause, about Tom's last voyage and about their plans for further improving their house.

Amalia felt sure that only they—and probably Lena, although she did not mention it—realized that Amalia slept in one room and Tom in another across the hall.

Some nights, though, Amalia did not sleep very much. She lay there wondering if he too was awake, and if so, what thoughts were going through his head. Was he as self-controlled and quietly optimistic as he appeared to be during the daylight hours? Or did he at night give rein to dark thoughts about the future, a future in which he would live with a child who was not his, and with a wife who might not ever be able to love him as he loved her, with his body as well as his heart?

One gray, raw afternoon when Tom was away at the boatyard, Lena came home from the general store looking grim. "Angus MacFarlane followed me into Hobart's. He wants you to meet him on the beach at Sagaponack at three o'clock."

Amalia looked at her silently, surprised that she should have agreed to relay such a message. Lena answered her unspoken question. "He said that if you didn't meet him, he'd come here. I didn't want the mister to come home and find that fellow here." As if to emphasize that this was Tom's house and that Amalia was Tom's wife, she had taken to calling him "the mister."

"All right, I'll meet him."

"And what are you going to tell him?"

"I think you know, Lena."

"That he's to stay away from you from now on? That you're Mrs. Tom Fulmer, no matter what?"

"Yes."

Lena's voice was grim. "Just see that you stick to that, my girl."

Amalia saddled Molly. She rode briefly along the turnpike and then left the road for the woods. Only the pines and cedars and mountain-laurel bushes were green. Some oak trees retained their leaves—dead brown leaves, rattling in the wind—but all the other deciduous trees were bare.

A black horse with two white stockings stood tied to the hitching post near the path leading down between the dunes to the beach. She rode past it and down onto the sand. Angus was there, face somber, red-gold head bare to the winter wind. Beyond him were a few yards of driftwood-strewn beach, and then the sullen gray ocean stretching to meet the gray sky.

He helped her to alight, fastened Molly's reins to the half-buried tree root, and then turned around. "As soon as possible after Tom came home, you were going to tell me what you had decided to do. He's been home a week now."

"I thought you'd realize what I'd decided."

"Maybe I have. But that isn't why you didn't tell me yourself. It was because you were afraid to see me. Wasn't it?"

She ignored that. "Very well. I'll tell you now. I am going to stay married to Tom. As far as other people will know, my child will be Tom's child, born prematurely. You see, Angus, we both feel that you would never contradict that."

"You're right," he said bitterly. "I never would. Just the same, you're a fool, Amalia. You're going to regret this decision the rest of your life."

"Angus, I told you the last time we talked that if Tom was generous enough to forgive me and still want me, I'd stay with him. I hope I'll never give him reason to regret it. And I certainly can't see how *I* should ever have reason to regret it. I'll be married to a fine man who loves me, and who will be the best possible father to my child."

"There's only one thing wrong with that idyllic picture. You don't love him."

She looked at Angus, wanting desperately to get away from him. In another moment she would start remembering things she did not want to remember, most especially the night of the hurricane, and his long body covering hers. She said swiftly, "You'll get over this. It's mainly your vanity which is hurt."

"I wish you were right," he said. "Oh, how I wish you were right. But if more than two years, and an engagement to another girl, didn't enable me to get over you . . ."

He broke off, and then said in a flat voice, "You look as if you're cold and want to leave. Shall I lift you into the saddle?"

"No! I mean, thank you, but I can manage."

Without a word, he turned and walked up the sloping beach and through the gap in the dunes. She waited until he'd had time enough to ride off. Then she led Molly to the log which served as a mounting block.

On her way back through the woods, she urged fat, lazy Molly into a trot. She was eager to get home and to help Lena prepare an especially good supper for Tom. In her present mood—tenderness for Tom, and fear of what she felt for Angus—she almost wished that Tom would share her bed tonight. But no. Better that they wait, wait until she could desire him as he must have hoped she would desire him when he sent that letter to Belleville.

Two nights later the sound of a pistol shot jerked her up through layers of troubled sleep.

At first she did not know it was a shot. She only knew that downstairs someplace there had been a loud, explosive noise. For a second or two she lay rigid. There was a full moon, and its blue-white radiance flooding through a window made parts of the room almost as bright as day.

She swung out of bed. The room was cold, cold. Heart hammering, she thrust her feet into slippers, caught up her robe from a chair back. The part of the room that held her bedside stand and its lamp was in shadow. She groped for the flintbox on the stand, couldn't find it. No matter. She could hear Lena's familiar footsteps now, moving along the lower hall from the kitchen to the parlor.

Amalia went out in the upper hall. She saw, by lamplight coming dimly up the stairwell, that Tom's bedroom door stood open. Sick with fear now, she moved to the head of the stairs. "Tom? Lena?"

Lena's voice called, "Don't come down here, child!"

Unheeding, Amalia hurried down the stairs. Lena stood in the parlor doorway. Upward-striking light from the lamp in her hand gave her scarred face an unfamiliar look. "Your husband's been shot. But don't you look at him, child. Go upstairs while I run and fetch Dr. Marsden."

Amalia brushed past her into the parlor. Lena turned, then, so that light from the lamp she held fell directly on the man on the floor. He lay on his back, his eyes open and empty-looking, the entire front of his gray dressing gown soaked with red. Amalia knew in that first terrible instant why Lena had told her to go back upstairs. There was nothing she or anyone could do for Tom. Even before she knelt beside him and placed fingers on his wrist, she knew she would find no pulse.

Numb with grief and shock, she knelt there for a moment. Then, with a vague, illogical notion of protecting him from the icy air pouring into the room, she got up and moved toward the open window. "Don't touch that!" Lena said. "Better that the constable sees how he got in."

Amalia's numb lips moved. "He?"

"The one who shot him."

Amalia looked down at her feet. There it lay on the turkey-red carpet, the pistol Richard Fulmer had insisted she buy. She recognized it by the silver oval set into its handle.

She saw then that she had at least one thing to thank God

for. The gun lay more than ten feet from Tom's outflung hand, much too far for him to have fired the shot himself. And so no matter how bleak his thoughts had been as he lay alone at night in that room upstairs, they had not driven him to taking his own life.

Lena said, "I'd best put on my shawl and fetch the doctor."

For the first time, Amalia noticed that the other woman was fully dressed. "I was setting buns to rise for tomorrow's breakfast," she said.

She placed her lamp on a table and lit the one on the parlor mantel. Then, carrying her own lamp, she hurried away. Moments later, huddled beside Tom's body, Amalia heard Lena go out the back door and then hurry along the brick walk that led around the porch to the front walk.

Hands clasping his lifeless one, Amalia closed her eyes. She felt grief not only for Tom but also for what they might have had together.

Or would she ever have been able to make Tom as happy as he deserved to be?

That was something that now she would never know.

# 31

Two afternoons later, almost the whole village attended the inquest into Tom's death. At least that was how it seemed to Amalia. As she sat at the witness table, placed at right angles to the long jurymen's table, she was aware that all the spectators' benches in this upstairs meeting hall were filled, and that standees lined the walls.

The coroner, a rotund man who ran a sailwright's loft near Long Wharf, questioned her briefly and gently about what she had heard and seen and done that night. She realized that they had brought her to the witness table first to spare her the ordeal of waiting.

"And you say the window had been opened?"

"Yes. It was wide open."

As she spoke, she felt a sharpened awareness of a few of the people in the room. Richard Fulmer, grimly tight-lipped. The handyman, burly Sam Thorpe, and his moon-faced "simple" nephew, Toby. Lena, in the fur-trimmed black bonnet she almost never wore. Ruth MacFarlane, subdued-looking today, as if a little awed by the judicial atmosphere. And next to her, Angus, red-gold hair bright in the January sunlight coming through the windows.

All those rows and rows of people out there. And a murderer among them?

No, she told herself sharply. It must have been some stranger. No one who knew Tom Fulmer would have had any reason to kill him.

The coroner was asking, "You left the window open?"

"Yes. I started to close it because I couldn't bear to have him lying there with all that cold air pouring . . ." She broke off and then said, "But Lena—Miss White—said it was best to leave the window as it was."

He nodded. "Now, do you have any idea, Mrs. Fulmer, about who could have had reason to kill your husband?"

She said with an effort, "No, no one except a prowler. He probably tried the front door, and found it locked, and then opened that window. My husband must have heard him and come downstairs . . ." Again she broke off.

"We won't keep you any longer, Mrs. Fulmer." As she left the witness table, she heard him call, "Miss Lena White, will you come up here, please?"

Lena corroborated Amalia's account of that night. After that, Dr. Seth Marsden testified as to the cause of death—a pistol ball through the heart—and that Tom must have died almost instantly. After that the coroner summoned a frightened-looking Toby to the stand.

"Toby, were you down at the cove the night Mr. Fulmer was killed?"

Toby's eyes rolled like those of a frightened horse. "I wouldn't hurt Mr. Tom. He's always been good to me."

"Now, son," the coroner said, although Toby, at past thirty, could not have been more than a half-dozen years his junior. "We know you wouldn't hurt anybody. But we also know that on the nights of full moon you like to take walks down by the cove. You walk all over the village, in fact." When Toby, still obviously frightened, did not answer, the coroner said, "Lots of people like to walk in the moonlight. It's nice to do that, isn't it?"

Toby grinned then, and nodded vigorously. "Sure is!"

"And when you were down there near the Fulmers' house that night, did you see anyone?"

"No!" Fear was coming back into his round face. "And I didn't do anything bad!"

The coroner sighed. "No one has accused you of anything. You can go now." Moving very fast for such a big man, Toby scuttled back to sit beside his uncle.

The coroner said, "Well, that's the only witness I have to call. And so unless someone else has something to say about this case, I'll ask the jury to retire and decide upon their verdict."

One of the jurymen, a thin man who clerked at Hobart's, said, "If you ask me, it's an open-and-shut case. Some stranger off a ship, either a thief or just plain drunk, crawled in that window, and Mr. Fulmer heard him—"

"Dave!" the coroner said sharply. "You're supposed to discuss that with the other jurors, and then bring back your verdict."

The jury filed out through a door into a room which served as a pantry whenever covered-dish suppers were held at the meeting hall. Within ten minutes they returned. Their verdict was that Tom Fulmer had been murdered by a person or persons unknown.

With Amalia holding the reins, she and Lena drove home, past lawns lightly covered by yesterday's snow, past trees whose ice-encased twigs gave back the winter sunlight in rainbow colors, like so many prisms.

For Tom's funeral two days later, the church was even fuller than it had been for old Matthew MacFarlane's services. Amalia realized that perhaps a few had attended out of a morbid interest in Tom's violent and unexplained death. But most of them, she knew, were there because they had loved and honored him.

Tom's brother, Richard, had escorted her to the funeral in a surrey he had hired for the occasion. In the church he sat beside her, his dark, thin face even more serious than usual. Throughout the service, even though she did not look at him, she was aware of Angus MacFarlane across the aisle, seated beside his young sister.

Angus was not among the forty-odd people who, on foot, followed the casket from the church to the nearby Old Burying Ground. Amalia was glad. She did not want the distraction of his presence during these last minutes before the earth closed over the fine man who had loved her and whom, in a way, she had come to love. Head bowed, she stood there in the bright chill, listening to the minister read the last rites. Someone handed her a small shovel. She sent the first half-frozen chunks of earth rattling down on the coffin. Then she turned away. With Richard, she rode back to the John Street house, where Lena was preparing tea and sandwiches for fifty people.

They were only a hundred yards or so from the house when Richard said, "I hate to discuss business details at a time like this. But if it is all right with you, I can have the *Falcon* ready to put to sea again next Thursday, only five days later than she was scheduled to sail. The present chief mate has master's papers, so he can be in command, if that is all right with you."

"Of course it is. There's no question but what Tom would have wanted you to continue to manage such matters."

Because he had been Tom's closest friend, Angus had been invited to the Fulmer house that day, but soon she realized, again with relief, that he was not coming. As she moved among the guests, pale and beautiful in the same black dress she had worn after her mother's death, she was aware that these people regarded her not only with sympathy but also with a speculative curiosity. What would she do now, this well-off young widow in their midst? Amalia thought of how much more avid their curiosity would be if they knew that she carried a child, a child conceived more than two months before Tom's return to Sag Harbor.

The last of the guests left, the sound of their carriage wheels dwindling away down the road. Amalia and Lena had no inclination to prepare supper, nor the appetite to eat it. In the house which seemed more silent than it ever had before, they sat beside the parlor fire, teacups in their hands.

On an afternoon two weeks later, when a late-January thaw had set icicles to dripping from eaves up and down Main Street, Howard Lipson in his upstairs office read aloud Tom's last will and testament. Amalia was there, and Richard Fulmer. So was Lena, because, surprisingly, Howard had told them that she was named in the will.

The document was dated January 2, a few days after Tom had returned on the *Falcon*. It provided for the payment of ten thousand dollars in cash to "my brother, Richard Fulmer." Lena White, "my wife's longtime companion and friend," was left five hundred dollars. Everything else, including his half-interest in the Fulmer Boatyard and his full interest in the merchant ships *White Falcon* and *Goodspeed*, "with all assets pertaining thereto," was left to "my beloved wife, Amalia Moreno Fulmer."

There was a codicil: "It is my wish that for five years after my death my brother, Richard Fulmer, shall be not only the executor of my estate but also the business manager of the *White Falcon* and the *Goodspeed*, at a yearly salary of two thousand dollars plus five percent of the net profits. At the end of five years, my wife may dispense with his services or retain them, as she chooses. I make this provision because I feel that should I die in the near future, my wife will be too young to bear the burden of administering her financial affairs."

Afterward, as she and Amalia drove home in the gig Tom had bought, Lena said softly, "I know that he left me that money only because he loved you so much, but I thank him for it, I surely do."

Lena turned silent and moody that evening, and remained that way for several days. Finally at breakfast one gray morning she burst out, "So you are going to do nothing about him!"

Amalia set down her coffee cup. "Who on earth are you talking about?"

"That MacFarlane, that's who!"

Amalia felt an unpleasant tightening of her nerves. "What about him?"

"He murdered your husband! And you know it!"

"Lena! I know no such thing." When the brown-skinned woman just looked at her with sullen eyes, Amalia said, "And you don't really believe such a fantastic . . . I mean, if you did, you would have spoken up at the inquest."

"You know why I didn't speak up! I couldn't tell them he had a reason for doing it, because that would have meant saying the reason was you!"

Amalia's voice shook. "Lena, that's . . . that's nonsense."

"Is it? He wanted you, but as long as your husband was alive, he couldn't have you. You made him realize that." She paused. "At least you *said* you were going to tell him you'd decided to stay with your husband."

"Of course I told him that!"

"But now that MacFarlane fellow is better off than he'd've been if you'd decided to ask your husband to let you go. Your husband's out of the way permanently, and you're a rich widow. That must suit Mr. MacFarlane just fine, seeing how hard up he is, so hard up he's taken that little bitty old job carrying people and furniture and chickens and what-not between here and New York."

Amalia leaped to her feet. "I won't listen to this another moment!"

"Yes you will, because you know it's for your own good! Now, sit down. Hear me out."

Amalia sat down. "All right, but only because I had best

show you how absurd you are! That New York boat has been in and out of Sag Harbor several times since Tom's death, but Angus MacFarlane hasn't come near me or even written to me. And yet you claim that he . . . he shot Tom not only to get me, but to get Tom's money—"

"He's biding his time, child. It wouldn't do to draw attention to himself, courting you so soon after your husband's death. Unless he sees some other man is after you, he'll wait, maybe until after the baby is born."

"Lena, if you spread this wild story around . . ." Amalia's whole body was shaking now.

"Honey, you know me better than that. You think I'd spread a story that would have people calling you a bad woman, and your helpless little baby a bastard?"

Amalia tried to make her voice cool and scornful. "Then may I ask what you hoped to accomplish by telling me about this fantastic theory of yours?"

"Child, I just want you to let him know you know. He'll leave you alone after that, you can bet."

"But I don't 'know,' as you put it!"

"You've at least suspected, haven't you?" When Amalia didn't answer, Lena said gently, "Remember, honey, I knew you before you could crawl. You can't hide from me what you're thinking and feeling."

She paused, and then added, "I won't say any more about it right now." Knowing that she had planted the seed, she got up and poured Amalia and herself a second cup of coffee.

For more than a week Amalia tried to put Lena's words out of her mind, but could not. Twice in dreams she confronted Angus with the accusation. In the first dream he said, "You're wrong, dearest. How could I have killed my best friend?" His face was so gentle and convincing that she awoke with grateful tears on her face. She awoke from the second dream too, but in quite a different fashion. Face hard and mocking, the Angus of that dream said, "Of course I killed him, but no one will ever prove it. And it was what you wanted. You know it was. You wanted him out of the way so that we could have each other." He reached out for her, and she awoke with a strangled scream of shame and horror.

Lying there in the semidarkness of early morning, with wind whining around the corner of the house, she realized what she must do. She must confront him with Lena's suspicion of him, just as gently and tactfully as she could. "I know it is absurd," she would say, "but just the same I would like to hear *you* say it is, so that I can tell her." Surely, Amalia thought, his reaction then would put her own mind at ease.

And if it did not? If instead she saw a leap of anger and guilty fear in those intense blue eyes? But no. She would not even think of that possibility, not until and unless she had to.

This was Thursday. The *Paxton*, having tied up at Long Wharf the night before, would not sail until Friday. She knew that she probably would find Angus on the beach at Sagaponack. Even though, as she had pointed out to Lena, Angus had not called upon her or written to her since Tom's death, her instincts told her that he must be going to Sagaponack whenever possible, on the chance of finding her there.

She waited until afternoon, and then saddled Molly, realizing as she did so that this was about the last time she should risk riding horseback. The northeast wind had been increasing all day. Now it rattled the siding of the old barn and whistled through the cracks.

Because she wanted to set as few people as possible to wondering why she should be out on this gray and windy day, she took the route through the woods rather than along the turnpike. She was sheltered from the wind among the trees, even though it made a sound like that of a rushing river through the top branches. When she emerged from the woods, though, the wind struck her with full force. With a red woolen scarf swathing not only her head but also the lower part of her face, she rode across fields where winter wheat tossed like a green sea. As she neared the break in the dunes lining the beach, she saw, with a leap of her heart, that the black horse stood there riderless.

She rode down onto the beach, vaguely aware that the usually quiet rollers were huge today, and broke with the sound of cannon shot before hurtling toward shore. She turned to her left. There, seated in the shelter between two tall dunes, was Angus. He wore the sort of long heavy coat ship's officers wore on the quarterdeck in bad weather, and a knitted black cap covered his bright hair.

Swiftly he got to his feet. He tied the mare's reins to one

of those fanged roots and then reached up to lift Amalia to the sand.

"I knew you'd come," he said. "I knew that if I kept coming here whenever I could, sooner or later . . ." He broke off. "What is it? What's wrong?"

Standing there only a few inches from him, and with her body still tingling from the touch of his hands as he helped her to alight, she found that she had forgotten all those tactful approaches she had rehearsed. Unable to wait another moment for his answer, she burst out, "Did you kill Tom?"

For a moment his face was blank. Then slowly those blue eyes seemed to freeze. "You can actually ask me that? Ask me if I killed my best friend and then slunk away?"

Her stomach knotted, not just with shame, but with a kind of fear of this man with the coldly blazing eyes.

"And why, in your view, did I kill an unarmed man I'd been fond of since we were boys? Because I felt that was the only way of getting you?"

She wanted to say, "It was Lena who put the idea into my head." But that would not only have sounded cowardly. It would not have been entirely true. Even before Lena had spoken, the thought had crossed Amalia's mind more than once that Angus was the only person with a reason to . . .

The blue eyes had grown even icier. "Or did you think I had still another motive? Did you think I wanted not only his wife but also those two ships I'd sold to him and that half-interest in the Fulmer Boatyard?"

When she just stood there voiceless, he said, "You don't have to answer. I can tell by your face that you thought I might have killed him to get his money as well as the woman he married."

Pain had mingled with the rage and scorn in his voice. "That settles it," he said. "I'm getting out of here."

After a moment she managed to move her lips. "Getting . . ."

"I've been offered the captaincy of the *Excelsior*."

She said haltingly, "The . . . the *Excelsior?* But that's a whale ship. And you said that you would never again—"

"There's no other seagoing ship I can get at the moment. And after today, I'll hate being in Sag Harbor more than I hate whaling."

Feeling numb, she asked, "How long will you be gone?"

"You've been in this town long enough to know the answer to that. If we manage to kill a lot of whales, we may be back in a few months. If we don't, we may be out there scouring the South Atlantic and the South Pacific for as long as three years."

After a moment she cried, "Oh, Angus! I'm so sorry."

He sounded tired now. "Don't be. I guess I can see how you might suspect me. Anybody who knew the truth about you and me might suspect me." As she opened her mouth to speak, he added swiftly, "And don't bother to say you don't suspect me now. You always will, at least in a tiny corner of your mind, until and unless it is proved that someone else killed Tom. And that will probably be about the time hell freezes over."

He was right, she realized despairingly. Just as she could never quite forgive him for what he had done to her in New Orleans, she could never be entirely sure that it was not he who climbed through the parlor window that brilliantly moonlit night, and with the pistol from the desk drawer . . .

He managed a slight smile. "You know what the trouble is, Amalia? You and I are each other's bad luck."

She turned to unhitch the mare. Blinded by tears and blowing sand, she stumbled over a piece of driftwood and would have fallen if he hadn't caught her arm.

"Here." He lifted her into the saddle, untied the reins, and handed them to her. She thought: This is the last time he'll ever touch me.

His face, white and bleak now, looked up at her. She saw his lips move and knew he had said good-bye, although he had spoken so softly that his voice was inaudible through the sound of wind and surf. She turned the mare's head and rode toward the break in the line of dunes.

# 32

Three days later, when she called for a pair of shoes she had left at the cobbler's shop on Main Street, she learned that the *Excelsior*, under the command of Angus MacFarlane, had sailed that morning. Even though she had known what he intended to do, she hadn't expected him to leave quite so soon, and the news brought her an almost physical stab of pain. She carried her newly mended shoes out to the gig. Through incongruously bright winter sunlight she circled the cove to North Haven and drove along narrow lanes for more than an hour. Finally, feeling calm enough to face Lena's scrutiny, she drove home.

Two afternoons later she encountered Ruth MacFarlane in Hobart's store. When Amalia had completed her purchase—ten yards of dress muslin—the young girl followed her out to the street. She said, as Amalia was placing her package in the gig, "I want to talk to you!"

She turned to face Ruth. What a pretty girl, Amalia thought, even when her mouth had that sullen set. "Yes, Ruth?"

"Angus has gone!"

"I know."

"He left on a whaler! And he didn't take me with him!"

"Now, Ruth. Even if he'd tried to take you with him, you would have hated being aboard a whaler. Why, I've heard that sometimes when the men are cooking the whale blubber the decks are ankle-deep in oil. And the smell!"

"I know all that!" Ruth snapped. "I've lived in a whaling village all my life, and you've been here only since last summer. You don't even know that you don't call it *cooking* blubber. It's called 'trying out.' "

"Whatever it's called, it must be a very unpleasant process, something I should think you wouldn't want to experience."

"But I didn't expect him to sail on a whaler! I expected him to wait for a nice clean merchant ship." She added, blue eyes bright with fury, "I think you had something to do with his going so soon."

"Now, Ruth. That's absurd."

She had tried to sound unruffled, even faintly amused, but her heart was beating hard. How much had this strange, intense girl learned, or at least guessed? Probably she had guessed where Angus was going when he left the MacFarlane house the night of the hurricane. Perhaps he had even told his father and sister that he was going to see if "Amalia Fulmer is all right."

Very soon, Amalia knew, she would have to let people know she was pregnant. What if this young girl started a rumor that the child had been conceived the night of the hurricane, while her husband was still somewhere in the Atlantic? In that case, Amalia realized, she would have to leave Sag Harbor. She could not raise her child in a town where other children, sooner or later, were sure to hurl the word "bastard."

She said, still striving for lightness, "What makes you think that I had anything to do with Angus leaving on a whale ship?"

"I just think you did, that's all." Her tone was brooding now. "Of course, neither of you will ever admit it. Oh, I know you think I'm stupid and young," she went on, suddenly sounding very young indeed. "But I'm a lot smarter than you or Angus or anyone else thinks!"

She turned with what could only be described as a flounce and walked away. So the child didn't really know anything, after all. And that was what Ruth was, in spite of her fifteen years and ripening figure—a child clinging to the notion that she had a right to first place in her brother's heart.

Mrs. Hannibal Allerdyce called upon her a little more than a week later. Amalia confided to the older woman that she was expecting a child "in September."

"Oh, my dear! How wonderful and yet how sad! A widow before you are a mother. And how tragic that Tom did not live to see his child."

When Amalia went shopping the next afternoon, she became aware that already the news was all over town. She could tell it by the increased courtliness of men, and by the blend of sympathy and congratulation in the smiles women gave her.

The winter wore on, with mostly sunny February giving way to raw and blustery March. By the end of that month, though, the green shoots of daffodils had pushed through the muddy earth. Then quite suddenly spring was there, her first northern spring, with butter-yellow forsythia bushes blooming beside the back door, and coral buds on maple branches waving against the tender April sky. Soon, while taking the daily "constitutionals" Dr. Marsden had prescribed for her, she began to find indigo-blue wild iris at boggy spots in the woods.

In early May she laid aside her black mourning gown, which she and Lena had let out several times over the past weeks, for a "semimourning" dress of violet. As Lena fitted the garment to her, Amalia was grateful that the slender dresses she remembered from her childhood had given way to fuller-skirted fashions. Otherwise people might be wondering why a woman who did not expect her child until September should appear so well-advanced in pregnancy.

It was in May, also, that Sag Harbor had its first news of Angus MacFarlane since he had left. Another Sag Harbor ship, encountering the *Excelsior* off the southern coast of Argentina, had learned that MacFarlane's crew had sighted few whales and captured none. The news brought Amalia a strange mixture of emotions. She felt sympathy for Angus, and, in spite of herself, a twist of pain at the thought that it indeed might be three years before the *Excelsior*, its holds finally filled with oil, would head for Long Wharf. But also she felt relief. Now she would be able, during her child's early infancy, to devote all her attention to him or her, undistracted by the thought that at any moment she might come face to face with a man she still yearned for and yet could never quite forgive or trust.

On a night in July, after a prolonged labor both more painful and more exhilarating than she would have thought possible, her son made his squalling entrance into the world. Almost immediately she fell into exhausted sleep. When she awoke, morning sunlight filled the room. Dr. Marsden sat beside her, plump and smiling.

As she looked at him, groggy with sleep, he said, "No, I haven't been here all night. I went home around midnight and came back a few minutes ago."

She was wide-awake now. "Where is . . . ?"

"Your son? With Lena, in the next room. She'll bring him to you in a moment." He added, his smile broadening into a grin, "He's a fine-looking boy, especially for a premature baby."

After a moment she said, "Do you think people will really believe . . . ?"

"Of course they will, if I say so. True, he is a bit robust for a seven-month baby, but long ago I figured out how to handle that. I'm going to forbid you to show him to callers for the first six weeks. Child's too frail, you know, too apt to get colicky from the least excitement, or catch someone's cold. By the time he does go on display, people will be confused as to just how old he is or how he should look."

She said slowly, "Dr. Marsden, how can I ever thank you?"

He was not smiling now. "I'm not doing it just for you, Amalia, much as I have come to like you, or just for the child, although God knows the stiff-necked Presbyterians in this town would make this a rough world for him if they knew the truth. I'm doing it because Tom asked me to."

He paused and then went on. "Doctors see a lot of human behavior. If they didn't become tolerant, they'd probably die of acute self-righteousness before they'd practiced a year. If Tom was able to forgive you, and able to want to raise the child as his own, then certainly I am not going to sit in judgment on you."

He was smiling again. "And now I'll shut up and let you meet your son." He raised his voice. "Lena!"

For several moments after a smiling Lena laid the red-faced, fist-waving child in her arms, Amalia was conscious of nothing but awe and a flooding tenderness. Then she began to notice details. He had a fuzz of hair which, thank God, was plain yellow, with no hint of red. As for his eyes, she could not see their color because his lids were shut. If they were the intense blue of Angus MacFarlane's eyes . . . She asked nervously, "Are his eyes . . . ?"

"They're brown, like yours. What are you going to name him?"

She knew that it might be prudent to do the expected thing and name him Thomas. But something within her revolted at the thought of that additional bit of deception.

She would name him after his great-grandfather, Miguel Ramirez, that broom seller who might or might not be alive across the ocean in Spain. And as soon as she was a little stronger, she would write a letter to him, telling him he had a great-grandson and namesake in a small American town called Sag Harbor. Perhaps this time he would reply.

She said, "His name will be Michael . . . Michael Fulmer."

# 33

Amalia had a new kind of calendar now. It did not measure time by weeks and months but by events in Michael's very young life. The day he first smiled. The day he first crawled. The first time he said "Mama." The first time, held in Lena's arms, he patted the scarred face and said "Weena!" His first staggering footsteps.

She of course also was aware of time passing in the usual sense. The change of seasons, and of Sag Harbor's social life, with late-summer picnics on the sands east of Long Wharf giving way to fall suppers and dances, and then, in deep winter, to nighttime skating parties on Otter Pond, with bonfires at the pond's edge casting rosy reflections on the ice.

Amalia attended more and more of these gatherings, and even gave a few small parties of her own. At any sort of party, she drew masculine attention. The town had an unusually large number of eligible young bachelors, most of them whale-ship officers who had delayed marriage plans until they had made a respectable amount of money. Several of these men made it clear that, with any encouragement at all, they would become her suitors.

She did not give that encouragement. None of them had Tom Fulmer's gentle, humorous appeal, let alone the attractions which had made Angus such a devastating force in her life. Besides, she was fairly content with her existence just as it was. She had a small son who seemed to grow in good looks and intelligence every day. She had this comfortable, well-furnished house. And with Richard Fulmer managing her financial affairs, she was assured of a more-than-comfortable income.

She knew that the town had expected Richard to pay court to his brother's widow. Without relishing the prospect, she herself had rather expected it. But whether she conferred with him about financial matters in his office or her parlor, his manner, although courteous, was strictly businesslike. Sometimes she felt that Tom's brother had never really taken to her. Or perhaps, ever since his fiancée had failed to join him at the altar that long-ago day, he had disliked all women.

Now and then she heard news of Angus and the *Excelsior*. The ship was still plagued with bad luck, her holds far from filled. True, off Japan the *Excelsior* had captured two huge sperm whales, only to lose them when a typhoon struck. Amalia found herself unable to wish Angus continued bad fortune. But at the same time she felt that each additional month of his absence made the memory of him less disturbing to her.

Certainly his continued absence was having a good effect on his half-sister. Amalia felt confident that by the time Angus returned Ruth would have outgrown her somewhat unhealthily close attachment to him. One sign of Ruth's emotional change, Amalia felt, was the lessened hostility in her manner when their paths crossed.

It was certainly easy to understand why, at long last, Ruth should be losing her possessive attitude toward her brother. Sixteen now, and taller than Amalia, Ruth was like a young goddess—golden-haired and blue-eyed and classically featured. On May Day the porch of the old MacFarlane house, where during Angus' absence Ruth lived alone except for two aged servants and a middle-aged female cousin, was literally covered with flower-filled May baskets.

Not only boys her own age flocked around Ruth. She also attracted the attention of young whale-ship officers, including a captain, who although still under thirty, was a millionaire. After all, many Sag Harbor girls married at sixteen.

"But that one won't," Lena prophesied. "There's such a thing as a girl being *too* popular. The girl has so many men hanging around her that it takes her years and years to settle for just one."

As soon as the school Ruth attended, the Bridgehampton Female Academy, closed in early June, Ruth deserted all her admirers to spend the summer with distant relatives in Portland, Maine.

Three weeks later, Amalia and Lena took Michael down to the Fourth of July celebration on Long Wharf, even though it was well past his bedtime. His brown eyes, so dramatic a contrast to his curling yellow hair, grew wide with wonder at the sight of fireworks spangling the night sky. And a week after that, they celebrated his first birthday, with a cake, in the grape arbor Toby and his uncle had built near the barn.

And a little more than a month after that, Angus came home.

Amalia and Lena and Michael had driven to the business district that August morning to buy shoes for the child's active and rapidly growing feet. Leaving Lena in the gig, Amalia started to lead her son across the sidewalk to Hobart's store. Then she stood stock-still. Moving toward her up the slanted street was a man in a whaling officer's uniform. Dark blue trousers. Short blue jacket, with no tails to become entangled in the harpoon line once a boat crew "tied in" to a whale. Visored cap to shield the eyes from the tropic sun. He had a duffel bag slung over one shoulder. Even though the cap hid his bright hair and shadowed his face, Amalia immediately recognized him. A kind of paralysis held her there, hand clutching her son's hand, while Angus drew closer.

He said, "Hello, Amalia."

His face looked older and somewhat thinner, with lines which hadn't been there before radiating from the corners of his eyes. She said from a dry throat, "Hello."

His gaze dropped to Michael, then returned to her face. "I'm coming to your house this afternoon."

"No!"

"Yes. I have a right to see him, get acquainted with him."

Her voice was soft but vehement. "You have no rights."

"Perhaps not, legally. Let's just say that I am assuming certain rights."

"Leave us alone!"

"You had better smile, Amalia, and keep your voice down. Otherwise we will attract attention."

She understood the implied threat. If she did not capitulate, he would raise his own voice and create a scene that might make it impossible for her to go on living in this town.

He half-turned away to greet an elderly woman. Before the woman continued on down the sidewalk she said, "Welcome home, Angus." She must have sensed the tension in the air, because her face held curiosity as she added, "Hello, Amalia. Awfully warm day, isn't it?"

"Hello, Mrs. Armitage. Yes, very warm."

The woman hesitated a moment, as if wanting to linger, and then moved on. Smiling pleasantly, Angus said in a low voice, "I'll be at your house at two o'clock."

He tipped his cap and went on up the walk.

Trembling, Amalia turned back to the gig and lifted Michael onto the wide seat. Then she herself got into the gig and took the reins from Lena.

Lena said, "What did that devil—?" and then broke off as Amalia gave a meaningful look at the child between them and shook her head.

Michael extended his right foot and pointed at it. "Sooz?" he inquired hopefully.

"We'll get your new shoes tomorrow, darling. Right now we have to go home."

She turned the gig around. Evidently Angus had gone into some shop, because they did not see him as they moved along upper Main Street. Amalia waited until she was sure that she would sound matter-of-fact. Then she said, "Captain MacFarlane is coming to call at two this afternoon. He wants to see Michael."

"Me!" Michael said, sounding pleased.

"He's an old family friend, and he wants to become . . . better acquainted with Michael. I'll be too busy to see him, but you will join them, Lena, won't you?"

"That I will," Lena said grimly, "every minute."

At two that afternoon, waiting nervously in her bedroom, Amalia heard the knocker strike. Swiftly she moved to a window. She could not see the front door from there, but she could see, tied to the hitching post, the white-stockinged black horse.

She heard footsteps along the lower hall now, the slow footsteps of Lena, the running ones of Michael. She heard Lena open the door and say, "Mrs. Fulmer can't see you. But if you want to we'll go back and sit in the grape arbor for a spell."

"Thank you," Angus said.

Amalia heard the three of them walk to the back door. After a few moments she went out into the upper hall and looked through the curtained window at its end. She could see them down there in the grape arbor, with Michael sitting on Lena's lap. For a while only the two adults talked, their voices not audible to her at that distance. Then Michael, apparently having decided that he liked this big stranger, began to babble in his own language, a tongue that even Amalia and Lena understood only part of the time. Amalia caught the word "mamatat" and knew that he must be talking about the mother cat and kittens in the barn of their neighbor, Dr. Marsden. Still talking fluently if unintelligibly, he slid down from Lena's lap and leaned against his visitor's knee.

Angus no longer wore his whale-ship officer's uniform. Most likely he had changed it at the first opportunity for the gray trousers and open-throated white shirt he wore now. Without that visored cap, the expression on his face was clearly visible. She saw puzzled amusement in his face as he looked down at his son, and tenderness, and something else. Sadness, perhaps.

She felt her throat tighten, as if she might cry. Oh, why *hadn't* he stayed away for three years, instead of less than two? Why had he come back while she was still so vulnerable? Vulnerable to the pang she felt as he raised a big hand, rather hesitantly, and laid it on Michael's curly yellow hair. Vulnerable to the memory of that same big hand caressing her body. Worst of all, vulnerable to the realization that in spite of all she had—fine little son, comfortable house, assured income—she was still a young woman who slept alone every night.

Face unsmiling, Lena had gotten to her feet and taken Michael's hand. She said something to Angus, and he, after inclining his head in assent, walked quickly along the wide brick walk to the corner of the house. Seconds later, from the window of her bedroom, she saw him mount the black horse and ride back toward the center of town.

She heard Lena and Michael come in the back door. Going out into the hall, she waited for them to climb the stairs. "Me!" Michael said, with more than usual distinctness. "Comed to shaw me!"

"*Came* to *see* me," Amalia said. "And now you're going to stop talking and take your nap."

When Michael was in bed in the small room adjoining her own, Amalia and Lena went down to the parlor. "Well, what did he tell you?"

"Not much," Lena said. "I asked him what luck he'd had, and he said fairly good, after all. His ship came back with about two-thirds of the hold filled with oil. Then I asked him how soon he was going out again, and he said, 'On a whale ship? Never. I've made enough out of this voyage that I can wait a little while for a berth on a merchant vessel.' "

Amalia remained bleakly silent. No telling how long he would be here.

"Child, you won't let that devil upset you again, will you?"

"Lena, I keep telling you he's not—"

"And I say he is. And don't let him use that sweet little boy to get around you. He'll come back here in a few days, saying that all he wants is a few minutes with Michael."

"If he comes here, I won't let him in."

"See that you don't. Oh, child! I can tell you still hone for him. But just keep thinking how he treated you in New Orleans, and what it did to your poor mama. And just remember your husband. Remember nobody knows who it was that—"

"Please, Lena! Don't talk to me about that."

She got to her feet and went upstairs to her room.

# 34

Her peace of mind was gone now. So was her pleasure in simple things. She no longer enjoyed making bouquets from the zinnias and marigolds she had planted in early summer, or watching the half-grown birds—wings drooping, beaks opened to emit piteous cries—as they begged their now-indifferent parents to go on foraging for them. She took little joy in the sight of the tall reeds between her house and the cove bending in the August breeze. She even found less amused pleasure in trying to understand her young son's chatter.

Again and again she had to resist the impulse to saddle Molly and ride down to Sagaponack. If he were there, being alone with him like that could only increase her turmoil. And if he were not there? If she went there several days in a row and still did not see him? She had to acknowledge that that would disturb her even more. She knew that they could never join their lives together, and yet somehow she could not bear the thought that he might have grown indifferent, that if it had not been for Michael, he might have passed her on Main Street the other day with a polite "Hello, Amalia," and a tipping of his visored cap.

Restless, brooding, and confused, she sometimes thought of abandoning the pleasant existence she had achieved in Sag Harbor. She even thought of taking her son and Lena back to that sleepy little lumber-mill town on the Mississippi.

And then five days after Angus' return to Sag Harbor, as Amalia sat at breakfast with Lena, she suddenly realized that she had another course open to her. In about a week the *White Falcon* would leave on a long voyage to ports along the coast of North and South America and then cross the Atlantic to the Mediterranean and southern Europe. She and Lena and Michael could sail on it, in the spacious owner's cabin.

Why, she could go to Cádiz, and walk up that hilly street Juana so often had described to her, and climb the stairs to the three rooms once occupied by the Ramirez family. Perhaps her grandfather, Miguel Ramirez, was still there, even though he had not responded to her letter telling him of his great-grandson's birth. And if he no longer lived there, someone at his parish church should be able to tell her what had become of him.

And her own father, that handsome young aristocrat of the miniature? Should she try to see him? Perhaps he no longer even remembered Juana. Even if he did, the chances were excellent that he would not welcome the sudden appearance of a daughter and grandson from across the Atlantic. Still, she could hand the miniature to a servant, along with a message, and thus leave the nature of his response up to him.

Whether or not she met any of her Cádiz relatives, the trip would be an exhilarating experience. And perhaps by the time she returned, this lingering, troubling need for Angus would have worn itself out, or nearly so.

She said, "Lena, how would you like to go to Cádiz?"

"Where?"

"You remember. You must have heard my mother talk of it. Cádiz is in southern Spain. The *Falcon* probably is scheduled to stop there, and even if it isn't, I can see to it that it does stop there. After all, it's my ship." She paused and then added, "The *Falcon* will be gone eight months to a year."

A slow smile spread across Lena's face. "Child, that's the best notion you've had in a long time." Then, as Amalia shoved back her chair: "Where are you going?"

"To tell Richard Fulmer we're sailing on the *Falcon*."

Richard's office was on the ground floor of the narrow old Fulmer house on Union Street. It was typical of him, she reflected, that he had chosen a room on the north side of the house in which to transact much of the boatyard's business, as well as everything connected with the two merchant ships his brother had willed to Amalia. Because of projecting eaves as well as the northern exposure, the room was gloomy even on this bright morning. On winter days, Amalia knew, the room often was so dark that it had to be lamplit.

Leaning back in his chair, Richard made a steeple of his long fingers and peered at her over the apex. "Of course,

Amalia. You have the privilege of occupying the owner's cabin whenever you wish."

"I'd like to have an additional clothes cupboard installed. And I'll need some sort of trundle bed for Michael, something attached firmly to my own bunk in the event of rough weather. Could all that be done before the *Falcon* sails?"

"Yes, especially since the sailing will be delayed a few days. I've run into difficulties."

"Difficulties?"

"Jared Manning has left us."

"Captain Manning, the *Falcon's* master?"

"Yes, he's bought a ship of his own, a schooner he'll use in the coastal trade. The trouble is, when he left us he took the *Falcon*'s second mate with him. I do have a captain to replace Manning. I signed him on yesterday. But I'm still short a mate. Unless I can find a qualified man, the captain will have to stand a watch, in addition to all his other duties. And in my opinion, that never makes for a smooth-running ship."

He paused and then said, 'So the new sailing date is ten days from now. I dare not make it later than that, if I'm to fulfill my arrangements with all the shippers along the *Falcon*'s route. If she has to sail with only two mates, and she probably will . . . well, that's just the way it will have to be."

"What's the name of the new captain?" Somehow, even before her brother-in-law replied, Amalia knew what his answer would be.

"Angus MacFarlane signed on. I'd heard he was looking for a berth aboard a merchantman, so when Jared Manning told me of his own plans, I offered the captaincy to Angus. He jumped at it."

Amalia's voice was thick. "Dismiss him."

"*What!*"

"I'm the *Falcon*'s owner, and I will not sail aboard her with Angus MacFarlane as captain, so dismiss him."

Richard Fulmer's deep-set eyes studied Amalia's face. "MacFarlane stays. When I say that I signed him on, I am saying that I signed a legal contract with him. Anyway, I would not break that contract even if I could. MacFarlane is a capable captain. We are lucky to get him."

After a moment he added, "And so I suggest that you wait until your other ship comes home, about seven months from now. There is an owner's cabin aboard the *Goodspeed* too, you know."

She was trembling. "I want to sail on the *Falcon*, and I intend to. Legal contract or no legal contract, get rid of Angus MacFarlane." She paused. "After all, who is owner of this ship?"

"You are."

The corners of his upper lip had lifted in something that she recognized, startled, as more of a snarl than a smile. She knew then something that she should have realized long before. Richard did dislike her, and with reason. No doubt he felt that Tom should have left him his half of the boatyard, plus some sort of share in the two merchant ships.

Richard went on, "But according to the terms of my brother's will, I am to remain manager of the Fulmer ships, with all the powers pertaining to that position, for a period of five years. What is more, the day after the reading of the will, Howard Lipson drew up an agreement between you and me, reaffirming those particular terms of the will, and you signed it. Do you remember that?"

"Yes." Richard had insisted upon such a contract, and so she had assented.

"Of course," he went on, "you could go to court to have that agreement set aside, but even if you did win, it might take you years. And so, my dear, I would advise you not to try to countermand my decisions. After all, my management of your affairs has been satisfactory to you up until now, hasn't it?"

"You know it has. But Angus MacFarlane is not going to command the *Falcon*. If you can't or won't oust him, I will, somehow."

"Very well. But if you succeed, I'll have to find a new captain. That might take time. And if shippers who have signed to place cargo aboard the *Falcon* exercise the cancellation clause in their contracts, it could cost you a great deal of money."

"I'll chance that." Chin held high, she stood up. "Goodbye."

When she reached home she did not drive the gig back to the barn. Instead she hitched the horse's reins to the post beside the front gate. Evidently Lena had looked through a window and seen the gig drive up, because she came hurrying out of the house.

"What's wrong? Why aren't you driving back to—?"

"Because I don't want to unhitch now. I want you to use the gig to deliver a note for me."

Lena studied Amalia's face. "Pretty hot-tempered note, to judge by the look of you. What's riled you?"

Swiftly Amalia told her of her interview with Richard Fulmer. "If my brother-in-law won't keep Angus off my ship, I'll do it! I'll ask him to come here at four this afternoon. I want you to deliver the message to the MacFarlane house right away."

After a moment Lena said soberly, "Maybe your brother-in-law is right. Maybe we should wait for the *Goodspeed*."

"No! I'm sure Richard could discharge Angus if he wanted to. He just wants to prove to me that the reins are entirely in his hands. They aren't. The *Falcon* is *my* ship, and I wouldn't want Angus commanding her even if you and I and Michael wouldn't be sailing on her, which we certainly are going to do."

She paused. "Well, will you take my note to the MacFarlane house?"

Lena sighed. "I'd better. Otherwise you might take the note there yourself, and what would that cousin of his and the servants make of that?"

At three that afternoon Angus rapped the bronze knocker against the front door. Amalia led him into the parlor. As he sat opposite her before the unlit fireplace, sun flooding through the west window emphasized the reddish tint in his yellow hair and the sun-bronzed color of his face. Despite a certain guarded look in their depths, his eyes regarded her calmly.

She knew, though, that behind that unruffled gaze he must be remembering a night nearly two years in the past when this whole house had shuddered under the wind's assault. She suddenly realized that the night of the hurricane, the night when their child was conceived, was only the second time he had been in this house, at least during her occupancy of it.

Unless—the thought came unbidden and unwelcome—unless on a moonlit night only three months after the hurricane, he had slid up that window over there . . .

She said, "I suppose you know why I asked you to come here."

"I think so. I talked to Richard earlier this afternoon."

"Then you know I don't want you to sail as captain of the *Falcon.*"

"Yes, Richard told me."

"Well?"

"I'm sorry, Amalia. My signing onto the *Falcon* as master constitutes a legal contract. I intend to see it enforced, even if I have to get a court injunction to keep the ship in port until this matter is settled."

Her voice began to shake. "You'd do that? You have so little pride that you would *force* me to accept you as an employee?"

"What does pride have to do with it?" His voice was infuriatingly matter-of-fact. "The *Falcon* needed a captain, and I needed a job, so I signed on."

"Even though your family used to own that ship! I should think that fact alone would keep you from sailing on her, let alone the fact that the present owner doesn't want—"

"I told you. I need a job. My father didn't manage too well with the money from the sale of those ships. And a portion of what he did leave is set aside for Ruth's dowry."

"But surely you made enough from that whaling voyage so that you could wait to sign onto some other ship!"

"Why should I run the risk of waiting, when I can have the captaincy of the *Falcon*?"

"Because I plan to sail on that ship!"

"That's your privilege. You're the owner."

"Don't you see how impossible that would be? You and I on the same ship month after month—"

"Then wait for the *Goodspeed.*"

So he thought he could force her to stay off her own ship.

Although rage had caused her to clench her hands in her lap, she tried to make her face as calm as his. Silently and rapidly she considered the situation. Richard had said that in all probability Angus would have to stand a watch. During her two years in Sag Harbor she had learned enough seagoing lore to know about watch arrangements aboard ships. The senior officer always took the four-to-eight watch because those hours were the most perilous, with the light changing from predawn blackness to full day, and from presunset dazzle to full dark. It would be a simple matter for her to stay in her cabin during those hours when he was on the quarterdeck. As for the rest of the time, he would have to spend a good deal of it sleeping, taking meals in the officers' salon, and writing up the log.

Why, if she managed things properly, she might be able to avoid all but the most fleeting contacts with him.

"No, I shan't postpone my journey. Lena and my son and I will occupy the owner's cabin of the *Falcon*."

She saw surprise in his face, and something else, something she could not identify because it came and went so quickly. But at least, she reflected with satisfaction, she had succeeded in startling him. Obviously he had expected her to back down.

She said, "Lena and my son and I will take all our meals in our cabin."

"There is no reason you should not."

"And another thing. I don't want you to take advantage of this voyage to try to . . . to ingratiate yourself with my son. It is in only one sense of the word that he is your son too. Otherwise he is mine. Yes, and Tom's, because he bears Tom's name, and because Tom accepted him before he was born."

When Angus finally spoke, his voice was still calm. "Very well. I won't ingratiate myself, as you put it. Naturally I wanted to see him for those few minutes the other day, but I'll let that suffice." He paused. "Is there anything more you have to say?"

"No. If I need to communicate with you again before we sail, I will do so through my brother-in-law."

"Good-bye, then," he said, and got to his feet.

# 35

Sea turtles swam along beside the ship, only a foot or so below the water's surface. Ponderous and greenish-brown, they looked almost as old as time. On land, probably, they appeared awkward, even ridiculous. But they moved through water with graceful ease. Amalia loved watching them. Standing at the ship's bulwarks like this, looking at the turtles, and hearing the seethe of water past the hull, she could feel herself falling into a kind of pleasant trance.

She had found much on this journey to enjoy. With her appetite sharpened by sea air, even the plain meals she shared with Lena and Michael in their cabin seemed good. She enjoyed these early afternoons on deck, as well as the nights when, after Angus' four-to-eight watch was over, she slipped out on deck to look at the stars. Sometimes, though, she was poignantly reminded of a letter of Tom's, in which he said that some night in the future he would point out the Southern Cross to her. Well, as soon as the *Falcon* had traveled sufficiently far south, she would see the Southern Cross, but not with Tom's arm around her.

She had liked going ashore in various ports—New York, Philadelphia, Baltimore—as they moved down the Atlantic coast. Although she had no way of knowing it, in Norfolk, Virginia, she walked past the house from which Sara Davidson, while her respectable parents slept, had slipped away forty-odd years ago to start her career as New Orleans' most successful madam.

As for Angus, she had managed to avoid him almost entirely. And from the very first day he had kept his word about holding aloof from Michael. Within seconds after Amalia and Lena had climbed the gangplank from Long Wharf to the *Falcon*'s deck, the child had seen and recognized his visitor of about two weeks before. Breaking free of Lena's grasp, he ran toward the man with the intense blue eyes, shadowed today by his officer's cap.

Angus had said coldly, "Don't bother me, Michael. I'm busy. As long as you are aboard this ship, you are not to bother me. Do you understand that?"

Probably the little boy did not understand all the words, but he understood the tone. Small face hurt, he ran back to the two women. By the next day, apparently, he had forgotten the rebuff. According to Lena, who was on deck with him at the time, Michael ran toward the quarterdeck and looked up at Angus, who was pacing slowly back and forth behind the helmsman.

"Trunder!" he shouted. That was his term for the trundle bed which the ship's carpenter had attached to Amalia's bunk. "Me got trunder!"

The big man, who for some reason no longer wanted to be friends, looked down at him and said, "Do you remember what I told you yesterday about not bothering me?"

Face woebegone, Michael nodded.

"Well, I meant it."

This time the rebuff was effective. From then on Michael addressed most of his friendly if garbled conversation to two other men aboard ship, Phineas Smith, the assistant cook, and Brian Carr, the second mate. Small and balding, Phineas had seven grandchildren, which may have been why he could make sense of most of Michael's chatter. Slim and red-haired Brian Carr, on the other hand, was not yet twenty-five. The young second mate not only liked Michael. He made it clear, in his shy way, that he found Michael's mother attractive. At every opportunity he gave her information, naming the various sails for her and, now that they were in Caribbean waters, the names of distant islands they passed. Only minutes ago, as she stood watching the turtles, he had called down from his station beside the helmsman to tell her that the blue smudge on the horizon was the island of Haiti.

"That Brian Carr is sure a nice boy," Lena had said at lunch in their cabin one day.

Amalia nodded a wary agreement.

"And he comes from a fine family. That boy's going to inherit a lot of money someday. His father owns a bank in Providence, Rhode Island. Did you know that?"

"No."

"Brian says that when he gets married he'll quit the sea and go into his father's business." When Amalia didn't respond, Lena said, "Brian told me that himself. I figure he wanted me to tell you."

"I figure you figured right. But it's no use, Lena. I could never become interested in him."

Lena sighed. "No, I guess that would be way too sensible for you, getting interested in a nice boy who is going to inherit a bank."

Now Brian called down to her, "Mrs. Fulmer! Look toward the bow."

She looked, and caught her breath. A school of dolphins was playing in the bow wave, diving under the foam and then arching high into the air, bodies iridescent in the sunlight. They reminded her of those big cousins of theirs, those leaping whales who had been playing follow-the-leader off the beach at Sagaponack. That had been the same day that Angus, no longer engaged to be married, had come back to Sag Harbor from Boston . . .

Angus! Surely it must be almost four. Soon he would emerge from the passageway beneath the quarterdeck and climb up to where Brian now stood. She might even meet him in that narrow passage, as she had three days earlier. Emerging from his own cabin just as she was about to pass, he had stood face to face with her for a moment. Then, with a slight ironical smile, as if he guessed that the unruly pulse in the hollow of her throat was racing, he reopened his door and stepped inside his cabin, leaving her room to pass.

She had not slept well the night after that happened. Come to think of it, much as she had been enjoying this voyage, she had not slept well since the *Falcon* reached the tropics. The sun-dazzled waters by day, the warm dark nights, the wind that sometimes carried the spicy fragrance of some nearby island—somehow all that disturbed her, stirring memories and desires she had tried to put aside.

Throwing Brian Carr a quick smile and a nod, she hurried to her cabin, where, with Lena sitting beside him, Michael napped in his small bed.

A week later the ship put into Santos, Brazil. As she looked at the little town with its crowded wharf, its crescent beach fringed with palms, its wide dirt main street leading past structures of pink and blue and green plaster, Amalia found it hard to realize that the month was November. In Sag Harbor the trees would be bare, and all over town there would be the sound of axes splitting firewood for the long winter ahead. Here, some twenty-odd degrees below the equator, the subtropical summer was near its height, with moist heat that seemed to press down from a hazy sky.

She and Brian Carr and Lena were to have supper ashore that evening. He had approached her on deck the day before. "I wonder if I might show Santos to you and Miss White tomorrow night. There is a nice place, quite respectable, where we could have supper."

How nice he was, she thought. Most men would have said "your maid" or "your colored woman."

Aloud she had said, "That sounds very pleasant. But there is my little boy. I would not want to take him with us, and of course I cannot leave him alone."

"I thought of that. I am sure that Phineas Smith would be glad to stay with him in your cabin."

Amalia realized that Michael would enjoy having the undivided attention of a man who, more or less, spoke his own language.

"Tomorrow is the fete day of one of Santos' favorite saints," Brian went on. "There will be a sort of parade, with a band and street dancing. Upper-class people—planters and so on—don't take part, of course. But some of them come from as far away as São Paulo to sit in the cafés and watch the festivities."

"It sounds delightful. We'd love to go."

At eight the next evening she sat with Lena and Brian in an open-fronted café. They had finished their supper, a chicken-and-rice-and-red-peppers concoction which Brian had assured them was quite safe, and now sat drinking mild white wine which he poured from the bottle on the table. Almost every other table was filled with well-dressed people drinking wine or brandy and chatting in Portuguese. Most of these planters and merchants and their wives appeared to be of European stock, although a few of them obviously had some nonwhite ancestors, African or native Indian.

From down the street, now bathed in the light of a yellow

moon, came the sound of a strange kind of music, plaintively melodic, but with a rhythm Amalia had never heard before. "They are coming," Brian said.

"What kind of music is that?"

"It is a blend of Portuguese fado and the music the slaves brought with them from Africa. You won't hear this music anywhere in the world except Brazil."

They had come in sight now, many bearing torches whose wavering reddish glow mingled with the yellow moonlight. There were scores of them, most of them very black, some of lighter skin tones, all of them young, and many of them handsome indeed. The girls wore tight, brightly colored skirts and blouses knotted under the breasts, leaving their stomachs bare. Their headdresses were fantastic arrangements of feathers and flowers. The men wore ordinary white cotton trousers, some of them quite ragged. But their sleeveless long vests, hanging open to reveal naked torsos, were splendid with feathers and embroidery and spangles.

To the music of drums and trumpets and banjos, they danced. Sometimes couples, facing each other, stood in place and swayed to the music, palms touching, naked feet barely moving in the dusty street. Sometimes young men, like strutting roosters, circled around girls whose bodies wriggled a frank invitation. It could have been termed indecent, Amalia knew. But it was also very beautiful. The play of torchlight over muscled male bodies and rounded feminine ones. Flash of white teeth in dark faces. And that sensuous, insistent, throbbing music, which seemed to make her own blood throb in response.

Quite suddenly, a wave of rebellious longing swept over her. She felt something almost like envy for those laughing, wriggling girls. That was absurd, of course. She was white, in a world where white people ruled. If not wealthy, she was at least comfortably off. These girls, on the other hand, were poor, uneducated, and slaves or the descendants of slaves.

But one thing she felt sure of. Not one of them would go to bed alone tonight.

She looked at Brian's pleasant, slightly freckled face. Half-turned away from her, he was answering some question Lena had asked. Why couldn't she be sensible enough to turn to him, or someone like him? Why did she keep wanting a man who was good for her in one respect, and that respect only?

Her sense of bewildered loneliness, perhaps reinforced by the wine she had drunk, made her long to put her head on the table, right here among all these people, and burst into tears. Then she reminded herself sharply that she had no reason for self-pity. If it had been a mistake to sail on a ship commanded by Angus MacFarlane—and she admitted to herself now that it was—it was a mistake she had made of her own free choice.

Hoping that her face revealed none of her thoughts, she kept her gaze fixed on the whirling, foot-stomping, hand-clapping dancers.

Shortly after midnight a hired surrey carried Brian and the two women along the wharf to where the *Falcon* was berthed. A line of nearly naked black men was carrying bales up the gangway. Amalia knew what was in the bales. Raw cotton, destined for ports along the Mediterranean and southern Europe. The sight of that cargo was a reminder that Santos was the *Falcon*'s last port of call in the western hemisphere. Tomorrow they would strike out across the vast, lonely South Atlantic.

When the three of them stepped aboard, a voice from the quarterdeck called down, "Mr. Carr!"

Amalia looked up. Angus, tall in the moonlight, stood beside the unmanned wheel.

"Yes, Captain."

"Correct me if I am wrong, but it has always been my understanding that you have the twelve-to-four watch. It is now twenty past twelve."

Sarcastic, Amalia thought. Sarcastic and cold. Was it because that was the sort of man he became once he assumed command of a ship? Or was it because he didn't like the fact that Brian had taken her and Lena ashore?

"I know," Brian was saying. "But the street is still so crowded that our carriage had trouble getting here. Besides, sir, I didn't think it would matter much, since we are in port."

"Then you thought wrong. Mr. Saunders is not feeling well tonight." Saunders was the middle-aged first mate. "And so I want you to go down into the holds and see to it that these bales are being stored properly."

"Aye, sir, right away." Brian added hurriedly to Amalia, "Good night."

"Good night, and thank you for this evening."

Aware of the scrutiny of that tall figure on the moonlit quarterdeck, she walked with Lena toward their cabin.

# 36

Eleven days out of Santos, the *Falcon* and a Philadelphia merchantman crossed paths. With the canvas of both ships partially reefed, the two vessels kept each other company for an afternoon. In a longboat the *Falcon*'s officers rowed over to the Philadelphian. After a while they brought back the other ship's officers for a visit aboard the *Falcon*. Near sunset, both ships set their respective sails and then parted, the Philadelphia vessel heading for home and the *Falcon* continuing on a northeast course across the Atlantic.

Except for that one meeting, the *Falcon* and her crew and passengers might have been all alone in a watery universe. They met no other ships and sighted not even a distant island. Except at times of flat calm, when the sails hung lifeless and the tar calking the timbers seemed almost to bubble under the tropic sun, the ship sailed steadily on. Once in a while there was a rain squall, darkening the sky and drenching the sailors who swarmed aloft to shorten canvas. Most days, though, were monotonously alike. Again and again Angus wrote in the ship's log: "Skies partially overcast, winds westerly, seas moderate with slight cross-chop. Heat so intense that again today I ordered crewmen to avoid sunstroke by resting in shade ten minutes of every hour."

Amalia and Lena and Michael avoided the merciless equatorial sun by never venturing from their cabin until dark. But there was no way of escaping the heat. Except when the sea was too rough for her to have the porthole open, Amalia sat near it most of the day, trying to read or to write letters to be dispatched to Richard Fulmer and a few Sag Harbor friends when the ship next touched land. Often, though, she just stared out at the blue or gray ocean, which, in these latitudes, often had an oily look.

The day the *Falcon* dived to her unmarked grave was also

a day of comparative calm and moderate seas. When Angus came on watch at four o'clock, though, he saw dark clouds at several points on the horizon, and realized that there were squalls in the area. He hoped some of them would reach the *Falcon*. A squall would not only cool the air. Its winds, if favorable, might enable them to make more knots than they had been averaging these past few days.

Standing beside the helmsman, a Sag Harbor boy of eighteen making his first voyage, Angus turned his gaze from the horizon to the deck below. Then he stood motionless with shock.

The number-one hold was on fire. Smoke, seeping out around the edges of the hatch cover, wavered up through the brassy sunlight.

Even as he cupped his hand around his mouth and shouted for all hands, he was thinking: That goddamned boatswain. The night before at supper he had instructed young Brian Carr to send the boatswain down into the holds early the next afternoon to make sure there were no signs of leaks. The boatswain, who had been known to drink while on duty, must have left his pipe down there.

Or perhaps, Angus thought, as he clattered down the ladder, it was not the boatswain's fault. Perhaps this was a case of that strange phenomenon, spontaneous combustion. Whatever the cause, those bales of raw cotton, one of the most dangerous of cargoes, were on fire.

He thought: Amalia! That stubborn little fool. She had been determined that she and the boy make this voyage. And now . . .

The main deck had filled up with men swarming out from the officers' cabins and the crew's quarters in the forecastle, their faces taut. To Chief Mate Saunders Angus said, "Get both hatch covers off." To Brian Carr he said, "Get the pumps started, four men to a pump."

He caught the arm of a sailor hurrying past. "Go back and tell the ladies to stay in their cabin until they get further instructions."

Already a group of men was tugging at the cover of number-one hold. They had it halfway off when flames shot into the air, forcing the men to fall back.

Angus knew right then that it was no use. The pumps could never bring up enough seawater to quench a raw-cotton fire that well advanced. If it had not already eaten its way through the bulkhead to number-two hold, it would do so within a few minutes.

"Lower the longboats!" he shouted. "Abandon ship!"

Turning, he hurried down the passageway beneath the quarterdeck and, without knocking, opened the door of the owner's cabin. Both women stood in the center of the room, Amalia with the frightened-looking child in her arms. Above his yellow curls her face was deathly pale.

"We're leaving the ship," he said. "Get out on deck as fast as you can. Bring shawls for yourselves and some sort of head covering for the child. Nothing else. There won't be room in the boats."

Leaving the door open, he hurried away. There had been no need for him to tell them the ship was on fire. They could smell the smoke and hear the roar of flames, punctuated by explosive sounds. While Lena snatched down shawls from the wardrobe to cover her own black cotton dress and Amalia's blue one, Amalia wrapped the now-whimpering Michael in a white blanket from his trundle bed.

They hurried out on deck, out into a confusion of smoke and spiraling yellow flames and shouting, hurrying men. Both longboats were in the water now, and men were climbing down the rope ladders flung over the *Falcon*'s side.

Amalia thought: The miniature! That portrait of Enrique Villega which Juana had cherished all her life, and which Amalia hoped would prove her identity to the father she had never seen. It was in the portmanteau under her bunk. Getting it would be a matter of seconds.

She thrust Michael into Lena's arms. "I'll be only a minute."

Smoke had backed into the cabin. Coughing, she knelt and drew the portmanteau from under the bunk. Its clasp resisted her fingers momentarily. Then it opened. Eyes half-closed against the thickening smoke, she fumbled for the miniature. She found it, thrust it down the bosom of her dress, then ran down the smoke-filled passageway to the deck.

No sign of Lena and Michael.

She flew to the bulwarks, looked down. One of the boats was entirely filled and already pulling away from the ship. Lena was among its passengers, with the blanket-wrapped Michael in her arms.

"Michael!" Amalia screamed. And then: "Lena! Make them bring the boat back."

Michael had seen her. Small face distorted with terror and tears, he stretched out his arms. Through the crackle of flames and the voices of men and the creak of oars, she could hear his shrill voice calling to her.

Frantically she looked around for Angus, and saw him not three feet away from her. "Call that boat back!"

"Don't be a fool. There's no more room in that boat. Now, climb down that—"

"I won't be separated from my son!"

"Then you should have stayed here to make sure you left in the same boat." He seized her arm. "Now, climb down the ladder."

With her free handed she pounded against his chest. "Call . . . that . . . boat . . . back!"

Still holding her arm with his left hand, he stepped back from her. She saw his big fist arching upward toward her chin. She felt brief, numbing pain, and then nothing at all.

A rocking motion. Creak of oars. Low, shocked-sounding voices of men. She opened her eyes and, with a sense of being in the grip of a dream, sat up. Whether in a dream or in reality, she was in the after end of a longboat. On a thwart perhaps three feet in front of her two men sat facing away from her, backs bending and then straightening as they pulled at the oars. In the west the brief tropic sunset flamed. And off to her right, across perhaps two hundred feet of ocean, something else flamed. The *Falcon*, her sails consumed now, her masts and spars and yardarms aflame, looked in the rapidly lessening light like some elaborate piece of fireworks.

Realization struck her then. This was no dream.

She screamed, "Michael!" and scrambled to her feet. Frantically she looked around. She saw the other longboat finally, a black shape many yards away across sunset-streaked water. "Michael!" she screamed again. "Lena!"

Angus eased his way between the two oarsmen. Standing inches away from her, he said, "Shut up!"

Through the swiftly descending darkness she tried to see if his visor-shadowed face was as harsh as his tone. "Please! Please! Call out to that other boat and tell those men to row over so that I can—"

"Amalia, any moment now the *Falcon* is going under. Do

you want the people in these two boats to be sucked under with her? The important thing is that both boats put distance between themselves and that ship as fast as they can."

He paused. "Now, the longboats will stay in touch with each other during the night. We'll keep hailing back and forth. In the morning, when it will be completely safe to do so, I'll transfer you to the other boat, or Michael and Lena to this one. Will that content you?"

She wanted to cry, "No! Make the transfer now!" But that demand, she realized, was unreasonable.

She nodded. "All right."

"Does your jaw hurt?"

"Not much." In her anxiety over her son, she had been scarcely aware of her jaw's soreness until he mentioned it.

"You were hysterical. I had to knock you unconscious. It was the only quick way of getting you off that ship and into the boat."

His last words were almost lost through a strange sound, a kind of seething roar. Amalia looked at the *Falcon*. Her once-proud head down, she was plunging into the sea. Her descent somehow arrested, she seemed to hang there for a moment, her stern a dull glow through the thickening dark. Then she disappeared, leaving only a ghostly patch of disturbed white water to mark where she had gone down.

Angus turned, stepped over the thwart where the two men still rowed, and made his way toward the longboat's bow. Despite her own distress, Amalia was able to feel a fleeting sympathy for him. To an owner, the loss of a ship was a misfortune, but one made bearable by compensation from an insurance company. But to a captain, whether or not he was also the owner, the death of a ship meant a loss of self-esteem, of pride in his competence.

She sat down again. From somewhere near the longboat's bow a voice she recognized as the ship's carpenter's called out, "Ahoy, there."

She held her breath. From what sounded frighteningly far away came the answering hail: "Ahoy!"

Minutes later there was again an exchange of calls. This time Amalia had the comforting feeling that the boats had drawn closer together.

Full darkness now. A few of the brightest stars, including those of the Southern Cross, shone through a thin overcast. It was Brian Carr who, in his shy, please-like-me way, had pointed out the Southern Cross to her. Now she recollected that he had been in the other longboat, standing near Lena and Michael with a distressed expression on his face. Part of his distress, Amalia realized, must have been because he had expected her to be a passenger in the same boat as Lena and Michael. But that boat had filled up while she was back in her cabin groping for the miniature, and so someone, almost certainly Angus, had given the castoff order. . . .

Again the boats exchanged hails. This time, too, she judged them to be less than a hundred yards apart, far enough to avoid colliding in the darkness, but near enough not to lose each other.

What, she suddenly wondered, lay ahead of them in this vast South Atlantic, where they had seen no islands and encountered no ships for many days? But she must not think about that. She must not think beyond the next morning, when at least she would be holding her son in her arms.

Huddled in the bottom of the boat, she drew her shawl closer around her. The tropic night was never really cold. But after the intense heat of day, the humid dark often seemed cool. She realized suddenly that the strain of the past hours had left her exhausted. Although she hadn't expected to sleep at all, she found herself slipping into unconsciousness.

Jagged lightning, so brilliant she was aware of it through closed eyelids. Crashes of thunder. Sheets of water drenching her. The boat pitching, stern rising dizzily and then dropping. Wide-awake, she sat up. The two men on the nearby thwart had shipped their oars. From the way they bent, straightened, turned sidewise, and then bent again, she knew that they were bailing rainwater from the boat, although in the darkness and the blinding downpour she could not tell what utensils they used. The rain fell so thickly that the boat seemed to pitch up and down in a small circle of wildly tossing whitecaps, its diameter only a few yards across.

When the prolonged squall finally passed, there was a brief respite from the wind and rain, although the boat still pitched. Then a second squall struck. Amalia clung with both hands to the gunwales. As she had ever since the first squall jerked her awake, she though of almost nothing but Michael. It seemed to her that through the howling wind she could hear his voice crying for her, and that through the blinding rain she could see his distorted small face.

Only minutes after the second squall passed, the eastern horizon began to lighten. There was a band of clear sky there between the sea and the murky overcast. Into that band of limpid sky the sun rose with tropic abruptness.

Amalia got to her feet. Her aching, agonized eyes searched the sea. There was no second longboat. In every direction the Atlantic stretched emptily away, its surface so drenched in sunrise glare that even the still-tossing whitecaps were dyed a pinkish bronze.

# 37

As it had most of the time for days now, the longboat's tattered sail hung limp. Seated on a thwart in the sail's scant shade, Amalia looked across the curled bodies of four semiconscious men in the bottom of the boat to where Angus sat on the midship thwart, big hands resting idly on the partially shipped oars. To preserve what was left of his strength, he would not start rowing again until late afternoon brought some slight lessening of the equatorial heat.

Around them the ocean stretched emptily from horizon to horizon. On this day of flat calm there were no whitecaps, only endless swells which rocked the boat gently from side to side. Vaguely she noticed that, as usual on days of haze-filtered sunlight, the swells had a brassy sheen.

Her gaze dropped to the inert men in the bottom of the boat. Just to prove to herself that she could, that her mind still worked, at least after a fashion, she recited their names to herself. There was eighteen-year-old Nate Dent, the galley boy who had worked under the direction of Michael's good friend, assistant cook Phineas Smith. There were the Hazelton twins, Jim and Silas, who had been going to sea for almost half of their thirty-odd years. And then there was Johnny, a Sagaponack Indian with an unpronounceable last name. Despite his more than forty years, he had welcomed his turn as lookout in the *Falcon*'s lofty rigging.

There! She had remembered who they were. But on other points her mind was hazy. For instance, how long since the *Falcon* had gone down? Five weeks? Seven? Ten? Was it February now? March? She had long since lost track. She had a sense that both her mind and her starving body had shriveled under the merciless sun.

She could remember clearly, though, that first terrible morning in this boat when her frantic gaze, sweeping the sunrise-dyed water, had found no sight of the vessel which had held her little boy. As she stood screaming, she became aware that Angus had made his way to her and grasped her shoulders. "Stop it!" he said harshly. "Stop it!"

Not heeding him, she screamed, "Michael, Michael!" Then, with her distraught gaze focusing on his face: "You killed my son!"

"That's not true! If it hadn't been for those squalls, we would be transferring him to this boat right now." He lowered his voice. "And aren't you forgetting that he is my son, too?"

Despite her own agony, she was aware of pain in his voice and in the blue eyes beneath the cap's visor.

He went on in a normal tone, "And anyway, it would be foolish to assume that the other boat foundered in those squalls. We were just driven on separate courses, that's all. We may sight them at any moment. And even if we don't, they have just as good a chance of surviving as we do. The other longboat, like this one, is stocked with food and water. And I saw the second mate carrying his sextant aboard with him, so they will have no problem navigating." He paused. "Do you understand what I've been telling you?"

She said distractedly, "I suppose. . . . Yes, I understand."

"Good. Now, as soon as I've passed out rations, we'll rig a sail. If there's enough canvas in the locker, I'll also rig a curtain aft here so you'll have some privacy. Now, sit down, Amalia. And for your sake and the sake of all of us, try to be as brave as you can."

Yes, she could remember that morning clearly, and most of what happened for about the next two weeks. For instance, she remembered the morning when the early-dawn light revealed that the first of their number had died. He had been the *Falcon*'s carpenter, a six-foot-four giant of a man, half Sagaponack Indian and half Fiji Islander. He lay half in and half out of the boat, his long black hair trailing in the water.

Soon after that her memory had begun to blur. The other deaths—had there been ten of them? twelve?—seemed to blend together, with one exception. That was the death of the middle-aged sailor she had often seen manning the wheel during Brian Carr's watch. Sometime in the night, a black night of thick overcast, he had begun to shout. The weak, angry voices of men torn from the brief oblivion of sleep demanded that he shut up. He had replied by jumping overboard.

In the morning those left in the boat—there had been almost a dozen of them, it seemed to Amalia now—had made an appalling discovery. The precious sextant was gone from the boat's locker. For some reason known only to his own crazed mind, the man had taken it with him into the ocean's depths.

With the aid of that instrument, Angus had been able to keep the boat on a fairly consistent northeasterly course. Even if they were not picked up by some ship, he had told them, they would have a good chance of reaching the bulge of Africa or one of the several islands in those latitudes before their supplies of jerked beef and hardtack ran out.

But after the sextant's loss he had to navigate as best he could, relying on visual sightings of the sun and stars, and trying to estimate the speed of the various currents either helping or hindering their progress. On days of flat calm, like this one, the makeshift sail was of no use, and only oars could propel them forward. Often squalls of wind and rain decided their course for them. After such squalls, Amalia and the others sometimes knew, by the grimness of Angus' face, that the storm had left them even farther from their goal.

For one reason, though, they welcomed squalls, despite the danger that the boat might be driven far off course or even founder. They caught rain in bailing buckets and added it to the contents of the kegs Angus kept in the locker. Thus even though water always was so scarce that he rationed it, none of them actually suffered from thirst. It was because of the ever-dwindling supply of food that all those men had died. That, and the equatorial sun. It not only blistered faces and arms. If Amalia's hazy memory was correct, Angus had said that at least three of the men appeared to have died from sunstroke.

Whatever the reason, one by one they had succumbed and been lowered over the side. The carpenter's mate, a bearded, pious man from New Bedford, had at Angus' request recited a brief prayer as the bodies were lowered into the water. But then he himself, after a night and half a day of delirium, had died. After that, any prayers for the dead were said silently.

Now Amalia thought: With so many dead, how is it that I am alive? Was it because, as Dr. Seth Marsden had once casually remarked, women had an extra layer of fatty tissue, and so could go longer without food? Was it because women, although weaker of muscle, had greater powers of sheer endurance? Perhaps women were better equipped emotionally to survive some sorts of ordeals. Women—and tough, stubborn men like Angus.

She knew that she should retreat behind that canvas curtain Angus had rigged up for her and try to sleep during this, the hottest part of the day. But she felt too tired, too stupefied, even to move. Instead she sat there and gazed at Angus' hands resting on the oars, those big hands with the red-gold hair curling along the backs.

Memory stirred. That house on John Street, with the hurricane howling outside, and the caresses of those big hands bringing her to such a state of desire that she had cried out for him to bring her release. Not only her mind seemed to remember that, but her body too. She wondered how that could be. How could she, only half-alive, remember so vividly the warmth of his lips around the erect nipples of her breasts and the weight of his long body on her own?

Her gaze lifted to his face, red and blistered where it was not bearded. His beard was the same red-tinged gold as his hair. Was it in one of the squalls, she wondered, that he had lost his cap? Then she became aware of the expression in his blue eyes, sad and wry and yet touched with mockery. Somehow, she felt, he had sensed her thoughts of a moment ago. Somehow he, too, was remembering the passion-tormented creature she had been that stormy night.

She felt a wave of humiliation, and then of rage. All of her bitterness toward him came rushing back. During these last few days she had even begun to blame him again for depriving her of Michael. It seemed to her suffering-hazed mind that if Michael were in her arms he would be safe, they would both be safe. She wanted to cry out, as she had yesterday—or was it the day before that, or the day before that?—"Where is my son? Why did you separate me from my little boy?"

But if she said that, he would only tell her, as he had before, that he had done what he had to do the day the *Falcon* went down. Perhaps, too, he would remind her once again that Michael was his son as well as hers.

And so, with an agonizing effort, she wrenched her mind

away from her child, her child who might still be floating in that other boat, or long since at rest in the ocean depths, or, pray God, alive and healthy aboard some ship which had sighted that second longboat. Eyes closed, she forced her mind back to the distant past, back to her growing-up years in that peaceful little Mississippi town, back to her mother's stories of her own childhood in Cádiz.

Cádiz, and that steep street she had hoped to climb with her son in her arms, so that he could meet his great-grandfather. . . .

As sometimes happened, she fell asleep while still sitting upright.

An unmeasured interval later she heard a hoarse voice shouting, "Do you see it, Captain? It's land! I'll swear it's land!"

Eyes still closed, Amalia frowned. Even half-asleep, she had recognized the voice of Nate Dent, the galley boy, who had spent the last few days curled up on the boat strakes, seldom stirring except to receive his tiny ration of beef and hardtack. But about a week ago he twice had imagined he saw land. She bitterly resented him for interrupting her dream, a pleasant one in which she and the nuns had been harvesting peaches from a tree in the convent garden in Belleville.

Then she heard Angus say, "By God, boy! You're right!"

She came wide-awake then, and twisted around on the thwart to follow the direction of their gaze. There it was, surely not more than a few miles away, the bluish shape of a small island.

# 38

It took three hours' hard rowing to bring them close to the island. Angus was not the only one who rowed. As if the sight of land had been a magic elixir, Nate Dent and the Hazelton twins and Johnny of the unpronounceable last name also manned the oars, their gaunt faces filled with half-incredulous joy.

They could see details of the island now. Obviously it was of volcanic origin. Its central hill, rising about eight hundred feet, was still roughly cone-shaped. But the lava that had flowed down its sides perhaps millions of years ago had now turned to rich earth, supporting a tangle of trees and vines. The lower slopes of the hill ended in a crescent of beach fringed with scrub palms. The sand of the beach was neither white nor pink, but the black of that ancient lava flow.

The boat's hull grated over pebbles. Angus and the other men jumped into the water and pulled the boat high onto the glistening black sand. Holding her under the elbows, Angus helped Amalia out of the boat.

She said, "Where . . . ?" Her voice had a hoarse, unused sound.

"This island must be somewhere off Africa. That's all I can feel sure of." He turned to the Sagaponack. "Johnny, you wait here by the boat. The rest of us will walk a ways, but we'll be back by sunset."

They set out along the black sand. Amalia wondered if the others, too, felt a weakness in long-unused leg muscles. She said, "Could there be people?"

Angus answered, "On this island? Why not? It may be part of the Cape Verde chain. Some of those are inhabited." His voice quickened. "But one thing I'm sure of. We're not going to starve." He pointed ahead to where some lumbering green shapes moved toward the water. "Turtles. And where there are turtles, there are turtle eggs."

A few moments later Silas Hazelton said, "Look!" Following the direction of his pointing finger, Amalia saw a horned goat, body hidden by ferns, peering down at them from the lush hillside.

"You think that's a wild goat, Captain? If it isn't, it must be that people are here."

"Or have been. Sometimes people settle islands and then abandon them."

For a while after that they walked in silence toward a headland. Just offshore were black rocks with harsh-voiced seabirds hovering over them. Gull's eggs, Amalia thought. Would they taste like hen's eggs? She tried, and failed, to remember how eggs had tasted.

And then every other thought was driven from her mind because a man was coming around the headland, a man in tattered blue trousers and white shirt and ship's officer's cap. He had some sort of basket over his arm, and walked with his gaze directed downward. In the late-afternoon light his beard was fiery red.

Amalia said hoarsely. "Isn't that . . . ? Oh, it is, it is!"

Nate Dent, the galley boy, yelled, "Mr. Carr, Mr. Carr!"

Brian's head jerked up. He ran toward them. Amalia and Angus and the other two men also were running. Amalia thought: Oh, please, God, have Brian tell me that my baby is alive too.

Brian Carr said to Angus, "Lord, Captain! We thought we'd never see you again, none of you." Then he turned swiftly to Amalia. "He's fine! Your little boy's just fine."

She burst into tears and flung herself into the second mate's arms. He said, sounding both pleased and embarrassed, "Why, I think he's even grown some." He patted her sob-shaken shoulder. "Miss White is fine too."

She stepped back. "*Where* is he?"

"They're all about a mile the other side of that headland." He laughed excitedly and held up the basket he carried. It was made of woven palm bark. "I often find buried turtle eggs along this beach, but I'm sure not going to look for them today!"

They all moved toward the headland. Will he know me? Amalia wondered feverishly. And what do I look like? So terrible that I will frighten him? She raised a hand to her sun-blistered lower lip, then to her hair. She had long since lost her hairpins, and so she had just let her hair hang, grateful for the slight protection it gave the sides of her face. After weeks of sun and salty air, her hair felt harsh to the touch. She had a terrible presentiment that Michael would run screaming if she tried to take him in her arms.

With the small part of her attention not given over to thoughts of her son, she was aware of the men's swift, excited conversation. The other boat, she heard Brian say, had landed on this island a little more than three weeks ago. Because their ordeal had been less prolonged, the people in the other boat had fared better. Ten had survived and seven had died, one of them Phineas Smith, the assistant cook. When she heard that, Amalia wondered what Michael had felt about his friend's death. Because of all the strangeness and fear surrounding him, perhaps he'd had no room in his small self for grief.

Angus asked, "What's your guess as to where we are?"

"One of the Cape Verde islands."

"That's my guess, too."

"But it must be well away from the main group," Brian Carr went on. "Even from this island's highest point no other island is visible, and neither is Africa."

"And you didn't find any inhabitants, of course."

"None. But there have been people here, probably years in the past. On the other side of the island, only a few feet above where we've built huts, there is a patch of sweet potatoes which is still producing, even though it is badly overgrown. Other places we've found what is left of small plantings of tobacco and cotton. Maybe most of the people who made these plantings died in some sort of epidemic, and the others just left. I guess there could be all sorts of reasons why they gave up. Anyway, they didn't take all of their animals with them. There's a species of goat here that I remember from my grandfather's farm in Rhode Island. We killed one and cooked it the afternoon of the day we arrived. It was sure a change from bully beef!"

Again he laughed excitedly. "If you have to be a castaway, you probably couldn't find a better spot than this. Plenty of water. Springs all over the island. And wild bananas and coconuts and tamarinds."

They had reached the headland now. They rounded it. Soon the black sand became grayish, then white. Looking at the hillside, Amalia saw that apparently on this, the eastern side of the island, the lava at least partially had been eroded away, revealing the limestone which the volcano had thrust up from the seabed. She saw chalky white boulders, one of them just above a spring that sent a rivulet running down the hillside to sink in the sand.

About a hundred yards away was another headland. As they moved toward it, she heard Angus ask, "But I assume that even if this is a miniature Eden, you're not averse to being rescued. Do you light a signal fire?"

"Every night, on the highest point of the island. And by day we fly a distress flag up there. Miss White donated the flag. It's a yellow shawl."

Amalia thought of Lena, wrapped in that yellow shawl and with a sobbing child in her arms as the longboat pulled away from the burning ship. She had an almost irresistible desire to break into a run. But she knew she must conserve what little strength she had, if she was to go the rest of the way on her own feet.

They rounded the headland. And there only about fifty yards away were a number of palm-thatched huts, with men moving about between them. Near the water two men were adding wood to a fire. A woman, back turned, stood watching them. She held a yellow-haired child by the hand.

Amalia's throat closed up, so that she could not have screamed Michael's and Lena's names out even if she had wanted to. And she did not want to. Michael must not see her as a witchlike woman in the throes of hysteria.

It was Brian Carr who shouted. The men moving about among the huts and the two men and woman and child beside the fire all turned, stood motionless.

Then the two groups were running toward each other. Even Amalia allowed herself to run a few steps before she stopped in her tracks. Lena had swept the boy up in her arms and was still running.

She halted a few feet from Amalia. "Oh, my child! Oh, my poor little girl!"

"Please, Lena. Please don't . . ." She wanted to say: Please don't let him know that *you* think my appearance is strange. But she could not get the words out.

Lena, though, must have realized what Amalia wanted. She set Michael on his feet. "You see, darling? It's just as I have kept telling you. Here is your mama, safe and sound."

For a moment Michael stared at Amalia, one of his hands entangled in Lena's skirt. Then the confused, doubtful look in his brown eyes gave way to delight. He ran to Amalia and encircled her legs with his arms. "Oh, Mama, Mama!"

She sank onto her knees and held him close. His small body felt firm. He was taller and heavier than she remembered. She thought fleetingly: They must have given him extra rations in the longboat. And then, still holding him close, she allowed herself the luxury of bursting into tears.

# 39

Leaving Michael in the care of Second Mate Brian Carr, Amalia and Lena climbed the next afternoon to a spring-fed pool high on the verdant hillside above the huts. While Lena watched the path, ready to give warning if one of the men started to climb toward them, Amalia stripped naked. Neck-deep in the limpid water, she washed not only her thin body and salt-encrusted hair but also her garments. Then, after spreading her tattered muslin dress and her brown shawl and her chemise and petticoat and drawers out on limestone rocks to dry, she wrapped herself in a length of sailcloth. It was from the locker of the longboat in which she and Angus and the others had existed for so many terrible days. Two of the men had rowed the boat around from the other side of the island near sunset the day before.

Lena sat down beside her. "Child, you sure got thin."

Amalia said, rubbing a long strand of dark wet hair between her palms, "I know. I must look hideous."

"Don't talk foolish. You're beautiful. Losing ten pounds or so doesn't change that. Neither does getting sun-blistered. All you need is a few days of good eating and of staying out of the sun."

"And a few more nights of good sleep."

The night before, in the hut the men had built for Lena and Michael, she had slept long and well. After weeks of fitful slumber on the hard, often water-soaked strakes of that always rolling longboat, the bed of ferns upon which she had slept in the hut had seemed to her like the most luxurious of mattresses.

"That reminds me. Why is Brian Carr's hut so close to yours?" A good fifty yards separated those two huts from the others.

"It was his idea." Lena hesitated, looking faintly embarrassed. "You see, Amalia, I'm not good-looking, and never was, even before I got this scar. But it's been a long, long time since all those men were ashore in Santos. And after a time men get considerably less choosy. So Brian Carr felt it was better for him to build his hut close to mine and Michael's."

"So he's been protecting you."

"That's about the size of it."

Seeing the troubled look in Lena's eyes, Amalia said lightly, "Now, don't go worrying about *me*. For one thing, we just can't be stranded here much longer. If this is one of the Cape Verde islands, some ship is sure to pass here soon." She turned and looked up the path. "Is it very far up to where you light the beacon fire each night?"

"No. When your clothes are dry, we can climb up there, if you want."

"All right. And in the meantime I'm going to braid my hair and wind the braids around my head. There's enough ribbon left in my chemise to tie the braids in place."

"Good! Your hair looks . . . peculiar, hanging down like that."

Amalia knew Lena did not mean "peculiar." She meant "wanton." Amalia thought of the day on the beach when Angus had told her harshly to put her hair up. But the night of the hurricane he himself had taken the pins from her hair . . .

Quickly she swerved her thoughts. "I wonder who they were, the people who planted crops on this island and then left."

Lena shrugged. "Maybe Portugee. I heard someone say that the Cape Verde islands belong to the Portugee. Or maybe black people from Africa. But anyway, I know there were children here."

"How do you know?"

"Well, Michael kept wanting to climb to the top of the hill, so one day I said yes. We rested here by this pool for a while and then started up the rest of the way. All of a sudden he darted off the path and out of sight. I got my skirt snagged on a bush, so it was a minute or two before I could catch up with him. And when I did, he was looking into this cave. Not a deep cave. More like just a floor of that white rock . . ." She hesitated.

"Limestone?"

"That's it. A wide limestone floor with a half-dome over it. We walked inside, and there on the floor was a little doll somebody'd made of wood, with shreds of palm bark for hair. It had had a painted mouth and nose and eyes, I guess, but those had pretty much worn away. It still had part of its dress, though, a piece of pinkish cotton, although maybe it was red to start with. I'd like to show it to you, but Michael left it on the beach one day and the tide must have swept it away."

"But you could show me that cave."

"All right. We'll stop there on the way up."

"Imagine Michael discovering it!" Amalia gave a proud laugh. "He's growing so fast. And he's giving up a lot of that funny language. I can understand nearly everything he says."

A little more than an hour later, as they climbed toward the hill's summit, Lena said, "See that limestone boulder up ahead? The spot where Michael slipped away from me is just beyond it." Moments later she added, "Here it is. You see, there must have been a fairly wide path branching off here once, although it's almost all overgrown now."

They left the main path and followed a barely discernible one through a tangle of palmettos, trailing vines, and giant ferns. Then they reached the cave's lip. Amalia stood looking in at the clean sandy floor and the dome-shaped roof, about eight feet above the cave floor at its highest point. What a marvelous place those now-vanished children had to play.

She turned around. From below the cave the green hillside sloped quite steeply away toward the beach. She could see far out over the water, a sparkling blue on this clear day. Africa was over there somewhere beyond the horizon. She wondered just how far beyond.

Returning to the main path, they climbed the rest of it. As they neared the rim of what had once been an active volcano spewing molten rock down its side to the steaming sea, the palmettos and tamarind trees thinned out. Up here the vegetation was mostly wild grasses and vines. As for the volcano's crater, over the aeons it had filled up with earth eroded from the volcano's rim, so that now it was like a tableland. If Amalia had not seen the island's shape from the sea, she would not have realized that now she stood at the edge of what had once been a bubbling pool of lava.

Amalia saw the distress flag, Lena's yellow shawl fastened

to a wooden pole. At the moment, it was of little use. On this windless day the shawl hung limp. Near it was a pile of driftwood about five feet high.

"Each day at sunset," Lena said, "one of the men climbs up here and lights the signal fire. In the morning they bring up more driftwood. We'd better get back," she added. "Night comes awfully sudden."

"I know."

About halfway down the path, Lena said, "Child, there's something I've been wanting to ask you. It's about Angus MacFarlane. You haven't held what he did against him, have you? I mean, his knocking you unconscious and then putting you in the boat?"

"Yes, I'm afraid I have."

"Well, you shouldn't. You know what I think of him. I'd a lot rather you favored someone like Brian Carr. But just the same, the day the *Falcon* went down, he did what he had to do. And . . . well, fair's fair."

"I know." Perhaps now that she had been reunited with her child, she would be able to really feel the truth of Lena's words. Perhaps she would be able to put aside the bitterness which, even now, filled her at the thought of all those weeks when she had believed she would never see Michael again.

Near the bottom of the path they encountered a man, one of those who had been in the same longboat as Lena and Michael. He had a flintbox in his hand. He greeted them politely and then moved on.

Amalia and Lena stepped onto a beach dyed with mauve and pinkish sunset light. At the water's edge, Michael walked hand in hand with Brian Carr. Both man and child were barefoot, and Michael was kicking at the froth of spent waves. With Lena still beside her, Amalia started toward Brian and Michael and then stopped, suddenly aware that Angus MacFarlane was moving swiftly toward her along the beach. As he drew closer, Amalia saw that he had thrust a pistol into the waistband of his trousers.

He nodded to Lena and then said, "Amalia, will you walk a short way with me? I want to talk to you."

In spite of herself, she felt her pulsebeat quicken at the look in his eyes. It was telling her how much he liked the newly laundered dress and the clean, shining braids wrapped around her head.

"All right."

Lena said, "I'll take Michael into the hut and try to get him to take a short nap so he won't be cranky at supper." She turned away.

Amalia and Angus walked slowly over the sand. She asked, "Where did that pistol come from?"

"The longboat's locker."

"The boat we were in? I never saw you wear it."

"It wasn't needed in the longboat."

"And it is now? Why?"

"Do you want a frank answer?"

"Of course."

"You are the main reason. You are a beautiful young woman on an island with a dozen men. I've let it be understood that any one of them who lays a hand on you gets shot."

She had an impulse to ask, "And will you apply that rule to yourself?" She did not ask it, of course.

He went on. "Thank God there's no rum on the island. There were two bottles in the locker of the other longboat, but they were drunk before the boat even landed here. Just the same, I think you should keep aloof from the men as much as possible. For instance, you and Lena and the boy had better take your meals by yourselves."

"What about Brian Carr? Are you going to order him to move his hut?"

When Angus finally replied, his tone was curt. "No, not unless you want me to."

"I'd rather he stayed there. Lena has felt safer for his presence, and I imagine I will too."

"Very well. It's hard to picture Carr as a danger to women, anyway."

Her voice was sharp. "That is true, but not for the reason you are implying. He's not . . . insufficiently masculine. He's just a gentleman, that's all."

He asked coldly, "Are you trying to tell me you find him attractive?"

"Frankly, I cannot see how that is any of your business."

"Of course it is my business! I am still in command of the *Falcon*'s passengers and crew, even though the ship itself has gone down. And I say there'll be no dallying on this island. Do what you want to with him after we are away from here.

For all I care, you two can be married by the captain of whatever ship picks us up. But if while we're on this island you start giving your favors, as the saying goes, to that second mate, it's going to cause a lot of jealousy among the rest of the men. And I won't have that!"

Through the rapidly fading light, she looked sidewise at his set, angry face. She thought, feeling a surge of vengeful pleasure: Jealousy among the other men, poppycock! *He's* the one who is jealous right now, so jealous he would like to strangle poor Brian.

Aloud she said, "Hadn't we better turn back now, so that Lena and I can get a cooking fire started before dark?"

"I meant what I said, Amalia."

"Very well. In the interest of keeping Brian from getting shot, I'll see to it that he keeps his distance. Now, let's go back."

Turning, they for a while walked in silence. Then he said, "I'm glad the boy looks so well." He added quickly, "Don't worry. I'll keep my promise not to—what was the term you used?—try to ingratiate myself with him. All I am saying is that he looks well."

There was a gruff note in his voice, as if his throat had tightened up. Her malicious pleasure of a few minutes before vanished entirely. What had he felt, seeing the child he had fathered, the child that all these weeks he must have thought dead, walking along the shore with his small hand in Brian Carr's? She wanted to say: You don't have to keep that promise. But, no. Better to leave things as they were. Better to try to keep her son from becoming any sort of bond between her and Angus, because certainly she should know by now that they indeed were, as Angus had once said, each other's bad luck.

He said, "One more thing. There are several paths leading up from the beach to the high point of the island. I'll see to it that the path you and Lena used today is off limits to the men."

"Thank you."

"Well, I'll leave you here. Good night." Turning to his right, he crossed the beach to where, near the water's edge, several men had already gathered around a driftwood fire.

As she neared the hut in which she had slept the night before with Lena and Michael, she saw that Lena, also, had gathered driftwood into a small pile a few feet from the hut's door. Amalia asked, "Is that to be a cooking fire?"

"That's right."

"How on earth did you know that Angus would want us to eat by ourselves?"

"It figured, that's all. There's no way that man would want you taking your meals with all those other men."

Straightening, Lena looked up through the thickening dark at the hilltop. Amalia followed the direction of her gaze and saw the beacon fire, its flames leaping straight up on this windless night.

# 40

For Amalia, the days that followed had a dual aspect. On the surface, she was living those days in the sort of tropical paradise she had heard about. True, rainstorms sometimes passed over the island, ripping palm fronds from the huts and, if it was night, quenching the signal fire. But most of the time the weather was idyllic, neither too warm nor too cool, with sunny days and with nights when the stars gleamed like diamonds strewn on dark blue velvet.

There was no shortage of food. At their separate fire, she and Lena cooked fresh fish wrapped in palm leaves, made turtle soup in one of the bailing buckets from the longboats, and roasted sweet potatoes from those now-reclaimed plantings on the hill slope. They had wild coconuts and wild oranges, small and very sweet. There were flowers to enjoy, also. On her almost daily walks up the path Angus had reserved for her and Lena and Michael, she found a species of pink lily, and numerous small tree orchids, white with spotted throats, on vines wound around palm and tamarind trunks.

But always underneath was the thought that she knew must haunt everyone on this island. What if they had to spend the rest of their lives here, with no books or magazines or newspapers, no knowledge of what was happening in the rest of the world? Whenever that thought came into her full consciousness, she managed to suppress it. Before long they would be rescued. It could be only freakish ill fortune which so far had kept ships from sighting their distress signal.

For Amalia there was still another sort of tension. She knew that the men were keenly aware of her. True, except for Angus, who brought them food supplies each day, men seldom approached the hut she shared with Lena and Michael. Even Brian Carr, who continued to occupy a hut only a few yards away, did not linger there in the daytime. Instead he joined the other men in their endless tasks of wood gathering, renewing the palm thatch on the huts, cultivating the reclaimed garden patches, and searching for turtles and turtle eggs.

On the few occasions when she did encounter one or another of the crew members, she was greeted with polite respect. But she could not help but sense their awareness, could not help but realize that, out of Angus' hearing, they must talk of her.

The knowledge made her cringe. At the same time, it brought her an inner excitement. Unfortunately for her, the excitement was not tenuous, diffused. Instead it was focused on the tall, curt-mannered man who, in the late afternoons, brought her and Lena and Michael their food for the next twenty-four hours. And as her body, recovering from those days of near-starvation in the longboat, grew stronger, that inner excitement increased. Often in the early morning, awakening in the hut where her little boy and Lena still slept, she would feel her face grow hot with the memory of some dream of Angus. Even though in some of the dreams the setting seemed to be that Sag Harbor house, it was the Angus of this island, bearded and sun-browned, whose kisses and caresses brought her to such a state of tension that she woke up aching for him.

Some days she and Lena, suiting their steps to Michael's, climbed with him up to the pool or even to the top of the cone-shaped hill. Other times, too keyed-up to bear even the company of those two she loved, she would climb the path to the pool and then continue on to the cave. Because the sand was uncomfortable, she had strewn the cave floor with the long ferns which grew in profusion all over the island. The first few times she had climbed the path alone she had been a little afraid that, in spite of Angus' injunction, someone might follow her. But apparently here on this island his authority still held, a ship captain's almost mystical authority. To oppose it would constitute mutiny, a crime almost as heinous as treason. And so she was left undisturbed to look out over the blue ocean stretching emptily between the island and invisible Africa. She would try hard to think of distant, pleasant things—the flicker of candles in the convent school's chapel or the way the tall reeds between the John Street house and the cove bent in the wind.

On a night when she had been on the island a little more than three weeks, she sat beside the embers of the cooking fire. Lena and Michael had already gone into the hut. She turned her gaze to where some of the men, out in the longboats, were spearfishing. With torches made of resinous wood, some of them attracted fish to the surface, where others could spear them with pointed sticks. Probably, she reflected, that was the way all people had fished up until the time someone had thought of fashioning fishhooks out of bone. For a few moments she looked at the torchlight reflections on the water and listened to the shouts and occasional laughter of the men. Was Angus out there with them? She turned her head and looked into the fire, hoping that the flickering pattern of the embers as they cooled would soothe her into drowsiness.

She did not know how long she had been staring into the fire when she heard the crunch of footsteps over the sand. Her head jerked around. Angus was approaching, a bucket in one hand, red-gold beard bright in the upward-striking glow of the embers. Startled, she got to her feet so quickly that her ankle turned in the soft sand. His free hand shot out to grasp her upper arm.

"God! You almost went into the fire."

He set down the bucket, grasped her other arm. Aware that the pulse was pounding in her throat, she did not move. His gaze went over her face, as if reading the evidence of what his touch was doing to her. A look, pleased and almost triumphant, leaped into those brilliant blue eyes.

Then he stepped back from her. He nodded toward the bucket and said, "Fresh-caught pompano for your breakfast. Good night."

She managed to murmur a thank-you. He turned and moved away into the darkness.

Amalia went into the hut. The dying fire cast enough light that she could see that Lena's eyes were open. What was more, from where she lay on her fern pallet she must have been able to see Amalia and Angus standing in near-embrace. But she made no comment. Amalia reflected that perhaps Lena, once so opinionated and bossy, had come to feel that when the *Falcon* had gone down she had lost all control of events. She could only wait to see where they carried her and the young woman and little boy she loved.

In midafternoon the next day Amalia went up to the pool to bathe. Afterward she dressed and, with wet hair hanging free, climbed to the cave. She sat with legs curled around her on the sunny limestone ledge, drying her hair. Not wanting to define the tension she felt, she looked out over the blue sea, a sea as empty as if ships had never been invented.

Sounds. Sounds of someone approaching, not from the direction she herself had come, but the opposite one. She got to her feet. Angus emerged from the tangle of ferns and vines and dwarf palmettos. She said, past the pulse hammering in the hollow of her throat, "Why have you . . . ?"

He stood close to her. "Why have I come here? Because last night you asked me to."

Much as she might have wanted to deny that, she found herself unable to. Remembering that moment beside the fire's embers, she was sure that her need of him must have been plain in her face.

He raised his hands, lifted the two long dark wings of her hair, let them fall back into place. He cupped her face in his hands and kissed her very gently. Then he was undoing the buttons of her worn cotton dress. She stood there, knowing she was helpless to stop him even if she had wanted to. And she did not want to. Suddenly and feverishly she knew that she desired him as much as he desired her.

But when he pushed her dress from her shoulders, baring her breasts, she said faintly, "What if someone—?"

"No one will come up here. But we had best go inside anyway."

Arm around her, he led her into the cave. At his bidding she lay down on the soft, springy ferns. Already she had a sense of warm inward melting. Eyes closed, she let him strip her of her dress and chemise and ankle-length drawers. He took off her garters and drew her stockings down over her narrow feet. For a moment after that his hand lingered on the dark triangle where her slender legs joined. Without her realizing it, she arched her body upward against the pressure of his palm.

She heard the sounds of his undressing. He lay down beside her. For a moment her eyes opened and looked up into his blue, gravely tender ones. Then again her weighted lids closed. She felt the silkiness of his beard as his lips caressed her throat, her shoulders, and closed softly, warmly, around the erect nipples of her breasts. By contrast his palm, stroking the inside of her thighs, felt callused. The very roughness of that hand, toughened by the hardships they had both been through, intensified the hunger deep within her. She felt herself moving, heard herself saying, "Please—"

His naked body lay on hers. She gave a little moan of pleasure at the first long thrust of him deep within her. For a while she lay passive, content to feel each thrust and withdrawal, thrust and withdrawal. But soon her need began to sharpen. Within seconds it had reached an almost painful intensity. Dimly she was aware that her fingernails bit into his shoulders and that she had wrapped her legs around him, wanting feverishly to have him plunge deeper and deeper into her desire-swollen body. But she found no surcease from the exquisite torment. Instead that rhythmic thrusting, faster now, seemed only to increase her almost unbearable hunger. Body arching upward to bring him still deeper into the demanding core of her, she moaned for release.

She found it. With a final thrust he brought her to climax, a climax so sharp and ecstatic that she cried out. For several seconds the long shudders of release swept down her body.

Quiet now, his body still weighted hers. Finally she opened her eyes and looked into the blue ones so close above her own. He said softly, "Just rest for a moment."

Seconds later he began to move again. Her climax of only minutes ago had been so complete, so satisfying, that she'd had no idea he could reawaken her desire so soon. But she was feeling it again, that slowly mounting urgency. And this time when he had carried her to the heights and the long, ecstatic fall, she felt the throb of his own release.

For a while they lay side by side in silence, her head on his shoulder. Then she said, "I didn't know—I mean, how is it you can—"

Only minutes ago her body had been shameless in its need. And yet now she felt too embarrassed even to ask her question.

He laughed softly. "How is it that I was able to hold back and wait until after I'd made love to you a second time? It's called control, my darling."

After a moment he added, "I'm sorry about the beard."

"Oh, no! I like it."

"Well, I'll have to shave it off before we get back to Sag Harbor. The town doesn't believe a man deserves the dignity of a beard until he's past thirty-five."

"Then . . . then you do think we'll get back to Sag Harbor?"

When he finally answered, his tone was sober. "I don't know. It seems to me that we should have been picked up long before this. But anyway, I'm going to wait one more week. Then I'll spend another week making one of the longboats as seaworthy as possible—mending the sail, recalking the seams, stocking the locker with food. Then I'll sail with a few men toward Africa. It can't be too far off."

"No!" she cried. "Please, please, don't you go."

"It will be all right, Amalia. I'll leave Brian Carr in charge, and I'll leave the pistol with him and give strict orders that the men are to obey him. He's a good man, no matter what I've said of him, and he'll take good care of you and the boy and Lena."

"I'm not thinking of us. I'm thinking of you! Anything might happen to you. The boat may founder in a storm, and we'd never know . . ." She broke off.

After a moment he said quietly, "Then you love me, Amalia? It was not just a matter of physical desire? You really love me?"

"Yes." She found she could admit it now. "I guess I never stopped loving you, from almost the first time I saw you."

He propped himself on one elbow. "Then you'll marry me if we get back to Sag Harbor?"

Unbidden, the scene flashed before her mind's eye. That moonlit New Orleans night when he had told her that he could not marry her. And then that time months later when the doctor, speaking of Juana's malignancy, had said that so often such a tumor develops after a severe emotional blow. . . .

Amalia said, "You're absolutely sure you want to marry me, Juana Moreno's daughter? You're absolutely sure that those Presbyterian ancestors of yours wouldn't start whirling in their graves?"

"Amalia! Why can't you put that out of your thoughts? Why can't you?"

She said, her voice subdued now, "It's because of the way

my mother . . ." She broke off. "You don't know much about my mother's death, do you?"

"Only that she died."

"In the past I haven't been able to talk to you about it. But now I will." Trying not to visualize how Juana had looked during those last weeks, her gentle, once-pretty face so thin between the graying black braids, Amalia told him the cause of her mother's death.

"The most terrible part is that the doctor said that malignancies often follow an emotional shock. It was I who gave her that shock. You gave me what felt like a death blow, and I passed it along to her, stupid and cruel young creature that I was, and to her it really was a death blow. . . ."

"Oh, my darling, my darling." She was crying now. He held her close to him. "No wonder you . . . But try to forgive me, darling. Can't you try?"

"I don't know," she said brokenly. After a moment she added, with sudden insight, "Maybe it is partly because I can't forgive myself for what I did to her."

"Amalia, I'm sure she forgave you ten times over before she died."

She pondered that for a moment. "Suppose we could go back to that summer in New Orleans. Suppose you again heard about my mother and Sara Davidson. Would you act differently this time?"

"Oh, Amalia! If the circumstances were the same, I would behave the same, not because I wanted to, but because I felt it was the right thing to do. There is no magic way of going back and altering the past, my darling. We just have to accept what we have done, and what we have become, and yet forgive each other for it. Don't you see that?"

"I suppose so," she answered slowly.

"And you'll think about marrying me?"

"Yes, I'll think about it."

For several minutes they lay silent in each other's arms. Then Amalia asked, "Do you think all those men will . . . know about us?"

"I'm afraid so. Even if we leave here by separate paths, they'll know. People who become lovers sometimes think they can hide it, but they can't. It shows in the way they look at each other and in the tones of their voices." He paused. "Will you mind very much?"

She said, after thinking it over, "Some. Not as much as I'd have expected I would." She turned and looked at the light beyond the cave mouth. It had taken on a golden tone. "It must be not too long until sunset."

"Yes, we had better go."

When they had dressed, they walked out to the ledge beyond the cave entrance and stood embraced for a moment. He said, "Tomorrow, at about the same time?"

She nodded. "Tomorrow."

They kissed, holding each other close. Then they parted, she taking her usual path down to the beach and the palm-thatch huts, he following another.

As she neared her hut, she saw that Brian Carr was there, helping Lena build the evening fire. Michael sat nearby, scooping up sand in a large clam shell.

Smiling, Brian Carr looked up at Amalia. Almost immediately she saw the expression in his eyes turn to something pained and wry. Perhaps he—or someone—had noticed that she and Angus were missing from the beach at the same time. Perhaps, too, lovemaking had subtly but unmistakably altered her appearance. Whatever the explanation, it was plain that he had guessed that only a short while ago she had been lying in Angus' arms.

He said, "Good evening, Mrs. Fulmer." He stood up, brushed sand from the worn and baggy knees of his once-spruce uniform trousers. "Well, I had best go on up the beach."

During supper Amalia realized from the very lack of expression on her brown-skinned face that Lena also knew. Neither of them said anything about it, though, until the meal was over and they had put Michael to bed. Then, as they sat beside the remains of the cooking fire, Amalia said, "Today, up in the cave . . . What I'm trying to say is that Angus and I . . ."

"I know what you are trying to say."

"I thought it best to tell you, because it won't be the last time."

After a while Lena said, "Maybe it's for the best. At least now the others will give up any notions they may have had about you. And anyway, I suppose it was bound to happen."

She did not ask what Amalia intended to do about Angus once they returned home. With an inward shiver, Amalia realized that perhaps Lena had given up hope that any of them would ever reach home.

Amalia said, "If we're still here two weeks from now, Angus intends to launch one of the longboats with a crew of several men."

"What for?" Lena asked sharply.

"To look for help. Maybe it will encounter a ship, either between here and Africa or in some African port."

"Talk him out of it! At least we are all safe as long as we stay on this island."

"I'll try."

But she did not try, not once during all the hours she spent with Angus during the next few days. She did not even ask him to send someone else to command the longboat, if it was ever launched. She knew it would be no use to try to persuade him. He would not ask other men to risk their lives while he remained in safety.

And so she did not mention the subject during their hours together, even though after a few days she observed men readying one of the longboats, mending its sail, storing food aboard, and calking its seams with resin from the scrub conifers that grew high on the volcanic hill. Instead she kept telling herself desperately that soon—perhaps tonight, perhaps tomorrow morning—a ship would appear.

Nor did she and Angus again discuss their possible marriage, even though she sensed it was on his mind just as it was on hers. Lying in his arms, languid with fulfilled desire, she sometimes felt she could not do otherwise than try to stay close to him her whole life long. But once they were away from this island, if they ever did get away, would she feel the same, or would she find her old bitterness and mistrust coming to the surface again? Perhaps if they ever reached Sag Harbor she would find it best to try to rebuild the sort of life she had achieved during those many months when Angus was away on that whaler, a somewhat lonely life, but busy and serene.

Then, feeling his lips warm on hers, and his callused hands stroking her body, she banished tormenting questions about the future. They might not have a future. Best to take what delights they could give each other in the present hour, the present moment.

But one day she did bring up the subject of his broken engagement to Barbara Weyant, the Boston shipowner's daughter. "You said it was because of a journal she found."

"Yes. I'd written about you in it. She found it in a drawer of my bureau. You see, on her father's advice I had taken rooms in the home of some cousins of the Weyants', two elderly ladies who had seen better days. While I was away on one of her father's ships, Barbara found the journal."

"You mean she invaded your rooms when you weren't there, and went through your belongings? But how can that be? Wasn't she . . . well, a lady?"

"Very much so. I don't know to this day what made her behave like that. I only know that when I got back to Boston there was a letter from her waiting for me. In it she said that during one of her visits to her cousins she had found my journal, and so she knew that I was in love with someone else. She also said she never wanted to see me again."

Imagining the dismay on Augus' face as he read that letter, Amalia felt a pang of jealousy. "How did her letter make you feel?"

He said after a thoughtful moment, "Embarrassed. Sorry that she had been hurt. And yet I also felt a vast relief. I'd asked her to marry me because I liked and admired her, knew that she would make a suitable wife, and felt that it was high time I married. Also, I hoped that marriage would make me forget you. But when she threw me over, and I felt that surge of relief, I knew that such a marriage would have been unfair to both her and me." He stroked Amalia's hair. "Is there anything else you want to know about her?"

Arm across his naked chest, she pressed her cheek closer to his shoulder. "No. Perhaps I've always been a little jealous of that fine Boston young lady of yours. Now I'm not."

Their eighth afternoon tryst up at the cave coincided with the full moon. It rose out of the east, a huge silver globe, while the last of the sunset still flamed in the west. Amalia felt she had best hurry down to Lena and Michael, but Angus held her back.

"Please, darling. Please stay a little while. They won't worry. Lena knows where you are."

And so she stayed, and they made love, while outside the sunset faded with tropic swiftness and only brilliant moonlight shone through the cave's wide opening onto their entwined bodies. After a while they dressed and stepped out onto the limestone shelf.

Amalia cried, "Look!"

The ship had anchored many yards offshore, obviously afraid to make a closer approach until morning. Moonlight flooded its dark hull, its square-rigged sails. And somewhere up in its rigging a yellow light, visible even through the moon's radiance, swung back and forth in an arc. Amalia pictured the man astride a lofty spar, swinging a lantern back and forth in answer to that beacon fire that had flamed unseen for so many nights.

# 41

Matthew Bowen, captain of the New Bedford whaler *Josephus Slate*, was almost as glad to find the *Falcon*'s survivors as they were to be found. For the last eight months of a voyage that had begun more than two years before, the *Slate* had been shorthanded. On a South Pacific island, eight of his crew had deserted, apparently unwilling to continue an arduous voyage that promised only a small profit for them to share. Unable to find the deserters, Captain Bowen had lifted anchor and set sail for the South Atlantic by way of Cape Horn. During the passage of the Straight of Magellan with its howling winds, black skies, and giant waves studded with chunks of ice, his first mate and two of his seamen had been swept overboard. Once in the South Atlantic, the *Slate* had captured several whales and might have successfully pursued several more if there had been enough crewmen to man all the whale boats.

No wonder that Captain Bowen, a stout man of middle age, was pleased to find a dozen experienced seamen, including two officers, even though, unfortunately, the castaways included two women and a small boy. With barely discernible reluctance he turned his cabin over to Amalia and Lena and Michael. Along with Angus, whom he had named acting first mate, he moved into the former first mate's cabin. Brian Carr shared the second mate's cabin, and the other *Falcon* survivors occupied those vacant bunks in the forecastle.

Grateful as she was to Captain Bowen, Amalia from the first disliked being aboard his ship. The cabin she shared with her little son and Lena was more cramped than the owner's cabin on the lost *Falcon*. What was more, like the rest of the *Slate*, it was none too clean. For a while the supplies of fresh fruit and vegetables taken from the island held out. But once they were gone, the only food they had, including weevily bread, was revolting. Worst of all was the ship's smell. According to Captain Bowen, weeks had passed since whale blubber had been boiled down in those big try pots on the ship's deck. The greasy smell, though, lingered on.

One early morning, awakened by the lookout's shout and by the pound of running feet on deck, she knew that a whale must have been sighted. Giving in to Michael's pleas, she allowed him to accompany Lena out onto the deck. Minutes passed, though, before she herself, irresistibly drawn, went to the porthole.

Out there on the calm ocean, sparkling in the sunrise light, a drama was taking place, one that probably would end with more money in the pockets of various humans—the ship's crew and its owners and the grog-shop proprietors and bordello keepers in New Bedford. For the harpooned whale the drama almost surely would end in death. She saw the enormous creature leap high into the air, trying to shake itself free from what must have been the agonizing pain of the harpoon in its side. Then it swam straight ahead, towing the whale boat and its crew at the other end of the taut harpoon line. Again the whale leaped, its magnificent body shedding water that gave off prism colors in the rising sun. If she had not known that the creature must be in its death agonies, she might have thought the sight beautiful. Turning, she went back to her bunk and sat down on its edge, hands clenched together in her lap.

The dead whale was brought alongside the *Slate*. After a while she heard the creak of winches and felt the ship actually shudder as the huge body was lowered onto it. Even though she stayed in the cabin the next few days, she knew, from the remembered talk of Sag Harbor people, what was happening on deck—the stripping of blubber and whalebone and the boiling of the cut-up blubber in the try pots.

Even though she could escape the sight of all that, she could not avoid the pervasive smell. What was worse, she happened to be standing at the porthole when the whale carcass, stripped of all that could bring money to its captors, was cut loose and allowed to drift back along the ship's side. In sick horror she stared at the bloody mass which that huge, beautiful, and harmless creature had become.

It was then that she decided upon a course she had been mulling over the past few days.

Knowing that Angus, as acting first mate, probably had just come off his morning watch, she went to the cabin he shared with Captain Bowen. She was almost sure Angus would be alone. The captain at this hour usually was taking breakfast in the officers' salon.

When Angus admitted her, she saw that he indeed was alone. She said, "I want to get off this ship. I want to take Michael to Cádiz, just as I first planned."

It was not a desire impossible of accomplishment. They were in the main Atlantic sea lanes now. On an average of at least once a day they encountered Europe-bound merchantmen as well as other whale ships. For a fee, almost any merchantman would accept her and Michael as passengers.

Despite the dismay in his eyes, Angus kept his voice calm. "I've realized how you must hate being aboard. As you know, a whaler is far from my favorite kind of ship." He paused. "But I can't go to Cádiz with you, my darling."

"I know."

"We all owe Captain Bowen a great deal. For me to go back on my agreement to act as first mate for the rest of the voyage . . . well, that would be pretty shabby."

"I know," she said again.

After a while he said, "You have still another reason for wanting to leave this ship, haven't you?"

She said painfully, "Yes. I haven't been able to make up my mind about . . . us. Maybe if I am away from you for a while I can."

"I thought that was it."

"I want to be sure, Angus. For the sake of all three of us, I want to be sure that I can bury the past and give us every chance of building a fine life together."

"I too want you to be absolutely sure. I'll hate like the very devil to let you go now, but if it is what you need . . ."

After a moment he asked, "Will Lena go with you?"

"I doubt that she will want to. The sooner she gets back on dry land, the better she will like it. And I doubt that it will be long before the *Slate* lands you at Sag Harbor."

"No, not long, now that the holds are almost full."

"There is one problem. I have no money to pay for passage to Cádiz."

"That is no problem. Captain Bowen will make you a loan. He knew Tom quite well." A certain constraint came into his voice, as it always did when he mentioned the husband she had lived with so briefly. "And he is at least acquainted with Richard Fulmer. He will know your credit is good."

She gave an unhappy little smile. "Besides, he will be glad to be rid of at least one woman aboard."

His smile echoed her own. "There are some captains like that. They hate the very idea of a woman on a ship."

Then his smile died. As they looked into each other's eyes, Amalia knew that he too was remembering the cave and their joined bodies on the bed of ferns.

For a moment she wanted to cry: Don't let me leave you! But, no. She still had unresolved emotions to sort out. Until she did, they might well go on tormenting themselves and each other. And it was best that she sort out those feelings away from his distracting physical presence.

They both knew that the captain might come in at any second. But they also knew that this might be their last chance for a real good-bye away from the gaze of others. And so she went into his arms, and his warm mouth covered hers in a long farewell kiss.

Three days later, after messages had been passed back and forth between the *Slate* and a Mediterranean-bound merchantman, the *Sea Queen*, two seamen rowed Amalia and her son over to the other ship. Holding Michael's hand, she stood at the taffrail until her eyes could no longer discern the tall figure standing in the *Slate*'s bow.

# 42

As the hired carriage drew her and Michael up the steep cobblestoned street, Amalia kept watching the numbers painted above the doorways of the various old houses. Finally she said, "*Párase, por favor.*"

The driver reined in. Still drawing on what she remembered of the Spanish Juana had taught her, she asked him to wait. In the green poplin dress she had bought in a Cádiz shop that morning, she got out of the carriage and lifted Michael down into the warm afternoon sunlight. They crossed the sidewalk and entered a doorway. As she led Michael slowly up three flights of rickety stairs, she was aware of smells—wine and olive oil and garlic, all underlain with the mustiness of decaying wood—and of the sounds of people talking and laughing and quarreling behind the closed doors.

On the fourth floor she knocked at a door. After a few seconds it opened. A plump woman of about thirty stood there, a naked baby on her hip. Amalia asked haltingly, "*Está aquí el Señor Ramirez?*" She paused for a moment, unable to remember the Spanish phrase for "broom seller," and then added, "*Señor Miguel Ramirez, el vendedor de escobas?*"

The woman stared at this visitor who spoke with such a strange accent. "*Señor Ramirez! Es muerto.*" As people do when addressing a foreigner, she spoke very loudly. "*Hasta quatro años.*" She held up four plump fingers.

Dead for four years. So Miguel Ramirez would never see his great-grandson and namesake. "*Gracias, señora.*" Aware that the woman stared after her, she turned and led Michael down the stairs.

Out in the street she lifted him into the carriage and got in beside him. She felt heavy with disappointment. To have come so far, and through such hardships, only to find her grandfather dead.

The driver had turned on the front seat to look at her inquiringly. Still she remained silent, wondering what to do. Go back to the inn where she and Michael had slept the night before, and wait there until a New England-bound merchantman sailed three days from now? Go to the church of the parish and see if any of the priests there knew what had become of Juana's brothers and sisters? No, she did not want to do that. From things Juana had said, Amalia had gathered that her mother had never felt very close to her quarrelsome brothers and sisters. Besides, these uncles and aunts Amalia had never seen no doubt were too poor and hard-pressed, too busy with their own families, to welcome a niece whose very existence they probably had forgotten.

But there was still her natural father, Enrique Villega. Now that she was actually in Cádiz, she quailed at the thought of trying to thrust herself upon him. Still, what was the worst that could happen if she tried to see him? He could have his servants turn her away at the gate. That would be humiliating, but she could survive it.

Besides, that morning at the inn she had written a note, just in case she did decide to try to see him. In it she had said, "I am the daughter of Juana Ramirez Moreno, and I would like to see you." She had signed it "Amalia Moreno Fulmer" and placed it in the reticule which, along with a portmanteau and articles of clothing for Michael and herself, she had bought that morning.

In her halting Spanish she asked the driver if he knew where the Castle Villega was. He answered that everyone in Cádiz knew that.

"Do you know if the *conde*'s son, Enrique, is there now?"

"Señora, Enrique Villega *is* the *conde*. The old *conde* died twelve years ago."

"I see. But is he in the castle now?"

He shrugged. "I cannot say. I heard that he and his family travel a lot to places like Paris and London. But perhaps he is there now."

"Please drive us to the castle."

For a moment more he stared curiously at this beautiful foreigner who first had asked to be taken to one of the city's poorest neighborhoods, and now wanted to go to Castle Villega. He turned around and slapped the reins against the back of his scrawny horse.

The carriage rattled down steep streets to a gate in a crumbling wall that must have been there since before the Middle Ages. Beyond the gate a few farmhouses stood in small fields. Then the carriage was moving between blossoming orange groves—the *conde*'s orange groves, the driver said—to a steep hill. On its crest, massive against the blue sky, rose the ancient walls and turrets of Castle Villega.

The old horse drew the carriage slowly up the hill and stopped at the castle gates. No doubt once they had been of foot-thick wood. Now they were of a gracefully patterned wrought iron that reminded her of New Orleans. Beside the gate, affixed to the wall of yellow stone, was a bell with a dangling lanyard. Alighting from the carriage, she pulled the lanyard. The bell's metallic clamor was loud in the afternoon stillness. For several moments the flagstoned courtyard beyond the gates remained empty. Then a man of about fifty, short and wide-shouldered and with a rather stupid face under graying dark hair, moved toward her.

*"Qué desea?"*

She answered in Spanish that she would like to see the Conde Villega.

The gateman stared suspiciously at this would-be visitor who had arrived, not in her own coach with a liveried driver and footman, but in a shabby carriage-for-hire. He said, "The *conde* does not see just anyone who comes to the gate."

She reached into her reticule and took out the miniature and the folded note. Reaching through the grillwork, she handed them to him. "Please take these to the *conde*."

He frowned down at the miniature for a moment, then placed it along with the note in the pocket of his loose blue peasant blouse. "Wait here," he said, and turned away.

In far less time than she had expected, he came back, moving swiftly, face wreathed in a deferential smile. "The *conde* welcomes you, señora."

While he opened the gates, Amalia took Michael down from the carriage and paid the driver. Holding her son's hand, she moved across the flagstones in the wake of the now obsequious gateman. A liveried servant stood in the opened half of the castle's front door. He said, "Will the señora and the señorito please come with me?"

Still holding Michael's hand, she followed the servant across a vast marble-floored hall, illuminated dimly by windows of leaded glass set high in its twenty-foot-high walls. She was aware of a barrel-vaulted ceiling where painted nymphs frolicked, of classical statues and suits of armor standing against the walls, and of twin marble staircases sweeping upward. The manservant stopped before a heavily carved door and knocked.

A voice called out in Spanish, "Enter, please."

The servant opened the door, bowed, and turned away. Amalia led Michael a few feet into a big room, bright with sunlight streaming through casement windows, and then stopped. A man had risen from behind a massive desk. He laid something—she was sure it was the miniature—on the desk's surface and then moved toward her, smiling.

He was not, of course, still the striking youth of the miniature. But in middle age he had remained handsome, with a tall, slender body, well-cut features, and graying brown hair.

When he stood before her, his gray eyes moving from her to Michael and then back again, she said, "*Señor, está usted—*"

"I speak English, my dear. And, yes, I am Enrique Villega." His smiling gaze went over her face. "Yes, you are Juana's daughter." He looked down at Michael. "And this?"

"My son, Michael."

"Ah, yes. Miguel. Did you name him after Juana's father?" She nodded. "That must have pleased her."

"She did not know about it. She . . . she died several years before Michael was born."

She saw surprise and genuine sorrow in his face. "Then she died young, far too young . . ." He broke off and then said, "But you can tell me about it in a few minutes. Right now I would like to speak to Michael."

With the air of a man used to children, he crouched down and said, "Would you like to sit behind my desk over there? In one of the drawers there is a picture book that my son used to look at when he was about your age."

Michael said eagerly, "A book with pictures?"

The *conde* took several heavy volumes down from the shelves that lined one wall, placed them in his desk chair, and sat Michael down on top of them. He opened a desk drawer, took out a book, and laid it before Michael, its pages open to a picture of plumed knights in combat.

Leaving the child absorbed in the book, Villega and Amalia sat on a small sofa across the room. He said, "My grandson is a fine-looking boy. I assume you know that I am his grandfather and your father. Otherwise you would not have come here."

"Yes, I know."

"Did Juana have more children by that man she married?"

"Manuel Moreno? No, he died before they reached America."

"Died? Oh, poor Juana, poor little Juana. What happened to her, all alone in a foreign country?"

That, Amalia vowed silently, was something this sensitive-faced man would never know, not from her. "Shortly after my birth—that was in New Orleans—a friend of my mother's advised her to make a certain investment. It turned out so well that she was able to buy a house in a little Mississippi River town and live off her income."

"How did she die?"

"A malignancy." Before he could ask any more questions about Juana's death, she hurried on. "I married a man named Thomas Fulmer and went to a little Long Island town to live. But I'm a widow now. My husband died in an accident."

"My dear child! How very sad."

"Yes. But he left Michael and me well provided for."

"That at least is good. Will you wait here for a few minutes? I want to tell my wife of your arrival and bring her to meet you."

He was gone quite a while. Sitting there with hands clasped nervously in her lap, Amalia reflected that probably the *condesa* was not taking kindly to the thought of welcoming a byblow of her husband's youth.

He returned finally, bringing his wife with him. She was a woman of forty-odd, blond and ample and quite handsome. If she resented Amalia's presence, she hid it well.

"Welcome, my dear." Her English was more heavily accented than her husband's. She threw a smile at Michael, who, from his throne of books, looked solemnly back at her. "How long will you be staying with us?"

"You mean, in Cádiz? A ship is sailing for American ports three days from now. It is a sister ship of the one on which I arrived. Until it sails we are staying at the inn on Calle Mayo."

"Nonsense," Villega said. "You are staying with us. I will send someone to the inn to fetch your trunk."

"I have only a portmanteau."

Both Enrique and his wife looked surprised but made no comment. He said, "I will send someone for it right away." He turned to his wife. "My dear, do you think that one of the rooms overlooking the herb garden . . ."

"Yes, and an attached room for the little boy and Ana. Ana," she said to Amalia, "is a housemaid now. But she was nursemaid to our son and later on to our twin daughters. I'll ring for her now so that she can help us with your little boy."

Minutes later Amalia and the *condesa* climbed the marble stairs. Behind them Ana, a big woman with a faint dark mustache, led Michael at a slower pace. On the second floor the *condesa* stopped beside a door midway of a wide corridor. She turned, said something in rapid Spanish to the maid, and then smiled down at Michael. "Go with Ana, little one. Your mother will be with you soon."

Michael looked at Amalia, saw her reassuring smile, and walked away beside the nursemaid. The *condesa* said to Amalia, "Our son is at the university in Madrid, but if you are to be here for three days, you should meet our twin daughters now. At the moment they are taking their watercolor lessons." She hesitated, and then went on, "My dear, would you mind if I tell them merely that you are a friend from America? It would be so . . . awkward to tell them the truth. You see, they are only ten years old."

"I understand. And of course I don't mind." She added, meaning it, "You have received me far more cordially than I would have expected."

"You are my husband's daughter," she said in a low voice. "How else would I treat you?"

She had not said "my beloved husband," but the endearment was in her tone. From what Juana had told her, Amalia knew that the Villegas' marriage, like those of most European aristocrats, was an arranged one. But it was obvious that the *condesa* had come to love the handsome man chosen for her.

She opened the door and gestured for Amalia to step ahead of her into a sun-flooded room. The girls, identical twins, were blond and classically featured and gave promise of greater beauty than their mother's. They stood at easels, with white daisies in a glazed blue bowl, evidently the subject of their watercolors, on a high stand between them. Peering over the shoulder of one of the girls was a thin little woman, black-clad and of indeterminate age.

The *condesa* said, "Forgive us for interrupting, Señora Hernandez." She turned to Amalia. "May I introduce my daughters' governess, Señora Hernandez? And these are our girls, Angelina and Dolores. This is Mrs. Fulmer, a family friend from America."

Bowing slightly, the governess gave the insecure smile of someone who is neither of the servant class nor of the upper classes, but something in between. The girls, perfectly composed, dropped curtsies and said, almost in unison, "*Enchanté, Madame Fulmer.*"

The *condesa* laughed. "No, no! Not in French. Mrs. Fulmer is from America. One speaks English there."

After only the slightest hesitation, one of the girls said, almost immediately echoed by her sister, "It is a great pleasure to meet you, ma'am."

They were smiling, but, being children, they could not hide a certain critical curiosity in their gray eyes. It told Amalia that her green poplin dress was not the sort of garment usually worn by their parents' friends. She smiled back at them, realizing with wonder that these exquisite young aristocrats were her half-sisters.

"Please return to your painting, girls," the *condesa* said.

When she and Amalia were out in the hall she said, "I will take you to your room now."

Spaniards dine late. It was not until past nine that Amalia sat with the *conde* and *condesa* beneath the crystal chandelier in the dining salon. Obviously so their visitor would not feel uncomfortable in her green poplin, her host and hostess had not dressed for dinner. The table, though, was splendid with gold-banded china, crystal wineglasses, and tall scented tapers whose reflections wavered in the room's rosewood paneling.

The Villegas had never been to America. In response to their questions, Amalia described New Orleans to them, and the sleepy little river town where she had grown up, and the lively whaling port where she now lived. There was much that she did not tell them. She did not describe the circumstances of Tom Fulmer's death. She made no mention of the

*Falcon*'s fiery plunge, nor of the weeks in that longboat and on the island. Such topics seemed to have no place in this exquisitely civilized room, and she shrank from the thought of the dismayed speculation that would come into their eyes if she told them that she had spent weeks on that island with the *Falcon*'s crew.

But the *conde* and *condesa* obviously enjoyed what she did tell them, and were curious to learn more. Had she, they asked her, ever met President Monroe? Were the Indians still a threat along America's eastern coast? Had she ever been a passenger on a steamboat?

Toward the end of the meal Enrique Villega said, "Don't sail on that ship three days from now. Stay at least a week with us. I will see to it that you secure passage on a later ship."

After an almost imperceptible hesitancy, his wife echoed, "Yes, do stay."

Amalia remained silent for several seconds. It would be pleasant to stay longer in this beautiful place. Besides, she had not yet made what was almost certainly the most important decision she would ever face, the one concerning Angus and herself.

She said slowly, "Thank you. Thank you more than I can say. There are . . . problems waiting for me at home. But perhaps I can stay a little longer. I will think it over, if I may."

In late afternoon the next day Amalia sat on a marble bench in the herb garden. Behind her was a flagstoned arcade, with ground-floor rooms opening onto it. On the other three sides of the garden stretched a high wall of yellowish stone. She was alone. Her host and hostess had excused themselves, he because he had business matters to attend to, she because she needed to confer with the castle's majordomo. As for Michael, he was napping now, with the ex-nursemaid Ana sitting beside him. If she turned around, she could look up at the window of his room and at the windows of her own larger and more luxurious one, furnished, not in the heavy Spanish style she had expected, but with graceful English furniture of the last century.

She felt too lazy and content, though, even to turn around. The sun fell on the closed eyelids of her upturned face. There were the mingled fragrances of thyme and rosemary and basil and sage. Bees made a drowsy hum. The question she had been pondering—about Angus, about whether she should linger in Cádiz a while longer—slipped from her mind. Feeling a sense of timelessness, of contentment and peace, she fell into a state of somewhere between waking and sleep.

Then, even though she did not turn around, she seemed to become aware of a presence in the shadowy arcade behind her. It was the presence of a young girl in the coarse blouse and skirt of a servant, a girl with a gentle face between two thick braids of dark hair. Amalia thought, quite calmly: Hello, Juana Ramirez, hello, my little mother.

That young girl, a half-dozen years younger than Amalia was now, was speaking to her. Amalia heard her words, not in the usual fashion, but with a kind of inner ear.

"My child," Juana was saying, "forgive yourself. Don't you know that I forgave you, freely and completely, long ago?

"And forgive Angus. Be happy, my darling. That is what I have always wanted most. If you feel you have anything to make up for, then that is how to do it. Accept your happiness, and hold it close to you always."

Amalia did turn her head then. Through the tears in her eyes she saw that the arcade beyond the archways was empty of everything but afternoon shadows. Had she been there, that young girl of long ago? Amalia did not know. She only knew that words had seemed to sound in her mind. She turned and looked at the herb garden, vision blurred by the tears now running down her cheeks. Underneath the throb of an old and reawakened grief, she felt a grateful joy.

Tonight she would tell the Villegas that she wanted to return home as soon as possible.

She dried her tears and then walked along that arcade to the foot of a staircase leading upward.

# 43

Helped by favorable winds, the merchant-passenger ship which Amalia and Michael had boarded at Cádiz sped across the North Atlantic in less than a month. Despite her feverish impatience to be with Angus, she enjoyed the voyage. She spent much of her time, whether in her cabin or out on deck, thinking of their future. Should she and Angus, after their marriage, build a ship to replace the *Falcon*? Even if the insurance money did not cover the cost of building a ship, she probably had enough money now, thanks to Enrique Villega.

On her last morning at the castle, the *conde* had sent a servant up to her room with a note requesting her to come to his study. In the big room where she had first seen him he opened a desk drawer and handed her the miniature.

He said, smiling gently, "Your mother stole it, you know."

"Yes, she told me."

"I saw her slip it into her skirt pocket. It pleased me, pleased me so much that I could not mention it, lest I burst into tears. In those days, you see, I too was very young. Perhaps someday you will show it to Michael and tell him who the young man in the miniature was."

He reached into the drawer, brought out a small leather pouch, and held it out to her. She knew that it must contain gold pieces. She also knew, from the reminiscent look in his eyes, that he was remembering how once he had given a similar pouch to Juana.

She shook her head. "Thank you, but that is not necessary. As I told you, my husband left me well provided for."

"Then take it to please me. You are not only my daughter. You are my firstborn. Use it for my grandson's education, or whatever purpose you choose. But take it."

She had accepted the pouch, but had not opened it until she and Michael were in their cabin aboard ship. She discovered that it held Spanish gold pieces worth about five thousand American dollars. Surely that plus the insurance money would be enough to build another *Falcon.*

She wondered if Angus would agree to share both the money from her father and the estate left her by Tom. Perhaps he would be stiff-necked about it, and insist that they live off whatever he himself could earn. Well, all that was secondary. The important thing, the wonderful thing, was that soon she and Angus would marry. As she sat in the passenger dining salon, or stood at the bulwarks looking out over the whitecapped blue sea, there was usually a little smile curving her lips, a smile so happy that the others aboard, even though they did not know the reason for her content, found themselves smiling too.

It was the very happiness of those days that made the foreboding dream she had, the last night of the voyage, seem so inexplicable.

In the dream she stood with the Gypsy in that New Orleans doorway. But everything had changed. The time was night rather than day. The street did not look like any New Orleans street she had ever seen before. She and the Gypsy were alone, and the Gypsy was old. The hand that held Amalia's, palm up, was bony and dry. Amalia wondered how it was that the Gypsy could read her palm in the darkness, but apparently she could.

"No happiness," the Gypsy was saying. "No happiness until you come face to face with the evil that haunts your life, and destroy it."

Chilled and sickened, Amalia cried, "But I *am* happy!"

"No. You have only the hope of happiness. And that hope will never come true. Not until you overcome . . ."

And then Amalia saw movement along the narrow hallway that stretched behind the Gypsy, and knew that it was back there, that nameless evil, and that she must flee it lest it destroy her. She snatched her hand from the Gypsy's cold, dry grasp, turned, and tried to run down that street that did not look like a New Orleans street. But her legs felt weighted, as if she moved against some invisible current. Behind her there were swift footsteps. They did not sound like ordinary footsteps, but like the clang-clang-clang of hooves over a metal roadway. Something unspeakable was drawing closer and closer to her on this dark street. Breath labored, heart hammering, she struggled against the invisible tide.

Even though it was nighttime, that strange light which illuminates bad dreams showed her that just ahead stood something she recognized, the wrought-iron gates of that cemetery where she had met Sara Davidson. If she could get inside, slam the gates . . .

With a prodigious effort she flung herself against the gates. She groped for a handle, could not find it. And then she knew that the unspeakable something was right behind her. In another second it would touch her, and she would surely die.

A scream, strangling in her throat, awoke her.

She lay there sweating. The gray light of very early morning filled the cabin. She looked at Michael, still sleeping beside her in the wide berth.

What could have caused a dream like that, especially now, when in a very short time she would be in Angus' arms? How short a time? Last night the captain had told her that he expected to anchor at Sag Harbor's Long Wharf by midmorning.

Sliding out of bed, she crossed the cabin barefoot and looked through the porthole. Was that Shelter Island out there, taking shape in the dawn light? Yes, it was. That meant that the ship had traveled faster than the captain had anticipated. But even so, Angus surely would be down on the dock to meet her. From Cádiz she had written the approximate date of her arrival and dispatched the letter by a ship scheduled to reach Sag Harbor before she would. For the past several days he must have come to Long Wharf to meet each arriving merchantman.

The oppressed feeling left by that nightmare was slipping away now. She turned back to the berth and shook Michael's small shoulder. "Wake up, my darling. We're home."

The ship docked a little before six-thirty. Since she and Michael were the only passengers leaving the ship at Sag Harbor, there was no one on deck except officers and crewmen. Long Wharf was even emptier. At that hour most of the villagers were either at breakfast or still asleep. But Howard Lipson was there, plump face upturned. Her gaze swept the wharf. With apprehension knotting her stomach, she saw that Angus was nowhere in sight.

She lifted the still-sleepy Michael into her arms for the steep descent of the gangplank. Carrying her portmanteau in her free hand, she moved down to the wharf.

"Hello, Amalia. Hello there, Michael." Howard wore a strained little smile. "You're looking *very* well, Amalia."

"Thank you." Then, swiftly: "I had thought that Angus MacFarlane would meet us."

With a meaningful look at the drowsy child, Howard said, "I think it would be better to talk after I've driven you home." He took the portmanteau from her hand. "My surrey's at the foot of Long Wharf."

As they walked over the wooden planking, she asked tautly, "Can't you at least tell me where he is?"

"He's here in Sag Harbor."

"*How* is he?"

"Physically he's well enough. But he's . . . in trouble. I'll tell you about it later."

They got into the surrey and drove along lower Main Street, deserted except for a drunk sleeping in a grog-shop doorway, and then through the equally quiet business district to the big houses beyond. Vaguely she noticed that in the front gardens some dahlias still bloomed. When she had last seen Sag Harbor, dahlias were blooming.

He said, "You've been gone a year."

"A little more than that."

They were passing the MacFarlane house. Was Angus in it right now, at breakfast or still asleep? The flutter of a sheer window curtain on the second floor caught her eye. She saw a slender hand let the curtain fall back into place.

Amalia asked, "Is Ruth MacFarlane here?"

"Yes. She came back from Maine only a few days after the *Falcon* sailed."

"She's still unmarried?"

"Yes. Can't make up her mind, I guess, what with all those fellows after her."

To distract herself from the apprehension weighting her, she asked, "How is my brother-in-law?"

"Richard? He was mad as a wet hen when he heard the *Falcon* was lost. He blamed Angus, of course. Shipping companies and their managers always blame the captain. But after the insurance company paid the claim, he quieted down."

The surrey turned onto John Street. While Howard was

tying the horse's reins to the hitching post, Lena came running out of the house. Both weeping, the women embraced. Then Lena lifted Michael into her arms. With a crow of pleasure he fastened his arms around her neck.

Lena said to Amalia, "Have you had breakfast, child?"

From the strained look on the scarred face, Amalia realized that Lena knew about Angus' trouble, whatever it was. "I had coffee aboard ship, and that was enough. But you might give Michael something. Anyway, keep him with you for a while. Mr. Lipson and I have to talk."

Minutes later she sat with Howard beside the parlor's unlighted fireplace. Early-morning sunlight slanted into the room. With some part of her mind not wholly given up to dread, she noticed how clean Lena had kept it—the windowpanes sparkling, the furniture polished, the andirons shining.

Howard said, "The trouble started with Toby."

"Toby! The handyman's nephew? That—"

"Yes, that half-wit, or maybe three-quarters-wit. Anyway, an evangelist came to town last month and preached at the Presbyterian church every night for a week. You've never heard such hellfire-and-brimstone sermons. Night after night people stood up to confess all sorts of sins. Lying, cheating, fornication, blasphemy. Toby didn't get up in church. Maybe those sermons had him so scared that his legs wouldn't hold him. But after the preacher left town, Toby went to the coroner and told him that he had lied about Tom Fulmer's death. The coroner had asked him if he had seen anyone down at the cove that night, and Toby had said no, and that had made him a liar or maybe even the same as a murderer, and he was headed straight for hell. The coroner says Toby was crying so hard he almost couldn't understand him."

Amalia's heart was beating suffocatingly fast. "What was it . . . he hadn't told?"

"Now he says that he not only was down by the cove that night. It was a night of bright moonlight, remember? He says now that he saw a man lying half-hidden in the rushes across the road from the house. The man had yellow hair."

Amalia whispered, "Oh, no!"

"I'm afraid that is how it is. And you see how that places Angus. There are a few other yellow-haired men in town, but none of them besides Angus had any motive for killing Tom.

That is why the coroner has called for a new hearing into Tom's death."

She said sickly, "What is to be done?"

"I'm going to represent Angus at the hearing and question Toby. In the state Angus is in, he might well lose his temper with that dull-witted creature, and that would prejudice the coroner's jury even more."

"Even . . . more?"

"Yes. You see, after the survivors of the *Falcon* arrived here, it was spread all over town that . . . that on that island you and Angus . . ." He broke off, looking embarrassed.

"Was Brian Carr one of those who spread the story?"

"Carr? Oh, I remember. That young second mate. No, he went home to Rhode Island as soon as he had picked up his pay from Richard Fulmer. I heard somewhere that he'd left the sea and gone into his family's banking business. No, it was the crewmen who spread the story."

"And the town . . . condemns us . . ."

"Not at first. Oh, a few of them at least pretended to be shocked, but most of them didn't. They looked at it realistically, and realized that as far as Angus and you knew, you might have been destined to spend the rest of your lives on that island.

"But after Toby told his story, everybody remembered what they'd heard about you two on the island, and about your being engaged to each other several years back, and . . . well, that seemed to underline the fact that there was no one else with a motive for killing Tom, especially no one else with the appearance of the man Toby says he saw."

After a while she asked heavily, "What does Angus say about it?"

"That he is innocent, of course, and was nowhere near this house that night."

"Why . . . why wasn't he there to tell me that? At the wharf this morning, I mean?"

"For one thing, I've advised him to stay away from you until after the verdict is given at the hearing. For another, he feels he doesn't want to see you until and unless the jury decides not to indict him. As he told it to me, shortly after Tom's death you told him you were suspicious of him. . . ."

That blustery winter day on the beach at Sagaponack. Angus' blue eyes blazing down at her as he demanded, "And why, in your view, did I kill an unarmed man I had been fond of since we were boys? Because I felt it was the only way of getting you?"

For a long moment there was silence. Then Amalia managed to speak. "Do you think he . . . killed Tom?"

"Candidly, I don't know. Angus has a temper. He might conceivably kill in a rage. But it's hard to think of him as a stealthy murderer. One keeps coming back, though, to the basic question. Who else, of *any* sort of appearance, had a reason to kill Tom? Why, he was the most popular man in town. I can't think of anyone who had a reason even to resent him, except that brother of his. I guess Richard had always envied Tom, for a number of reasons. Still, would he have waited that long to kill him? And anyway, it certainly doesn't sound as if it was Richard Fulmer Toby saw that night."

Beneath Amalia's confusion and fear, anger stirred. "If you go before the coroner's jury with *that* attitude, how do you expect to help Angus?"

"I won't show them this attitude. I've shown it to you because I felt you had the right to know how I viewed Angus' situation. But at the hearing I'll do everything I can to raise doubts about Toby's testimony.

"How will I do it?" he went on. "By getting that poor dummy so mixed up that he won't even be sure any longer that he was even in Sag Harbor that night. The jury, I hope, will feel that they can't rely on anything he says."

Howard left soon after that. Amalia walked back through the house. Lena sat on the low back step. Michael knelt out under the apple tree, piling up the wooden blocks Amalia had bought him shortly before they sailed on the ill-fated *Falcon*.

Amalia sat down beside Lena. Lena asked, "Is he gone?"

"Yes. Lena, do you think Angus . . . ?"

"Do I think he killed your husband? Of course not, child, of course not!"

"You once thought he might have."

"That was before I got to know the man. That was before I'd seen him close up, so to speak, the way I did when he was running the ship and running things there on the island. He's bossy and hot-tempered, but I don't think he would be a sneak, at killing or anything else."

Amalia reached over and squeezed the other woman's

hand, hard. Then she said, "I think I'll go upstairs and rest. A . . . a dream woke me early this morning, and you know how that always leaves you tired."

Once in her room, she found she was too oppressed with fear to even try to rest. Shortly before noon, she went back to the barn. After idle months in the livery stable, and idle weeks back here in her own stall, Molly seemed even fatter and lazier than before. Amalia saddled the mare and then rode through the leafy woods and down the narrow roads across dark green potato fields to Sagaponack beach. She hitched Molly to that same half-buried tree root and then walked up and down the beach, half-hoping, half-dreading that Angus would appear.

He did not. After about an hour she rode home.

Late that afternoon she was in her room, trying to distract herself with small tasks—searching the clothes in her wardrobe for moth holes, mending a broken chemise strap—when she heard Michael's laughter, mingled with a young girl's voice, from the garden below. Amalia went to the window and looked out.

Down on the garden path, Michael and Ruth MacFarlane were playing "horsey." Seated astride her neck, his ankles in her grasp, he cried, "Faster, faster!" as she galloped up and down. Amalia watched for a few moments and descended to the kitchen.

Lena was seated at the table, shelling lima beans from the trellis near the barn. She said, "Ruth MacFarlane's out there."

"I know."

"I hope you don't mind. I wanted to start supper, so I left Michael with her."

"No. I don't mind." On the contrary. From Ruth she might obtain some news of Angus, something that might lessen this numb foreboding. If his sister, who loved him so much, was able to play lightheartedly with Michael, then perhaps Angus' situation was less dangerous than Howard Lipson had implied.

Amalia went out the back door. No longer galloping, but with the child still astride her neck, Ruth walked toward her. "Hello! I hope we weren't making too much noise." She swung Michael to the ground.

"Not at all. Shall we sit in the grape arbor?"

As soon as they were seated, Michael insisted upon being lifted to Ruth's lap. Amalia could understand that. Almost any male, whether going on three or going on ninety, would be drawn to Ruth. In a cornflower-blue dress that matched her eyes, she was lovelier than ever.

"What a year you've had!" Ruth said. "The *Falcon* going down, and then that island, and then Spain—"

"Yes," Amalia said hurriedly. "And how about you? What have you been doing since I last saw you?"

Ruth made a face that a less lovely girl would not have risked. "Nothing. Just living here in this poky little town."

"I should think, with all your young men . . ."

Ruth shrugged. "It's still a poky little town."

Michael reached up and tugged at a lock of Ruth's hair. "Horsey! Let's run, horsey."

"Michael! Stop pulling Miss MacFarlane's hair. Now, go into the house and ask Lena to put you to bed for your nap."

He whined a little, but finally obeyed. Ruth said, "I'll have to go now."

"Oh, please don't! Wouldn't you like some tea?"

"Thank you. But I have some friends calling for me at four-thirty, and it will take me about fifteen minutes to walk home."

"I'll go to the front gate with you."

It was not until they had almost reached the gate that Amalia summoned up the courage to ask, "Ruth, do you think that the coroner's jury will . . . ask for an indictment?" When Ruth didn't answer, she went on haltingly, "I mean, do you think they will believe that Angus could possibly have—"

The girl whirled on her then, face angry and scornful. "Of course not. No one in this town could believe my brother would do such a thing. Oh, maybe *you* could believe it!"

Speechless, Amalia looked at the girl who only moments ago had seemed amiable. "But if he does hang, you're the one to blame." The blue eyes were glittering now. "You've always been to blame for everything. And when I came back from Maine and heard *you'd* sailed on the *Falcon*, not me, you—"

Evidently aware that she had become incoherent, Ruth broke off. Then she said, her voice merely sullen now, "When Angus came back on that New Bedford whaler early this summer and told me you'd transferred to a ship going to

Spain, I hoped you'd never come back. I hoped that ship too would catch fire, or you'd just decide to live in Spain, or—"

Again she paused and then said, "No, that jury won't accuse him. Even if there were some people in town who might believe that half-wit Toby for a little while, they won't after Howard Lipson gets through with him."

She turned and walked rapidly down the road. Amalia looked after her. What a strange, strange girl! Amalia thought of the rage and panic she must have felt when she first heard that someone had killed Tom, thus leaving Amalia free to accept Angus' attentions.

Why had she come here today, with all that hostility bottled up inside her? Perhaps, Amalia thought dryly, it was hope that drew her, hope of finding that this past year had turned me into an aged wreck.

Plainly Ruth had not outgrown her unhealthy attachment to her brother. Perhaps that emotion would still be there twenty years from now, barring her from any normal happiness.

But Amalia had far more pressing and immediate worries than Ruth's final destiny. She turned and walked slowly into the house.

# 44

She went to Sagaponack twice the next day, once in midmorning and once in the late afternoon. Each time, the beach was empty.

As she made her way back and forth through the fields, she had been aware of the scrutiny of farmworkers who crawled along the rows between the plants, looking for yellow-and-black potato bugs. She could imagine them talking among themselves and to others about "Tom Fulmer's widow, that woman Angus MacFarlane had on that island. Bet she made those two trips to the beach in hope of meeting him. Maybe she did. Maybe he got down onto the beach farther on toward East Hampton."

Well, it did not matter. If the jury decided tomorrow in Angus' favor, he would marry her, and after a while the town would forget all the old scandal. If the jury did ask for his indictment, and he was tried and convicted, if they took that long, splendid body and hung him by the neck until he was dead, then what those farmworkers said today would not matter either. Nothing would matter very much. She would sell the house, and take Michael a long way away from here, and try to get through the rest of her life as best she could.

The reopened hearing into Tom's death was scheduled for two o'clock the next afternoon. Amalia waited until a few minutes after two before hitching Buttons to the gig. She hoped to slip unnoticed into an already filled meeting hall and find a seat in the back row. Through heat so intense that the maple trees along Main Street had a wilted look, she drove to the business district. Near the meeting house, vacant carriages and tethered saddle horses lined both sides of the street. She had to turn around and drive back about a hundred yards before she found a hitching post not in use.

Pulse fast, she walked back to the meeting house and climbed the narrow stairs to the open double doors of the hall.

His moon face frightened, Toby sat at the small witness table. He was saying, ". . . didn't tell anybody because I was too skeered, that's why."

The back-row bench, Amalia saw, was empty except for a man and woman, perhaps newcomers to Sag Harbor. At least she did not recognize them. Feeling relieved, she sat down at the end of the bench.

But her entrance had not gone unnoticed. People she knew had turned to look at her. Mr. and Mrs. Hannibal Allerdyce, and the Hobarts of the general store, and Mrs. Arnshaw, at whose boardinghouse she had stayed, and at least a score of others. Among them was Richard Fulmer, his gaunt face grim. For the first time she realized that her brother-in-law and business manager had made no attempt to see her these past two days. She wondered why. Could it be that he felt that Angus had indeed killed Tom, and that she had been the reason? Or was it just that he, like everyone else, had heard the story about her and Angus on the island, and deep in his lonely, misogynist soul, hated them both for it? Despite the color she could feel flaring in her cheeks, she looked at him squarely.

A hum of conversation had arisen. The coroner banged his gavel. "Let's have some order here."

As the voices subsided, Amalia saw that Angus, with Howard Lipson beside him, sat in the first row. On the other side of Angus was Ruth. Had any of those three turned to look at her? She was sure Angus had not. Despite all those other eyes turned in her direction, she would have felt the special impact of his gaze.

The coroner said, "All right, Toby. So you didn't tell anyone about seeing the man there in the reeds because you were afraid to."

Toby nodded vigorously. "I was skeered he'd kill me too!"

"But after the evangelist was here, you did come and tell me about seeing a yellow-haired man hiding in the reeds. Now, why did you tell me?"

"Because I got more skeered of hell than I was of him."

Several spectators tittered. "All right, Toby. I have no more questions." Then, as the moon-faced man hastily rose:

"No, sit down. Mr. Lipson has notified me that he wants to ask you a few things."

Howard Lipson rose and walked over to the witness table. He said in an easy, conversational tone, "You like to walk at night, don't you, Toby?"

The witness nodded warily.

"I do too, but I don't really know why. Why do you like to walk at night?"

Toby frowned with the effort of framing an answer. "Not many people around," he said finally. "Jist dawgs. I know all the dawgs, and they know me, so I ain't skeered of 'em."

To Amalia, Howard Lipson had always seemed a soft, rather ineffectual man. But now, seeing how skillfully he had gained the witness's confidence, she revised her estimation of him.

"But you *are* afraid of people?"

Toby nodded.

"Why, Toby?"

"Some people laugh at me and say I ain't right in the head."

The lawyer said sympathetically, "I can see how you wouldn't like that. Now, let's talk about the night Mr. Fulmer was shot. About what time was it when you saw a man lying in the reeds?"

"It was nighttime."

Howard Lipson did not pursue the matter but merely threw a glance at the jury which said: "You see what sort of witness this is."

"Now, was there a moon that night?"

"Oh, yes. A big round one."

"A full moon. You especially like to be out when the moon is full, don't you?"

"I sure do!"

"What color was it?"

"Yaller. Big and yaller."

The lawyer nodded. "The way a full moon often is before it rises more than about thirty degrees above the horizon. But, Toby, then how can you be sure it was a yellow-haired man you saw? In moonlight that color, wouldn't white or gray hair look yellow?"

Toby appeared bewildered.

Howard went on. "So you can't really be sure of the color

of his hair, or even if it *was* hair. Mightn't it have been the sort of wig some young boys wear on Halloween?"

"Warn't Halloween. I'd never go out on Halloween!"

"I don't blame you. Some boys can be pretty mean, can't they? All I am saying is that it could have been a man in a wig."

Toby nodded vigorously. "Sure! Sure!"

"It might even have been a small dog lying there in the reeds, mightn't it, or maybe an old mop somebody had thrown away. After all, you didn't go over and look, did you?"

"I sure didn't."

"What did you do?"

"I lit out and run."

"Why?"

"It was night and it was winter and a man was layin' in the reeds where you wouldn't expect nobody to be. And so I run."

"But why?" Howard Lipson persisted.

"Because I was skeered it was a ha'nt."

This time it took the coroner almost half a minute to quell the laughter. When the room was quiet once more, Howard Lipson said, "I am sure that we all appreciate Toby's testimony, just as we appreciate the fine work he does for so many of us. Thank you, Toby."

The witness beamed. Turning to the jury table, the lawyer said in a voice too rapid for the slow-witted Toby to follow, even if he had understood the words, "I think we can concur that the credibility of this witness is such that it would be a miscarriage of justice indeed were this jury to return a recommendation for indictment of anyone. I have finished my questioning."

He sat down. The coroner asked, "Does anyone else have questions for this witness?" When no one spoke, he said to the still-beaming Toby, "You can leave now." He turned to the jurymen. "You may retire and consider your verdict."

While all eyes were on the jurymen moving toward the back room, Amalia slipped out of her seat. She descended the narrow stairs to the blazing heat outdoors and hurried to the gig.

She waited there nearly half an hour. The jury was taking longer than it had at the end of the first hearing into Tom's death. Surely these fellow townsmen of Angus would not indict him. Surely now they realized that if poor Toby had seen anything at all, it had not been a person.

But suppose there *had* been a man lurking in the reeds that night. With her hands turning cold, she again realized how unlikely it was that the person had been anyone except Angus. Howard Lipson had suggested that it might be someone wearing a wig, or someone whose white hair appeared yellow in that deceptive moonlight. But now she realized that anyone bent upon concealing his identity probably would have worn a mask rather than a wig. As for a white-haired man, who among the village's older population could have held a grudge against Tom, particularly a grudge so strong that it would lead him to lie in the damp reeds on a winter's night, waiting to slip into that house and kill its owner?

People had begun to leave the upstairs hall now. The couple who had shared the rear bench were among the first to appear. Heart beating hard and fast, she watched them approach. She leaned out of the gig and asked, "Will you please tell me the verdict?"

The man said, "They didn't recommend an indictment." He sounded rather disappointed. "The verdict was the same as I hear it was last time, death at the hands of a person or persons unknown."

For a moment relief left her limp and speechless. Then she said, "Thank you." She got out of the gig, unhitched the reins, and then, even though the couple still lingered, obviously eager to talk, drove off through the hot sunlight.

At the John Street house she found Lena in the upstairs hall polishing a mirror that hung near the room where Michael lay napping. "It's all right," she said softly, "it's all right! They didn't accuse Angus."

"Thank the good Lord!"

"I'm going to Sagaponack," Amalia said rapidly. "I think he'll come there right away. But if he should come here first, tell him where I am."

She went out to where she had left the gig at the hitching post and drove through Bridgehampton and along the roads through the potato fields to the beach. She left the gig where the road ended between two dunes and, heart singing, descended to the sand.

It was cooler here. Although the sky was cloudless, evidently there was a storm somewhere out in the Atlantic, because the usually gentle rollers were booming today, tossing back spray that held miniature rainbows. She had a giddy feeling that even nature reflected her own exultation. Too restless to stay still, she walked up and down the beach.

He arrived, finally, striding through the gap between the dunes. As swiftly as she could through the soft sand, she ran toward him. Then, with sudden cold foreboding, she realized that he was not moving toward her now, but standing motionless. She herself stopped for a moment, and then walked toward him. Beardless now, his face watched her impassively.

She said, "Oh, Angus! I'm so happy, so happy for both of us." Then, when he did not speak, but just looked down at her: "Oh, God, Angus! What is it?"

"It is something I just heard from my sister." He paused. "Did you ask her the day before yesterday if she thought I'd killed Tom?"

She said falteringly, "I guess I said something like—"

"But *you* were the one who was afraid I'd killed him, weren't you?"

She looked up at him, feeling that the blood drained, not just from her face, but from her heart. "No, not really."

"What does that mean, 'no, not really'?"

"Please, please, Angus! Try to understand. The ship had docked early that morning, and Howard Lipson instead of you met me, and he told me what Toby had said—"

"And you believed it was me that the poor half-wit saw, or thought he saw."

"No, no!" Then, despairingly: "All right! I couldn't think of anyone else it might be."

His voice had a constricted sound. "And so, even after we'd been so close on that island, closer than most human beings are ever lucky enough to be, you still believed that I might be a killer, and a sly, cowardly killer at that."

She said faintly, "I . . . I at least had this little fear you might be, but after Howard got Toby to talking—"

"How do you know Howard isn't just a clever lawyer who could have, if he'd wanted to, thought of a way to make me look guilty as hell? You shouldn't have needed this afternoon to convince you I was innocent. You should have known in your heart that I was."

"Angus, listen! I love you. I had only the tiniest doubt of

you. But even if it had been a big doubt, I would have gone on loving you."

His voice was quiet now. "Even if you thought I was a murderer?" When she didn't answer, he said, "I don't think much of that kind of love, Amalia."

Her voice too was quiet now, and tired. "I'm sorry. I'm trying to be as honest with you as I can."

"I know you are." He paused. "And now I want you to answer this question honestly. Suppose we marry. Will a marriage ceremony erase that tiny doubt you mentioned?" When again she didn't answer, but just looked up at him with wretched dark eyes, he said, "You see? Nothing could end that doubt except knowing definitely that someone else killed Tom, some would-be thief, some escaped lunatic." He gave a little laugh that held no humor whatever. "But there's no evidence that the killer even tried to steal anything. And as for escaped lunatics, none were reported."

For a moment there was silence except for the crash of a wave, followed by the seething sound of its withdrawal. Then she said, almost in a whisper, "What are you telling me, Angus?"

"That we're still each other's bad luck. Perhaps we always will be. That's why we mustn't marry. We can't go on destroying each other's lives."

He paused for a moment, and then added, "I'm going to go to Connecticut tomorrow and look at a small merchantman for sale there. If I can make the down payment—and I think I can scrape it up—I'll go into the coastal trade, with New London as my home port."

She said, numb with shock, "You mean you are leaving Sag Harbor tomorrow, and won't be back?"

"Of course I don't mean that. I'll go over on the early-morning ferry and come back on the noon one. But as soon as I can settle a few things here—arrange for Howard to handle the sale of my house, and so on—my sister and I will move to New London."

She said bitterly, "You mean you've made all those plans just this afternoon? It sounds to me as if, even before I came home—"

"Of course I made plans earlier. I thought that since I didn't want to touch the money Tom left you, I'd buy that small ship after we were married and sail her out of Sag Harbor. It wasn't until this afternoon, when Ruth told me about her visit to you, that I decided that New London would be my home port."

Beyond all pride now, she reached out her hands to him. "Please, please! Don't do this to me. I love you."

He said harshly, "Don't you think I love you? Don't you know that right now it's all I can do to keep from taking you in my arms, and then driving with you somewhere deep in the woods, and making love to you the way we used to make love on the island? *But it's no damn good, Amalia.* Maybe you could live with that tiny doubt you mentioned, that nagging little suspicion that your husband was a killer. But I couldn't live with the knowledge that my wife felt that way about me.

"You're still young, Amalia. We both are. Let's stop destroying each other, right now." When she just looked up at him with her white suffering face, he said, "Good-bye, Amalia," and turned away.

She watched his long, straight back until he disappeared between the dunes. She thought: The last good-bye. Oh, they might see each other again before he left Sag Harbor, and even exchange a few polite, meaningless words. But today had been good-bye.

As if afflicted with actual physical torment, she began to walk up and down. That dream, she thought distractedly, that early-morning one aboard ship. The dream in which some nameless evil had pursued her down a New Orleans street to those cemetery gates. To escape its touch, the touch that would destroy her, she had awakened.

But she really had not escaped. These last few minutes had brought the destruction, not of her body, but of all her hopes of a happiness she had expected to unite her and her son's father until they died.

It was sunset now. Sky and water and sand, curving dune grass and breasts of circling seabirds, all were colored exquisite shades of pink and mauve. The very beauty of it was more than she could bear. She fled up to where she had left the gig.

# 45

Jim Wycherly, New Orleans' commissioner of police, was one of that city's most popular political figures. Much of that public esteem rested on the fact that he was said to be a great family man. Every night the neighbors saw him arrive home at six to have supper and spend the evening with his wife and three grown daughters.

Therefore it was in the late afternoons that he went to Sara Davidson's.

This particular afternoon, as was always the case when important clients arrived, Sara invited him to have a glass of her very best brandy. "And you and I can have a little chat while you are waiting for Celia." Celia, his usual choice among Sara's girls, was otherwise engaged at the moment.

With a sigh, Jim settled his ample body against a sofa's backrest. "The brandy will do me well enough, Sara. Right now I'm not interested in Celia."

She poured his brandy from the decanter on a rosewood side table. Handing it to him, she asked, "You've had a strenuous day?"

"Unpleasant, anyway. I had to go down to this waterfront rooming house and inspect the body of a man who'd shot himself. He did it about three days ago, but his body wasn't discovered until around noon today."

"But, Jim! I shouldn't have thought that a man in your position would have to go down there."

"If he'd been just some ordinary derelict, I wouldn't have. But years back this fellow was the richest planter for miles around, so I felt I'd better go down there to make sure he'd died by his own hand. Maybe you've heard of him. His name was Mountjoy, Lawrence Mountjoy."

"Of course I knew him. He was here one day about . . .

oh, it must have been four or five years ago. I almost didn't recognize him. White hair, and seedy clothes."

"Believe me, he looked worse than that when I saw him this afternoon."

"How long had he been there?"

"In this cheap rooming house? The landlady said he'd moved in more than five years ago and never left."

"That's strange."

"Why?"

"The last time I saw him I had the distinct impression that he would go east, to a little town on Long Island. Perhaps he wanted to, but could never get up the energy or the money."

Well, she thought, so Lawrence Mountjoy had not been able to revenge himself, through the daughter, on that little Spanish bitch, Juana. Even so, maybe things had not gone well for the daughter. Sara hoped that was the case.

# 46

On eastern Long Island, the next day dawned as hot as the previous one. For most people, a thick cloud cover made the heat even more oppressive. But Amalia, eyes heavy from lack of sleep, was too wretched to be more than vaguely aware of physical discomfort.

She had arrived home the evening before to find Michael already in bed and Lena washing the plate upon which she had served the little boy's supper. Standing in the lamplit kitchen, Amalia had said harshly, "It's over. He isn't even going to stay in Sag Harbor." Then, as she saw the dismayed questions in the other woman's eyes: "No, I don't want to talk about it. Not now. I'm going to my room."

"Without supper? Child, you mustn't."

Amalia turned and walked to the stairs. In her room she sat at the window staring through the moonless dark at those reeds where, on a winter's night, someone perhaps had lain. Finally she went to bed. Sleep, though, was impossible. She stared up at the ceiling, incapable of any thought beyond: How am I going to get through the rest of my life?

Shortly after dawn she did fall into exhausted sleep, only to be awakened a couple of hours later by Michael in the next room, singing the tuneless little song with which he often greeted a new day.

Lena asked no questions. But around two in the afternoon she came out to where Amalia sat in the grape arbor staring straight ahead. "Amalia, I think we'd better drive to East Hampton."

"What?"

"That big store in East Hampton. The general store here has stopped carrying the kind of furniture polish we like. And we can order coal for the winter at that East Hampton yard. And we—"

"All right. Go to East Hampton."

"Girl, a drive would be good for you."

Amalia leaped to her feet. "Go by yourself! Go anywhere! Just leave me alone!"

She went into the house by the back door and climbed the stairs. Through the open doorway of the room next to hers she saw that Michael, seated on the floor, was making a tower out of his wooden blocks. In her own room she sat down on the bed's edge. After a while she heard Lena drive out in the gig. Beneath her wretchedness, Amalia felt a stir of shame for having shouted at the other woman. Well, she would apologize when Lena returned.

And until then?

She realized that she not only felt incapable of getting through the rest of her life. She did not even know how to get through the rest of the afternoon.

They needed coal for the winter, Lena had said. What else did one do to prepare for winter? Why, one inspected heavy blankets and winter clothes for moth damage. Yes, that was something she could do with the rest of the afternoon.

For a few moments more, though, she just sat there. Then she went to the doorway of Michael's room. "I'm going up to the attic. You be a good boy. Stay right where you are."

Michael said, with mild indignation, "I'm always a good boy," and placed another block on a precariously leaning column. As she looked at him, she was poignantly aware of something she had first noticed weeks before. Michael's hair, once a very pale gold, was taking on the reddish tinge of his father's. Swiftly she turned away. She walked to the end of the hall and pulled down the steep ladderlike stairs leading up to the trapdoor.

The attic seemed at least ten degrees hotter than the rest of the house. She moved through the gray light, opening windows. Then she lifted the rounded lid of the large tin trunk that held winter blankets.

She had finished inspecting the blankets and had opened a trunk that held winter clothing when she heard footsteps on the stairs leading up from the ground-floor hall. Why had Lena returned so soon? She could not possibly have driven to East Hampton and back. What was more, Amalia had not heard the sound of the gig going past the side of the house to the barn. Perhaps for some reason Lena had left the gig out front. Well, Amalia would know in a moment. Lena would see that the attic stairs had been lowered, and would come up here.

She lifted a gray woolen cloak, stared at it dully for a moment, then turned it to look at the back. No, no moth holes. She folded it, added it to the stack of garments on the seat of an old chair.

Michael's soft giggle, followed by someone saying, "Sh-h-h!"

Amalia said, "Lena?"

Michael's face rose into view through the trapdoor, then Ruth MacFarlane's face, then the little boy's chubby legs, crooked over Ruth's shoulders. As the girl climbed the rest of the way into the attic, Michael shouted gleefully, "Surprise!"

"Ruth! What are you doing here? And you shouldn't climb those steep stairs with Michael on your shoulders. It's dangerous for you both."

Ruth smiled. Not replying, she walked toward one of the open windows. She reached up, swung the child off her shoulders, and then sat down on the windowsill, with him sitting in her lap. Still smiling, she reached into the pocket of her yellow cotton dress and brought out a metal-capped glass jar filled with dark liquid. She bent over, still holding Michael, and rolled the jar across the attic floor. The sound of its rolling was loud in the stillness.

It stopped against the toe of Amalia's shoe. She said, bewildered, "What on earth . . . ?"

"There's rat poison and coffee in the jar." Her smile broadened. "The coffee may be a little stale. I made it three days ago, right after you came back here. But you won't mind the taste, at least not for long. Cyanide works fast."

Amalia stared through the hot gray light to where the smiling girl, like a nineteenth-century Madonna, sat with the gleeful-faced child in her lap. Amalia thought: Is she mad? Or was *she* the one who had gone mad? Perhaps that was it. Heartbreak and sleeplessness and this terrible heat had combined to bring her a flash of insanity. Unless, of course, the girl was making some sort of macabre jest.

"Ruth, if this is some sort of joke . . ."

"I'll show you what sort of joke it is." She wasn't smiling now. Still supporting Michael's shoulders with one arm, she slipped her other arm under his knees. Swiftly she rose, turned, and swung the giggling child out into the void above that brick garden path some thirty feet below. Amalia watched, too frozen with terror even to scream.

Ruth turned around with the little boy still in her arms. "I could have dropped him then. Drink it, Amalia. If you don't, I will drop him. And don't try to make a lunge at me. If you do, he'll be out of that window while you're still a half-dozen feet away."

Michael must have sensed then that this was no game. Amalia saw his small face turn pale and his lips open to scream. The girl clamped her hand over his mouth, and with her other arm held his now-struggling body close to her. "Don't you dare scream!" she said fiercely. "And stop fighting me. If you don't, I'll throw you out this window before your mama can stop me. Do you understand that, Michael?" She gave his head a little shake, her thumb and fingers pressing hard into his round cheeks. "Do you understand?"

Brown eyes wide in his green-white face, the child nodded.

"Not that anybody would be apt to hear you," she said, taking her hand away from his mouth. "It's just that I don't want to have you yelling."

At last Amalia's paralyzed mind had begun to work. "Ruth, Lena will be back here any minute. Now, put Michael down and we'll go down to the kitchen and talk this—"

"You're a liar." Ruth was smiling again. "Lena won't be back for at least an hour, and probably longer. I saw her on Bay Street less than thirty minutes ago. She turned onto the road to East Hampton. I went right home and got that drink I'd fixed for you." Her smile broadened. "I've got a knife, an old pocketknife of my brother's. I intended to hold it to your boy's throat. But I like this window idea better." Her smile vanished. "Now, pick that up and drink it. It'll be so quick you won't feel anything. I'll take Michael back to his room and then just walk away from here."

Amalia looked down at the jar lying against the toe of her shoe. She could not save Michael by drinking that poison. He was old enough to describe what had happened. Ruth knew that.

When Lena came home an hour from now and found her dead of poison in the attic, and Michael's small, shattered body lying on the brick walk, what would she think? What would everybody think? That in her despair over Angus she had dropped her child to his death and then taken poison of her own concoction.

She moved her numb lips. "Why?"

"You know why." Ruth's face had twisted. Incredibly, she no longer looked lovely, or even passably pretty. She looked hideous. "It's Angus. You're not going to have him."

Amalia cried, "But there's no need for you to . . . Why, Angus and I have said good-bye to each other. He's going to—"

"I know. He told me. He's going to leave Sag Harbor as soon as he can. We'll move to New London, and he'll sail a coastal schooner out of there. So he *says*. But that doesn't mean he won't change his mind."

Her tone was brooding now. "Twice before I managed to break things up between you and Angus. I did it in New Orleans. I did it here in Sag Harbor, and after I had, Angus sailed on that whaler." Her voice gathered speed. "But when he came back, he took command of the *Falcon*. And you went with him. Not I. You! Now, pick up that jar."

Because she did not know what else to do, Amalia obeyed. She stood with the jar in her hand, gaze fixed on the girl and Michael. Apparently terrified beyond speech or movement, he stared with distended brown eyes at his mother.

Amalia said thinly, "I don't understand. You said that in New Orleans . . ."

Her voice trailed off. After a moment Ruth smiled. "I think I'd like for you to know about that. Yes, I'd like very much for you to know. I'm the one who wrote that letter to Angus, the letter telling him to go see a woman named Sara Davidson."

Amalia's numb lips moved. "You couldn't have. You were a child."

"I was twelve. Twelve-year-olds can listen at doors. I'd been doing it since I was seven! I liked listening outside the servants' dining-room door down there in New Orleans. It was a lot more fun than listening to that stupid old pair who've worked for us since before I was born. Anyway, one day I heard them talking about some cook they knew, a cook who'd once worked for a woman named Sara Davidson. The cook had told them that there used to be a Spanish woman named Moreno at Sara Davidson's place on Oak Street and that she had a little girl named Amalia. I didn't understand everything they said, of course, but I could tell from their tone that it was something Angus wouldn't want to know about you. So I printed that note and mailed it to him."

Then here it was, the evil that the New Orleans Gypsy had mentioned, the evil which would shadow her life for years. Here it was, in the form of an outwardly lovely young girl with a deathly pale little boy in her grasp.

"When Howard Lipson brought you here to Sag Harbor, I didn't mind too much. After all, you were Mrs. Tom Fulmer by then. I was young and stupid in those days, only fourteen, so I thought your being married meant that Angus would be safe from you. I thought he'd be safe even though I knew that his engagement to Barbara Weyant would soon be broken, and he might come back here from Boston."

Even to her own ears, Amalia's voice had a dazed sound. "You . . . *knew*?"

"Of course." Her smile broadened. Amalia had a half-unbelieving sense that Ruth was enjoying herself, much as she might have at a party, or a picnic on Shelter Island. Her face, ugly only minutes ago, had regained its prettiness. "You see, I'd found that journal of Angus' in which he'd written all those things about you, how he couldn't get you out of his mind, and so on. I found it in his portmanteau after he and I came back from New Orleans." Her face had turned ugly again. "After he went up to Boston, I couldn't find the journal so I figured he must have it with him. I printed an unsigned note, telling Barbara that if she could get a look at the journal Angus kept, she'd read something she ought to know. I guess it took her quite a while to get over her ladylike squeamishness and look for the journal, but she finally did, and that was the end of that."

She looked broodingly past Amalia to some point on the opposite wall. "Later on, I wished he'd married her. After all, I could tell he didn't love her. I could still have had a chance to be first in his life. Yes, I made a mistake there. But as I said, I was young and foolish enough to think that your proxy marriage to Tom would keep you and Angus apart. But it didn't, did it?" Her voice rose. "He made you pregnant, didn't he? The night of the hurricane, that's when it must have happened. He told Papa and me he was coming here to see how you were that night. So don't think *I* didn't count nine months from the hurricane to the time you had this one."

She looked down bitterly at the child she held tightly against her. His terror-distended eyes rolled upward, then toward his mother, then back to the face of the person, once his friend, who might at any moment hurl him to that brick walk down there. Ruth said, "Why, his hair is even getting that red tinge."

Amalia could feel the girl's rage building again. She said swiftly, desperately, "You were going to tell me all of it."

Ruth smiled. "You think you're pretty smart, don't you, Mrs. Fulmer? You think that if you keep me talking long enough, Lena will come back, or maybe Angus, or maybe someone else. But it's sixteen miles to East Hampton and back, and it will take time for Lena to shop, if that's what she's over there for, and I can't think of why else she'd have gone. As for Angus, the ferry from Connecticut doesn't even dock until four o'clock. And I don't think you'll get any callers on a day like this. So I can tell you all of it, if I want to. And I do want to. For instance, Mrs. Fulmer, wouldn't you like to know who it was that made you a widow?"

Amalia felt utter unbelief. The last thing in the world this obsessed girl would have wanted was for Tom to die, leaving Amalia free to accept Angus' love. "You . . . you couldn't have been the one. You had no reason to kill him."

"Of course I had no reason! It was an accident. I'll give you one guess, Mrs. Fulmer. Who did I come here to kill that night?"

Incapable of speech, Amalia made no answer. Ruth said almost playfully, "And how did I know that pistol was there in the parlor? That's a harder one, isn't it? But think back to the first afternoon I called on you in this house. You and Lena were alone here then. Tom's brother had persuaded you to buy that pistol. I heard about it. In a town this size, everybody hears everything before long. And so that day I came here, I started to leave and then asked if I could get myself a glass of water, and you said yes. I went in by the kitchen door and just kept going until I reached the parlor. It seemed to me you'd keep the pistol there, rather than in your room, so that either you or Lena could get to it quickly if you needed to. I was right. It was in the top drawer of the desk.

"And if you're wondering why I wanted to know where the

pistol was," she went on, "let's just say I had a feeling I might have use for it. And I was right about that, too." Her voice turned bitter and accusatory. "When Tom came back, you didn't even try to be really married to him, did you? If you had, maybe I wouldn't have felt I had to get rid of you. But you didn't even sleep in the same bedroom with him, did you?"

As if from a long way off, Amalia heard herself asking, "How did you know that?"

"How do you think, you stupid thing? Several nights in a row I lay over in the reeds watching this house. I saw each of you drawing the curtains, you in one bedroom, and Tom in the one opposite, above the parlor. The night that half-wit Toby came along, I'd made up my mind that after the lights had been out in both rooms for about an hour, I'd go in through that window, get the pistol from the drawer, and slip up to your room. I knew the shot would wake Tom and maybe Lena too, but people are groggy for a little while after they wake up. I figured I could be out of the house and fifty yards or so down the road before Tom could cross the hall to your room, and get a lamp lit, and see what had happened. And after that he'd have to get dressed enough so he could run to get Dr. Marsden.

"And so that night after both lights were out I waited there in the reeds. I had on a dark dress and cloak and a dark shawl over my head. I don't know how the shawl slipped enough to show my hair, but I guess it did. When Toby started running, though, I had no idea he'd seen me. I just thought he was running because he was a loony. I mean, who knows why loonies do things?

"After a while I crossed the road to this house. The window went up easily enough, and once I was inside the parlor, there was enough moonlight for me to see the desk. But when I reached inside that drawer for the pistol, I couldn't find it. I pulled the drawer out farther—too far—and it fell to the carpet.

"I guess I should have gone out the window then and run away as fast as I could. But the sound hadn't been loud, not on that thick carpet, not loud enough to wake Tom in the room above the parlor. Besides, I was only fifteen then, and I thought I could do anything. So I got down on my hands and knees and started feeling around for the pistol."

She stopped speaking for a moment. When she went on, her voice was sullen. "I guess the trouble was that Tom hadn't been asleep. He'd heard the drawer fall. I found the pistol, all right, but by that time he'd slipped down the stairs. I looked up and saw someone in the doorway. It was just a dark shape. It might have been you as well as him, but whichever it was, I wasn't going to let myself be caught, so I fired the pistol, and then dropped it, and then climbed out of the window and ran."

Still with that brooding look Ruth stared at the floor. Amalia stood motionless, with every muscle, every nerve in her body pulled taut. She had thought of a way, perhaps the only way, by which she might hope to save both Michael and herself. But she must attempt it before Ruth's rambling discourse—sometimes boastful, sometimes brooding and sullen—brought her back to the present moment. Back to the jar of deadly brew in Amalia's hand, back to the terror-petrified child in her own grasp, the child who, in a second's time, could be hurled out that open window.

"If I'd been able to kill *you* that night . . . But everything went wrong, all wrong. Angus went off on that whaler, and then, while I was in Maine, you both sailed on the *Falcon*. When Angus came back alone, I hoped and hoped you'd be in another shipwreck, or that you'd decide to stay in Spain, or *something*. But instead, you've come back . . ."

Amalia thought: Now! And pray God Ruth would lunge immediately to try to stop her. Pray God she would not take time to whirl around, with Michael in her grasp, to that open window . . .

Amalia dropped the jar and ran toward the open trapdoor.

She heard a shout, heard a thump as Michael's small body struck the attic floor. From the corner of her eye she saw Ruth, a streak of yellow in her summer dress, hurtling toward her. And then Amalia was grappling with her at the trapdoor's edge. She saw the girl's now hideously ugly face close up, the blue eyes glittering, the upper lip lifted at the corners to show the incisors. She felt Ruth's nails carve grooves in her cheek. And she heard Michael. As if he had been released from a spell, scream after scream ripped out of him.

Ruth had gotten her hands around Amalia's throat. She was taller than Amalia, and six years younger, and strong, with the strength of the maniacal. The terrible pressure of those long-fingered hands made Amalia's lungs feel as if they were about to burst. A red haze was gathering before her eyes. In another moment or so she would lose consciousness, leaving this creature free to do as she chose with herself and with Michael.

With a last desperate effort, Amalia managed to pull backward a few inches. Her right foot shot out, and its instep hooked behind Ruth's ankle.

Feeling her feet go out from under her, feeling her body fall backward toward the void below, the girl let go of Amalia's throat and tried to save herself. For an instant or two after she tumbled backward her hands caught and held the edges of the trapdoor opening. Amalia caught a last glimpse of the hate-and-terror-distorted face. Then the weight of Ruth's own body sent her falling to the floor below.

Dizzy, and with that red mist still before her eyes, Amalia stepped back from the brink, lest she too fall. She felt Michael's hands clutching her skirts. He was still screaming, with tears streaming down his upturned face.

She said hoarsely, "Let go of me for a moment, my darling. Yes, that's my good boy."

She took a step forward, looked down. Ruth lay motionless on the upstairs-hall carpet, her neck bent at an odd angle. Shaking all over, Amalia turned to her son. He no longer screamed, but tears still rained down his face.

"Now, I'm going to pick you up, Michael. You are to hold very tight to me, with your arms and legs both." She lifted him. With his sob-shaken body pressed tight against her breast and his arms clasped around her neck, she moved backward down the ladderlike steps, her hands holding to the side rails. Sickened at the thought that she might step on that motionless body, she looked over her shoulder just before she reached the stair's foot.

She hurried to Michael's room, went inside. Even though she was almost certain that the fall had killed Ruth, she shot the bolt in the door's barrel lock, lest somehow Ruth manage to come after them. Then, feeling sick and dizzy, she put Michael on his small bed and lay down beside him. After a while his sobs quieted. Feeling less dizzy, she said, "Stay right here, Michael," and got up. She unlocked the door, looked out. The girl in the yellow dress still lay beneath the attic opening.

Amalia went to her, bent, forced herself to place fingers on the slender wrist. The pulse was thin and irregular, but it was there.

So she was alive. Perhaps just barely so, but alive. That meant that Amalia must fetch Dr. Marsden at once.

But even now she was afraid to leave Michael alone in the house with Ruth MacFarlane. "We're going to Dr. Marsden's," she said when she returned to the child's room. Because they could move faster that way, she lifted him into her arms, carried him from the house and out into the humid gray heat. Gasping for breath, she hurried down the road. And there, coming around the bend in John Street, was the gig.

Lena reined in beside them. "Child! Your face! What happened?"

Amalia realized that her fingernail-slashed cheek must be bleeding. "I'll tell you on the way," she said, handing Michael up to Ruth. "Just turn the gig around and drive us to Dr. Marsden's as fast as you can."

# 47

For almost a minute after she awoke, Amalia was wondering if the very dim light falling through her bedroom window was that of almost morning or almost night. Then the fact that she wore, not a nightdress, but a robe over her underclothing, reawakened memories of several hours before, and she knew that now it must be early evening.

She remembered herself and Lena and Michael driving back to this house in the gig, with Dr. Marsden and his man-of-all-work following in his surrey. After he had knelt beside the unconscious girl for a few moments he said, "Davey and I had best carry her downstairs and then take her back to the examination room in my house. But first," he went on, opening his black leather bag, "I want you to take these pills, Amalia. They'll give you several hours' sleep. And, girl, you look as if you need it."

She had gone to her room and, aided by Lena, had taken off her dress and swallowed the pills. The last sounds she had heard were the slow footsteps of the men carrying Ruth toward the head of the stairs.

Amalia sat up in bed. "Lena!"

The door opened. A figure too tall and wide-shouldered to be Lena came into the darkened room. "She's with Michael," Angus said. "I've been waiting just outside your room for you to wake up."

"Is Michael . . . ?"

"He's fine." He was fumbling with the chimney of the lamp on her bedside table. "Still a little upset, but otherwise fine." He struck a flint against the box and light bloomed. "Why don't you lie down again?"

Because she felt a little light-headed, she sank back against the pillow. Angus brought a chair to the bedside and sat down. Even in the soft lamp glow his face looked strained, older.

He said, "Your cheek! And there are bruises on your throat. Oh, Amalia! Do they . . . ?"

"My throat still hurts a little, but not my cheek." She had a drowsy recollection that after she had swallowed the pills, Lena had bathed her scratched face. "Angus, is your sister . . . ?"

She broke off. When Angus finally spoke, his voice was toneless. "She's dead. She died about two hours ago."

"Oh, Angus! I'm sorry." When he didn't answer, she went on. "I suppose you could say I made her fall. But you see, she tried—"

"I know what she tried. Dr. Marsden sent his man to get me from my house around four-thirty. I'd just gotten back from Connecticut. Ruth was still alive then, and talking in a disjointed way. I heard part of it. How she'd shot Tom, and why, and . . . and a lot of other things."

"Angus, I'm sorry, so sorry! I know you must have loved her."

"Yes, even though I always knew there was something . . . wrong about the way she loved me. I tried not to think about it. A man doesn't like to acknowledge that his own sister has incestuous . . ." He paused and then went on. "Yes, her death grieves me. But oh, God, Amalia! Not as your death would have, or our son's."

Our son. He had never referred to Michael that way before. She began to feel the ache of tears in her bruised throat. "Angus, can you ever forgive me?"

"Forgive you for what?"

"For believing for an instant that you might have been the one who . . ."

"Of course I can forgive you." He added after a moment, "Now that we know the truth about Tom's death, can't we forgive each other for everything? Forgive, and go on together?"

Unable to speak, she nodded. He leaned over her. Because of her bruised throat and lacerated cheek, his kiss upon her lips was very gentle.

He straightened. After a moment he said, smiling down at her, "Maybe it's better that you were not, after all."

She said, puzzled, "Were not . . . ?"

"Pregnant. From the time we left that island until I received your letter saying you were on your way back to Sag Harbor, I kept hoping that I had made you pregnant again. I figured that then you would have to marry me. But if you had been pregnant . . . Well, today you might have lost her."

She said, joyful but bewildered, "Her? You are sure that our next child will be a girl?"

"No, I am sure only of how much I want her to be."

"But why, dearest, why?"

"So that we can name her Juana."

The joyful tears slid down her face. She knew then that he loved her very much, so much that he wanted more than just her own forgiveness. He wanted to reach out, in contrition and to do her honor, to the gentle spirit of that young Spanish girl who had given Amalia life.